UNVEILING THE PAST

UNVEILING THE PAST

KIM VOGEL SAWYER

THORNDIKE PRESS
A part of Gale, a Cengage Company

GALE
A Cengage Company

LIBRARY OF CONGRESS CIP DATA ON FILE.
CATALOGUING IN PUBLICATION FOR THIS BOOK
IS AVAILABLE FROM THE LIBRARY OF CONGRESS

ISBN-13: 978-1-4328-7952-5 (hardcover alk. paper)

Published in 2020 by arrangement with WaterBrook, an imprint of Random House, a division of Penguin Random House LLC.

Printed in Mexico
Print Number: 01   Print Year: 2020

For *Mom* —
I miss you every minute of every day.
I'm doing my best to make you proud.

And for *Daddy* —
Of all the fathers God
could have given me,
I'm so glad He gave me you.

A father to the fatherless . . .
  is God in his holy dwelling.

— Psalm 68:5, NIV

ONE

June 1992
Little Rock, Arkansas
Margaret Diane DeFord

While her daughter happily crunched a big bite of off-brand sugar-frosted flakes, a cereal reserved for summer consumption only, Diane sipped her second cup of coffee and perused the Sunday paper. Bright midmorning sunshine flowed through the sliding glass doors that led to their small balcony and glared against the newsprint. Diane angled the folded pages away from the light. A short article caught her attention, and she laughed as she finished the paragraph.

"What's so funny, Mom?"

She peeked over the top of the paper at her daughter. "It's snowing in Colorado."

Meghan's fine dark eyebrows shot up and her mouth formed an O, revealing a gap where her bottom front teeth used to be.

9

"But it's summertime. It's not supposed to snow in summertime."

Diane shrugged. "Tell it to Colorado." She glanced out the sliders and winced when the sunlight met her eyes. Not a cloud in the sky. Today would be a scorcher in Little Rock.

"You know what?" Meghan swung her bare feet and grinned, holding her spoon like a sword. "It'd be neat if it snowed in the summer. Snow is nice and cold, and it would cool us down when it's so hot outside."

A six-year-old's logic. "It'd be neat, but it isn't possible. You need cold atmospheric conditions for snow to form, and you don't get that in the summer."

Meghan's face puckered. "Then how come it snowed in Colorado? It's summer there, too, isn't it?"

"Sure it is, but the elevation is different."

"What's elebation?"

"Elevvvvvation." Without conscious thought, Diane slipped into her teacher's voice. "Elevation is the height of a land area above sea level. The higher the elevation, the cooler the temperature. Colorado's average elevation is probably six thousand feet higher than Arkansas's. It makes a difference."

10

"Ohhh." Meghan's expression brightened. She clanked her spoon onto the table and half scooted off her chair. "Can we go to Colorado and see the snow?"

Wouldn't it be wonderful to go on an impromptu vacation and experience snow in June? But a single mom on a teacher's salary didn't have the luxury of taking impromptu vacations. Or even planned vacations beyond day trips to local museums or the zoo. She shook her head. "Sorry, no can do."

Meghan's bottom lip poked out. She slumped into her seat.

"But later you can go to the pool and cool off that way." She'd had to pay more in rent than she preferred to live in an apartment complex that included a private pool and playground area, but it was worth it. Meghan could go swimming whenever she wanted.

"Okay." Little enthusiasm colored Meghan's tone.

Time for distraction. Diane pointed at Meghan's bowl. "Finish up your cereal before it gets soggy."

"I like it soggy."

"The sooner you finish eating, the sooner you can head to the pool."

"Okay."

11

Diane raised the paper and focused on an article about an agreement between President Bush and Russian president Boris Yeltsin on arms reduction, ideas forming for discussing the potential ramifications of the pact with her history students when school started again in the fall.

"Mom? Mom!"

Diane snapped the paper down. "What?"

Meghan scowled. "I asked you a question."

She'd been more caught up in her thoughts than she realized. "What was it?"

Meghan tapped the paper. "I read a new word on there. Hold it where I can see."

Diane lifted the pages.

Meghan squinted at something. "What is *uh-bit-you-are-ees*?"

Confused, Diane flipped the paper around. "Oh. You mean obituaries."

"What's obituaries?"

This child had more questions in her than Diane ever imagined a small head could hold. "An obituary is the printed record of a person's death."

Sadness pinched the little girl's face. "You mean it says somebody died?"

"I'm afraid so." Diane glanced at the columns. At least a dozen names were listed, and postage stamp–sized black-and-white pictures gave a face to each name. Her gaze fixed on one, and for a moment she forgot to breathe.

"Like my lizard died?"

Diane stared at the name — Charles (Chuck) Harrison — and the grainy image beside it.

"Mom, like Lenny the Lizard died?"

"Meghan, enough questions already. Eat your breakfast. It's turning into a soggy mess."

"I like it —"

"Eat!"

Meghan yanked up her spoon.

Diane bent over the page and read the entire obituary. Slowly. Underlining the words with her trembling finger.

Charles (Chuck) Harrison, of Fort Smith, Arkansas, age 52, died on June 15, 1992, in his home. He was born February 25, 1940, in Fort Smith, the fourth child to Frank and Edna (Collins) Harrison. He graduated from Fort Smith High School and earned degrees in business adminis- tration and accounting from the University of Arkansas, where he graduated summa cum laude in 1963. He owned and man- aged Harrison Accounting, a successful business in Fort Smith, for almost thirty years. He married his childhood sweetheart, Melinda Garland, in September 1962. To their union was born one child, Kevin, in 1965. Charles was preceded in death by his parents. He is survived by his wife, Melinda; his son, Kevin, of Fort Smith; his brothers, Richard and James; his sister, MaryAnn (Harrison) Walker; and several nieces and nephews. Cremation has taken place. No service is planned.

She gave a jolt at the final line. No service? Why wouldn't the family have a service for someone who held lifelong connections to a community? And how had the man died? "In his home" was such an ambiguous explanation. More questions than Meghan could ask in a day formed on Diane's tongue, but all of them remained unstated. She couldn't — she *wouldn't* — ask the person who could answer.

She slid her gaze to a name in the middle of the impersonal recitation. Kevin. Her blood went as cold as the snow covering the mountaintops in Colorado. A dozen images flashed through her mind's eye, and she winced with each remembrance. Mother always said she had a stubborn streak a mile long, and she'd put it to good use when she determined not to think about Kevin Harrison. She'd succeeded. Until now.

These people — Charles, Melinda, Richard, James, MaryAnn, the unnamed nieces and nephews . . . She had a connection to them. Well, not directly, but Meghan did, which meant Diane did by default.

She glanced at Meghan, who sat with her chin in her hand, stirring the last few sodden flakes in her bowl with a stubby finger. She'd slept in yesterday's pigtails, and they hung askew with stringy wisps of darkest brown framing her flushed cheeks. The stretched neck of her favorite Care Bears nightgown sagged, and a squiggly thread stuck out from the seam of one shoulder. Such a disheveled mess and yet so beautiful. Not a single resemblance to her blond-haired, blue-eyed father.

Thank God.

She closed her eyes, wishing she hadn't seen the obituary. Wishing she hadn't seen Kevin's name in print. Now she'd have to start all over in wiping him from her mind. She popped her eyes open and tapped her daughter's wrist. "Hey."

Meghan didn't lift her face, but she shifted her eyes and peered across the table through a fringe of messy bangs.

"Are you done?"

She offered a barely discernible nod.

15

"Put your bowl and spoon in the sink. Then do your morning stuff."

Meghan nodded wisely. "I know. Wash my hands, brush my teeth, and get dressed."

"But don't put on your swimsuit."

"No swimming?"

"Nope. We're going to do something else."

A hint of curiosity flashed in Meghan's brown eyes. "What?"

"It's a surprise." It would be a surprise to Diane, too. She had no idea where they'd go or what they'd do. She'd probably end up using her credit card, spending money she couldn't afford to squander. But she needed a distraction.

She flicked her fingers at Meghan. "Go on now. Hurry. We don't want to be late."

Giggling, Meghan hopped down from the chair and grabbed her bowl. She scampered to the sink, her bare feet slapping the linoleum. She clattered the bowl and spoon into the sink, then flashed a grin over her shoulder. "We're gonna have fun, right?"

"C'mon, Di, we're gonna have fun."

The voice from the past — the voice she had steadfastly blocked from her memory for seven years — attacked. He'd given her a lot more than fun.

Diane gritted her teeth. "Hurry, Meghan."

Two

May, Twenty-Five Years Later
Carson Springs, Arkansas
Sean Eagle

Chinese takeout for the third time that month. And it was only the fifteenth. Sean picked up his fork but didn't aim the tines for the mound of steaming chicken-fried rice on his paper plate. He glanced across the kitchen table to Meghan, intending to ask if they could forgo bringing home any more little white wax-coated boxes until at least the end of June, but the sight of his wife expertly wielding chopsticks diverted his attention.

She paused with the bamboo eating utensils halfway to her mouth and grinned at him. "What?"

He pointed with his fork at the pair of sticks holding a clump of food, then met her curious gaze. "You handle those things like a pro. Are you sure you're Italian and

17

not Chinese?"

He'd meant to joke, but when her smile faded, he recognized his error. When would Meghan decide to do more than stare at her biological father's name on the paper in her desk drawer? The sooner she found the man and satisfied her curiosity, the sooner they could stop living under the shadow of someone neither of them had ever met.

She put the bite in her mouth, chewed, and swallowed. Pinching a chunk of chicken with her chopsticks, she shrugged. "Mom always said if you're going to eat Chinese food, you shouldn't use a fork. And Grandma said that adage about being hungry a half hour after eating Chinese is only true because you lose part of each bite to your lap."

Sean gave the expected laugh and finally plunged his fork into the rice. They ate in silence. Well, except for the mumble of news reporters from the television around the corner in the living room. Years ago, he'd developed the habit of keeping the television or radio on. For noise. His house was too lonely without it. He hadn't expected to need a source of noise after he got married, though. They'd been husband and wife three years already, and —

"Are you done?"

Meghan stood beside him, hand out-stretched. He glanced at his plate. The food, with the exception of a few stray pieces of rice, was gone. He didn't even recall eating it.

"Yeah, I guess I am." He handed her the grease-stained circle of white paper, then picked up the fork, wooden chopsticks, and pair of empty water bottles and followed her to the kitchen. He placed the fork on the counter near the sink and tossed everything else in the recycling bin while she dropped their plates and napkins in the trash can.

Leaning against the counter, he folded his arms over his chest and observed her put the fork in the dishwasher. He was capable of doing it, but she had a "system," and she didn't want him messing it up. Always so independent and self-sufficient. Sometimes he admired the traits. Sometimes he wished she needed him a little more.

"All done." She clicked the door closed and shot a smile over her shoulder.

"Not quite." He bobbed his chin at the appliance. "You didn't start it."

"It isn't full yet. No sense in wasting water." She grabbed a handful of paper towels and a spray bottle of cleaner and crossed to the table.

Sean remained in place, staring at the dishwasher's stainless-steel door. She'd put things in the racks every day for more than a week, and there still wasn't enough in there to warrant running it? Something wasn't right with that scenario. His mom hadn't gotten a dishwasher until he was a junior in high school, but he recalled the appliance humming every other day at least. But then, Mom had made use of her stove every day.

He understood why Meghan didn't cook much. Investigations took them away from home, sometimes for days at a time. Even when they were tied to their desks in the Arkansas Cold Case Investigations Department, the commute from Little Rock to Carson Springs put them home past the normal supper hour. Grabbing something quick was easier than preparing a meal and eating at eight o'clock or after. Before their wedding, how many suppers had he grabbed at a drive-through window?

Sure, he understood, and he didn't blame her for not wanting to cook. He was tired, too, at the end of the day. But memories of home-cooked meals and conversations around the table sent feelings of *family* rolling through him — a longing for the life he'd had with his parents. The kind of life he always thought he and his wife would share.

He shifted his attention to Meghan, who spritzed the laminate tabletop and wiped it down with the crumpled wad of paper towels. Her mink-colored ponytail swayed beside her cheek, giving her a girlish look. But she wasn't a girl anymore. She'd be thirty-two this year. Thirty-two . . . and he was thirty-six already. When his mom was thirty-six, he'd been a seventh grader. Even if he and Meghan had a baby tomorrow, he'd be forty-one by the time their child started school and fifty-four — three years older than Meghan's mom was now — when the child graduated.

Urgency propelled him across the floor. He snagged Meghan's wrist and, with a gentle tug, pulled her into his embrace. She melted against him, slipping her arms around his torso and resting her cheek on his shoulder. A sigh escaped. Ah, the contentment of holding his wife. He couldn't love her more if he tried. His very love was the reason he wanted a child with her.

He rocked her side to side and whispered against her silky hair, "Meg, can we talk?"

She leaned back slightly, still caught in the circle of his arms, and looked at him, her brown eyes holding a smile. "What about?"

His gaze roved her upturned face. He could imagine their child — dark-haired and dark-eyed, given her Italian coloring and his father's Native American ancestry. Of course, his mother had been from Scandinavian stock. Blond-haired and blue-eyed. If Meghan's father had similar genes, they could have a little blue-eyed blond instead. Wouldn't that be something?

She bumped his backside with the spray bottle. "Hey. Where'd you go? You said you wanted to talk."

He searched her eyes for a moment, gathering courage, then took a sideways step that separated them. "Put those down, huh?" Her brow furrowed, but she placed the damp wad of towels and the bottle on the table. He captured her hand, linking fingers with hers. "Let's sit."

Laughing softly, she scuffed alongside him to the sofa. "It must be important if you want to sit."

He flopped into the corner of their overstuffed L-shaped couch, and she immediately nestled — head on his shoulder, legs tucked underneath her — the way she did when they watched television or worked on a crossword puzzle together before bed. She loved him. He knew that. So wouldn't having a child be a natural way to express their love?

He ran his fingers through the thick strands of her ponytail. "Meg, do you think we make a good team?"

She tipped her face and smirked at him. "For that we had to sit? What a silly question." She wrinkled her nose. "No, we don't make a good team. We make a *great* team. The best. We wouldn't be the first husband-wife investigation pair in the history of the state's cold-case unit if we weren't." She kissed the underside of his jaw and settled close again.

He cleared his throat. "I wasn't talking about our work relationship."

She toyed with one of his buttons. "No?"

"Hm-mm. I meant as husband and wife."

She went still for the count of three, then abruptly swung her feet over the edge of the sofa and sat up. "What's wrong?"

A commercial advertising toilet bowl cleaner came on. Good grief. He grabbed the remote control from the fold-down armrest and turned off the television, then took hold of Meghan's hand. She didn't pull free from his grasp, but she didn't curl her fingers around his, either. She sat tense, chewing her lip.

"Honey, nothing's wrong." Which wasn't exactly the truth. How could he phrase things so she'd understand? "You and me, we're good together. Really good. Maybe . . . too good."

She eased against the sofa cushions but kept some distance between them. "What do you mean?"

"We've got this routine that we follow. Up early, hitting the exercise equipment, then driving to work, and" — he gestured to the living room — "hanging out. Always the two of us. Just the two of us."

She released a little huff. "We don't have a lot of extra hours every day. If we didn't get up early or have our drives to and from work, we wouldn't have any you-and-me time at all."

"That's my point." He leaned forward and propped his elbows on his knees, sandwiching her limp hand between his palms. "Our day is so structured, with work and the commute eating up a chunk of time, that we're kind of caught in a rut." He gazed steadily into her unblinking eyes. "Not necessarily an unhappy rut, but a rut all the same. What we have now, that's all we'll ever have. Unless we change something."

"Are you wanting to move to Little Rock? I mean, I love our house here, but that'd get rid of the commute."

He, too, loved the three-bedroom Craftsman-style bungalow they'd purchased in a town near Little Rock after their *I do's.* "No. We chose the commute to give us some separation from our job. We need that."

"So you're happy with . . . this?" She waved her hand, and he surmised she meant the house in general.

"Yes."

Meghan shook her head, making her ponytail bounce. "Then what do you want to change?"

He puffed his cheeks and blew out a breath. "I want to use one of our extra bedrooms for something other than a home office or an exercise room."

Her eyebrows pinched, and she tapped her chin with her finger. "Hmm . . . We could put the exercise equipment in the basement. The rec room is long enough to use half for a workout space. But I don't really want our desks and computers down there." She tilted her head. "What're you wanting to use the room for instead?"

"A nursery."

She drew back, shock registering on her face. An uneasy chuckle left her throat. "I thought we already talked about that."

He tightened his grip on her hand. "A year

ago. You asked for time to think about it."

"No, I asked for time to get ourselves established before we thought about it."

He raised his brows. "We've taken three years. Our routine is down pat. I'd call that established, babe."

She slipped her hand free and sat back, folding her arms across her chest. "At the bureau and here at home, yes, but what about our goal of going independent?"

Her goal. Not his. He liked the promise of a steady paycheck, and he started to tell her so. Again.

"Besides, it wouldn't be fair to have a baby when we have so little free time. I like having you to myself. I'm sorry if that sounds selfish, but it's the truth." She scooted to the other end of the sofa, leaned against the armrest, and pressed the soles of her bare feet against his thigh. "And while I'm being truthful, I have to admit . . . I'd be a terrible mother."

Sean squeezed her foot. "I don't believe that."

She made a face. "Because you are innately optimistic. Believe me, I admire that about you, but sometimes you aren't realistic. I love Mom — of course I do — but she wasn't the huggy, lovey-dovey, cookie-baking, take-your-kid-to-the-circus kind of mom yours was. That's what you want from me, right?"

He couldn't deny it. Her description fit his expectation. He shrugged.

A sad smile lifted the corners of her lips. "Sean, I still haven't gotten the hang of being a wife. I'm not — I can't —" She swung her feet to the floor and stood. "I'm sorry." She scurried through the arched opening that led to their bedroom.

Sean sighed. He said to the empty room, "I'm sorry, too."

THREE

Meghan DeFord-Eagle

Meghan closed herself in the master suite's bathroom and perched on the rolled edge of the soaking tub. She wrapped her arms across her aching middle and stared at her somber reflection in the mirror above the sink.

"A baby . . ." She whispered the words, forcing them past her dry throat. Why did something as helpless and harmless as an infant strike such fear into her? She snorted. How ridiculous to ponder the question when she knew the answer all too well. She could never subject an innocent baby to the DeFord Curse.

She grimaced and jerked her gaze to the tub's gleaming brass crisscross faucet knobs. Grandma DeFord had admitted to a rocky relationship with her mother. Mom had spent the majority of her childhood and adult years resenting Grandma. Meghan couldn't honestly say she resented Mom, but neither did she want to emulate her. At least not Mom's style of parenting. But what other parenting style did she know? She'd only add another generation of mother-child conflict to the family history. Would that be fair to the baby? Not to mention burdening Sean, who'd end up being the buffer between his wife and child.

Having filled the position of peacemaker more years than she wanted to count for Mom and Grandma, she wouldn't wish that frustration and heartache on anyone, much less the man she loved more than she knew how to express.

A tap at the door intruded, and she gave a start. She blurted "What?" more sharply than she intended.

"Can I come in?"

She swallowed. Sean sounded so kind, so hopeful, so patient. He'd be such an amazing dad. She grabbed one of the spigots and gave it a vicious twist, then called over the sound of water splashing against the porcelain tub. "I'm gonna take a soak, Sean. Relax a little bit."

She held her breath. Would he ask to join her, as he so often did?

"Okay. I want to look over some notes on the computer about the Dunsbrook murders, then turn in. Enjoy your soak."

Her breath eased out, and she slumped forward, half-relieved and half-disappointed. Probably the same way he was feeling. Guilt struck hard. She undressed and eased into the tub, willing the steamy water to dissolve the unpleasant emotion. But the guilt refused to budge. Sean deserved to be a father. But how could she watch him develop a relationship with their child and not be envious? Envy rotted the bones — wasn't that what it said in Proverbs?

She closed her eyes and tried to imagine herself cradling a baby. The picture wouldn't gel. Mom sometimes joked that she hadn't inherited a maternal gene. Apparently neither had Meghan. She'd been born to a non-maternal mother and an absentee father. She'd be the worst kind of parent. Why couldn't Sean understand?

And these thoughts weren't helping her relax. She might as well get out. Using her toe, she flipped the drain lever and then dried off while the tub emptied. Her feet met the slate tiles, and gooseflesh broke out over her frame. She grabbed her terry-cloth robe from the hook on the back of the bathroom door and tossed it on. Her damp feet left marks on the plush carpet as she crossed to the closet. She chose a T-shirt–

style nightshirt printed all over with dachshunds, then exited the closet. Sean entered the bedroom from the hallway at the same time. He shot her a tight smile but didn't say anything.

Temptation to run to him, to apologize, to beg his understanding twined through her. But what could she say that she hadn't said before? Sean knew her. Knew her better than anybody else. Even so, he didn't fully understand her. Or at least he didn't understand her fears. She could talk until she was blue in the face and he wouldn't understand because his up-bringing had been so different from hers.

The contrasts of their childhoods bounced in her mind like a tennis ball flying back and forth over the net. Him raised in a two-parent household, her raised by a single mom. Him attending church every time the doors were open, her going only on Christmas and Easter. His parents cheering him on at sporting events and school programs, her mom shooing her out the door with a bright "Do good, Meghan" and staying home to grade papers. Him playing board games with his folks and sharing bouts of laughter, her trailing Mom through musty museums and listening to lectures and explanations. Different. She and Sean were

31

so different.

A person couldn't change her past. Her background would never match his. Did that mean —

"Are you coming to bed?"

She blinked twice. He was already in bed, his puzzled face illuminated by the glow from his bedside lamp. She must look like an idiot, rooted in front of the open closet door, staring into space.

"Sorry. I guess I was lost in thought."

Amusement glittered in his dark eyes. "Ya think?"

Another difference between them. He was always so quick to forgive and move on. She forgave. Sure she did. But move on? That part was hard.

She closed the door and crossed the floor in a few quick strides. She slipped between the sheets and clicked off her lamp, then flopped onto her back. Sean rolled toward her and raised up on one elbow. The room was dark, the shadows heavy, but she made out his handsome, chiseled face tipping near, and she closed her eyes in readiness for his customary nighttime kiss. Sometimes the kiss lengthened and they ended up staying awake for a while. For reasons she couldn't explain, she hoped tonight they'd stay awake.

His warm breath brushed her cheeks, and then his lips touched hers — firm, moist, tender. She wrestled her arms from beneath the light covers, ready to draw him close, but before she caught hold of him, he lifted away from her and rested his head on his pillow. " 'Night, Meg."

She swallowed the lump in her throat and whispered, " 'Night." A few seconds ticked by, and then she added, "I love you."

His hand slid across her belly. His fingers splayed, but he didn't pull her to him. Moments later, his deep, even breathing told her he'd fallen asleep.

It was Monday. They'd made love twice over the weekend. Monday led to Tuesday, a workday, and they needed their rest. He wasn't rejecting her. He was being practical and responsible. She should follow his lead. She placed her hand over his and closed her eyes, but sleep refused to claim her.

An image of the folded slip of paper in her desk drawer — the piece of paper bearing a single name, written in her mother's strong penmanship — lingered behind her closed lids. Mom had never wanted to talk about the man who'd gotten her pregnant in college and then told her to get lost. Meghan had learned not to ask questions about him. Why get Mom all worked up?

Her telling Meghan his name was a huge concession.

Meghan knew the traits she'd either inherited or learned from her mother. But half of her genetic makeup came from someone else. A total stranger. All she knew about him was that he hadn't wanted to be a father. At least not back then. Maybe not now, either. After all, to her knowledge, he'd never made any effort to find her. Irresponsible and apathetic — those were the characteristics she applied to him. But no one was all bad. There had to be something admirable about him or Mom wouldn't have been drawn to him in the first place.

What if he'd made a mistake with Mom and didn't want to disappoint his parents, so he'd run away rather than admit he messed up? What if, out there, she had grandparents and aunts and uncles and cousins who would welcome her with open arms? What if her paternal genetic half was, for the most part, stable and loving and nurturing? Would there then be a chance that some of those genes would rise up and make themselves known if she bore Sean's child? The question tormented her well past midnight until she finally fell into a restless sleep.

In the morning, she forced herself to

complete a half hour on the elliptical while Sean made use of their weight bench. They rarely talked during workouts, but the silence felt heavy and almost funereal. Relief flooded her when the timer buzzed and they could shower and dress. To expedite their leave-taking, it had become their routine for him to grab his shower in the hall bathroom — would he still do that if they had a child? — and her to use the one in the master bath.

As usual, he was out, was dressed, and had a pot of coffee ready by the time she left the shower. He handed her the *Mrs.* travel mug of the *Mr.* and *Mrs.* set they'd received from Grandma for their wedding.

She inhaled the wisp of steam rising from the little sip hole and sighed. "Mmm, smells great. Almost as good as your aftershave."

He gave her a light nudge with his elbow, grinning. "Aw, I bet you say that to all your husbands." He'd made the teasing comment before in response to a compliment, and she'd always laughed, but this morning the statement stung her heart.

She touched his arm. "Sean, you do know . . . I don't want any other husband but you. There are things I wish I could've learned from Grandma and Mom" — like how to be a wife and a good mother — "but they did set one example for me that means a lot. They didn't man hop. Grandma is still faithful to her husband even though he's been gone almost forty years. Mom never married, but she was never with anyone except my father. We DeFord women aren't perfect. Not by a long shot. But we're faithful. You can trust me on that."

He gazed at her, his brow puckered, for several silent seconds. Then he set his mug aside and cupped her face with his hands. "I do trust you, Meghan. And you can trust me. We made a commitment before God and a church full of witnesses to be faithful until death parts us. Remember what we said? In sickness and in health, in want or in plenty, for better or for worse." The corners of his lips twitched into a lopsided grin. "Whatever comes our way, you're stuck with me."

"Even if —" She gulped, worry making her mouth go dry. "Even if I don't ever want to be a mom?"

He kissed her forehead and lowered his hands. "My love won't change. Now, c'mon, we better hit the road."

She wished he sounded more convincing, but she followed him to their old Bronco without asking anything else.

The commute to the cold-case department offices in Little Rock took thirty minutes, with half that time spent getting through downtown traffic and stoplights. Sean drove in silence, which wasn't out of the ordinary. He took his position as investigator seriously, and Meghan knew without asking he was mulling over the information he'd explored on the computer yesterday evening, sorting it and searching for potential leads. The murder of the eight-year-old Dunsbrook twins, Dominic and Xavier, which had taken place in the late seventies, plagued him. Whenever there were children involved, Sean always worked extra hard to solve the case. He had a soft spot for kids.

The thought led her back to his desire to be a father. Guilt crashed over her, and she forced her attention to the scene outside the window. She'd grown up in the city and spent several childhood summers in Las Vegas — an even bigger city — with her grandmother, but she didn't much like big cities. Which was why she and Sean had purchased a house in tiny Carson Springs instead of keeping his house or her apartment in Little Rock. If they established a private investigation office, they could work out of their home and avoid this daily crush of traffic, noise, and busyness. She made a mental note to bring up the idea with Sean again over dinner.

He pulled into the four-level parking garage a half block from their office building. She didn't need her sunglasses in the shadowy interior, so she tucked them into her attaché case for easy access when they vacated the garage. Sean located a spot on the second level and parked. The moment she stepped from the air-conditioned cab, humidity prickled her flesh. They took the concrete steps to the street level and set off up the sidewalk at a brisk pace.

Scattered clouds hid the sun, so she left her sunglasses in her case, but the clouds did little to cool things. Summer wasn't due for another month, but here it was, not quite eight in the morning, and the thermometer on the bank building across the street showed seventy-one degrees. The air was still, and the smell of exhaust permeated the area. Meghan wrinkled her nose and couldn't hold back a soft snort.

Sean glanced at her.

She waved her arm in the direction of the street. "If we worked from home, we wouldn't have to breathe in exhaust fumes. Or make that commute." Sean's clenched jaw let her know she'd said too much. Why hadn't she stuck to her original plan to bring up the going-independent idea over dinner?

She reached for his hand. "Ignore me. I didn't sleep well last night, and I guess I'm a little grumpy."

He offered a quick smile, squeezed her fingers, then let go. Although demonstrative at home, Sean never showed her affection on the job. He was always a gentleman, though, which he proved by opening the door for her and gesturing her into the building.

Two of their coworkers, partners Tom Farber and Greg Dane, were waiting beside the tarnished doors to the ancient elevator, coffeehouse disposable cups in their hands. Tom grimaced when Meghan and Sean reached them.

"We'll probably have to take the stairs. I think it's stuck again." Tom pushed the activation button three times, grunting with each thrust of his thumb. He muttered a curse under his breath. "Worthless piece of junk."

The four of them trudged to the enclosed staircase at the rear of the building, both Tom and Greg mumbling complaints as they went. More reasons to work from home — no faulty elevators and no dealing with co-workers' foul language. Not that the other detectives or their supervisor swore like sailors. She'd heard worse in her college dormitory.

But Sean never swore. After working closely with him and then having the privilege of being his wife, she'd become more sensitive to cursing. Sean said it was because her spirit was growing more in tune with the Holy Spirit, and she liked that idea. She'd include not having to listen to unwholesome talk as a reason for working from home.

The other two cold-case detectives, Tyler Roach and Anthony Johnson, were already at their desks when Meghan, Sean, Tom, and Greg entered the cold-case unit's area. So was their captain, Ken Ratzlaff, who sat on the edge of Sean's desk. The captain glanced at what Meghan called his Dick Tracy watch and scowled.

"The elevator's not working." Tom yanked out his chair and slumped into the seat. "So we had to hoof it. It's three flights, you know."

Greg swiped his sweaty forehead. "Gotta be ninety-plus degrees in that staircase. I thought we'd croak."

Captain Ratzlaff released a rare chuckle. "Eagle and DeFord don't seem winded." To avoid confusion on the job, the team had continued to call Meghan by her maiden name, but when she and Sean went independent, she'd name their agency Eagle Investigations.

Anthony tilted his computer screen and squinted at it through his glasses with thick lenses. "Of course they're not winded. Everyone knows the two of them are" — he made his voice high and squeaky — " 'practically perfect in every way.' " Tom and Greg groaned, and Anthony grinned. "Sorry. Watched *Mary Poppins* last night with my nine-year-old daughter."

Meghan set her attaché case on her desk and slid into her chair. Sean sat at his desk, which butted Meghan's so they were facing each other. He winked at her.

"Intriguing." Captain Ratzlaff stood and folded his arms over his chest. "Well, practically perfect Eagle pair, would you follow me to my office? I want to discuss a new case with you."

Meghan sent the man an uneasy look. "But we haven't solved the Dunsbrook case yet."

The captain headed across the floor, poking his thumb over his shoulder. "Pass it to Farber and Dane for now. They closed their investigation yesterday, so they can pick up where you left off."

Meghan followed Captain Ratzlaff with Sean on her heels. She didn't look, but she suspected Tom and Greg were shooting glares after them. No one wanted to take a half-completed case. She wouldn't blame them a bit for being disgruntled, and she couldn't help worrying about why the captain wanted to pull her and Sean from a case they'd spent two months investigating. If Ratzlaff was unhappy with them, they'd know soon enough. The man had never been one to mince words.

Their boss snapped his office door closed and nodded toward the worn leather sofa stretched in front of a trio of tall windows overlooking the street. They sat, and he leaned against the edge of his Volkswagen-sized desk. The desk's metal creaked, and the sofa's leather squeaked in unison. Then the room fell silent.

Ratzlaff gripped the edge of the desk, his elbows jutting outward, and aimed a frown in their direction. "I'm not generally in the habit of letting someone else dictate who will investigate which case. But I've got what I'd call a kinda special situation, and the person who alerted us to it requested a female investigator. DeFord, that means you."

The tension in her shoulders released. She and Sean wouldn't receive a reprimand. Questions crowded her brain, but before she could ask any of them, Ratzlaff crunched his face into a rueful scowl and continued.

"Eagle, you've been pretty gung ho about finding the killer of those two little boys, so I'm gonna give you an option here. I'd like to put DeFord on the new case, but if you want to stick with the Dunsbrook murders, I'll pair her with either Farber or Dane. Then you can finish the investigation with whichever of those two are at loose ends."

Captain Ratzlaff drummed his fingertips against the desk's metal front, creating a discordant percussion solo. "What's your pleasure on this one?"

Sean leaned forward, resting his elbows on his knees, and Meghan fully expected him to offer to step away from the Dunsbrook case. "Before I let you know, would you tell us what the new case is about?"

FOUR

Sean

Meghan's soft huff of breath let Sean know she wasn't thrilled by his question. He wasn't even sure why he'd asked it. Why hadn't he told Ratzlaff he wasn't interested in switching partners even for one case? Maybe he'd gotten himself more tangled up in the Dunsbrook murders than he'd realized. Or maybe he was holding a hint of resentment about Meghan's stubborn refusal to consider starting a family and needed some separation.

Ratzlaff reached behind him and picked up a folder. He held it like a choir book and scowled at it. "March 22, 2002, Anson Menke, a loan officer at Union National Bank and Trust in Fort Smith, was reported missing by his wife, Carleena, when he didn't return home from work. The same day, someone from UNB&T told the bank president that Menke had embezzled close

44

to a million dollars over a fourteen-year period. Although the Arkansas Bureau of Investigation did quite a bit of digging, no direct evidence was ever found connecting Menke to the theft. Even so, his sudden disappearance, coupled with testimony by two employees at the bank that Menke had been acting edgy in the weeks before he disappeared, was enough to convince a judge that he'd taken the money and fled the country."

Sean raised his hand. "Excuse me for interrupting, but we've done missing-person and embezzlement cases before. None of this sounds all that special." Certainly not worth putting aside the Dunsbrook case.

Ratzlaff lowered the folder and frowned at Sean. "I didn't say the case was special. I said the situation was special."

Meghan shifted to the edge of the cushion. "What's special about it?"

The captain dropped the folder on top of a stack of papers on the corner of his desk and stared at it. "The people left behind."

Sean waited for him to explain his cryptic statement, but the man seemed to have drifted off somewhere. He glanced at Meghan, who sat with her concerned gaze pinned on their boss.

Sean cleared his throat. "Cap?"

Ratzlaff gave a jolt and looked at Sean.

"Did you know Anson Menke?"

Ratzlaff grunted. "Not personally. But I know about him. Anson Menke had three kids — a girl and two boys. They were only ten, seven, and three years old when he left. The younger boy, Brandon, joined my Boy Scout troop when he was eight. He graduated from high school this past Sunday, and I was there to watch him walk across the stage and get his diploma. Not the same as having his father there, but . . ."

The captain rounded his desk with plodding steps and sank into his desk chair. He linked his hands on his stomach and sent a sad look across the desk. "Brandon had to walk that stage without either of his parents watching him. Obviously his dad wasn't there, and — to make things worse — his mother died a little over a month ago. Liver failure, brought on by lupus."

Tears flooded Meghan's eyes. "Oh, that's so sad."

Even though they were on duty, Sean couldn't resist putting his hand on her knee. She covered his hand with hers and held tight. He welcomed the touch. He hadn't been much older than Brandon was now when he'd lost his parents, and he remembered the pain and confusion of that time.

At least the Menke boy had a brother and sister. He wasn't totally alone.

"Won't argue with you there. Carleena went to her grave believing that Anson didn't abandon his family." Ratzlaff released a soft snort. "His kids don't know what to think. But they need answers. The girl — her name is Sheila — talked to me at Brandon's graduation party and asked if I'd try to find out what happened to her dad. These kids want answers. They deserve answers."

Meghan gave a slow nod. "I can see why the case is personal to you, but I'm still not clear on why you need me, specifically, on it."

The captain sat forward and stacked his arms on the edge of his desk. "Lemme be blunt. Carleena was sick from the time Brandon was born, so Sheila had to grow up overnight when her dad disappeared. She helped raise the boys and took on a lot of responsibility in the house even though she was still pretty much a little girl. She carries a load of resentment, and she doesn't trust men. She asked for a female detective because she wants to be fully involved in the investigation, and she feels more comfortable talking to a woman."

He sat back and held his hands wide.

"Like I said earlier, I'm not in the habit of letting someone tell me how to assign my cases, but this time I'd like to honor the request. Besides . . ." A slight smile lifted the corners of his stern lips, and he pointed at Meghan. "I trust you. I trust your instincts, and I trust your ability to tactfully handle Sheila's interference. Because I'm pretty sure she'll poke her way into the middle of everything. She's a do-it-herself kind of gal."

Sean swallowed a chuckle. Sheila sounded a lot like Meghan. "She probably had to be, given the circumstances." The same way Meghan had grown up fast, saddled — in his opinion — too early with responsibility by her single mother. Meghan would be able to understand Sheila's resentment about being abandoned, too, since her father had disappeared even before she was born.

Unease wriggled through his center. Maybe Meghan had too many connections to Sheila Menke. Would it be detrimental to her emotional well-being to take on the case? He sent a sidelong look at his wife. The sharp V of her eyebrows and her sucked-in lips gave evidence of deep thought. Or deep uncertainty.

He turned to the captain, prepared to ask him to consider allowing Dane and Farber to head the investigation.

Meghan pushed up from the sofa and crossed to the desk. "I appreciate your confidence in me, Captain. I'll investigate, and I'll do my best to put Sheila at ease. But I don't want to work with Tom or Greg. Nothing against them personally. It's just that I work best with my partner." She angled herself and pinned Sean with a hesitant yet hopeful half smile. "Are you in, partner?"

He stood. "Cap, would it be okay if Meghan and I had a private conversation? It shouldn't take long."

Ratzlaff shrugged and pushed out of his chair. "The only private place up here is my office. I'll go touch base with the other detectives while you two decide what you want to do." He strode out and closed the door behind him.

Sean took Meghan's hand and drew her back down on the sofa. "Meg, I don't think you should rush into this one."

She slipped her hand free and pushed a stray strand of brown hair behind her ear. "I know you'd like to see the Dunsbrook case through to the end, but doesn't it seem as if this one should take priority? Captain Ratzlaff has a personal connection to the case. He was willing to set other things aside and put you on the case that was personal to me a few years ago — finding Grandma's lost sister. Don't we kind of owe him this one?"

He searched her expression. "Is that the only reason you want to take this case?"

"Isn't it reason enough?"

"No."

She looked aside.

He pulled in a deep breath. "I'm gonna be honest with you. I'm not sure this case is right for you."

She jerked her face toward him so sharply her ponytail flopped over her shoulder. Defensiveness glittered in her eyes. "Why?"

"Searching for a father who might have abandoned his family?" He spoke softly, kindly, unwilling to hurt her. The subject of her absent father had always been a prickly one. "Is that really something you want to take on, considering your father abandoned you and your mom?"

"Yeah. I think it gives me an . . . edge. I can relate to these kids. I know how they feel."

Sean cupped her upper arms and rubbed his hands up and down the sleeves of her plaid lightweight blouse. "Which is why I think it might be hard for you to be objective. You know Cap's rule about investigat-

50

ing — don't get personally involved, because it affects your ability to reason."

She laughed, shaking her head. "Don't preach at me when you don't take his advice. You throw your whole self into every case we're assigned. It's why you're such a great investigator. You really care about solving the mystery. It makes you dig deeper, look harder, explore every angle."

"And even then, sometimes I fail." If they failed on this one, it would hit Meghan harder.

"But mostly you succeed." She grabbed his hands, and a sheen of tears brightened her eyes. "I want to try to find their father. And . . ." She glanced down at their joined hands, swallowed, then pinned him with a fervent look. "I want to find my father."

Three or four times a year since they'd exchanged wedding vows, he'd suggested searching for her father, and she always resisted. She wasn't manipulative. She wouldn't pull that out of the air to sway him to her side. So he knew she was being honest. But the timing seemed odd. "Why now?"

"I need to know who I am. All the way through. I won't until I meet my father and get to know him. Once I've uncovered all the parts of me, maybe I'll feel better about having a baby."

She'd said "maybe," which was a far cry from absolute certainty, but at least she'd cracked the door of possibility open. Still, he needed her to understand something. "Meg, who your parents are doesn't define who you are. Sure, you inherited your looks and some of your mannerisms from them, but a gene pool isn't the only thing that makes you who you are. Your personal convictions, your desires and determination, and — mostly — your commitment to honor God with your life . . . those are what matter. If you ask God to mold you into the person He designed you to be, He will. You only have to listen for His voice and follow where He leads."

She twisted slightly, dislodging his hands, and stood. "That's easy for you to say. You had such great examples, and your parents taught you about God from the time you were tiny. I'm kind of like a toddler Christian. I still have a whole lot to learn. I need you to be patient with me." She folded her arms. "And I need you to work with me on this investigation."

He stared at her stiff frame and her unsmiling face. She wouldn't budge on this one. He really wanted to finish the Dunsbrook case. He'd already spent two months on it and developed a rapport with the twins' parents, and he sensed he was close to a breakthrough. He couldn't guarantee how close, though. A day? A week? A month? The captain wanted Anson Menke found now for the sake of the man's motherless children.

Sean rose. "Before you tell Cap you want to jump cases, how about we have a sit-down with Sheila Menke? Make sure the two of you are compatible."

Meghan pursed her lips. "It's an investigation, not a courtship."

"I know, but Ratzlaff said the girl likes to be in charge. Even though she wants to work with a female investigator, it might not be in your best interests to work with her." Especially since Meghan intended to also search for her own father. Two cases, so similar, might be too emotionally taxing. He wouldn't put Meghan through it. "So let's chat first, get to know her a little bit, then decide. Okay?"

FIVE

Kendrickson, Nevada
Diane

Diane closed the cover on the folder containing Student 14's term paper about black holes and dropped it on the graded stack in the middle of the breakfast nook's round table. Two more to go . . . She slipped her glasses to the top of her head, closed her eyes, and rubbed her temples.

A chuckle sounded from the kitchen. "That bad, huh?"

Diane shot a wry grin over her shoulder at her mother. Who would have thought four years ago that she would not only choose to live under the same roof as Hazel Blackwell-DeFord but actually come to enjoy her mother's company? And her mother's baking. Mother made some mean vegan chocolate cookies. If her nose served her correctly, the first batch of tonight's offering was about ready to come out of the oven. She'd have two with a glass of almond milk as a reward for getting through these term papers.

She settled her glasses back on her nose. "It's not bad at all. This one was fascinating, really — the student did a great job with the research and explanations. It's gratifying to see all the things I taught over the course of the year about sentence structure and citing sources done so well."

Mother wiped her hands on her apron's gingham skirt. The bibbed apron protected her floral blouse and hot-pink pedal pushers. With her classy way of dressing and her always perfectly bobbed snow-white hair, she could be a model for *Seniors Are Us* — if such a magazine existed. There probably wasn't a more stylish eighty-three-year-old in Kendrickson than Hazel Blackwell-DeFord. She glanced at the stack of term papers, then smiled at Diane. "So you don't regret having to shift from political science to English?"

Diane held up one finger. "Honors English. Remember, these are the cream-of-the-crop kids." She lowered her hand and sighed. "No. Oh, I admit I was apprehensive at first. I'd taught political science for so many years that it felt like second nature, but I've really come to enjoy teaching literature and English." She loved teaching, period. Loved interacting with and inspiring the kids. The paperwork? That she could do without. "The grading is just . . . time consuming."

Sympathy lined Mother's face. "Well, you've been sitting there since you got home from school. You sat there yesterday all the way to bedtime. Maybe you could space them out a bit. So it doesn't feel so overwhelming."

"I've got history finals to grade, too, and the end-of-year scores are due Thursday afternoon. I can't waste any time right now." She reached for another folder. "I'll have plenty of time to relax this summer, though. The principal called a special meeting after school to let us know that the summer tutoring program went kaput. Funding issues."

Dismay flooded Mother's features. "Oh, no. So no extra income this summer?"

Diane shook her head. "I was counting on it, too, to put new tires on my car. But" — she shrugged — "it is what it is. That means I'll be at loose ends and underfoot all summer."

Mother's expression brightened. "Maybe you can join our book club. The ladies would welcome you, and —"

The oven timer buzzed, and at the same time, Diane's cell phone sang "My Girl," the ringtone for her daughter. Diane glanced at the clock. Five past eight, which meant five past ten in Arkansas. An odd time for Meghan to call.

She tapped Accept Call on the phone as Mother removed the tray of cookies from the oven. "Meghan. What's wrong?"

"Why do you think something's wrong?"

"The hour, that's why. Isn't it bedtime over there?"

Mother placed the cookie tray on a stack of hot pads on the counter and crossed to the table. She gazed down at Diane, worry furrowing her brow.

"It's definitely getting close, but —"

Mother tapped Diane's shoulder and then pointed at the phone. Diane pressed the speaker icon.

"— I wanted to make sure I didn't interrupt your dinner."

Mother leaned over the phone. "Hello, Meghan. How's my favorite granddaughter?"

Meghan's laughter rang out. "Sure am glad I don't have competition for that title or I might not hold it. I'm fine, Grandma. How are you?"

"Fair to meddlin'. And you know I meddle a lot."

Meghan laughed again.

Mother returned to the cookie tray and transferred cookies to a cooling rack.

Diane turned off the speaker option and put the phone against her ear. "What's up? Is everything okay with you and Sean?"

"Everything's fine." A hint of tension in Meghan's tone said otherwise. "We're taking on a new case." Sean's low voice rumbled in the background. "Well, we're thinking about taking on a new case. We'll know tomorrow for sure after we've talked to the person who asked to open the investigation. Captain Ratzlaff said she works nights as a certified medication aide at a rest home and sleeps until three or so. So she'll come to the office later in the afternoon to discuss it with us."

Diane fiddled with the corner of a waiting term-paper folder. If this wasn't an emergency, she should probably ask to table the conversation until she'd finished her grading.

"But I wanted to let you know I've made a decision. I'm going to contact my father."

Diane went still. Even her breath caught in her lungs and forgot to escape. Mother placed a saucer of cookies in front of Diane. The sweet aroma of chocolate filled her nostrils, a contrast to the bitter taste of regret flooding her tongue. "Why?" Her breath whooshed out with the word.

Another laugh came, but this one sounded nervous. "Why not?"

When she'd given Meghan her father's name four years ago, she'd expected Meghan to contact Kevin Harrison right away. But as time went by, Diane had decided Meghan was content not knowing. What had changed her mind? "I mean, why now? Has something happened — a health issue or something?"

Mother sank into the chair next to Diane and picked up one of the cookies, but she didn't carry it to her mouth. She watched Diane's face the way a first-time mother might watch her colicky newborn sleep.

"No, no, nothing like that. I've just decided . . . it's time. Time for me to know who he is. To know about the other side of me." Another nervous chuckle. "You're okay with that, aren't you? I mean, you did tell me I could find him if I wanted to."

Yes, she had. So why did it bother her that Meghan was following through? "If that's what you want to do, then you should do it. Are you planning to email or call?"

"I was actually thinking about showing up

in person. This new case — if we take it — will mean going to Fort Smith, since that's where the family lived at the time the father disappeared. So I can arrange to stop by his office. If I have a face-to-face meeting, I ought to get a pretty good read on him. Especially if I take him by surprise. His response ought to tell me right away if I'll have an actual relationship with him or not."

"He's still in Fort Smith?"

"Yeah. A simple internet search turned up his name and company address. Apparently he's in corporate real estate — owns office buildings all over the U.S."

Diane always knew Kevin would be successful. He'd had the drive to excel. At least in business. "When do you think you'll go to Fort Smith?"

"It really depends on how the investigation pans out. But soon."

Mother's intense scrutiny was making Diane want to squirm. She'd be bombarded with questions the moment she disconnected the call. But that wasn't the reason she extended the conversation. "Meghan, may I make a suggestion?"

"What's that?"

"Reconsider the idea of surprising him."

"Why? I just said —"

"I understand why you want to surprise

him. But I also understand . . . him." He hadn't liked surprises. She'd always wondered if things might have gone differently if she had chosen another way of breaking the news of her pregnancy. She'd also never forgotten the pain of his crushing rejection. She couldn't set up her daughter for the same kind of treatment. "It would be better to give a little advance notice. The meeting will be less . . ."

She taught honors English, but she couldn't come up with an appropriate word.

"Volatile?"

Meghan had chosen well. Diane nodded. "Yes. That."

"Well, Mom, I've encountered volatile situations before in my line of work. I can handle it if he gets verbally combatant with me."

"Those situations had to do with other people's lives, Meghan, not your own. There's a difference." Silence fell at the other end of the call. In those few seconds of quiet, Diane sent up a quick prayer for guidance. An idea seemed to fall from the sky. "Will you do me a favor?"

"What?" She sounded apprehensive, but at least she was willing to listen.

"Give me his contact information. Let me get in touch with him first. Prepare him for your meeting."

"Mom, I —"

"I know you're an adult and capable of doing this yourself. I know you want to see his honest reaction to meeting you. But believe me" — Diane released a rueful snort — "Kevin Harrison was never one to hide his true feelings. Even with advance notice, you'll get the real McCoy when you meet him. But let me tell him his daughter wants to meet him. Let me be the one to —"

"Take the brunt?" Meghan was catching on.

Diane squeezed her forehead, where a headache began to throb. "Yes. I wasn't the world's most protective, involved mother. Let me make up for some of that now. Please?"

A heavy sigh met Diane's ear. "All right. I guess I can do that. I'll text you the contact information I found online. But don't wait too long, okay? I'm kinda eager to get this over with."

"Let me finish grading all the final-semester tests and so forth and get scores turned in to the office." The headache changed from a throb to a pound. "Then I'll get in touch with him."

"She's here."

Meghan acknowledged Sean's statement with a nod, closed the file on her computer screen, and looked toward the double doors that led to the cold-case unit. A woman with shoulder-length straight blond hair and a petite frame stood talking to Captain Ratzlaff. Her tunic-styled tank top, holey capri jeggings, and gladiator sandals identified her as young, but her tense, unsmiling countenance gave her a hardened yet weary appearance. Apparently the burden of responsibility — or maybe dragging around a boulder of bitterness — had aged her. Sympathy struck.

The captain led the young woman toward the cluster of desks, and Meghan and Sean rose. Captain Ratzlaff gestured to Meghan first. "Detective, this is Sheila Menke. Sheila, Detective Meghan DeFord."

Sheila extended her hand, and Meghan took hold. She had a strong handshake. What Meghan would call a commanding grip. The corners of the young woman's lips jerked upward into a brief, stiff not-quite-smile. "It's nice to meet you." She turned to Sean but didn't offer to shake his hand. "You must be Detective Sean Eagle. I hope

63

you won't mind if I call you two Sean and Meghan. Detective and Detective feels stuffy."

Sean nodded. "Sean and Meghan is fine, Sheila. Or do you prefer Miss Menke?"

"I prefer to not need your services. But that's moot."

One of the other agents snickered. The captain sent a quick frown in the direction of the sound, then ushered Sheila across the floor. "Let's go to my office. We'll be more comfortable there."

Meghan and Sean trailed the captain to his office. He rolled his desk chair out from behind his desk and offered it to Sheila. Sean and Meghan took the sofa, as they'd done yesterday, and Captain Ratzlaff sat on the edge of his desk and folded his arms over his chest. "Sheila, I've told the detectives the timeline for when your father went missing. They also know a judge ruled that he fled the country with stolen money. As much information as you can give them about what you remember from your dad's last days at home will help guide their investigation. So the floor is yours."

Sheila crossed her legs, then placed her hands in her lap. It seemed a relaxed position, but she wove her fingers together so tightly her fingertips reddened. Every fingernail was bitten down to the quick. Tension seemed to pulse from her, and a nerve pinched in Meghan's neck — a telltale signal of discomfort. Yet sympathy still rested heavily on Meghan's chest.

"First, my mother swore my father was an upstanding man who would never steal. She said he loved all of us and wouldn't walk away without a word. What I remember about him would support that. I have good memories of him reading to us kids, taking us for ice cream on payday, helping me with homework, and tossing a ball back and forth in the yard with my brothers, Wayne and Brandon. I thought he was a good dad."

She recited pleasant memories, but her tone was flat and her expression blank, as if she shared details of someone else's life. The nerve in Meghan's neck throbbed.

"Mom worked as a school secretary until my youngest brother, Brandon, was born. She got sick during the pregnancy, and her health fell apart. She got worse and worse. Now she's dead." Sheila bit her lip and lowered her gaze.

Sean leaned forward slightly. "We're very sorry about the loss of your mother. You have our condolences."

Sheila's head lifted, and determination gleamed in her blue eyes. "She never went back to work after Brandon was born, so even though I wouldn't say we were poor, we didn't have a lot of extra money. Then Dad left and we didn't have any money except Mom's disability. Mom wanted to keep our house in Fort Smith. She wanted to be there when Dad came back. But the bank — the same one Dad had worked for — foreclosed, and we ended up moving into subsidized housing here in Little Rock because the complex had an opening. Mom stayed in touch with our old neighbors, though. They promised to let her know if they saw Dad come around. But, of course, he never did."

She turned to the captain. "I don't really remember anything significant about the days before Dad left. He seemed uptight, but Mom was going through a rough patch. She had those — times when the sickness was worse than usual. He always got uptight then, worrying about her and worrying about the doctor bills and worrying about us kids. He worried a lot. I remember that."

Captain Ratzlaff rubbed his chin and pinned Sheila with a frown. "You said your dad seemed uptight before he disappeared. You also said he got uptight when your mom wasn't doing well. Do you remember anything he might have said — to your mom

66

or on the phone to a friend — that would shed some light on whether there was something more than your mom's health bothering him?"

Sheila shrugged. "If there was something related to his job, we wouldn't have known. Dad had this habit of leaving work outside the door. He never talked about anything work related. At least not in front of us kids."

This investigation was supposed to be Meghan's. If she was going to take it on, she needed to connect with Sheila. She braced her elbow on the sofa's armrest, bringing her a few inches closer to the younger woman. "What about something personal? Illness, and the stresses that accompany taking care of someone who's sick much of the time, can really take a toll on a relationship." Grandma had often talked about how hard it was on her family to watch her father's health fail due to alcoholism. His addiction ruined his relationship with his wife and daughter. "Did you hear them fighting, maybe about bills or about him spending time with someone else or doing things your mother didn't approve of?"

A short, half-amused, half-disgusted huff left Sheila's lips. "He and Mom didn't fight.

Not where us kids would hear. They took their private conversations behind their closed bedroom door, and they never got noisy. My mom said she made Dad promise to never fight in front of us because she spent her childhood witnessing explosive arguments between her parents. She didn't want us to feel afraid in our own home."

"Sounds like your mom was a very loving person."

Tears glistened in Sheila's eyes. She sniffed, then blinked, and her expression turned sullen. "Loving, yeah, and naive. I wanted to have my dad's disappearance investigated years ago, but Mom wouldn't hear of it. She told us over and over again he had to have met with foul play or he would've come back to us, but she wouldn't let us try to prove it. I think deep down she was scared I was right — that my dad got fed up with taking care of a sick wife and three kids. He saw the chance for a new, better life, and he took it. Mom didn't want us to find him living on some tropical island, free of responsibilities."

Sheila seemed to examine her ragged thumbnail. "Now that she's gone, I don't have to worry about sparing her feelings. And I need help. Financially, I mean. If my dad's dead, I need to know. There's a sizable life insurance policy through the bank that would sure make things easier for us. And if he's alive, then I want to know why he left. He owes us an explanation."

Meghan wanted an explanation from her own father, too. Why had he so easily walked away from her and Mom? Her life would have been so different if she'd had both a father and a mother.

Sheila rocked the chair, her gaze darting between Meghan and Sean. "It's been fifteen years. Do you think it's possible to figure out where he is?"

Meghan nodded. "Of course it's possible."

"But it's not a given." Sean gave Meghan's knee a light squeeze. "None of our cases are."

Sheila's eyes narrowed to slits. "Are you saying you won't try?"

Meghan met Sean's gaze. She knew him well enough to recognize apprehension in his tight lips and wrinkled brow. They'd worked with needy people and angry people and hurting people. With some who were needy, angry, and hurting all at once. Resentment seemed to be Sheila's main emotion, but who could blame her? The girl believed that she'd been duped by the man who should have nurtured and supported her.

The nerve in Meghan's neck continued to pinch, proof that Sheila's hardened attitude put Meghan on edge, but she wanted to find Anson Menke. As Sheila had said, the man owed his children answers. She wanted those answers for Sheila. And she wanted them for herself.

Six

Sean

The clock showed 5:40 — ten minutes past their official quitting time — when Sean, Meghan, and Sheila left the captain's office. The other detectives had clocked out for the day, and the room was quiet.

Sean went to his desk, and Meghan walked Sheila to the doors. They paused at the opening, and Sean slid into his chair. The two women spoke briefly, Meghan with her head tipped, leaning in ever so slightly, and Sheila holding her stiff, folded-arms pose. Even though Meghan made no attempt to touch the younger woman, kindness and understanding showed in her expression and attentive frame.

His heart rolled over. She seemed . . . motherly.

Sheila departed, and Meghan scuffed to Sean, her brow puckered and her lower lip caught between her teeth. She perched on the corner of his desk and sighed. "That's a very angry young woman. Part of it is probably mourning. I got the feeling she's struggling to hold it together and using anger as a means of protecting herself."

Sean gave a slow nod. "You could be right. Or she could be perpetually angry. Some people don't have a positive attitude. They're not the easiest folks to get along with."

A teasing glint flickered in her eyes. "And what do you always say about folks who are hard to get along with?" She nudged him. "Those are the ones who need love and acceptance the most, right?"

He rubbed his nose and chuckled. "Yeah, yeah, quote me when I'm trying to get you to think logically."

She laughed, but she sobered quickly. "I want to help her, Sean. If you decide to stick with the Dunsbrook case, I'll try to understand. And I hope you'll understand why I want to step away from it and pursue this one instead."

Sean already understood. Meghan saw herself in Sheila. She was already tangling herself in this missing-person case as much as she had when they set off in search of her grandmother's long-lost little sister. Meghan was thinking that if she uncovered the truth about Sheila's father, she would discover truth about herself and her feelings toward her absent father.

Of course he understood. But he wasn't yet sure if he supported her desire to jump investigations. He also wasn't sure he was ready to give up his current case. Didn't the boys' parents deserve answers, too?

He pushed his chair backward and stood. "Let's talk about it more on the drive home, okay?"

Captain Ratzlaff strode toward them, carrying a manila folder. "If you're gonna talk about it, you might as well have all the information available." He flopped the file into Meghan's hands.

Meghan rose, cradling the file as if it were made of glass. "When do you need it back?"

"I've got it saved on my computer, so I don't necessarily need it back. But if you're asking when I need to know whether you'll take the case, how about you tell me Friday?"

Sean looked at Meghan. She nodded, and he said, "Sounds fine, Cap."

"All right, then. Head out of here so I can lock up."

Meghan grabbed her purse — the one that reminded Sean of an old-fashioned mail pouch — and tucked the folder into it. Then she headed for the doors without a backward glance. Sean shut down his computer and trotted after her.

Someone had taped an Out of Service sign on the elevator doors. Sean pointed at the sign. "Bet Farber had some choice words about that." If Sean and Meghan ended up working with different partners, he'd steer her away from Farber. The detective knew his stuff, but his crassness and penchant for cursing weren't a good match for Meghan. Or for any female, as far as Sean was concerned.

Meghan changed course and crossed to the staircase. Sean caught up to her and opened the door. They headed down side by side, the thump of their soles on the concrete steps echoing against the cinderblock walls. Halfway to the main level, Meghan wrinkled her nose. "I hope they get the elevator fixed fast. Or put some air fresheners in here. Ugh, it smells like old gym socks and mold."

He waggled his eyebrows at her. "I think I know a way to clear our noses of the scent."

"Iriana's?"

"What else?" They both loved the downtown pizzeria's doughy crust topped with everything but the kitchen sink.

She grinned. "I like the way you think,

but it'll get us home too late to get to Bible study."

How could he have forgotten it was Wednesday? He looked forward to the Bible study at their small interdenominational church every week. Too often, investigations took them away for days at a time and they were forced to miss fellowship with their local body of believers. He shouldn't skip when they had the opportunity to go. But when they reached the main level, he caught Meghan's hand.

"Give Iriana's a call, and place a to-go order for a Clean the Floor pie. We'll eat it when we get home." They'd have leftovers for two lunches, too. The pizza loaded with a variety of meats, vegetables, and mozzarella was a four-course meal in a single slice.

She grinned and fished her cell phone from her purse. "Great compromise."

Yes. Compromise. He hoped they'd be as successful in finding a compromise concerning the Dunsbrook and Menke cases. And — his heart caught — parenthood.

Meghan

The riverside-area shops were all doing booming business. Or so it appeared by the lack of parking spots. After their second unsuccessful sweep up and down the block, Meghan sighed.

"Drop me off at the corner. I'll run in, and you can keep circling until you see me on the curb."

"I guess we'll have to unless we want to leave it behind." He turned off the main street, braked, and unlocked her door. "Hurry, huh?"

"I'll be out as soon as I have our food in hand." She jogged up the block. The tantalizing aromas of fresh bread and spices met her nose even before she opened the door to Iriana's, and her mouth watered as she entered the restaurant. The interior was dim, which lent an intimacy despite the crush of tables and the cacophony of laughter, conversation, and kitchen noise.

She wove her way between tables, heading for the cash register counter, wishing she and Sean had time to take a table and enjoy their pizza in this wonderful atmosphere. When she'd nearly reached the counter, someone called her name. She turned a puzzled look in the direction of the caller and spotted the other four detectives sharing a booth. Greg Dane waved her over.

She crossed to the men.

Greg said, "Great minds think alike."

Meghan smiled. "Hard to resist the pizza

here. I ordered ours to go so Sean and I can get home in time for Bible study."

Tom Farber smirked and glanced at his buddies. "Then I guess we won't ask you to join us."

The others had given up on inviting Sean to their get-togethers even before she married him. They'd never invited the two of them. She knew why, too. Their means of winding down after work always involved alcohol. Today it was beer, evidenced by the nearly empty pitcher in the middle of the table, but they weren't averse to harder stuff.

When Meghan was a teenager, Mom had told her about her alcoholic great-grandfather who'd died before Mom was born — *"We could have inherited an alcoholic gene, Meghan, so be careful about drinking."* She'd also witnessed her friends acting like a bunch of idiots when they tipped a bottle. She'd never had any desire to lose control of herself that way. As a result, Meghan stayed away from liquor. Sean avoided it, too, but for scriptural reasons.

Tom meant to goad, something he seemed to thoroughly enjoy, but she refused to take the bait. She punched him lightly on the shoulder. "Since you've got a jump on dinner, you'll probably be done in time to go to Bible study with us. Wanna come? We always have snacks during the break. Those ladies know how to bake."

Tom laughed, blasting her with his warm, beer-scented breath. He jabbed Greg Dane with his elbow. "How about it, partner? Wanna go to the BS session? Get it? Bible study — BS?"

Greg cringed, and Tyler and Anthony exchanged embarrassed looks. Greg sent Meghan a weak smile. "He's had one too many. Ignore him."

Tom laughed again and reached for the pitcher. He emptied its contents into his glass. "There's no such thing as one too many after you've finished an investigation. This is celebration time." He half stood and waved clumsily at a bleached-blond waitress taking the order at another table. "Hey, you — Sunshine Girl. Bring another pitcher."

Greg grabbed Tom's arm and pulled him onto the seat. The two began a terse exchange.

Meghan bent down to Tyler Roach, who sat across from Greg, and whispered in his ear. "He isn't driving, is he?"

"We won't let him. Don't worry."

"Good." She straightened and inched backward, gesturing to the counter. "I better get my pizza and scoot. Y'all are welcome to come to Bible study anytime — you don't need a personal invitation."

"Don't save me a seat." Tom nearly growled the comment. For the first time, Meghan noticed a second pitcher on the table, also empty. Tom must have downed most of it by himself to be so intoxicated already. "Had enough of that Bible thumpin' when I was growing up to last me four lifetimes." Scowling, he flapped his hand at Meghan. "Go on. If you aren't gonna join the fun, then get outta here."

Meghan hurried off, more than happy to let Greg deal with his partner. She paid for the pizza and left, but a worry followed her. The captain had said if he split her and Sean, he'd pair each of them with Tom or Greg. Working with Greg would be easier — he wasn't openly obnoxious. But if she took Greg, Sean would be stuck with Tom, who would rather torment Sean than cooperate with him.

Sean's Bronco rolled up to the curb, and she clambered in, careful not to dump the steaming cardboard box holding their supper. The moment she snapped her seat belt in place, Sean rolled the old SUV forward, and she said, "Please pass the Dunsbrook case to Tom and Greg and stay partnered with me on this new one."

His eyebrows rose, but he kept his eyes on

the traffic. "That's not exactly the start of a discussion, Meg. It's more like an appeal."

"It is definitely an appeal. A heartfelt one."

"I thought you said you'd understand if I wanted to see the Dunsbrook case through."

"I know I did, and I meant it when I said it, but" — the aroma coming from the closed box was so tantalizing, she had a hard time ignoring it — "I really don't want to work with anybody but you. And I don't want either one of us to have to work with Tom. It's like he takes delight in being difficult, you know?"

Sean glanced at her, worry creasing his forehead. "I saw Farber's car, as well as Dane's, parked outside the pizza place. Can I presume they were inside and gave you some trouble?"

"You're a good detective. Yes, and yes." She put the box on the floor between her feet, where it wouldn't tempt her to dive in. "Actually, Tyler and Anthony were in there, too. The four of them were celebrating Tom and Greg's closed case."

Sean set his lips in a grim line. "I can imagine how they were celebrating. They didn't get obscene with you, did they? Because if they did, I'll —"

"No, nothing like that. Just Tom's usual antichurch stuff. Grandma would say he's as prickly as a hedgehog when it comes to religion. At least I got some insight about why Tom's so antagonistic. He said he'd had enough Bible thumping to last him several lifetimes. Do you think his folks took him to a legalistic church when he was young?"

They left town behind and got on the highway. Sean passed an older-model sedan and eased back into the lane. "I suppose it's possible. Some churches push grace aside and preach condemnation. It'd be hard to know without visiting the church myself. It's also possible he's fighting the Spirit's tug. We've both witnessed to him, and we live out our faith in the workplace. He might feel guilty because he's strayed from what he was taught, and he may use the Bible thumping as an excuse."

Meghan tapped the edge of the pizza box with her toe, willing the miles to pass.

Sean shot a grin at her. "Go ahead and eat a slice while it's hot and fresh. It's okay."

She should wait — how fair was it to eat in front of him? — but temptation got the best of her. She balanced the box on her lap, lifted a slice, and took a big bite. The mingled flavors of seasoning, meat, vegetables, and bread flooded her taste buds, and she couldn't resist a soft groan of approval. "Well, as unpleasant as my exchange with him was, this pizza makes it worth it." She took another bite and spoke around it. "Greg seemed pretty embarrassed, and he said Tom was drunk. Greg's used to working with him — he knows how to handle it when Tom gets unpleasant. I think we should leave Tom and Greg to each other and we should stick together."

Sean drummed his fingers on the steering wheel. "I think we should thoroughly discuss the pros and cons and pray about it before we make a decision. I get where you're coming from, and it makes sense from our point of view, but sometimes God leads us to places we wouldn't necessarily choose in order to help us see something we wouldn't grasp any other way."

She gaped at him. "You think it might be God's will for us to split up?"

He reached across the console and squeezed her wrist. "Not necessarily for the long haul. But maybe for this one case." He released her wrist and gripped the steering wheel again. "And maybe not even for this case. Like I said, we need more time to look at it, to pray about it, to make sure we know what we're supposed to do. Running ahead of God only gets people into trouble. So let's use the time Captain Ratzlaff gave us to seek God's will. Okay?"

SEVEN

Kendrickson, Nevada
Diane

Diane stared at the lines of text filling the email memo box. She'd written the message three different ways, and she still wasn't satisfied with it. Shouldn't an English and literature teacher be able to compose a simple email? But then, she was fairly new at teaching English and literature, and this wasn't exactly a *simple* email. Toss in her exhaustion from surviving the final full days of the school year — always a challenge between the kids' excitement and all the end-of-year grades to compute — and her brain didn't want to function.

She set the laptop aside and tipped her head against the sofa recliner's puffy headrest. Her trio of dachshunds snuffled in their sleep, and Miney bumped her nose against Diane's knee. She automatically ran her hands through the dog's thick ruff.

Funny how empty the sofa felt with only three dogs lounging around her instead of four. She sure missed Ginger, the matriarch of her doggy family.

The sweet old girl had succumbed to heart failure after the first of the year, and she and Mother had cried for days. Mother even bought a little wooden box with the phrase *Pets Leave Paw Prints on Your Heart* carved into its top. They put Ginger's ashes in the box, which now rested in Mother's china curio. Diane never would have imagined her mother mourning a dog, let alone allowing its ashes to be displayed like a prized possession. How much Mother had changed since Diane's childhood.

Had Kevin Harrison changed over the years?

Miney sat up and whined, her pointed nose aimed at the hallway leading to Mother's private suite. Diane peered toward the shadowed opening, and Mother stepped into the living room. Her pert gaze landed on Diane.

"Are you still up? Gracious, Margaret Diane, it's almost midnight. If you don't get some sleep, you aren't going to be worth a plug nickel tomorrow."

Diane chuckled. In some ways Mother would never change, including using her daughter's full name. At least Diane had come to appreciate it, now that she knew its origin was Mother's beloved sister. "Friday's only a half day. End of the school year, you know, so I'll be all right."

Mother stared at Diane for a few seconds, her snow-white brows pinching into a V, and then her expression relaxed. She lowered her slender frame into her wingback chair and propped her bare, wrinkled feet on the chair's matching island-sized ottoman. Miney hopped down and joined Mother, who smiled and scratched the dog's curly ears with her arthritis-bent fingers.

Diane pulled Duchess into the spot Miney had vacated. "Why are you awake?"

"I need to sit up awhile. Heartburn." She grimaced, shaking her finger at Diane. "No more spicy food for supper. My constitution can't take it."

Diane bit back a laugh. The vegan fried rice they'd eaten nearly six hours ago had been anything but spicy. Diane suspected the real culprit was the box of Junior Mints Mother had consumed while watching television. No sense in chiding Mother with the reminder, though.

Mother's frown dropped to the laptop balanced on the sofa armrest. "Are you still figuring final grades?"

"No, I finished an hour ago."

"But I heard you tapping on the keys until right before I got out of bed. What else are you working on?" Awareness dawned across her lined face. She dipped her head in a slow nod, as if agreeing with herself about something. "Ah. Still giving you fits, hmm?"

Diane sighed and put the laptop back on her lap. She opened it and squinted at the unsent email. "What if he doesn't even remember me? If he writes back 'Who are you?' I'll be mortified. But I don't want to write our whole history — short as it was — as a memory jog. I'm starting to wish I'd told Meghan to surprise him and leave me out of it."

Mother smiled, shaking her snowy head. "Your protective instincts wouldn't allow it, and I'm proud of you for stepping in even though it's hard for you to contact him."

Hard didn't seem a strong enough word. After decades of squelching every thought of the man who'd fathered her child, intentionally bringing him to the forefront of her thoughts was torture. If he was still the self-centered, manipulative, apathetic person he'd been when they were in college and he took aim at her precious daughter, she wasn't sure how she would react.

"Why don't you read me what you have?"

Mother crossed her ankles and lifted Miney into her lap. "I'll give you some constructive feedback."

There'd been a time when Diane would have run from her mother's constructive feedback. She realized how much she'd changed when she nodded and angled the laptop for the best view. "All right. Here goes . . . 'Dear Kevin.' " She shot a look at her mother. "Should I use Mr. Harrison instead? We aren't exactly on friendly terms, you know."

"Mr. Harrison is too stuffy. Kevin is better."

Mother's firm tone made Diane smile. She returned her attention to the email. " 'Dear Kevin, in 1985, you and I were sophomores at —' "

"Wait."

Diane shifted her gaze to her mother's frowning face. "What?"

"Drop the *Dear*. Start with Kevin." Her brow puckered. "That man was not a dear. And this isn't what we would call a friendly letter. So start with his name."

Diane deleted *Dear*. "Okay. Here we go. 'Kevin, in 1985, you and I were sophomores at the University of Arkansas. We had a brief relationship, and I became pregnant. You weren't interested in becoming a parent at that time, so —' "

"I wonder if he's ever become a parent . . ."

Diane gave a jolt. "I — I don't know." Why hadn't she contemplated the question? If Kevin had other children, then Meghan had siblings. Something Diane had never given her. How the girl had begged for a baby brother when she was six. Diane had tried to explain it took a mommy and a daddy to make a baby brother, but Meghan then asked how come a daddy hadn't helped make her, and Diane nearly swallowed her tongue trying to talk her way around that one. She'd finally told her precocious daughter they didn't have room in their apartment for a brother.

Meghan might very well have brothers or sisters out there. If so, she would probably be over the moon. But would those siblings want to form relationships with her, or would they be like their father was — disinterested?

"I'm sorry I interrupted. Go ahead, Margaret Diane." Mother hid a yawn behind her hand, then blinked at Diane.

"Yes. Um . . ." Diane cleared the troublesome thoughts and focused on the email. " 'You weren't interested in becoming a parent at that time, so I raised our baby — a girl — on my own. Her name is Meghan D'Ann DeFord-Eagle. She is now a cold-case detective for the state of Arkansas, is married to a fine man, and is a responsible, loving Christian woman. She is also interested in knowing her biological father. She will be in Fort Smith as part of an investigation in the near future and would like to meet with you. I realize my email has probably come as a surprise, and if you need a few days to process this information, I understand. But I would appreciate a response at your earliest convenience.' "

She shrugged. "And that's where I'm stuck. What do I say in conclusion?" Mother didn't answer. Diane glanced over. Mother's eyes were closed, her jaw slack. Sound asleep. Diane released a huff and looked again at the email. She whispered to the dogs, "Well, I guess I'm on my own." She should be used to that by now.

She reached to close the laptop, and her fingers brushed against the screen. A *whooosh* met her ears, and she gasped. She frantically tapped on keys, but it was too late. The email had already whisked through cyberspace to Kevin Harrison's inbox.

"Good morning, Mr. Harrison."

" 'Morning." Swishing his pant leg with a leather portfolio, Kevin strode past the new hire seated at the receptionist's desk. What was her name? Gina? Georgia? He couldn't recall. But why bother learning it? None of his receptionists from the temporary-employee agency lasted longer than a few weeks. Kind of like his marriages. But he did recall all his wives' names. Most of the time.

He paused at his office door and tapped the glazed surface with the edge of the portfolio. "I'm expecting a call about the property in Nevada. I don't want to deal with anything else today. Unless it's Floyd Turner on the other end, take a message."

"Yes, sir."

"That applies to my email, too. Forward anything from Turner. The rest can wait."

"All right, Mr. Harrison."

He glanced over his shoulder at the woman. Young — probably midtwenties. Neatly dressed in black slacks and a white blouse, straight red-blond hair pulled into a ponytail. What his father would have called passable in the looks department — a down-to-earth pretty, not the kind of over-

90

the-top pretty that tempted one to engage in flirtation. And she sure was polite. A breath of fresh air after the last one, who rolled her eyes and sighed every time he gave her an instruction. He hoped this one would stick around. "Do you remember how I take my coffee?"

"Strong and black."

That was more than Wife Number Two could ever remember. "My travel mug's clean and ready to go. Gimme five minutes to settle in first."

"Yes, sir."

Allowing the coffee vendor to set up a cart inside the front doors of his office building was one of the best decisions he'd ever made. Coffee at a moment's notice without having to deal with a pot and all the mess that accompanied it.

He dug his key card from his pocket and placed it against the reader pad. "Get yourself some, too, if you want."

"Thank you. I will."

He closed himself inside his office and crossed the sculpted sage carpet to his brass-and-glass desk. He hated that monstrosity. No drawers, which meant everything he used on a regular basis had to sit on top of the desk in trays or cups. The shiny surface always wore fingerprints no matter how many times he made use of the glass cleaner in his closet. If he'd been in his right mind, he never would have let Wife Number Four talk him into replacing the functional oak banker's desk he'd purchased from an antiques dealer when he and Wife Number One were on their honeymoon.

With a grunt, he dropped the portfolio on his desk and eased into his high-backed, wheeled chair. The supple tan leather was like butter against his frame, and he released a sigh of pure bliss. Tawny had wanted him to replace the chair, too. She'd picked out something that looked like a giant boiled egg with its guts scooped out. He'd dug in his heels on that, though. Even so, she'd talked him into a lot of things he wished he could undo.

He absently rubbed his upper arm, where a purple-and-green — her favorite colors — tattoo of the triquetra symbol hid underneath his sleeve. After only thirteen months of matrimony, he'd decided he needed to get rid of her before she ramrodded any other changes to his ordered existence.

He sat forward and turned the portfolio so it aligned with the corner of his desk. Then he folded back the flap and slid out the contract he'd printed at home last night. These days, he found it easier to proofread on a hard copy than on a computer screen. Evidence that the years were creeping up on him. Which was why he'd paired himself with Tawny. He'd thought being with a girl half his age would make him feel half his age. One of his dumber ideas.

A tap at his door scattered his musings. "Come on in, Gentry." That was the new receptionist's name — Gentry. He congratulated himself for remembering.

The door opened, and she entered, carrying his stainless-steel mug. She placed it on his desk between his oversized computer monitor and the tri-level wooden tray that housed folders. "Here you are."

Kevin grabbed the mug and took a hesitant sip. Hot but not scalding, robust in flavor, and strong enough to kick his brain into overdrive. Perfect. He took a second, longer sip, then set the coffee aside, jammed his black horn-rimmed reading glasses onto his face, and fixed his attention on the contract laid out in front of him.

Gentry didn't move from her spot on the opposite side of the desk.

Without lifting his head, he shifted his eyes and gazed at her over the top of his glasses. "Is there something you need?"

"You said you didn't want to see email except from Floyd Turner."

"That's right."

A pink flush crept across the young woman's cheeks. "Well, there's one that . . . It's . . ."

Kevin sat up and yanked off his glasses. "Is it from Turner?"

She shook her head.

"Then use one of my standard responses to answer it." He slid his glasses into place and bent over the contract.

"Well, the problem is —"

Kevin held back a grunt of aggravation and sat up again.

"— none of your standard responses really . . . fit."

He had pat messages ready to go for people seeking employment, people asking for donations, people wanting him to sample their products, people with questions about renting office space, people interested in selling him property, and lawyers trying to finagle alimony out of him. Nothing else landed in his business email box.

Polite or not, if she couldn't figure out which message to cut and paste into an email, he'd send her back to the temp agency at the end of the day. "Can't you improvise something?"

"I — I don't know."

He blew out a huff of breath. "Fine. Go

ahead and forward it on. But unless any of the others come from Floyd Turner, deal with them."

"Yes, sir." She scuttled out.

Kevin closed his eyes, centered his thoughts, and leaned over the contract again. Moments later, a soft ding signaled the arrival of the email that had so befuddled poor Gentry. What in the world could have created the girl's blush and stuttering? Probably Tawny sending him selfies in a string bikini again. He wouldn't be able to focus on the contract until he'd satisfied his curiosity.

He bumped his mouse, and the computer screen came to life. A few clicks on his keyboard, and his email program opened. He adjusted his glasses and zeroed in on the first address in the inbox. Somebody who went by loves2teach. He snorted under his breath. He could imagine what Tawny wanted to teach him. Well, she had a few lessons to learn, too, most notably that he couldn't be wrapped around her gorgeous little manicured finger anymore.

With a jab of his thumb, he opened the email. "Kevin, in 1985, you and I were sophomores at the University of Arkansas. We had a brief relationship . . ." He drew back, frowning. What kind of scam was this?

He scrolled to the signature at the end of the short email.

"Ms. Diane DeFord, Instructor, Southwind Private Academy, Las Vegas."

He jolted with such force that the chair slid backward a few inches. Diane DeFord? The girl he'd . . . His mouth went dry, and his pulse doubled its tempo.

He'd rather hear from Tawny's lawyer.

EIGHT

Little Rock, Arkansas
Sean

"So what did you two decide?"

Sean looked aside to avoid Captain Ratzlaff's intense gaze. He'd agreed to pass the Dunsbrook murders to Farber and Dane and work with Meghan on the Menke disappearance. Now that it was time to say so, however, he couldn't find the words. Where was the peace he'd prayed for last night? With or without it, they had to move forward.

He looked his captain in the eyes. "Well, Cap, we —"

The desk phone jangled. Captain Ratzlaff grimaced and yanked up the receiver. "Ratzlaff, Cold Case Department . . . Hello, Mrs. Dunsbrook."

Mrs. Dunsbrook? Of course. Her Friday-morning check-in. She'd probably called Sean's number first, and when he didn't answer, she called the captain. Guilt smacked him with as much force as a baseball bat. How could he abandon this case? The Dunsbrooks trusted him.

"Yes, ma'am, he's right here." The captain held the phone toward Sean. "It's for you."

Meghan touched his knee. "Why don't you let Greg or Tom talk to her?"

He shook his head. Sure, it'd be easier on him to let either Dane or Farber let the Dunsbrooks know they were taking over, but he owed the couple an explanation. He stood and took the phone, then pressed it to his ear, aware of Meghan's uneasy frown aimed at his back. "Good morning, Mrs. Dunsbrook."

"I'm sorry. I must have interrupted something important if you're in the captain's office." The woman sounded hesitant and apologetic. And sad. She always sounded sad.

"It's fine, ma'am. You don't need to apologize. I needed to talk to you anyway."

"Has there been a breakthrough?"

The eager note in her tone pierced Sean to his core. "No, ma'am. No breakthrough. Not yet."

"Oh." So much disappointment in a single syllable.

His instincts told him he was close, but he

couldn't throw vague instincts at this grieving mother's feet as an offering. He needed more. She deserved more. And, maybe selfishly, he wanted to be the one to give it to her. From his first meeting with them, Mr. and Mrs. Dunsbrook had reminded him of his own parents — stable, soft spoken, completely dedicated to their family. Maybe he was too entangled in this case, the way he feared Meghan would get too caught up in the Menke case, but the phone call coming in the midst of indecision had confirmed something for him.

"But I haven't given up, and you shouldn't give up, either. There's always hope, right?"

"Yes, Detective Eagle." Her voice quavered, but it held a small measure of strength. "We'll hold on to that hope."

He disconnected the call, then turned to the captain. "I'm staying with the Dunsbrook case."

Captain Ratzlaff raised one eyebrow. "You sure?"

"Yes, sir." It would be tough parting ways even temporarily with Meghan, but the peace he'd requested had now arrived. He'd made the right choice.

The captain shifted his gaze to Meghan. "You okay with this?"

Meghan sat with her hands gripped in her

lap and her lips set in a grim line. She glanced at Sean, fury glinting in her dark eyes, then shrugged. "Yeah. It's fine." If her blunt reply wasn't proof enough, her body language screamed disapproval. The captain was astute enough to recognize it. And he probably realized their job had created marital discord — the very thing he'd warned them about when they told him they were engaged. Up until now, though, they'd balanced work and marriage fine. The Menke case was the problem.

She thought he was being stubborn. She'd told him so during previous discussions about the cases. He'd probably get an earful when they were alone, and he probably deserved it after saying he'd stick with her and then bailing. But he needed to see this one through, with or without Meghan. Sadness sagged his shoulders. They'd come to an impasse about starting a family. Now they'd failed to find an acceptable compromise on another important issue. He prayed it wasn't the start of a trend in their relationship.

"Well, then" — the captain rounded his desk and yanked open his door — "let's get Dane and Farber in here and get your new partnerships established."

"This is just for one case, though, right?"

Meghan's words blasted like rifle shots.

Captain Ratzlaff sent a brief look over his shoulder. "Hope so."

Sean didn't take great comfort in the reply. He turned to Meghan, intending to explain why he'd chosen to stick with the Dunsbrook case after all, but the headstrong jut of her jaw changed his mind. He'd wait until she'd cooled off some. She'd be more apt to listen and understand then.

Farber and Dane sauntered into the captain's office. Dane leaned against the doorjamb, one hand in his pocket, seemingly unconcerned, but Farber planted his feet wide and folded his arms over his chest, his muscles taut. He reminded Sean of a firecracker with a lit fuse, ready to explode at any moment. If he had his choice, Sean would rather work with Dane, but he wouldn't wish Farber on Meghan. Farber was a good investigator, maybe the best in the department, but he held no sensibilities toward females. Or Christians. Tom Farber had been the burr under Sean's saddle for years.

Sean gritted his teeth. No matter how this went, it wasn't going to be pretty.

Captain Ratzlaff returned to his desk chair, sat, and aimed his unsmiling gaze at the pair of men near the doorway. "Here's the deal. We've got a new investigation — a missing-person case — and it's a touchy one. Requires kid gloves. I've assigned it to DeFord. But Eagle's going to finish up the Dunsbrook investigation. That's where you two come in."

Farber grunted. "I kinda figured this was coming when you tossed the Dunsbrook case in our laps." He flung one hand in Sean and Meghan's direction. "So who gets who?"

"As I said, we need kid gloves on this one. Farber, that's not your specialty. So I'm putting Dane with Meghan."

Relief flooded Sean. Meghan would be spared Farber's crusty crassness. But a tingle of resentment also teased him. He wasn't eager to spend the next however-long-it-took dealing with Farber's insults and innuendos. A silent prayer went up for a quick close to both investigations so they could all get back to their usual partnerships.

"You're sticking me with Beagle?" Farber plowed his fingers through his salt-and-pepper hair, making the thick strands stand up like an angry porcupine's quills. "Why can't he work with Roach or Johnson?"

Sean forced a laugh. "C'mon, Farber, you're making me feel like the nerdy kid who never gets picked for playground games."

Farber snorted. He didn't even glance at Sean. "Seriously, Cap, Johnson ought to put in some time on the Dunsbrook case. He's never worked a murder investigation. Good experience for him."

Captain Ratzlaff aimed a scowl at Farber. "I'm not playing Fruit Basket Upset with the entire department. The decision's made. You're with Eagle and Dane's with DeFord for the duration of these two cases. Then you'll get back to your old partnerships." He slapped his desktop with both palms and rose. "Sooner y'all get started, the sooner you'll be back to normal. So get to it."

Dane opened the door and gestured Meghan out. She whisked what Sean interpreted as an apologetic grimace in his direction as she passed him, but she didn't hesitate in leading Dane out the door.

Sean stood and slipped his thumbs into his trouser pockets. "Wanna show me what you and Dane covered with the Dunsbrook case the past couple days?"

Farber's thunderous expression bellowed no, but he nodded. "Yeah. Let's get to it. Like Cap said, the sooner it's done, the sooner we can be rid —" He coughed. "The sooner we can get back to normal around here."

Sean had been praying to find the murderer for weeks, but he sent up another, even more fervent request for answers. He wouldn't say it out loud, but he wasn't any keener on working with Farber than Farber was on working with him.

Fort Smith, Arkansas
Kevin

Kevin braced his hand on the window frame and stared at the street below. Traffic flowed in a regular pattern — idle and drive, idle and drive — guided by the stoplights, the same way it did every day. But for him, the world had come to a halt. Well, not a halt. More like a fast reverse. Backward in time to the day pretty Diane DeFord knocked the wind out of him.

March 1, 1985
Little Rock, Arkansas

Something nudged him in the ribs and then yanked the covers. Kevin grunted into full wakefulness. He squinted past a dull throb behind his eyes and glared blearily at Diane. Even with her makeup smeared and her dark hair spread across the pillow in tangled strands, she was beautiful. What his friends called a hottie. She was smart, too — dean's list every semester. And she'd chosen him.

His aggravation at the rude awakening faded as quick as a blink. "You goin' back to your dorm?"

She shook her head and pushed hair away from her face. "Not yet."

"Good." He rolled sideways, slipped his arms around her, and pulled her close. He kissed her hair, then aimed a kiss at her lips.

She turned her face aside. "Kev, go brush your teeth, huh? I have something important to tell you."

He grinned and tightened his grip. "I don't much feel like talking, but I do feel like —"

She shoved his chest. Hard. "No. Go brush your teeth, okay?"

Anger swelled. Who did she think she was, pushing him away? But nature was calling, and he needed to answer. Grumbling, so she'd know for sure he wasn't happy, he crawled out of bed and staggered into the bathroom. How many beers had he consumed at the party last night? Mom would say if he couldn't remember, it'd been too many. Dad would say if it was less than six, he wasn't worth his salt. Kevin always made sure he was worth his salt and then some.

The liquor had erased his memory of much of the evening, but the fact that Diane was in his bed let him know the night hadn't been a bust. He didn't intend to waste the morning, either.

He removed the sour-feet taste from his mouth with mint-flavored paste, then returned to the bedroom. Ignoring the throb in his head, he flopped across the bed and nuzzled Diane's sweat-moist neck.

"Kevin, guess what?"

Hadn't he said he wasn't interested in talking? He slid his hand under her head, his fingers catching in her hair, and lifted her face. "Can't guess." He closed his eyes and leaned in.

"I'm pregnant."

He went as still as a mannequin. He'd heard her wrong. He must've heard her wrong. "What?"

She laughed — the shrillest, most uneasy laugh he'd ever heard. "I'm pregnant. Isn't it wonderful? We're gonna have a baby."

Fear roared like the sound of ocean waves beating against rocks. His mouth went dry, and he jerked away from her. "What makes you think it's mine?"

She sat up and scooted on her bottom to the headboard. Her hurt-filled gaze locked on his face. "I haven't been with anyone else." She swallowed. Tears swam in her brown eyes. "Ever."

He couldn't say the same, but this pregnancy announcement was a first. He swung his feet to the floor and bent low, elbows on knees, fingers in his hair, palms massaging his throbbing temples. "This can't be real . . ."

Hands — warm and trembling — curled over his shoulders. Her breath whisked past his ear. "I know it's a shock. It took me by surprise, too."

Kevin shrugged loose. Questions he knew his father would ask poured out of his mouth. "How'd it happen? Aren't you smart enough to use birth control? Of all the —"

"I'm not the only one who could take precautions." Her tone changed from sweet to abrasive. "You —"

He jumped up and spun to face her. He jabbed a finger at her. "Don't you dare pin this on me." She scrambled to the headboard and huddled there. He leaned in, fury and panic making his chest burn as if a bonfire had ignited under his skin. "You did it on purpose, didn't you? Thinking you'd get me to marry you. My family has money — is that what you're after?"

Shock registered on her face. "No! I don't need your money. I thought . . . I thought . . ." Tears spilled down her cheeks, and she reached for him. "Kevin, please, we're gonna be parents. I need you to —"

He lurched away from her outstretched hand, shaking his head. "I'm not gonna be a parent. No way. Not now. Not with you."

She covered her quivering lips with the back of her fist. Tears rolled, and sobs shook her entire frame. It took every bit of self-control he possessed not to gather her in his arms and cry with her. But he had to stay strong. He had to think. Dad always told him to keep the upper hand. To never get caught with his guard down. Dad would call him every kind of fool if he let some unplanned pregnancy destroy the plans they'd made for his future.

He lowered his gaze to the carpet, blocking out the sight of his distraught girlfriend, and forced his beer-soaked brain to function. What would Dad do? *Eliminate the competition.* The voice boomed through his mind as loudly as if Dad were standing in the room.

Kevin sucked in a fortifying breath, organized his thoughts, then slowly rounded the bed and sat next to Diane's feet. "Di, honey . . ." He waited until her brown eyes shifted and met his. He smiled and ran the pad of his thumb down her tear-stained cheek. "Do you love me?"

She nodded fast. Tears made fresh trails past her puckered lips. A girl so pretty shouldn't be all red eyed and blotchy faced. She shouldn't ruin her perfect figure with a bulging belly, either. What he wanted was best for both of them.

He cupped her jaw and stroked her lower lip with his thumb. "Then you'd do anything for me, right?"

She tipped her head, pressing her cheek into his palm, and gulped. "Yes. Anything."

"I want you to get rid of it."

She jolted, shaking the whole bed, and stared at him. "W-what?"

"Get rid of it. We aren't ready to be parents. And you can't be far along, right?" He settled his hand on her belly. Completely flat. Nobody would ever have to know he'd been stupid enough to get her pregnant. "It's not worth ruining our lives for, is it?"

She flung his hand aside and scuttled to the opposite side of the bed. She stood and gaped at him. "No. I can't. I can't kill it."

He huffed. "People do it all the time. That's why abortion's legal — so you don't have to have a baby if you don't want to."

She clutched her stomach and shook her head. "But I . . . I want to have it."

He glared at her, daring her to change her mind.

She whispered, "With you."

She didn't get it, did she? He couldn't have a baby. Dad would kill him if he shamed his folks with an out-of-wedlock baby. And a shotgun wedding was out of the question. How could he finish school if he had a wife and kid to support? He stomped past her to the closet and grabbed jeans and a button-up shirt. He dressed, watching her out of the corners of his eyes. She put on her jeans and sweater, then sat on the edge of the bed, hugging her shoes. Staring at the floor. Biting her lip. Soft whimpers begged him to comfort her, but he couldn't. He had to hold his ground. As he tied the laces on his sneakers, he threw a snarling look in her direction.

"If you have it, it'll be yours. Not mine. If you decide to get an abortion, I'll pay for it. Then we can keep going out. But if you have it, you're on your own. Don't expect anything from me."

She tightened her arms around her shoes. "I . . . I . . ."

"Make up your mind, Diane. Do you want a kid, or do you want me?" He held his breath, waiting — hoping — for her to make the right choice.

Without answering, she bolted past him and out the door. Her sobs carried from the hallway to his ears. Stung, he sank onto the edge of the bed. She hadn't even met the kid, and she picked it over him. How much more of a loser could he be?

Present Day
Fort Smith, Arkansas
Kevin slapped the window frame, snorted, and returned to his desk. He slumped into his chair and propped up his head with his fist. Diane had been smart to dump him. He'd proven himself a loser in relationship after relationship. First with Julie and her son, Kip, who called him Dad. Then Sherry, then Veronica, and finally Tawny. Every marriage had crumbled. Or combusted.

He had his thriving business, though — evidence that he wasn't a total failure. So he might as well get to work. He opened the file, slid his glasses onto his nose, and leaned over the stack of pages.

The acquisition of the four-story building in the heart of the Las Vegas Strip promised to be his most lucrative deal to date. Even though he hadn't seen the property in person, online photographs of the loft apartment and various offices on the lower three levels looked good. Once his agent had finished a personal inspection and deemed the property acceptable, he would hand over a check, and then —

His frame jerked as if someone poked him with a fork. He tapped keys and brought up his email. He checked the message from Diane DeFord. Her email signature indicated she worked in Las Vegas.

"I would appreciate a response at your earliest convenience."

Wheels turned in his mind. Why pay an agent to inspect the property when he could do it himself and maybe have the chance to inspect Diane, too? He'd also be out of town when her daughter was in Fort Smith, which would buy him some time to decide whether he really wanted to meet the girl Diane had refused to abort.

He clicked Reply and began to type.

NINE

Little Rock, Arkansas
Meghan

Sean didn't utter a word during their drive home Friday, so Meghan didn't talk, either. A part of her wanted to tell him she was sorry he'd gotten stuck with Tom Farber. Another part wanted to thank him for not asking Cap to partner her with the crass agent. But most of her was so disappointed he hadn't chosen to stay with her that she couldn't get the other words to come out. She'd never had a partner other than Sean, and she'd never wanted a different one.

If only the captain had waited until she and Sean closed the Dunsbrook case before bringing the Menke case to the table. Then she wouldn't have to sit here in this uncomfortable silence with her husband. But she wouldn't have to sit in silence if she'd asked to see the Dunsbrook case through, either.

She gritted her teeth and stared out the

window at the green landscape. They'd made their decision, the captain's pronouncement finalized it, and now they had to follow through. She hoped they could do so without freezing each other out.

Sean pulled into the driveway and hit the garage door opener. Meghan started to ask if grilled cheese sandwiches and tomato soup — one of the comfort meals of her childhood — would be okay for supper. Her cell phone's ring interrupted, and Mom's face showed on the screen. She pressed Accept Call and put the phone to her ear while Sean drove slowly into the garage.

"Hi, Mom. Are you celebrating?"

Mom laughed. "You know me well."

"How could I forget last-day-of-school festivities?" When Meghan was a kid, they'd gone out for ice cream to celebrate the close of a school year. Mom didn't eat dairy products anymore, but she might buy herself a half pint of the vegan substitute made with cashew milk and bananas.

Sean parked the SUV and turned off the ignition. He pointed to the door leading to their utility room and mouthed, "I'm going in." She nodded, and he headed inside. She popped her door open for ventilation but stayed put.

"Before I celebrate, though, I've got an

email you need to hear."

Chill bumps broke out over Meghan's arms. "From my father?" How strange to hear herself use the title. The word never rolled from her tongue but emerged stilted and overly formal. Yet she couldn't bring herself to say *dad. Dad* denoted relationship, and she had none.

"Yes." Mom's reply was clipped, too, as if she'd prefer not to continue. "Do you want me to read it to you or give you the *Reader's Digest* abridged version?"

Meghan's stomach growled, reminding her that she and Sean needed supper. "Abridged is fine, but you can forward it to me and I'll read the whole thing later."

Mom huffed a laugh. "Well, it won't take long. He was never much of a conversationalist, and it appears that transfers over into written communication, too. Basically he says not to bother trying to look him up when you're in Fort Smith because he won't be there. He's flying to — you won't believe this — Las Vegas to finalize a business transaction, and it might take a week or two."

Meghan sagged against the seat, torn between deliverance and disappointment. "If he's gonna be in Vegas, will you try to see him?"

Silence fell at the other end of the call. A silence so lengthy that Meghan wondered if the connection had been lost. She hopped down from the SUV and stepped out onto the driveway. "Mom?"

"I'm here."

"I thought I'd lost you."

"No. Just thinking. He suggested meeting up while he's in town — to talk about you, he said — but I don't know. I'm not sure I'm ready for that."

"Then don't." Guilt about Sean having to spend time with Tom prompted the firm statement. "I can take over communicating with him from this point on. He knows now that I'm out here and interested in connecting with him, so the surprise element is gone. You can move completely out of the picture."

"Can I?"

Meghan wasn't sure if Mom was asking permission or questioning her ability.

A heavy sigh met Meghan's ear. "I need to think it over. Either way, at least you know not to waste your time going by his office. I'm sorry about the timing of his trip."

"Yeah. Me, too." The evening sun was surprisingly bright. And warm. Meghan ducked into the shaded area right inside the garage opening. "But it's probably just as well. I need to focus on the case, and meeting him would distract me. Especially since it won't be Sean with me in Fort Smith. My new partner probably wouldn't want me wandering off on a personal errand while we're on the job."

"New partner? Why aren't you investigating with Sean?"

Meghan inwardly kicked herself. She hadn't meant to tell Mom or Grandma about her and Sean dividing up. "It's only temporary." She forced a light tone she hoped Mom would accept as legitimate. "Sean is going to finish our old case while I investigate the new one. So the captain split Tom Farber and Greg Dane, too. Tom will work with Sean, and I've got Greg."

"Are you all right with that?"

The worried tone let Meghan know she hadn't fooled her mother. She laughed. "Truthfully, not a hundred percent, but as I said, it's temporary. Might actually turn out to be a good thing — it'll let us see how well we function independently. When we open our own agency, there'll be times we'll probably have to juggle more than one case. This will give us some practice."

"So you're still planning to leave the department and branch out on your own?"

"We're waiting for the right time." Why did she feel as if she'd lied to Mom? She pushed off from the house and headed for the door. "I should get supper fixed. Congrats on finishing another school year. And thanks for playing go-between for Kevin Harrison and me. I'll take it from here so you can bow out."

Kendrickson, Nevada
Diane

Diane placed her phone on the end table and smiled at her mother, who sat in her favorite chair with an open book in her lap but her gaze pinned on Diane. "Now that I'm done talking to Meghan . . . have you decided where you want to go for dinner?"

"The Salad Palace for one of their avocado-and-tomato concoctions. But before we go, what was that about Meghan getting a new partner? Why isn't she working with Sean?"

Diane swallowed a chuckle. Eighty-three years old and Mother's ears worked as well as a teenager's. Diane needed to close herself in her bedroom if she wanted a private conversation. "It's a temporary thing — for one case, I think."

"Oh." Mother closed the book with a snap. "Well, then, I won't worry about it.

But you need to forgive Kevin Harrison."

The abrupt change in topic sent Diane's head spinning. "What?"

"You heard me. You need to forgive Kev —"

Diane waved her hands. "Yes, yes, I heard you. That *what* was rhetorical. I meant, what makes you think I haven't?"

Mother tipped her head and gave Diane a "you're not fooling me" look. "Your hesitance to see him face to face, of course. If you'd forgiven him, you wouldn't perceive him as a threat."

Diane sat straight up at the edge of the sofa cushion. "A threat?" From her spot on the corner of the sofa, Duchess began to whine. Diane automatically reached out and toyed with the dog's ears. "Honestly, the things you say."

Mother shrugged. "I'm old. I might not have a chance to talk tomorrow, so I have to say what needs saying today."

"Oh, Mother, you're too stubborn to die."

"Don't flatter me." Mother's still-bright brown eyes twinkled. "Seriously, though. Think about all the things you've overcome by meeting them head on. You pushed past your fear and chose to have a baby all by yourself. You ignored the naysayers and finished college while caring for a newborn and toddler. Then you single-handedly raised a wonderful daughter. You give of yourself every day to your students, inspiring them to be their very best. You're strong and courageous. And yes, stubborn. Like me."

Diane laughed. "Just when I thought you were getting all warm and mushy, you have to go and insult me."

A smile twitched at the corners of Mother's lips. "Being stubborn isn't a bad thing, Margaret Diane. Stubbornness could be defined as determination on steroids. As long as it's aimed in a God-honoring direction, being stubborn can be a gift because it gives you stick-to-itiveness." She tapped her manicured fingernail on the cover of the book in her lap. "What was it Alice said in *Alice's Adventures in Wonderland*? 'I can't go back to yesterday . . .' "

Diane gave a slow nod. " '. . . because I was a different person then.' "

"Yes. Different." A thoughtful frown pinched Mother's face. "You are a different person now than you were in your rebellious college years. Christ has redeemed your heart. So you don't need to be afraid of seeing the person who fathered your child."

Diane raised her eyebrows. "You think I'm afraid?"

"I do. I think you're afraid of revisiting your past because there's a part of you that hasn't forgiven it. You haven't forgiven him for leaving you to handle the consequences of the pregnancy on your own, and — since I'm being so bold — you haven't forgiven yourself for letting him get you pregnant."

Diane pulled Duchess close and rubbed the dog's soft neck and chest while considering all that her mother had said. For years, she'd pushed aside memories of Kevin. She'd tried to bury the hurts and snubs and difficulties the unwed pregnancy had brought. As Mother claimed, she'd overcome it all. She was, by anyone's account, a success story. But deliberately coming face to face with Kevin Harrison after all these years?

She set the dachshund aside. "No promises, Mother, but I'll think about it."

Mother planted her hands on the chair's armrests and pushed herself to her feet. "Think about it, yes. And pray about it. While you're praying, ask God to help you forgive Kevin and forgive yourself, because until you do, you'll drag around an iron ball of regret." She looked down and wriggled her bare toes. "Now, where did I leave my shoes?"

TEN

Carson Springs, Arkansas
Meghan

Meghan set the table with plates and bowls from the set they'd received as a wedding gift. Amazing how much more appealing they were than flimsy Styrofoam. Even the simple sandwich and soup looked more appetizing. She should use the real stuff more often. It might make Sean think her cooking had improved.

She peeked around the wide doorway between the eat-in kitchen and the living room. Sean slouched at the end of the sectional, chin in hand, eyes closed, television blaring. She cleared her throat. He didn't budge. Swallowing a chortle, she crossed the floor and tapped his knee. He awoke with a start.

She smiled. "Sorry to disturb you. Supper's ready."

"Can't believe I fell asleep with that noise

going." He clicked the television off and stood. He stretched, groaning. "I don't know why I'm so tired."

At least he was talking again. Maybe the nap had erased his irritation. She hoped so. "Grandma would say if you fell asleep without intending to, you needed the rest."

"I guess so."

She suspected his tiredness was for the same reason as hers. She hadn't slept much last night, worrying about their differing views about the Menke case. She returned to the kitchen with him trailing her. He sat at the table, and she realized she'd neglected to add beverages. She hurried to the fridge and grabbed two water bottles. Then she grimaced and turned to Sean. "Do you want your water poured over ice in a glass?"

"Why?"

She gestured toward the dishware and reached to open the cabinet door that shielded their glasses from view. "It'll match better."

He glanced at the plate and bowl in front of him, then shrugged. "Whatever you want to do."

She hesitated, fingers pinched on the cabinet knob.

"Meghan, it's okay."

Sighing, she joined him at the table and

handed him one of the condensation-dotted bottles. "I know we don't stand much on formality around here. I'm sorry." The apology was meant to cover a lot more than her practice of using disposable plates, but she wasn't sure he'd read it that way. A lump filled her throat and prevented any other words from escaping.

He slid his hand toward her. "As long as we get fed, it's not a big deal."

She took his hand while he asked a blessing on the food, and she tried to accept his statement as truth. But she knew she disappointed him far too many times when it came to her domestic insufficiencies. He'd never complained or nagged, but from remembrances he'd shared about his mother, his home, and his childhood, she'd gathered how unconventional their lives were compared to what he'd grown up with. She hated letting him down, yet she couldn't imagine doing things any differently, given their work schedule. But if they worked from home . . .

Sean dipped his sandwich in the soup and aimed the dripping corner toward his mouth.

"Sean?"

He paused and looked across the table at her.

"That was Mom who called."

"I figured. Did you have a good chat?"

"I told her that maybe us splitting up as partners could end up being a good thing."

"Oh, yeah?" He took the bite, chewed, swallowed, and dipped another corner. "How so?"

He sounded curious, not defensive. She tore off a small piece of her sandwich and popped it into her mouth. "It could let us see how well we do as individuals. In case we ever have to, you know, handle more than one case at a time."

"Are you talking about if we open a private agency?"

She preferred *when* instead of *if,* but she nodded.

He placed his sandwich on the plate and brushed his hands together, dispelling crumbs, then rested his elbows on the table. "Have you actually researched independent investigation companies? Gathered statistics for an agent's average caseload or income expectations? Because I'll be honest — the idea worries me."

"Don't you think we'd be successful?" Meghan plopped her sandwich onto the plate, no longer hungry.

"I think we're successful now. We make good salaries at the bureau. I'm comfortable with our lifestyle. And I think we need to be practical. What if we go out on our own but the cases don't come in? How will we pay for our house, utilities, and vehicles? Plus, with self-employment, there are different taxes to cover and insurance issues. There's a lot we need to carefully consider before even thinking about opening a private agency. Most important, we need to be in prayer — individually and as a couple — and seek God's will. I've never received so much as a nudge from the Holy Spirit about leaving the bureau. Have you?"

She chewed the inside of her lower lip. She couldn't honestly say the Holy Spirit had nudged her, but what difference did that make? "If we're operating an honest business, using our skills as detectives to help people, isn't that good enough?"

Disappointment tinged his features. "Meg, anything we do — no matter how unselfish or profitable it appears from a human viewpoint — is useless if it's outside God's will for us. I can say with all certainty God put me at the Arkansas Cold Case Investigations Department. I've always believed He placed you there, too — to be my partner in both work and marriage. I love you, and I don't want to hold you back from pursuing a God-planted dream, but I've got some real apprehensions about it."

She had always appreciated his honesty, but in that moment she wished he'd be less straightforward and more supportive. She toyed with her spoon, her gaze low.

"We better eat before the soup gets cold. We can talk more later, okay?"

She nodded and dipped her spoon into the soup, but he didn't bring up the subject after supper, and neither did she. Saturday they performed the usual weekend household and yard chores. Sean mowed the lawn and raked and bagged the cuttings while Meghan did laundry, cleaned the bathrooms, and swept and vacuumed the floors — roles traditionally assigned to their respective genders. As she pushed the vacuum cleaner across the carpet in their bedroom, she couldn't help but think back to when she and Mom shared cleaning chores in their apartment.

They hadn't lived in squalor, but neither could she say they'd been neat freaks. Mom always complained that Grandma had kept their house so perfect a person couldn't relax in it, and Mom wanted their apartment to feel lived in. As a kid who'd rather play than clean, Meghan was perfectly content with lived in, too. She and Sean often put up with lived in because of long workdays, but she suspected that his mother kept their home closer to what Grandma had done.

For some reason, on this Saturday, performing the mindless and often thankless tasks so many generations of women had done before her left her lonesome for Grandma. A desire to talk to the woman who'd been her anchor throughout her childhood overwhelmed her. She turned the vacuum off and dropped onto the bed. She retrieved her cell phone from her pocket, pulled up the list of names and numbers, and aimed her finger for Grandma's contact.

The phone rang twice, and then came a pert "Hello, Meghan."

Meghan smiled, memories of her grandmother rushing through her mind. "Hi, Grandma. Am I intruding on your day?"

"As if you could ever be an intrusion."

Her reproving tone made Meghan grin. "That's not what you said when I barged into your bathroom in the middle of your bath."

"Ah, yes. Well, there was that one time . . ."

Meghan laughed. It felt good to laugh. She needed to call Grandma more often.

"So what are you and Sean doing today? Anything exciting?"

"Cleaning house. And grocery shopping a little later."

"Us, too. In fact, your mother is at the market right now stocking up on organic vegan products. I told her to be sure to buy me one thick, juicy, grass-fed T-bone."

"Do you think she'll do it?"

"If she knows what's good for her, yes, she will."

Chuckling, Meghan reclined against the pillows and lifted her feet onto the bed.

"Your mother tells me you and Sean are working on separate cases."

Funny how Mom talked to Grandma about everything these days. When Meghan was a kid caught between them, she wouldn't have imagined the closeness they now shared, but their relationship rifts had all been mended. It gave her hope that she and Sean would weather their current differences. "Yeah, we are."

"And that you intend to connect with your father."

Meghan stifled a snicker. They really did discuss everything. "What do you think about that? Is it a good idea?"

"I've been praying for years that God would direct you concerning a relationship with your father. If this is His timing, then I'm all for it."

The same uneasy feeling that had attacked when Sean asked if the Holy Spirit had prompted her to leave the cold-case department tingled through her again. "I'm not sure if God directed me on this or if it's my own curiosity." She shared her desire to know more about who she was, genetically and biologically, then added, "How do you know when God's telling you to do something? I mean, in the Bible it was so obvious. A burning bush, a talking donkey, angels who showed up and delivered messages. God doesn't do those kinds of things anymore."

Grandma's chuckle rumbled. "You're right that He doesn't prompt donkeys to speak, and I'm pretty sure I've never been visited by an angel. But, honey, He does talk to us. He speaks to me every day."

Meghan almost dropped her phone. "He does? How?"

"Why, through His Word. The holy Scriptures. Every part of the Bible is God speaking to His followers. And then there's His Spirit, who resides within you. The Holy Spirit is always with us, guiding and directing us."

A hollow feeling inched through Meghan's center. She gripped the phone tighter. "Sean and I read some verses together every morning at breakfast, we go to Bible study at church, and I read the Bible on my own, too." When she carved out the time. "But the Bible was written for so many people. How can it speak to just me?"

"What I've discovered" — Grandma's voice quavered, as if she battled emotion — "is that the Spirit brings a scripture to mind or brings a new understanding of a scripture when I'm seeking. When my heart is open and His timing is in place, then I know it's His voice."

Meghan's chest went tight with a longing she couldn't define. "I still don't understand. How do you *know*?"

"It's hard to explain. But I . . . I know. I experience a peacefulness. Or a settledness. Or a new resolve." She fell silent for a few moments, and Meghan listened to her own pulse throb in her ears. Finally Grandma's sigh carried through the connection. "Proverbs 19:21 says it well. 'Many are the plans in a person's heart, but it is the Lord's purpose that prevails.' Following God's will should always be first and foremost in our lives. We can't be at peace when we're outside His will. Not if we're truly His children. So, honey, if you aren't absolutely certain that God's leading you to seek a relationship with your biological father, then maybe you should wait until you receive His confirmation."

A lump filled Meghan's throat, making it hurt to talk. "But I want a father, Grandma. I think I always have."

"And you've always had one, dear girl." Even though Meghan couldn't see her grandmother's face, she could tell by her voice that she was smiling. "You've had your heavenly Father. God is Father to the fatherless. He's the best Father because He never leaves us or forsakes us. You aren't fatherless, Meghan. Remember that."

Grandma's words seemed to reiterate what Sean had said about her needing to honor God with her life and follow His direction. She nodded. "I'll try to remember. Thank you."

"I'll pray for God to speak clearly and for your heart to be open to His voice so you know what you're to do. And speaking of hearing . . . I hear your mother in the kitchen. I should go help her put the groceries away and make sure she brought my steak."

Laughter bubbled and spilled from Meghan, chasing away the melancholy pall that had fallen. "You do that. Thanks for talking to me, and thanks for praying. I love you."

"I love you, too, honey. Goodbye."

Meghan tucked the phone in her pocket and returned to vacuuming. She replayed her conversation with Grandma while she cleaned the carpet, and by the time she was finished, she'd decided maybe it was best that her father wouldn't be in Fort Smith while she was there. She needed to do more thinking — and praying — before meeting him.

The problem was, she'd already set a ball in motion. And it was rolling straight for Mom.

ELEVEN

Las Vegas, Nevada
Kevin

Kevin set his suitcase on the folding stand in the corner of his hotel suite. The metal frame and sagging woven straps seemed rickety and out of place in the otherwise plush surroundings. He shrugged out of his summer-weight dove-gray suit coat, which he'd worn over a plain white T-shirt and jeans *Miami Vice* style, and hung it on a hanger in the closet. He'd need it again for his meeting with the Realtor tomorrow, but for now there wasn't any reason to keep even that small bit of formality in place. Tonight's agenda included ordering room service and watching television.

Because he'd made reservations for an eight-day stay, he unzipped his suitcase and spent several minutes transferring everything to drawers in the low, sleek dresser that stood sentry on the wall opposite the king-sized bed. Socks and underwear in a top drawer, T-shirts and polos in the second-row drawers, and jeans, khakis, and athletic shorts at the bottom. The same way Mom had organized his clothes at home. He had no idea why she'd ordered the clothing articles that way, but it made it easy for him to find what he needed. Especially on those mornings when his brain was sizzling from too much imbibing the night before.

One more top drawer remained. He could store his wallet and wristwatch in there. He yanked the drawer open, and several items slid to the back of it at the force of his tug. He glanced in and grimaced. He had no use for the Bible, the Book of Mormon, the Teaching of Buddha, or the hotel-provided notepad and pen. He bumped the drawer closed with his hip, then returned to the closet and kicked off his leather sneakers.

His shaving kit and a pair of tasseled loafers remained in his suitcase. He plopped the loafers on the closet floor, then placed his shaving kit in the bathroom, pausing for a moment to admire the floating marble slab centered with a glass bowl sink — classy. He'd chosen well, considering he made the reservation online. But a person couldn't go too wrong when booking on the Strip in Vegas. Or purchasing property on the Strip.

Too bad Dad wasn't alive to see this deal go down. He might actually be impressed.

As abruptly as he'd closed the dresser drawer on the stack of religious books, he closed down all thoughts of his father. On the desk near the window, a folder with the hotel's insignia imprinted in gold foil caught his attention. The restaurant menu should be inside. His growling stomach propelled him across the thick carpet. He flopped the folder open and chose the tab marked Room Service. Within minutes he'd made a selection, and he called the kitchen and requested garlic shrimp and roasted Roma tomatoes over angel-hair pasta, as well as a bottle of their best rosé.

Kevin hung up the phone, then sat on the edge of the bed. Tomorrow was Sunday — a whole day of settling in before his Monday-morning meeting with the Realtor. He should find a grocery store and stock some basics for the week, make good use of his kitchenette. Room service was convenient, and he could afford to order every meal if he wanted to, but his waistline would take a direct hit if he went a full week eating rich foods.

Sometimes being middle aged leaning toward old stunk. He caught a glimpse of his reflection in the full-length mirror next to the bathroom door — steel-gray hair, high brow, prominent jaw, lanky frame. Great Scott, he looked more like his father every day.

What about Diane's daughter? Did she look like *her* father?

And where did that thought come from?

With a grunt, he grabbed the television remote and aimed it at the big screen tucked inside the armoire in the sitting area of the suite. He didn't turn it on, though. Curiosity held him captive. Who did Meghan D'Ann DeFord-Eagle resemble? Was there any hint of him in her at all? He tried to envision a child born to him and Diane. No picture formed. But he bet he could find out what she looked like. If she'd been involved in any noteworthy cold cases, there could be news reports online. There might even be photographs of the detectives if the cold-case unit had a website.

He tapped the remote on his knee, debating with himself. Watch television, or do a little sleuthing?

Someone knocked on the door, and a female voice called out, "Room service."

Dinner already? He strode to the door and swung it open. A blond-haired young woman and a skinny Hispanic man wearing matching blue uniforms and chef aprons crossed the threshold. The woman carried a tray containing a silver dome-covered plate, silverware rolled in a linen napkin, miniature canisters of salt and pepper, and a single wine glass turned on its rim. The man toted a bucket of ice. A wine bottle's neck poked up like a buoy. She set the tray on the kitchenette counter, her long braid sliding forward, and gestured for the man to place the bucket next to it. Then she flipped her braid over her shoulder and aimed a smile at Kevin.

"When you're finished, please put the tray in the hallway, and someone will retrieve it. Is there anything else you need?"

Kevin glanced at the wine bucket. "A cork-screw?"

"You'll find a corkscrew in the drawer next to the sink."

Kevin lifted the dome and peeked at his food. He quirked his brow. "Parmesan?"

The young man pulled a small shaker bottle of grated parmesan from the pocket of his apron and handed it to Kevin.

Kevin stifled a chortle. Maybe he should ask for a dining companion since they'd managed to provide everything else. "Looks like I have what I need."

The woman whipped a black leather check holder and pen from her pocket and held them out. "Sign, please, and we'll leave you to enjoy your meal."

Kevin added a tip to the amount, signed the check with a flourish, and handed it back. He couldn't resist winking — flirtation came far too naturally, his mother used to berate — even though the woman was probably a year or two younger than Tawny. She fluttered her eyelashes, proving she was practiced in the art of flirtation, before she ushered the man out the door.

Alone again, Kevin made use of the corkscrew, smiling at the satisfying *pop!* as the cork slid free. A sweet essence accompanied the gentle *glug-glug* of pale liquid filling the glass, and he drew in a slow breath to absorb the slightly fruity aroma. He took a sip as he lifted the silver dome and set it aside. The savory-smelling steam rising from the food mingled with the sweetness of the wine, and his mouth watered.

He slid onto the barstool, sprinkled parmesan over the pasta, tomatoes, and pink shrimp, then added a dash of pepper. He jerked open the napkin bundle and picked up his fork. Before he plunged it into the pasta, though, he glanced at his computer bag. Why not multitask?

He clanked the fork on the counter, grabbed his laptop from the bag, and booted it up. Over the next twenty minutes, he alternately tapped keys with his left forefinger, sipped wine, and ate every bit of the well-seasoned pasta and toppings. By the time he finished eating, half the bottle of wine was gone and he'd saved three photographs of Meghan DeFord-Eagle to his computer.

He pushed the plate aside, pulled the computer closer, and opened all three images. He leaned close, holding the wine glass near his jaw, and examined the photos side by side. None of them held even the slightest resemblance to him. But he sure saw Diane in the girl. She had her mother's olive complexion, dark hair and eyes, and delicate profile. Pretty girl. Very pretty girl.

For several seconds he stared at the center image. Even while draining his glass, he kept his gaze locked on the face of his daughter. Shouldn't he feel something? Stirrings of pride? Curiosity? Regret? He waited, but nothing within him changed. Maybe because this girl wasn't his daughter after all. Diane said she was, but she could be wrong. After all, he wasn't so hard hearted that he wouldn't experience the tiniest niggle of some kind of emotion when looking at the face of his one and only biological child for the first time. Or was he?

Uncomfortable with the direction his thoughts had taken, he turned the chair away from the bar. He grabbed the bottle and glass and trudged to the long green-and-brown-checked sofa stretching along the wall. He flopped onto the center cushion, poured another glass, then sat and sipped, the bottle still gripped in his hand. He stared at the wall, seeing in his mind's eye the images of the seemingly successful, satisfied-with-her-life young woman Diane had raised.

Curiosity rose. But not about the girl. About the girl's mother. How'd Diane done it? How had she raised Meghan by herself and managed to produce a well-rounded, competent adult? He'd had help raising his adopted son. Mostly from the boy's mother, Julie, of course. But Wife Number Two, Sherry, had been good with Kip — probably because she hoped it would convince Kevin to let her have a baby. By the time he married Wife Number Three, Kip was a cocky high school junior who rebelled against every authority figure, but Veronica had at least tried to form a relationship with him.

Experts said it took a village to raise a child, and he'd had a whole village involved in Kip's upbringing. A mother, two stepmothers — well, three, but Tawny didn't count because she was too close in age to Kip to even pretend to mother him — and a host of nannies. Oh, and for a year or two, a child psychologist. Even with all those people lending a hand, Kip was now a twenty-three-year-old college dropout living in his mother's basement and holding an on-again, off-again job as a deliveryman for an itty-bitty pizza joint in one of the less glitzy parts of town. Not exactly what a father proudly proclaimed in the annual Christmas letter.

So what was Diane's secret? There was only one way to find out. Ask. Assuming she'd be open enough to answer. Back when they'd dated, her chattiness sometimes drove him to distraction. He hadn't been interested in conversation then. Sometimes he wasn't now. But if Diane was willing to talk, he'd be willing to listen.

She hadn't included a telephone number in her email. If school were in session, he could reach her there, but this was summer break. No sense searching online for a telephone number. She probably used a cell, and she was savvy enough to keep her personal number off internet informational sites. He'd contact her the only way he

could — via email — and hope she'd answer.

TWELVE

Kendrickson, Nevada
Diane

"Margaret Diane, your phone is making noises."

Diane took another bite of her garlicky steamed string beans. "I know. I heard it. It's telling me I have a new email."

Mother stabbed a button mushroom with her fork tines. The trio of dachshunds lined up at the slider door to the patio watched the mushroom lift from the plate toward Mother's mouth. "Email on your phone?" She shook her head and made a *tsk-tsk* sound. "Picture taking, text messaging, shopping . . . and even email. A person can do just about anything on a phone these days."

Diane grinned. "Like living in *The Jetsons* cartoon, isn't it?"

Mother chuckled. "Beyond anything I could have imagined. Having access to others so easily is an advantage. One needn't search for a phone booth in case of an emergency." The phone dinged again. She shrugged and popped the mushroom into her mouth. "But you also have a constant intrusion. I suppose there's a positive and negative for every new piece of technology."

"That's true enough." Too many people Diane knew kept their cell phones locked in their palms like an extension of themselves. She especially disliked seeing phones used during what should be social times — meals or gatherings. The gadget that connected people to family and friends, services, information, and media was a good thing. But finding a balance — even with good things — was important, she preached to her students, and she practiced what she preached. Which was why the phone wasn't at the table.

Ding!

Mother frowned in the direction of the sound. "My, someone is persistent. You don't suppose it's from Meghan . . ."

Meghan would call or text if she really needed something, but the sound was distracting them from enjoying their dinner. Diane should turn off the volume until they were finished eating. "I'll go check."

Miney and Molly stayed behind and kept

guard over Mother, but Duchess trotted after Diane. She picked up the phone and held it toward the dog. "Be glad you don't have to mess with these things. Nothing but a nuisance." Duchess nosed the phone and whined, and Diane laughed. "All right, all right, I'll see who's pestering us."

She tapped the email icon. Kevin@HarrisonInc.net showed as the sender. Her mouth went dry. Had he changed his mind about coming to Vegas? She considered turning off the phone and waiting until after she'd eaten to look at it, but she didn't think she'd be able to take another bite until she knew what he wanted.

Her hand trembled, but her finger connected with the address, and a message popped onto her screen.

Diane, I'm in Vegas. I have appointments set up for the weekdays, but tomorrow is open. I wondered if we could meet. Talk. I'd like to catch up and learn a little more about your daughter. You can reply to this email or give me a call at —

"Margaret Diane, is everything okay?"

Diane jammed the phone into her pocket and returned to the kitchen. Duchess settled under her chair instead of joining the other two dachshunds. Diane offered her mother what she hoped was a convincing smile. "Yes. Everything's fine."

Mother's brows came together. "Try again."

So much for being convincing. Diane pulled the phone out and held it up. "The email was from Kevin. He wants to meet tomorrow."

"For what reason?"

"To catch up and talk about Meghan." She frowned. "Or so he says."

"You don't believe him?"

Should she? When she was young and foolish, she'd bought into his proclamation that she was special to him, that their relationship would be permanent. And look what it had gotten her — unwed motherhood. She stared at the email. "I'm not sure."

"Well . . ." Mother pushed the last mushroom around on her plate, a slow grin forming on her wrinkled cheek. "You could invite him to tomorrow's church service and then to brunch afterward."

Diane laughed. "That'd be a good way to get rid of him. He was adamantly opposed to 'organized religion.' " She cringed. "At the time of our acquaintanceship, it was one of the things I liked about him."

Mother patted Diane's hand. "Leave the past in the past, where it belongs."

Diane waved the phone. "Kinda hard to do when the past is knocking on your door."

"The past can knock on the door all it wants to. You don't have to answer."

Diane stared at the phone screen. Mother was right. She didn't have to answer. If he really wanted to get to know Meghan, he could ask for her contact information. Diane had done her part — removed the element of surprise. She didn't need to be involved any further.

"What are you going to do?"

Diane shifted her attention to Mother. Her mother's eyes twinkled, as if she already knew the answer. Diane huffed a laugh. Then she hit Reply and tapped out her response.

The world must be coming to an end. Brunch with her mother and her daughter's biological father? Diane wouldn't have imagined it happening in a thousand years. But here she was, sharing a high button-tufted booth seat with Mother and staring across the polished table at Kevin.

As she'd expected, he declined the invitation to church, but he was waiting at their favorite Kendrickson eatery, Viva la Quiche, when she and Mother arrived after the early service. Even if he hadn't sent a JPEG of his business card, which included his photo, she would have recognized him. Time had changed his sandy-blond hair to the color of a dirty nickel, but it was still thick, and he wore it combed away from his high forehead. Black horn-rimmed glasses now framed his blue eyes, but those eyes held the same intensity that had once captured her girlish heart. She found it difficult to focus on the menu with him peering at her through the glasses' lenses, elbows on the table and steepled hands against his fashionably stubbled chin. He watched her, and Mother watched him, and Diane wished she hadn't answered the knock on the door.

A waitress approached with three coffee mugs and a carafe. She poured steaming brew into cups for each of them, then set the carafe in the middle of the table. Her smile drifted across their faces. "Have you decided what you want?"

Kevin held his hand toward Mother. "You order first, Mrs. DeFord." He settled his penetrating gaze on the waitress. "One check, please — give it to me."

Diane anticipated an argument, but to her surprise, Mother only thanked him and then requested the crustless, egg-whites-only spinach and mushroom quiche with a side of fresh fruit. Kevin nodded at Diane, and she blurted, "I'll have the same, but with the vegan egg substitute."

"Make mine the gruyère, bacon, and asparagus quiche — good ol' chicken eggs, please, yolks and all — with a side of country potatoes." Kevin gathered their menus and handed them to the waitress with a wink. A far-too-easily-offered wink. Apparently his penchant for flirting hadn't changed, either.

The waitress nodded and scurried off. Kevin shifted his attention to Mother. "I didn't realize Diane would bring you, Mrs. DeFord, but it's nice to have a chance to meet you."

"Instead of the stuffy title Mrs. DeFord, which makes me feel as ancient as Methuselah, why don't you call me Hazel?"

He grinned. "Hazel. Now I know where Diane gets her natural beauty and spunk."

Mother took a sip of her coffee, her bright eyes snapping. "There's no need to flatter me, young man. I'm beyond the age of flirtatious chitchat."

Diane sucked in her lips to hold back a laugh. Mother wasn't ordinarily crusty, but she was straightforward. Kevin wouldn't be able to draw her in with smooth talk and overconfident charm.

Kevin chuckled and held up his coffee mug as if making a toast. " 'No legacy is so rich as honesty.' "

Mother raised one eyebrow. "Shakespeare?"

He nodded. "From *All's Well That Ends Well.*"

"You're a fan of the poet bard?"

"Not a fan necessarily, but I admire him. I mean, he lived . . . what? More than four hundred years ago? And we still remember him. Still see his works performed on stages. He left his indelible mark on the world. I find that impressive and even enviable."

Mother sipped her coffee and fell silent.

Kevin took a drink of his coffee, then set the cup aside. "Teachers leave a mark, too. Worthwhile profession. So tell me, Diane, how many years have you taught in Vegas?"

Diane preferred to talk about Meghan, but at least the topic wasn't too personal. And he'd set his flirtatiousness aside. "Three full years now. The school had an opening in subjects I am qualified to teach, and Mother graciously offered me half of her house, so I moved here." She didn't bother explaining how the move had mended her broken relationship with her mother. That was too personal.

"Like I said, teaching's an honorable career. My mother planned to teach, but Dad talked her out of it. He wanted her home, more available to him." An odd edge colored his tone even while an easy smile remained on his face. "She always volunteered at school. Was even PTA president a year or two."

Like her mother. The similarity made Diane squirm, but she wasn't sure why. Maybe because it made him seem too . . . average. Like any other man. She'd tried so hard to demonize him in her thoughts. Putting the majority of the blame on him made it easier for her to bear her burden of guilt. But he'd once been an only child with a PTA-president mother, the same as her. Even-steven, as they would have said in childhood.

He plied her with questions about teaching, which she answered, carefully planning her responses before uttering them, until their food arrived. She'd never been so relieved to see a plate of quiche. The worry about saying too much had created a dull throb in the base of her skull.

"This all looks great." He picked up his fork and aimed it for the pile of crispy, browned chunks of potato, but when Mother bowed her head, he laid the utensil on the table and folded his hands.

The respectful gesture made something roll over in Diane's chest, and at the same time, his voice roared from the past. *"People who talk to God are fools. Might as well talk to a pile of dirty laundry."* Was he pretending to respect Mother while inwardly scoffing? She slammed her eyelids closed and sent up a silent thank-you for the food and a request for God to guard her mouth and mind until she and Kevin could part ways.

While they ate, he turned his question asking on Mother — mostly about the advantages and disadvantages of living in Las Vegas. Mother answered openly, even injecting a few anecdotes Diane hadn't heard before about living in such a flamboyant area.

The waitress brought their check, which Kevin took care of, rejecting Mother's offer to leave the tip. Then they stood and headed for the door. Out on the sidewalk, Kevin rested his hand on Diane's arm and gave her a smile as warm as the sun beaming from the cloudless sky.

"Thank you for the invitation. I enjoyed the food and the company very much."

She took a slight side step, dislodging his hand, and managed a weak smile. "You're welcome. Thank you for brunch. I hope your business dealings here go well." She wanted to ask why he hadn't mentioned Meghan during their hour and a half together, but questions would delay their leave-taking. She cupped Mother's elbow and turned for their vehicle.

"I wonder . . ."

His musing tone stopped her. She looked back.

"I feel as if I caught up with you, but we didn't really talk about your daughter."

Her daughter, not *his* or *theirs.* She couldn't decide if she appreciated or resented his use of the pronoun. She started to suggest he deliver his queries to Meghan herself, but he spoke before she could form the sentence.

"If you aren't busy tomorrow morning, maybe you'd be willing to meet me and the real estate agent at the building I'm interested in purchasing. You could tour the building with us. I'd appreciate a feminine point of view on its aesthetics. Then I'll treat you to lunch on the Strip, where you can tell me about your daughter."

Diane examined his face, searching for signs of duplicity.

He must have sensed her uncertainty because he held up his palm, Boy Scout style. "Strictly business. You can even bring

Hazel again if that makes you feel safer."

If he knew that Mother carried a Glock in her handbag, he might not feel so safe with her around. Maybe she should mention the weapon and watch his reaction. She imagined his shock, and her lips twitched with the desire to grin.

Mother pressed her elbow to her ribs, squeezing Diane's hand. "I have book club tomorrow morning, so I'm not available. But if you'd like to go, Margaret Diane, it's fine by me."

Diane frowned at Kevin. "You said you wanted a feminine viewpoint. Couldn't your wife accompany you on the trip?"

His smile turned stiff. "I'm divorced." He twisted the unadorned platinum band on his finger. "I wear this for business because a married man appears more trustworthy than an unmarried one to some people."

Mother's pursed lips evidenced her disapproval, and Diane sensed it had more to do with him misleading people than the fact he was divorced. An uncomfortable thought struck. He'd used her once. Would he do it again?

She put her hand on her hip. "You aren't planning to pass me off as your wife with this real estate agent, are you?"

He threw back his head and laughed. The

reaction was so spontaneous that Diane couldn't help but believe it was genuine. The laughter lasted only a few seconds before he gruffly cleared his throat and ended it. He met her gaze. "No." He shook his head. "No."

Hmm, was he now insulting her?

A disarming smile formed on his still-handsome face. "I really would like to ask a few questions about Meghan."

He'd finally used their daughter's name.

"If you're not comfortable meeting me at the building, then maybe we can —"

"It's all right." She'd be safe meeting him in a public place. She'd see him one more time, satisfy his curiosity about Meghan, and then be done with him. Besides, she didn't have anything else to do except attend book club with Mother and her octogenarian friends. She pulled out her cell phone and opened the calendar. "Tell me the address and time, and I'll meet you there."

THIRTEEN

Little Rock, Arkansas
Sean

Could granola bars spoil? Sean braced his palm against his rolling stomach and opened the door to the cold-case unit's building. Meghan crossed the threshold, her lips set in a grim line and her face pale. She looked half-sick, too. Maybe they'd better buy name-brand breakfast bars next time. Ones without raisins and dates. It had to be the raisins and dates making him feel queasy.

Yeah, right.

Apparently workers had come in during the weekend and fixed the elevator, because the Out of Service sign was missing. Meghan pushed the Up button, and they waited in silence for the car to arrive.

Acid burned in Sean's throat, and he swallowed. Twice. The burn remained. He'd never been one to bemoan Mondays, but this one was going down as his least favorite

Monday ever. They'd stumbled through their morning routine, as slow and clumsy as a pair of sloths. Unlike themselves. He'd prayed plenty of times during the weekend in preparation for changing partnerships, and he sent up another prayer as he and Meghan stepped into the elevator car for their ride to the fourth floor.

Please give me Your patience, Your strength, Your compassion, Your discernment . . .

The doors opened, and Meghan got out. She took three steps across the tile floor, then stopped and spun to face him. He slid to a stop while the doors whisked closed behind him. "What's wrong?"

"I don't want to work with Greg. And I don't want you to work with Tom."

"It's too late for that, babe."

"No, it's not. Greg and I haven't officially started our investigation. You could still hand off the Dunsbrook case to Greg and Tom, and you and I could forge ahead on the Menke case." Her expression pleaded with him, making his stomach churn worse. "It doesn't seem right partnering with anyone else. I actually feel like I could throw up."

Sean grimaced. "Yeah. No more raisins and dates in our granola bars."

"What?"

"Never mind." He lightly gripped her upper arm and stroked with his thumb. "I understand how you feel. I feel pretty much the same. But we gave the captain our decision. If we go back on it now, it reflects on our professionalism."

"But —"

"We can still confer with each other about our cases, get each other's input, and be involved even if we aren't working as an assigned team. Splitting for an investigation doesn't mean splitting in everything else." Although they remained split on the subjects of starting a family and opening a private business. The queasiness intensified.

She seemed to search his face for several seconds, her brow pinched into worry lines, and then she lowered her head. Her chest rose and fell with a mighty sigh. "I think I messed up. I didn't listen for God's voice before I decided what to do."

Her distress pained him worse than thinking about spending the next weeks in constant contact with his nemesis. He caught her shoulders and turned her toward the case unit's doors. "Well, it was pretty much decided for you by the captain. You were assigned, remember? I'm the one who was given the choice of investigations."

She glanced back at him, her nose wrinkling. "And you chose Tom over me. Nice."

The hint of impishness removed some of his discomfort. He grinned. "You know what they say — absence makes the heart grow fonder."

"That didn't work so well for my mom and grandma."

Her melancholy returned so quickly that a fresh stab of pain slashed through his belly. He nudged her arm with his elbow, the kind of teasing bump junior high–age boys gave girls they liked. "That was a completely different situation, and it's all water under the bridge now, right?"

He waited for a response, but she only shrugged. He grabbed the door handle. "C'mon, we need to go in or Cap'll think we're playing hooky." He leaned down slightly and whispered, "It's only one case, Meg. Remember what you told your mom? It'll probably turn out to be a good experience for us."

"I said *might*."

"Let's go." He ushered her into the room.

Farber was sitting on the edge of Dane's desk, and he shot a sour look in their direction as they crossed to the cluster of detective desks. " 'Bout time you showed up. You get lost on the way to work, or what?"

161

Meghan draped her purse handle over her desk chair and released a short laugh that seemed as much cough as chuckle. "Now, Tom, we aren't that late. Did you get up on the wrong side of the bed this morning?"

Farber muttered something under his breath and rounded the desks. He stopped in front of Sean and folded his arms over his chest. "Cap called in. He's gonna be gone all morning — something about his wife getting a root canal and needing him to drive her home afterward. So he said get our notes together for a sit-down with him when he gets here."

"Sounds good." Sean always welcomed Captain Ratzlaff's input. He sat and slid his chair up close to his desk, then hit his desktop tower's power button. "Lemme make sure I forwarded everything to you so we've got the same information in front of us."

Dane held up his hand. "Before you get too ambitious over there, let's change the desk configurations. It'll be a lot easier for us to confer with the right person if we aren't talking over the top of each other."

Meghan's face fell. She gaped across their butted desks at Sean. "Do we really need to? I mean, it's only for one case, right?"

Farber huffed. "One case can take more

than one day to solve. So . . . who wants to move?"

Dane stood. "It's no big deal to me to change places. I haven't booted up yet, so I can unplug everything and go pretty easily."

"No," Farber barked. "Beagle's already got his computer on, but DeFord hasn't. Unplug hers and mine instead. Me and her will swap out. Beagle, get her equipment unplugged. DeFord, pull your chair out of the way. Johnson, Roach — give us a hand with these desks. The ancient behemoths weigh half a ton."

Sean gritted his teeth. Even though the captain often put Farber in charge when he was away, the man's dictatorial attitude chafed like a sand pebble stuck in a shoe. *Patience, Lord . . .* He shifted to his knees, ducked under his desk, and pulled the plug for Meghan's computer from the power strip. As he did so, nausea flooded his stomach — as if he'd disconnected the two of them.

"You done under there?" Farber was bending over, peering under the desk.

Sean backed out, forcing himself to ignore the uncomfortable ache in his gut. "Good to go."

"Johnson, Roach, move DeFord's desk. Beagle, help Dane with mine."

163

Everyone leaped into action.

Dane bobbed his chin toward Farber as they inched their way around Johnson's and Roach's desks. "He'd make a good drill sergeant, huh?"

Sean didn't answer, but inwardly he agreed. Farber got results. The fact that they all did his bidding without a word of argument proved it. The man was bucking for captain of the unit when Ratzlaff retired in a year or two, but Sean hoped the promotions team would talk to everyone in the unit before they made it official.

Farber's knowledge exceeded anyone else's on the squad, but his leadership skills needed some polishing before he'd be qualified to take command. Sean would rather see Dane, who'd served in the unit for as many years as Farber, receive the promotion. But if he and Meghan went out on their own, it wouldn't much matter who was in charge.

The thought startled him, and he lowered his end of Farber's desk with a thud.

"Hey! Careful!" Farber bounded over, scowling, and checked a couple of desk drawers. "Lucky for you nothing broke."

Their desks held office supplies and files. What could break? The discernment he'd prayed for gave him the wisdom not to ask the question out loud.

Panting, Roach leaned on Meghan's desk. "When we put these things back, let's empty the drawers first. It'd make 'em a lot easier to move."

"Stupid to take time for that." Farber grabbed his chair and angled it into position. "Y'all stop acting like a bunch of sissies and get to work." He aimed a glare at Sean. "Get me plugged in already, will you?"

Sean was still battling a floating sensation as his taut muscles relaxed. "Sure. Gimme a minute."

"*Now,* Beagle. I wanna get started. We've already burned up almost half an hour of our day."

Dane released a nervous laugh. "Why don't you plug it in yourself? Or did you wear yourself out telling everybody else what to do?"

Roach and Johnson snickered but shot wary glances at Farber. Meghan's gaze flitted back and forth between Sean and Farber, and Sean sensed her discomfort from ten feet away. Protectiveness welled, and sharp words formed on his tongue.

Patience and discernment, Lord . . .

Sean sent his wife a grin and wink, then turned to Farber. "I'd be glad to plug in your computer for you, partner, now that the blood flow's back in my brain. Then we can review those notes, all right?"

Farber grunted, but he nodded.

Sean bent down and pushed the computer cord's plug into the power strip. When he emerged from beneath the desk, the others — including Meghan and Dane — were focused on their own computers. Back to a normal day. Sean breathed a sigh of relief.

"Oh, DeFord and Dane." Farber turned his chair toward Meghan's and Greg's desks and frowned. "Cap said you'd be getting your travel papers by the end of the day, so prep for time on the field. And" — his scowl deepened — "the daughter of the missing man took a leave of absence so she can travel with you."

Just like that, the normalcy splintered.

Las Vegas, Nevada
Kevin

Kevin waited outside the building with Stan Fuller, the real estate agent, and watched for Diane's arrival. She wasn't late. He and Stan were early. So he didn't feel bad about standing under the morning sunshine while the agent repeatedly checked his watch and paced back and forth in front of the oversized doors leading to the building's lobby.

Odd how the invitation for her to explore

166

the property had left his mouth so easily. He'd used the excuse of wanting a female's reaction, which in hindsight was pretty smart, but it was sure out of the ordinary for him. He'd never involved any of his wives in his business dealings. Dad always said keep home and business separate. Kevin and Mom uncovered lots of ugly "business stuff" after Dad died, and Mom still carried a load of guilt over things she couldn't have controlled even if she'd wanted to.

Maybe if Dad had shared some of his worries about business, he would have lived longer and Mom would now live happier. But Kevin still followed his dad's example. All those instructions were deeply ingrained. He couldn't imagine changing now. For reasons beyond his understanding, he experienced a pinch of regret.

"Kevin?"

He gave a jolt. Diane stood near, rhinestone-studded sunglasses hiding her eyes.

"I'm sorry. I didn't intend to startle you. You must have been lost in thought." She pushed a strand of dark shoulder-length hair behind her ear and glanced in the direction of the real estate agent. The man gripped the door's ornate handle and nearly twitched in place. "Did I misunderstand the time? I thought you said ten thirty."

"I did say ten thirty." He gestured her toward the door. "So you're right on time. Thanks for coming. I don't imagine it's fun battling this traffic." The constant flow of cars, taxis, and buses up and down the Strip made Fort Smith traffic pale in comparison.

"Which is why Mother chose a house in Kendrickson. It's quieter there." She smiled at the agent, who opened the door as she approached. "Thank you."

Kevin followed her in. He enjoyed walking behind her and giving her a secret look-over from head to toe. Fifty-two — or was it fifty-one? — years old. Not quite as slender as she'd been in her early twenties, but definitely not overweight. Back when he'd known her, she'd dressed a little classier than the average college student. Yesterday's and today's outfits defined her curves without clinging to them. She was what his mother would call chic. Did she color her dark hair to hide gray? Not that he'd hold it against her — even Mom got a rinse every week to make her gray hair more silvery. He admired women who kept themselves up. Diane definitely kept herself up.

She slipped her sunglasses to the top of her head, mussing her bangs, and turned.

He made sure his gaze was aimed at her eyes when she looked up at him. "It's beautiful so far."

The comment confused him at first, and then he realized she meant the building. He glanced around the lobby and nodded. "Yes. I especially like the art deco touches. Art deco never goes out of style."

"I agree. It's classic."

Like her. He cleared his throat and shifted to face Stan. "When did you say this building was constructed?"

He pulled a detail sheet from his briefcase and handed it to Kevin. "In the late 1970s. The previous building was razed after a fire destroyed the top floor. But the builder tried to emulate the original blueprint in both layout and style."

"He did well. I wouldn't have guessed it was built in the seventies." Diane crossed to a doorway and ran her fingers over the marble doorframe. She raised her gaze to the medallion centered above the door. "What was its original purpose?"

Kevin held up the detail sheet. "Originally? A saloon and bordello."

Her eyes bugged, and red streaked her cheeks.

He laughed, partly at her reaction and partly out of his own embarrassment. He shouldn't have said that out loud. "I know, right? Hard to believe, smack-dab in the middle of town." Granted, prostitution was legal in numerous places in Nevada. For a lot of men, it was a draw. Not for him, though. If a man and woman were going to be intimate, at the very least there should be affection between them. Certainly no money changing hands. That's what his father had taught him, and he'd always followed Dad's instruction.

Of course, he'd also claimed affection for a number of women. The thought, for the first time, left him uncomfortable.

Stan cleared his throat. "By the 1940s, the building was home to several business offices. Not until it was rebuilt in the seventies was the top floor turned into an apartment. The zoning laws changed shortly afterward, so if a person built on this same location today, they wouldn't be able to use any part of the structure for residential. That makes this old beauty unique."

"I guess so." Diane's cheeks faded to a normal color. "Are you planning to live in the apartment, rent it out, or turn it into office space?"

Kevin scratched his chin. "I have no desire to live here." She seemed to release a held breath, and he couldn't decide whether he was insulted by her obvious relief. "I might offer it as part of a salary package for the person hired to manage the property, or I might lease it. I'm not sure yet."

"Why don't we go up and explore the apartment?" Stan headed toward an iron scissor gate standing guard in front of a metal door. "The owner has kept the electricity turned on so we can make use of the Turnbull traction elevator. Then, if you'd like, we can go to each level via the enclosed staircases — let you experience both means of accessing the different floors."

"That sounds fine." Kevin rolled up the detail sheet and used it to point. "Lead the way, Ms. DeFord." As he followed her into the mirrored elevator car, a question floated through his mind. Was she Ms. DeFord because she'd divorced and taken back her maiden name, or had she never married? He'd planned to talk about Meghan over lunch, but if he got up his nerve, he might ask a little more about Diane, too.

What a shame if a pretty lady like her had remained single her whole life. Especially if he'd been the one to scare her away from relationships.

FOURTEEN

Little Rock, Arkansas
Meghan

Greg lounged at one end of the sofa in the captain's office, and Meghan sat at the opposite end, fiddling with the straw in her soda cup while Captain Ratzlaff paced in front of his desk and went over the travel plans for her and Greg's trip to Fort Smith. Nothing unusual in any of it — state-arranged hotel accommodations, paperwork to keep track of their expenses, and a printout of the information gathered from the original investigation and Sheila Menke's statements.

The captain handed Greg the packet even though he'd said Meghan would be the lead on this case. "I'm not sure how it's going to work, having Sheila trailing you. She knows she's responsible for her own expenses. I almost hope her resources run out and she has to go home. I suspect she'll end up being a nuisance, but she's bullheaded enough not to listen to suggestions to stay out of it and let y'all do your jobs."

Meghan chuckled, forcing a levity she didn't feel. "When she said she wanted to keep up with the investigation, I expected frequent calls or texts, not a travel partner." She shrugged. "I think I understand why she wants to go with us, though. Think of everything she's lost — her father, her home, now her mother. She needs to hang on to something. This investigation gives her an outlet to regain some semblance of control."

A rare smile formed on the captain's face. "And that's why you're on this one, De-Ford. I know you'll be diplomatic." He shifted his gaze to Greg, who was paging through the file. "Dane, any questions?"

Greg plopped the envelope on the sofa between Meghan and him. "It's a standard investigation. With the exception of a third, unauthorized detective getting in the way. I'm more than happy to let DeFord handle the man's daughter."

"All right, then." Captain Ratzlaff opened his office door. "I'll let you two decide whose vehicle you'll take and how you'll meet up for tomorrow's road trip. Stay in touch, and good luck. I hope it goes quick."

Meghan carried the folder out with her, and she and Greg returned to their desks. He folded his arms on his giant desk calendar and pinned his gaze on her. "All right. Let's talk travel plans."

Meghan had suspected it would be awkward to make arrangements to travel with someone other than Sean, but the depth of discomfort startled her. She squirmed in her seat. "Um, do you mind driving? We usually take Sean's Bronco. I have my little Chevy, but it's not the most comfortable vehicle for distances."

"Yeah, I can drive. No problem. How about we meet up here tomorrow morning, usual start time, and load up and go?"

Glad to have it settled, Meghan nodded. "Okay. Sounds good." The sooner they got started, the sooner they could bring this temporary arrangement to an end and get back to normal.

Las Vegas, Nevada
Diane

Thank goodness for the fountains at the Bellagio. Diane had a perfect reason for gazing to the side rather than looking into Kevin's face during lunch. The intensity of his attention left her floundering and tongue tied — gracious, couldn't he have lost his magnetic attractiveness at some point over the past three decades? — but if she talked to the fountains instead of him, she could speak freely, almost passionately, about the girl she loved more than life itself.

She shared everything she considered important about Meghan, painting a picture of an adorable, inquisitive little girl who grew into an intelligent, respectful, responsible, caring young woman. As she spoke, pride welled up inside her and occasionally brought the sting of tears. She hadn't intended to talk so much or so long, but once she started, she couldn't seem to stop. And Kevin didn't seem interested in stopping her. Here they were, over an hour at this table, and she'd taken only a few bites of her salad of arugula, blue cheese, and shredded beets.

Diane took a sip of her water, moistening her dry mouth, then lifted one shoulder in a half shrug. "I'm not surprised she chose to go into investigative work. She always loved solving puzzles and unraveling mysteries. When she was a kid, she read every mystery series she could find at the library."

Kevin chuckled. His plate held only a few crumbs, and he pushed one of the larger bits of bread back and forth with his finger. "Nancy Drew and the Hardy Boys?"

"And the Boxcar Children, among others, yes." She sneaked a quick bite. "There were times her questions kind of got on my nerves, but I did my best to answer her. It was the teacher in me, I guess. I can't let questions go unanswered."

Except about Meghan's father. She'd squelched — no, stomped out — every one of those queries.

She took another bite and watched the fountains.

"Obviously Meghan's a great kid. Er, woman." Kevin's serious tone drew Diane's attention. Lines marred his brow, and he pursed his lips for a moment as if he'd tasted something unpleasant. He cleared his throat, but the worry lines didn't dissolve. "You raised her alone? Always?"

Diane swallowed. "What do you mean?"

"Did you ever marry? Have a live-in? Anybody to coparent with you?"

Now, that was too personal. She pushed her plate aside, no longer interested in the salad. "I really don't think that's your concern, Kevin."

He held up both palms. "Don't get defensive on me. I have a reason for asking."

Yes, being nosy. She'd agreed to talk about Meghan, but she wouldn't put up with him prying into her private life. "I'll answer, but then the subject is closed. I didn't marry. I didn't have a live-in boyfriend. Ever." She wouldn't divulge the reason she never married. She couldn't trust a man to be there for her. Her father died, her high school boyfriends never stuck around after meeting her overprotective mother, and then Kevin kicked her to the curb. She wasn't about to set herself up for more loss or rejection and put Meghan through it in the process.

"So how'd you do it?"

Diane shook her head. "Do what?"

"Raise such an amazing kid on your own." He rested his elbows on the table and leaned in, his blue eyes nearly blazing. "I mean, I have a son." He made a face. "Well, a stepson. He was three when I married his mother, and I adopted him when he was almost four."

Envy struck — a startling emotion. He'd raised someone else's child but refused to raise his own?

"His deadbeat dad didn't want anything to do with him, so somebody had to step up."

And yet he didn't see himself as a deadbeat dad? She gritted her teeth and forced down the ugly comments forming on her tongue. A public café was no place for a confrontation, and the same way she'd spoken openly about Meghan, she might let loose on Kevin. Mother was right. She hadn't forgiven him.

"His name is Kristopher with a *K,* but he goes by Kip." No pride lit Kevin's face when he spoke of his adopted son. If anything, he seemed embarrassed. Maybe even ashamed. "To be honest, he's a mess. He was always in trouble at school. Even got kicked out of a private school for picking a fight with one of his teachers. He was all of eleven at the time."

Diane had dealt with a few troubled students in her career. She'd always believed that kids who had problems needed a combination of compassion and consistent discipline. Most people either ignored the behavior, which left the child escalating in attempts for attention, or came down on the child with harsh punishment, which destroyed any hope for a relationship. She started to ask how Kevin had handled Kip's issues, but she decided she didn't need to know. She sat in silence, and after a few moments he went on.

"It wasn't as if we didn't try. We — meaning his mother and me — enrolled him in karate, Boy Scouts, Little League. Even got him counseling for a while. Nothing helped. He scared off half a dozen nannies and totally destroyed the relationship between Julie and me. He was just a . . . a brat."

Diane bristled. "That's not a very kind way to speak about your own child."

He held out his hands in a gesture of surrender. "Kind or not, it's the truth." He rested his elbows on the table again. "There was a whole army of people involved in Kip's upbringing. Even so, he's what just about anyone would call a first-class failure at life. Yet Meghan . . ." He shook his head, his brow furrowing again. "From what you've said, she's a complete success. So how'd you do it all by yourself? How did you produce a kid who could win the Good Citizenship award hands down?"

Diane started to say "luck." After all, she knew how much she'd failed with Meghan, sometimes bordering on neglect in her attempt to give her daughter the freedom she'd never experienced as a child. But when she opened her mouth, a surprising answer emerged. "Prayer."

Kevin drew back. "You . . . prayed?"

She couldn't suppress a laugh. His stunned expression matched her own shock. "No, I didn't. I pray a lot now. I returned to my childhood faith a few years ago. But I didn't pray when Meghan was growing up. Someone else did, though. My mother.

Faithfully. And I think God honored her prayers."

Kevin stared at her as if she'd started speaking in a foreign language.

Regret for the years she'd lost carrying resentment toward her mother and rejecting God's presence in her life created a painful pressure in her chest. She swallowed the lump forming in her throat and blinked against tears. "I actually blew it in a lot of ways, but in spite of me, God was there. I can't take credit for Meghan's stability, respectfulness, and success. She is who she is, in large part, because of who God crafted her to be and because her grandmother steadfastly prayed for her to become an honorable woman of faith."

Kevin stared at her through narrowed eyes for several seconds, seeming as if to forgo breathing during that time. Then he released a little huff of laughter. He lifted his napkin and wiped his mouth, and as he drew his hand downward, his puzzled expression changed to the overly self-confident expression she remembered him wearing in college.

"Well, this has been . . . enlightening. I appreciate you taking the time to tell me about your daughter."

So they were back to *your daughter* again.

"Congratulations on raising such an exemplary human being." He was complimenting her, but his tone held a note of derision. "I had hoped you would tell me something that would be beneficial for Kip. He's hardly a child anymore, but sometimes boys take their time growing up. I thought maybe you'd have suggestions for salvaging him before he wastes his entire life."

So he hadn't met with her to learn about Meghan but to harvest ideas for fixing his broken adopted son. He was still using her.

He stood. "I'll walk you to your car."

Diane remained in her chair. Irritation at Kevin warred with sympathy for the young man named Kip on whom everyone had seemingly given up. She snapped, "I did tell you something beneficial. You just chose to dismiss it."

His brows descended. He slid back into his chair. "Are you talking about prayer?"

She nodded. "I know you disdained religion when you were in college. To be honest, I did, too. Because I didn't understand the difference between religion and relationship."

"You aren't making sense, Diane."

His growling tone should have warned her into silence, but she'd spent too many years ignoring God. She wouldn't ignore opportunities to make up for her rebellion. She reached across the table and placed her hand over his clenched fist.

"I told you I pray now. But that's not because I have religion. It's because I have a relationship with God through His Son. When I was a little girl, I asked Jesus to be my savior, but then I let rebellion and anger at people separate me from Him. But He forgave me, and He welcomed me back into fellowship. So now I'm connecting with the One who created the universe and everything in it. I can't change or fix anyone, but He can. When I pray, I open the door for God to work. My mother's prayers impacted Meghan's life, and they impacted mine. A lot of people let me down, including you."

He yanked his hand free of her light touch and folded his arms.

"But God never did. He never will. That's why I know I can trust Him to continue to guide Meghan and me. You can trust Him to guide you and Kip. Open your heart to Him and let Him in."

FIFTEEN

Kevin

When Kevin played tourist and walked the Strip last night, he'd encountered a man carrying a Bible and hollering into a bullhorn for people to repent and be saved. Some other people pointed and laughed, but Kevin had skirted past, inwardly cringing. Did the man have any idea how foolish he looked and sounded? Now he cringed again, more ill at ease than he'd ever been, facing Diane's heartfelt but misguided sincerity.

"Are you done preaching at me?" He forced a light tone that directly contrasted the heaviness weighing on his spirit.

A grin briefly formed on her lips, then disappeared. "For now."

"Hmph." He pulled several bills from his wallet and dropped them on the table, then rose. He escorted her onto the sidewalk and paused. "Where did you park?"

"In the Caesars Palace parking garage."

He gained his bearings and then set off north up Las Vegas Boulevard. He tempered his stride slightly to match hers. She wasn't a petite woman — the top of her head reached his chin, and he was six two — but she'd worn a long straight skirt, and it restricted her progress. Of course, the numerous pedestrians crowding the sidewalk also slowed his pace.

They stepped around others, Diane murmuring "Excuse me" now and then. The red light stopped them at Flamingo Road, and he clenched and unclenched his fist inside his jacket pocket, counting the seconds until the walk signal came on. The crunch of people flowed forward, someone bumped him, and he and Diane got separated. He waited on the opposite curb for her to catch up. The little smile of thank-you she offered stabbed him with fresh regret he didn't understand.

Walking side by side became too difficult, so he fell behind her and followed her to the opening of the large garage behind the casino built to resemble Rome's Pantheon. She stopped beneath the covered portico.

"Thank you for the tour of the building, and thanks for lunch."

She sounded so formal. But what should

he expect? They weren't friends. They were barely acquaintances anymore. They were two people who, in their youth and stupidity, had created a baby and then gone their separate ways. They'd had a brief crossing of paths, satisfied their curiosities about the other, and now it was time to return to their regularly scheduled lives. Except for reasons he couldn't begin to understand, he didn't think he could return to his "regular" life unchanged.

He shoved his hands into his trouser pockets and rocked on the soles of his shoes. "Thanks for meeting with me, giving me your feedback on the property. It's helpful to see the building through a different pair of eyes than my own."

She'd been amazingly attentive to details, noticing things he would have overlooked. Her observations had already stirred ideas for improving the building and making it more visually appealing to female clientele. Women, after all, were the ones who spent the money. A wise businessman did what he could to capture their interest.

"It was fun. I hope the acquisition and remodel will go well for you." She pulled her keys from her purse and jangled them. "I better let you go. Enjoy the rest of your stay in Las Vegas." She took two steps and then turned back. "Kevin . . ."

He eased forward and closed the distance between them. "What?"

Pink crept through her cheeks, and she blinked rapidly, as if nervousness had suddenly gripped her. "I want you to know I . . . I don't hold a grudge against you. You know, for not wanting to be with me and help raise our baby."

He supposed her statement was meant to make him feel better, but it didn't. It made him feel like a sap. He angled his head and squinted at her. "Okay."

"Honestly, Meghan's a gift. A blessing. Even though it wasn't easy being a single mom and carrying the stigma of having a child out of wedlock, I can't wish we'd never been together, because that would mean I wish she hadn't been born. I could never wish her away."

What did she want from him? He shifted from foot to foot. "That's good . . . I guess."

She ducked her head for a moment, and when she looked at him again, complete peace glowed in her brown eyes. "All that's to say, I'm glad I had the chance to tell you about her. I hope you'll take the chance to get to know her someday. And I'll be praying for you and Kip."

Praying? For him? A snort blasted from

his throat — such a rude thing to do. Mom would be mortified. But if he'd tried to hold it in, he might have imploded. "Well, you go ahead if that'll make you feel better, but I don't see it doing much good. Praying is speaking. Using words." He leaned forward slightly, assuming a conspiratorial air. "There's no power in *words,* Diane."

She shook her head slowly. "You're wrong, Kevin. There is great power in words. 'In the beginning was the Word, and the Word was with God, and the Word was God.' That's John 1:1, from the New Testament. Words have staying power and changing power. *The* Word has the greatest staying and changing power of all. That's why talking to God is effective." She grinned, suddenly impish. "You'll see. Bye, now."

Kendrickson, Nevada
Diane

"I don't know what got into me, Mother." Diane stroked Duchie's soft ears and shifted into the corner of the sofa to better face Mother, who sat on her chair with her feet on the ottoman — the picture of relaxation. "First I was so uncomfortable, it was hard to talk at all. Then I got mad, like almost boiling under the surface, and it was hard to stay quiet. And then all of a sudden I felt so sorry for him, it made me feel like crying. Not for me — for him! What's with that?"

A knowing smile lifted the corners of Mother's pink-painted lips. "That's compassion, my dear. You weren't seeing him with your eyes but through God's eyes of love and mercy. You weren't seeing a man who wronged you but a man who is lost."

Diane thought about Mother's comments, and she nodded. "Yes. I think you're right. Otherwise I would never have quoted Scripture to him or promised to pray for him."

Mother's eyes widened. "You did what?"

Diane laughed. "I know. I was shocked, too. I sure didn't plan to, as he put it, preach at him. But it all came out so naturally, I can't help but believe God prompted me. And I'm going to do it. I'm going to pray for him." Steely determination stiffened her spine. "He says there's no power in words, huh? Hmph. He'll find out the power of words strung together into prayer."

Mother chuckled. "I'll continue praying for him. It'll be nice to know you've joined me."

Diane gaped at her mother. "You . . . you pray for Kevin?"

Tears winked in Mother's eyes. "Honey, I've prayed for him for years — even before

I knew his name. How could a man who abandoned his own child not suffer regret for it? How could that decision not impact his other relationships? So yes, I've been praying for him, for God to bring him to a place of need and healing." She smiled, giving a little nod. "It could be that God used you today to push Kevin over the brink of selfishness and into a relationship with Him."

Diane doubted it. Kevin was pretty hard. But God had reached her, and she'd been hard, too. She grinned. "That would be pretty cool. It would be best for Meghan, you know, to have a father who honored and followed God the Father."

"Yes." Mother's tone and expression turned thoughtful. "But even if Kevin Harrison avoids Meghan, she does have a Father. Just as you and I both do even though our earthly fathers are gone. God the heavenly Father is always there for us, so we needn't feel like orphans."

"Yes, I know. But if Kevin decides to contact Meghan, and if they end up forming a relationship, then it would be best for her if he had faith." Diane pulled Duchess into her lap and ran her fingers through the dog's smooth ruff, seeking comfort. She'd never wanted to share Meghan with her mother, and the old desire to keep her daughter to herself attacked. Maybe she should pray for herself, too, to allow a relationship to develop if it was what God willed for Meghan and Kevin.

"Will you let Meghan know you've been talking with Kevin?"

Diane shot a startled look at Mother. "I hadn't planned to. I mean, she's diving into a new case and adjusting to working with a new partner at the same time, which can't be easy. Kevin isn't in Arkansas right now, so there's no worry about running into him. Do you think I should tell her?"

Mother swung her feet to the floor and sat up. "I think that's up to you, but she might feel a little blindsided if Kevin does reach out to her and mentions that you and he have been seeing each other."

"We haven't been 'seeing' each other." Diane spoke emphatically, erasing the image Mother's choice of words painted in her head. "We've met — twice — to talk about Meghan. That's it."

Mother released a wry chuckle and rose. "That was poorly phrased. How about you've shared her history with him? She might like to know he's asked questions and they've been answered."

Diane chewed the inside of her lip for a

moment. She wouldn't want Mother and someone else discussing her behind her back. "You're right. I don't want her to feel blindsided if he suddenly sends an email or something. I'll tell her."

"I think that's wise." Mother shuffled in the direction of the kitchen. "I'm fixin' to get our supper started. Baked potato wedges and toppings okay?"

"Sounds good." Diane set Duchess aside. "I'll give you a hand." As she stood, her cell phone dinged. She pulled it from her pocket and glanced at the screen. A text message from Kevin stared up at her.

She hadn't even had a chance to pray for him yet and he wanted to meet. Again. Gripping the phone in her hand, she headed for the kitchen. Before she answered him, she needed Mother's advice. And prayers.

Carson Springs, Arkansas
Sean

Tuesday morning, Sean loaded Meghan's suitcase in the back of his Bronco. As the bag thudded into the bed, reality struck with force — his wife would be traveling with another man — and jealousy washed through him, an emotion he hadn't expected. He trusted Meghan. Truth be known, he trusted Greg Dane. Of the other married male agents in the unit, Dane seemed the most dedicated to his wife and children.

But Sean still didn't like the thought of Meghan heading to Fort Smith with another man.

Strength, Lord . . .

Her face flushed, Meghan trotted into the garage. "Okay, I think I'm ready. There should be enough leftover casserole from last night to cover supper for a couple nights, and there's lunch meat and cheese and a bagged salad in the fridge. Of course, you could always hit a drive-through if you want instead."

Affection trampled the jealousy. He caught her in a hug. After their tense days, it felt so good to hold her. He rocked gently to and fro, his cheek against her hair. "You forget how many years I took care of my own meals. I know how to open a can of SpaghettiOs and boil a hot dog."

She laughed against his neck, her breath warm and carrying the scent of their morning coffee. "I know you're able, but I feel guilty leaving you to fend for yourself." She pulled back slightly and met his gaze. "We'll for sure come back Friday evening and be home over the weekend, but I'm praying God will reveal the truth quickly so I don't even have to be gone that long. It feels so weird going without you."

"For me, too." He kissed the top of her head and released her. "You'll probably be so busy you won't realize I'm not there."

She rolled her eyes, teenage fashion. "Like that could happen."

He could hope. He opened her door. "Hop in. We better get moving."

As he backed out of the driveway, she pulled her phone from her bag and held it up. "Mom called last night after we'd gone to bed, and she left a voice mail. I haven't listened to it yet. Do you mind if I do that while you're driving?"

Sean put the SUV in drive and headed out of the neighborhood. He'd rather use their morning commute to talk to each other, but he shouldn't refuse. The message could be important. "Nope. Go ahead."

"I'll put it on speaker." She pushed a button, and moments later his mother-in-law's voice came through.

"Hi, honey. You must be sleeping. That's good. Just wanted you to know I've met with Kevin Harrison —"

Sean glanced at Meghan. She sucked in her lips and frowned.

"— a couple of times. He had brunch with your grandma and me on Sunday, and then

he and I had lunch together today. I told him all about how wonderful you are, and he was duly impressed."

Meghan blew out a little breath and grinned.

"We're actually meeting again tomorrow afternoon at the building on Las Vegas Boulevard he intends to purchase. Believe it or not, he wants my input on updates to the loft apartment. He hasn't yet said if he's ready to meet you, but I wouldn't be surprised if he lets me know that tomorrow. Just so you know, he doesn't have any other biological children, but he adopted his wife's son, so you kind of have a stepbrother named Kip." A nervous laugh rumbled. *"Kevin said Kip is pretty much a brat. Just what you always wanted — a bratty little brother."*

Meghan's frown returned.

"Anyway, I'll call again and update you after tomorrow's meeting. Grandma thought it was best to keep you in the loop concerning my communication with Kevin, and I agree with her. If you have any questions or worries, give me a call or shoot me a text. Tell Sean hi for me."

Sean waved at the phone.

"I love you. Goodbye."

Meghan placed the phone in her lap and stared at it. Sean waited a few seconds, but when she didn't speak, he bumped her shoulder. She looked at him.

"You okay?"

Meghan gestured to the phone, the movement choppy. "He adopted someone else's child, but he never once tried to get in touch with me. That makes me so . . . so . . ."

"Mad?"

"Yes. No. I'm not sure." She gripped the cell phone in both hands and squeezed. Sean wondered if she was pretending to squeeze Kevin Harrison's neck. "Disappointed maybe. Or . . . unworthy."

"Hey. None of that." Sean couldn't look at her — he needed to pay attention to traffic — but he used a stern tone he hoped would make an impact. "Don't let any feelings of unworthiness take hold of you. His decisions were his decisions, made without even knowing you."

"I know, but . . ."

Wisdom, Lord . . . He tapped her shoulder again. "Listen. What's to say he didn't adopt his wife's son because he felt guilty about not being your father? It could have been his way of making restitution."

She sighed and hung her head. "Maybe. I don't know."

Sean caught her hand and peeled it away from her phone. He linked fingers with her.

"Your value as a person has nothing to do with whether or not Kevin Harrison chose to be in your life. You are precious — to me, your mom, your grandma, and most especially God. We all love you. Don't you dare let a man you haven't met make you feel unworthy."

She leaned sideways and put her head on his shoulder for a moment. "Thanks, Sean. I love you."

"I love you, too. Why don't you call your mom . . . talk to her?"

She shook her head. "It's too early. Not yet six o'clock there. She and Grandma are probably sleeping. I'll call her later. Maybe on the road to Fort Smith."

They drove the rest of the way in silence, their fingers woven together. Maybe it was best Meghan was going to Fort Smith with someone else. If Kevin Harrison returned there in the midst of the investigation, and if by chance their paths crossed, Sean might be tempted to sock the man right in the nose for hurting Meghan.

Patience, Lord . . .

Sixteen

Fort Smith, Arkansas
Meghan

Meghan, Greg, and Sheila arrived in Fort Smith a little before eleven. Meghan didn't call her mother on the drive. She didn't want Greg or Sheila, who ended up riding in the back seat of Greg's SUV instead of following in a separate vehicle, listening to her conversation. She planned to call from the privacy of her hotel room as soon as they reached their destination, but when Greg asked about getting into their rooms, the hotel clerk said they had to wait until three. So she postponed the conversation with her mom.

She did send a text while on the road — a benign "Be careful, Mom." She received a reply, too — "I will. No worries." She wanted to say more, to ask more, but concern that either of her traveling partners might read the messages prevented her from sharing her thoughts or inner turmoil.

What was wrong with her? She'd wondered about her father for so many years, had imagined different scenarios. Now that she had some pieces of reality, why did the truth bother her so much? Because now she knew he hadn't bailed out of a desire to avoid fatherhood altogether. The fact that he'd raised a child — someone else's child — eradicated her long-held assumption.

He'd only bailed on her.

"How about we grab an early lunch and then go to the bank?" Greg angled his vehicle out of the hotel's parking lot. "What sounds good?"

Nothing sounded good to Meghan, so she peered into the back seat at Sheila. "Sheila, do you have a preference?"

The younger woman shrugged. She'd sat with her arms folded and the same unsmiling expression the entire two hours and twenty minutes it took to reach Fort Smith. Meghan felt sorry for her — Sheila couldn't possibly feel at ease with two strangers — but her taciturn nature was putting Meghan on edge. She wished the captain had talked Sheila into staying behind.

Meghan stifled a sigh and turned to Greg. "Let's see what's available on our way to the bank. Fast food's okay with me. We can plan a nicer dinner."

"That sounds fine."

Greg chose a taco joint, and the three of them sat around a tiny table and ate in silence. Meghan missed Sean so much her stomach hurt. When they were away on a case, they talked and laughed through meals, using the time to relax and revive from the tension of investigating. If she spent the entire time on this case uptight, with their only conversation centered around the missing man, she might have an ulcer by the time they went home.

They finished eating and headed for Greg's car, Sheila trailing well behind Greg and Meghan. The man sent a quick look over his shoulder, then whispered, "She's a strange one."

The protectiveness Meghan experienced surprised her. "She's a sad one. What else could she be after burying her mother a little over a month ago?"

Greg rubbed the side of his nose, sending his silver-rimmed glasses off kilter with the action. "S'pose you're right about that. But . . ." He glanced back again. "Have fun sharing a room with her."

Meghan gave a start. "What do you mean?"

"The hotel clerk said there's no reservation for Menke. Just the two rooms Cap booked for us. Looks like she intends to stay with you." He snickered. "She sure isn't staying with me."

Meghan hadn't planned on a roommate. She'd have no privacy at all. "But Cap said she understood she'd need to cover her own expenses."

Greg shrugged and dug in his pocket. "Maybe that's what she told him, but that's not how it's turning out. I mean, she got in my car without a word, she didn't reserve a room for herself . . ." He paused, key fob in hand. "She did buy her own lunch, though."

Yes. One taco and a small soft drink. Either Sheila didn't have money to cover her expenses or she had a very small appetite. Meghan suspected it was the former.

Greg pushed the fob, and the locks opened. Sheila hurried the last few feet and resumed her seat in the back. Greg and Meghan climbed in, and Greg started the engine. "All right. First stop — Union National Bank and Trust." He flashed a grin at Meghan. "Cap alerted the bank officials that we'd be coming, and they've set aside a meeting room for our use while we're in town. We can make it our home base. Beats using the extra bed in a hotel room, huh?"

"That's very kind and helpful of them."

Meghan shifted in the seat and looked into the back. "Sheila, did you bring a book or anything?"

The girl frowned. "No. Why?"

"You'll want something to pass the time while Greg and I talk to the bank representatives."

The most life Meghan had seen sparked in the young woman's eyes. "No way. I'm going in, too."

Greg harrumphed. "We brought you as a favor to Captain Ratzlaff. You aren't an investigator. You'll get in the way." He spoke as if to the windshield, but there was no doubt where — or to whom — his statement was directed.

"Mr. Ratzlaff knows I want to help. So I'm going where you go. I'm going to help."

Greg's eyebrows descended. "Listen here, Miss Men—"

"I'm going to help." Sheila glared at the back of Greg's balding head.

Meghan faced forward. "Let's talk about it when we get to the bank."

"There's nothing to talk about," Greg and Sheila said at the same time.

Meghan rolled her eyes. At least the two of them had taken her mind off her father. One small reason to be grateful.

Sean never would have anticipated being grateful for Farber's input, but he stared in pleased amazement at the piece of evidence Farber had brought to the forefront. "Why didn't I see that before?"

"Probably because your pretty little wifey is a distraction."

Appreciation whisked away, and anger swept in. But then Sean glimpsed Farber's smirk, and he tamped down the irritation. Farber meant to rile him. He wouldn't let the man win. *Patience, Lord . . .* "You could be right. She is pretty cute."

Farber snorted. "Actually, it's probably because you don't have siblings."

Sean turned a puzzled look on the man. "What does my only-child status have to do with it?"

"You never competed for attention. Never pestered a younger brother or sister." Farber hooked his linked hands behind his head and rocked in his chair. "My brother and me fought like cats and dogs when we were growing up. We hurt each other sometimes, too." He released a throaty chuckle and leaned forward, tapping the computer screen. "The age difference between the twins and the older cousin — three years —

is about right for rivalry. And an eleven-year-old is big enough to do some damage but still young enough to not fully comprehend the consequences of his actions. I think we need to look deeper into the relationship between the twins and this Stony Dunsbrook."

"It's an interesting theory. One that deserves a second look."

"Sure is. Says in the notes that the cousin was the last one to see the twins alive. And didn't you tell me the cousin's family moved across the country after the twins' funeral?"

"Yeah. Yeah, I did." That little tidbit should have created enough suspicion to support further investigation. How in the world did he not see it? Something else tiptoed through the back of his mind. Scowling, he clicked through a few notes on his computer.

"What're you doing?" Farber's tone held a note of derision.

"Something in the autopsy seemed strange." He found his highlighted notes and angled the screen so Farber could see it. "Here it is. The boys were found with dirt stains on their clothes, and they had dirt particles in their lungs, stomach, and mouth, as if they'd eaten dirt, but their faces and hair were clean." Sean raised one eyebrow. "I can't imagine little boys digging in the dirt or eating dirt clumps and not leaving residue on their faces."

Farber rocked his chair, his arms folded over his chest and a smug grin on his face. "So somebody washed them up."

Sean nodded. An idea was taking shape, and it wasn't pretty. "It's not easy to accuse a child, but you're right. We have to find out more about the last afternoon of the boys' lives, and that means talking to their cousin."

Farber snorted. "Stony Dunsbrook might've been a child when the twins died, but he's not a child now. He'd be close to fifty. So I don't feel too bad about asking him some questions."

Sean turned the screen and scrolled down the page. He found the cousin's parents' address in Stockton, California. After all these years, they might not be living there anymore. They might not be living at all. But it would give them a starting point. "Do you want to make the first contact, or do you want me to?"

Farber stomped around the desks and propped his hands on Sean's desktop, his eyes gleaming. "Oh, by all means, let me. Being a hound in hot pursuit of prey is my favorite part of this job."

Fort Smith, Arkansas
Meghan

Uncovering clues, seeing the puzzle pieces fall into place, was Meghan's favorite part of her job. But so far not even one puzzle piece had made itself known.

Did Sheila's presence intimidate the two employees who'd once worked closely with Anson Menke into withholding information? Or were Greg and Meghan so unaccustomed to working together they couldn't find the right questions to ask? Either way, the meeting was a flop.

After an hour of listening to the bank employees hem and haw and skirt questions, Greg thanked the men for their time and ushered Meghan and Sheila out of the room. The moment Greg closed the door behind them, Sheila whirled on him.

"Why are we leaving? They didn't tell us anything. They have to know more than they're saying. Go back in there and make them talk."

Meghan put her arm around Sheila's shoulders. "Sheila, we're investigators, not interrogators. We can't *make* them talk."

Sheila shrugged loose and held her hand toward the closed door. "Then ask again. And again and again" — she bounced her hand, emphasizing each *again* — "until they

205

say something that helps."

Greg scowled at her for a few seconds, then took off for the lobby. Meghan and Sheila trotted after him. Sheila muttered under her breath all the way to the car. Inside, she gripped the headrest on Greg's seat and shook it.

"I can't believe this. You aren't even trying."

Greg turned around and fixed Sheila with the kind of look Mom used to give teenage Meghan during rare arguments. "Miss Menke, I understand you have a personal connection to this case, and I'm not unsympathetic. But you have not been trained in investigative work, so you have no business telling me whether or not I'm doing my job."

Sheila slumped against the seat. She folded her arms over her chest and scowled out the side window, but tears glittered in her eyes. How much of Sheila's anger stemmed from the recent loss of her mother? Meghan was ready to cut the girl some slack, but Greg apparently didn't see the need.

"If you really want to help, try to remember everything you can about the weeks leading up to your father's disappearance and share that information with us. Otherwise, you really need to stay out of our way."

Sheila didn't answer. She didn't move, except to blink rapidly.

Meghan held up her hand. "Greg, I think you've made your point. Let's go see if we can check into the hotel now. You and I can meet up after dinner and go over our notes again, find a better direction to take with the bank reps."

Greg sent one more glowering look into the back seat, then faced the steering wheel. "All right." His lips remained in a grim line during the drive to the hotel. Although they were still an hour early, their rooms were ready, so the clerk allowed them access. Greg walked the women to their room. Meghan unlocked the door, and Sheila darted inside. Meghan started after her, but Greg stopped her.

"Listen, DeFord, you better come to an agreement with her or I'll be hauling her back to Little Rock in the morning."

Meghan cringed, imagining the scene if he followed through on the threat. "What am I supposed to do? Captain Ratzlaff gave her permission to be here."

"Cap didn't give her permission to ramrod the investigation. He threw the lead position in your lap, remember? So it's up to you to keep her reined in. You know as well as I do that those men clammed up because they didn't want to say anything incriminating in front of Menke's daughter. They're trying to protect her. It's chivalrous, but that won't help us. Or her, for that matter."

Meghan nodded, misery flooding her. She'd suspected the men were trying to protect Sheila's feelings, too. But how could she tell Sheila without crushing her? No matter what Sheila had said in the captain's office about wanting the truth, what she really wanted deep down was validation that her father hadn't embezzled money and disappeared with it. Because no girl wanted to think negative things about her father.

The recent truth Meghan had discovered about her own father left her heart bruised and aching. She didn't want to inflict that kind of pain on Sheila if she could avoid it. If only Sean were here. He'd know how to confront Sheila kindly and diplomatically.

Greg tapped his little room-card envelope on the wall, impatience marring his brow. "Well? Are you going to talk to her?"

"I'll do my best, okay?"

"I hope so." Greg set off up the hall, waving his card over his shoulder. "I'm in room 114. When you're ready for dinner, come get me."

Meghan took a deep breath, sent up a prayer for guidance, and entered what would be her home away from home for the next few days. Sheila's duffle bag was on the closest bed to the door, so Meghan plopped her bag on the end of the second bed. She looked around the simple, quiet room. "Sheila?"

"What?" The reply came from behind a closed door — probably the bathroom. Her voice sounded nasally, as if she'd been crying.

Meghan closed her eyes and sighed. This wasn't going to be easy. "Could you come out, please? I need to talk to you." Oh, how she missed her husband.

Seventeen

Las Vegas, Nevada
Kevin

Kevin's favorite part of acquisition was negotiating, but usually he didn't have spectators. Diane had brought her mother along for their meeting, which initially took him by surprise, but he'd largely ignored the older woman's quiet presence. She didn't matter. Not to him, anyway.

But what did Diane think, seeing him in action with the building's owner while the owner's agent and banker sat as if tongue tied and let the two of them verbally duke it out? He wanted to impress Diane, the girl with the high IQ who'd refused to kowtow to him all those years ago. He wanted her to label him as successful. Why? He wasn't sure, but he wanted her approval.

The building's current owner, Rodney Phelps, shook his head and glared at Kevin across the folding table set up in the lobby for their meeting. "I set a fair market price, and you know it. This piece of real estate is in the heart of the city, and it's an amazing old building — a unique piece of architecture."

"Unique, yes, but the greater emphasis is on *old.*" Using his fingertip, Kevin tapped a paragraph in the proposed contract and looked at the owner over the top of his glasses. "The plumbing system isn't up to code. The breaker box needs a major overhaul. Just those two things equal tens of thousands of dollars of expense right off the bat."

He turned to another page in the proposal document. "There's no private parking, which drops its value substantially if the building is to be used to house various businesses. Where are the employees supposed to leave their vehicles?"

Phelps huffed. "They can ride the bus or take a taxi. Buy a month pass for a public lot. It's what a lot of people who work the Strip do."

"Maybe. But it doesn't very well suit someone who makes the apartment their permanent residence." Kevin flipped several pages to a sheet bearing a series of grainy black-and-white photographs. "I agree with what you said earlier, that having a loft apartment is a distinctive feature, but the last updates were in 1985. No one wants a country kitchen or balloon shades on their windows anymore. Hiring an interior designer to bring the apartment up to date and ready for lease will put another major hit on the budget." He slapped the file closed and leaned back, pinning the soft-bellied, jowl-cheeked man with a firm look. "Carve forty-five thousand off the asking price, and I'll write you a check today."

A soft gasp came from the corner where Diane and her mother sat on folding chairs, but Kevin didn't look to see who'd emitted it. The sound itself told him he'd made an impact by intimating that his bank account could cover the cost of the building. *"Money talks, and people listen,"* Dad had always said. Kevin smirked. Money talk was more effective than prayers, he'd wager.

Phelps scowled. "All right, I admit the place needs some fixing up. So I'll come down thirty. But I won't be robbed."

"I'm the one being robbed if I pay what you're asking. You've heard my offer. Take it or leave it." Kevin glanced around the space, and longing twined through him. He wanted this property. If Phelps walked away, Kevin would kick himself all the way back to Arkansas, but he'd done his research. The building had sat empty for more than a year. The seller had to be on the verge of desperation. He also had to know the longer the building stayed on the market, the more it would deteriorate. Funny how empty buildings seemed to fall apart. The more deterioration, the less value it had. Kevin was doing the man a favor by taking the place off his hands before things got worse.

He looked at Phelps again and raised one eyebrow. "Well?" If he got shot down in front of Diane, he'd never forgive himself.

Phelps blew out a mighty breath and flung his hands in the air. "Fine. I'll sign." He pointed at Kevin. "But I still think it's thievery."

Kevin removed his corporate checkbook from his briefcase and laid it open on the table. He pulled his favorite gold-plated pen from the interior pocket of his suit coat and gave it a twist. "Make it out to you or your corporation, Mr. Phelps?"

By paying outright and not involving a lender, the transaction went smoothly and quickly. He signed his name at least a dozen times and forked over the biggest check he'd ever written, but when he escorted the three men to the door, he couldn't keep a smile from his face. He'd won. And the long-ago girl he'd wanted to impress had witnessed the whole thing.

He closed the door and turned to face the women. "Well, I think a celebration's in order. Where's the best place to get caviar and lobster on the Strip?"

Hazel DeFord stood, shaking her finger at him. "Young man, if I eat caviar and lobster, I'll fall asleep at the table from the gluttony and you'll have to carry me home."

Diane stood, too, and angled a wry grin at him. "Haven't you spent enough money?"

He'd impressed her. He could tell. His smile grew. "Not yet. The money he carved off the price will still be spent, and then some. But it'll be worth it in the end." He sent a slow look around the lobby, admiring the marble touches, crystal chandeliers, and stained-glass sconces. This lobby would make a perfect coffee-and-pastries shop. People could duck in and enjoy a snack or drink before browsing the specialty shops that would occupy the large rooms previously used for offices. A chill attacked. The best kind of chill.

He marched to the elevator and positioned his finger by the button. "Hazel, you haven't seen the best part of this place — the only loft apartment on this block of Las Vegas Boulevard's business district. Want to go up?"

Her lips quirked, and her eyes sparkled with mischief. "If it boasts a country kitchen and balloon curtains, then certainly I want to see it."

Kevin burst out laughing. He'd stop looking past her if she proved to be this amusing at every encounter. He pushed the button. "There's an amazing view, too. Ladies first."

The elevator creaked a bit getting started, but then the gears hummed like bees in a hive. It stopped at the fourth floor, and the doors slid open. Hazel stepped out onto the patterned carpet that reminded Kevin of a 1940s movie theater, and Diane followed her. Kevin came last but stepped past them and unlocked the apartment door.

With a wide sweep of his arm, he invited them to cross the threshold. "Diane, while you give your mother the tour, why not throw some suggestions my way for updating this space." He'd left his briefcase in the lobby, but he could make notes on his phone. "I don't want it to be the *only* loft apartment on this block. I want it to be the *best* loft apartment on the entire Strip."

She put her hand on her hip and gave him a cocky grin. "Well, to start with, burn the balloon shades. They're dust catchers." She patted one of the droopy poofs of sheeny pink. Dust motes floated through the air, and a spider ran up the curtain and over the top of the rod. She cringed. "And homes for critters, I see." She brushed her palms together and stepped away from the window.

Kevin made a note on his phone — *Hire exterminator.* "Eliminate the homes for critters. Got it." He repeatedly tossed his phone and caught it. "What else?"

Diane wandered from the window to the center of the open space that served as a sitting area, dining room, and kitchen. She braced her palm on the wedge-shaped island separating the kitchen from the other side of the large room. "What would you think about capitalizing on the original building's era and incorporating art deco elements? Like a patterned tile backsplash for the kitchen, plaster cornices, maybe even a focal wall with peacock-feather wallpaper?"

Kevin made a face — peacock feathers? Before he could voice the thought, Hazel gasped and clasped her hands beneath her chin.

"My, yes. Arch the doorway openings into the hallways, and perhaps add a mirrored sculpture of geometric shapes above the fireplace. You needn't go overboard, but the right touches would hearken back to the building's glory days while still blending well with the modern elements today's millennials want in their living spaces."

"Oh!" Diane's face lit. "What about Tiffany sconces on either side of the hallway opening?"

"Of course. Furnishing it with pieces that have low, clean lines, in solid colors that coordinate with the colors in a peacock's tail, would make things so inviting."

Hazel and Diane jabbered, sharing ideas so rapidly Kevin couldn't keep up. He finally waved his hands and laughed. "Ladies, ladies, please . . . I think I could forget about hiring a professional decorator and put the two of you on the job."

They paused and gawked at him, wearing identical "are you serious?" expressions. Then Hazel shrugged. "You've got the summer free, Margaret Diane. What do you think? Would you want to tackle the restoration of this loft apartment?"

Diane tapped her finger against her chin. "I don't know. Maybe. Would you help me?"

"Of course. It could be fun."

Kevin had been joking, but in hindsight, maybe he'd hit upon a good idea. He knew from past experience she had great taste. He still remembered what she'd done to his room in the frat house.

October 1984
Little Rock, Arkansas

"Look, if this is going to be your home for the next three years, you might as well make it homey, right?"

Kevin crinkled his nose and threw a sock at Diane. "Homey-schmomey. All I need is a place to lay my head."

She pursed her face, peeled the sock from her shoulder, and dropped it on the end of his unmade bed. "That might be enough for you, but if I'm going to hang around, I at least want someplace to sit."

"This'll suit." He bounced his hand on the edge of the mattress, hoping she'd catch his meaning.

She rolled her eyes and turned away. Yep, she'd caught it. But she wasn't having it. At least not now.

"I'm serious, Kev. It's not like you need to turn this place into *House Beautiful,* but right now it looks like a dump. How can you focus in here?" She snatched up articles of clothing he'd left on the floor and piled them on the end of his bed while she harped at him. "You've got a closet plus a dresser. There's no reason to leave clothes all over the place. This room is a great size. You could make a sitting area in this corner if you brought in a throw rug and a couple of small chairs. Maybe folding butterfly chairs — they're comfortable but can be tucked against the wall if you ever need the floor space. Your mini fridge would be perfect as a table between the chairs, serving dual purposes. Honestly, this is so much better than my dorm room. You ought to fix it up and really make it a great place for us to hang out."

He liked that she'd said *us.* He patted his back pocket where his wallet created a bulge. "I've got my credit card. If you want, we can go shopping." He slung his arms around her and pulled her tight against his frame. She fit there so perfect. Whatever he needed to do to keep her coming around, he'd do it. Except . . . "Don't do anything girlie in here. I'm living with a bunch of guys. I don't want them ragging on me, okay?"

She wriggled free and shook her head. "You're such a dork. I wouldn't make it girlie. But warm? Inviting? A place where people want to be instead of a place that people want to escape from?" She grinned, letting him know she was teasing. "Let's shoot for that."

His room had become the choice hangout spot for every guy in the fraternity, all because Diane had made it welcoming. The classy way she dressed told him she hadn't lost her touch.

He crossed the parquet floor to Diane and stuck out his hand. "Shall we make hiring DeFord" — he glanced at her mother, including her in the deal — "and DeFord official?"

Diane linked her hands at her waist and pinned him with a long, pensive frown. Then the corners of her lips twitched. "Hmm, Mother, what should we charge for our services?"

A teasing grin quivered on her rosy lips, and he couldn't resist winking at her. How long had it been since he'd engaged in playful chitchat with such a worthy partner? He slipped his hand in his jacket pocket and tipped up his chin, peering at her down his nose. "How about we negotiate over caviar and lobster tails?"

"I'd be fine with a vegan lobster-topped caesar salad from Lobster ME."

Kevin scratched his head. "What in the world is vegan lobster?"

"Believe it or not, it's heart of palm tossed

in lemon juice and seasonings. It's a great substitute for lobster."

He shuddered, and she laughed.

"You don't have to eat it. Lobster ME has plenty of traditional lobster choices, and it's within walking distance."

Walking would take longer than driving. Especially walking with a woman who had more than eighty years on her. But the added time was a bonus, not a burden. He angled a concerned look at Diane's mother. "Are you okay with us walking to the café, Hazel?"

The same impish expression Diane sometimes wore appeared on the older woman's face. "I've had eighty-three years of using these feet, so they're well practiced at walking. Let's go."

She headed out the door. Kevin glanced at Diane and found her grinning at him. Something seemed to sizzle. A connection that whisked him backward in time with such force that he felt like a goofy, smitten twenty-year-old again. He dropped his arm across her shoulders and aimed her for the door.

"You heard the lady. Let's go." And to his satisfaction, Diane didn't pull away.

EIGHTEEN

Fort Smith, Arkansas
Meghan

Meghan tapped on Greg's door. His grunt came in response. The door swung open, and she grinned at his tousled light-brown hair. "Were you napping?"

He rubbed his eyes and yawned. "Yeah. Dozed off in front of the television. Dinnertime, huh?"

"It's actually a little early for dinner, but I thought we might drive by Sheila's former house. Maybe it will stimulate some memories."

Greg narrowed his gaze. "Did you and her have a talk?"

Meghan glanced aside, shrinking her shoulders. "Well, no. She said she had a headache, so she napped, too."

He groaned. "DeFord . . ."

"I know, I know." She picked at a bit of loose wallpaper border. "I'll talk to her before we turn in tonight, but she seemed pretty upset after the meeting at the bank. I decided it was better to wait, let her calm down so she'd be more likely to listen to reason." Meghan also hadn't been much in the mood for a chat after texting back and forth with Mom and discovering what she and Grandma had gotten themselves into.

"You're probably right about that." Greg scratched his cheek, stretching the skin into a jowl. "My girls don't listen good when they're upset. But if I give 'em time to calm down and give myself time to cool off" — he shrugged — "things go better. Guess I kind of forgot that when I was giving Sheila the third degree."

The agents didn't talk much about their personal lives at the office. Meghan knew that all but Roach were married, and she'd overheard random comments about kids' sporting events and birthday parties, but she'd never asked for particulars. She tipped her head, trying to envision Greg with little girls. "How old are your daughters?"

"Sixteen, twelve, and ten. And my son's thirteen."

Meghan's jaw dropped. Four children?

He blew out a breath. A rueful scowl formed. "They're growing up fast, and I'm not there as much as I'd like to be." He shook his head, as if clearing his thoughts. "And this kind of talk isn't getting the job done."

An idea seemed to drop like a ceiling tile and bop her on the head. She straightened. "Greg . . . I'm not going to talk to Sheila about interfering in the investigation. I think you should."

He reared back. "Why me?"

"Because you're a father. What is Sheila missing in her life?" A lump filled her throat, and she swallowed. Hard. "I think she'd listen to you if you took a fatherly approach."

He scratched his cheek again. "I don't know. My girls listen to me because they've known me their whole lives. They don't have much choice. It's either listen or get grounded. But it's not like I can threaten to ground Sheila."

Meghan laughed. She could well imagine the outcome. "No, of course not, but you might be able to get through to her if you were more patient and kind than you were earlier. It's at least worth a try, isn't it? Wouldn't it be better if she could stay? Cap would be happier. You wouldn't have to eat up half a day driving to Little Rock and back in the middle of our investigation." She paused, giving him time to think, then added softly, "So what do you say?"

He rolled his eyes ceilingward and sighed. "I say we're both plumb loco for getting roped into bringing a civilian along on an investigation in the first place. But since she's here, we might as well make the most of it. Go get her. We'll do what you said — drive to her house, let her memory banks get poked some — and then, if it works itself naturally into the conversation, I'll see if I can convince her to stay at the hotel the next time we go to the bank."

Meghan smiled. "Thanks, Greg."

"Yeah, yeah, you just don't wanna be the bad cop in this partnership." His crooked grin ruined what could have been a derogatory comment. "Lemme grab my keys, and I'll meet you at the car."

Meghan encouraged Sheila to ride shotgun so she could more easily direct Greg to her former home. Although reluctant, she eventually slid into the front seat and fastened her seat belt. Meghan took the passenger seat behind her but sat on the edge and leaned sideways for a view out the front windshield.

Although it had been years since Sheila had lived there, she gave precise directions to the neighborhood. Greg turned onto Oak Street, and Sheila said, "Go slow, please.

There's lots of trees and stuff here that wasn't before. It's kind of confusing me. But our house was white with green shutters, and there was a flower garden in front of the picture window."

Meghan tapped Sheila's shoulder and pointed. "That one?"

Sheila's gasp gave the answer.

Greg pulled up to the curb and put the SUV in park, but he left the engine idling.

Sheila rolled down the window and curled both hands over the edge. "Everybody says when you go back home, it looks smaller than you remembered. But it doesn't. Not to me."

Greg rested his elbow on the console between the seats and peered out the window. "Nice house. Seems like a good place to grow up."

"It was." Sheila nodded, her blond hair bouncing on her shoulders. "It . . . yeah . . . really was." She fell silent, seemingly lost in thought.

Greg glanced at Meghan, dipped his eyebrows low, and bobbed his head toward Sheila. Meghan got the silent message. She cleared her throat. "What's the first thing that comes to mind when you look at the house, Sheila?"

A strange laugh burbled from the younger

woman's throat — half chortle, half sob. "Sitting on the porch steps, usually barefoot, scratching mosquito bites and watching the street. Waiting for Dad to come home."

Pain stabbed Meghan's heart, but she forced a soft chuckle. "Did you run to greet him when he pulled in?"

"Yeah." Sheila's fingers tightened, her knuckles glowing white. "He always scooped me up in a hug. That hug . . . it fixed things, you know? Even on the worst days, when Mom was really suffering, it seemed like when he got home and gave us all hugs, it helped."

"He was a good dad." Meghan stated it rather than asked, but it took every bit of strength she had to say it without breaking down.

"He was. Even up to the end. You know, the last day before he went away."

Greg said, "I know you've talked to us about the last day, but do you remember anything else? Something he said, something he did, that seemed out of the ordinary? Anything that might give us a clue about what he was thinking?"

Sheila stared out the window for several minutes, her frame stiff, and then she gave a little jolt and spun to face Greg. "That last night, Daddy didn't come to my room to kiss me good night like he always did. So I went looking for him."

March 21, 2002
Sheila

What were Mom and Daddy still doing at the kitchen table? The little clock on her bedside stand blinked 9:03. Supper was over hours ago, and she was supposed to be asleep already. But how could she sleep without her good-night kiss?

Sheila lay under her pink-and-white-checked comforter and listened to her parents' mumbled voices. Maybe they didn't know the time. After all, goofy Wayne had broken Mom's wall clock yesterday bouncing a basketball in the house, and the itty-bitty clock on the kitchen stove was pretty hard to read. They probably didn't know it was past her bedtime. She should go remind them.

She slid out of bed, padded up the hallway, and peeked around the corner into the kitchen. Mom sat kind of slumped in her chair with her elbows on the table. She held some papers, and it looked like she was reading them. Daddy sat across from her, watching her with his forehead all crinkled, the way he did when Mom was having one of her bad days. But they weren't talking anymore, so they wouldn't say Sheila was interrupting.

She stepped into the kitchen. Her bare feet met the cold linoleum, and her whole body shivered. She curled her toes and sucked in a breath.

Daddy jumped out of his chair so fast it almost tipped over. He took one step toward Sheila. "What are you doing out of bed?"

Sheila drew back, fiddling with the buttons on her Barbie pajama top. Why was he so mad? He only got mad when somebody did something really bad. Like bouncing the basketball in the house and breaking Mom's clock. "I . . ." She licked her dry lips. "I didn't get my good-night kiss."

A smile formed on Daddy's face, but it wasn't his real smile. More like the smile Wayne used when he got caught doing something he shouldn't and wanted to fool the person who caught him. "Sorry, punkin, I guess I forgot."

He forgot? How could he forget? He'd never forgotten to come kiss her good night. Not ever. She leaned sideways slightly and peeked at the table. "What're you —"

"Let's get you tucked in." Daddy reached her in two long steps and bent forward, putting his hands on his knees. "Hop on. I'll piggyback you."

She gawked at him. "But you said I was getting too tall to ride piggyback."

He laughed. A weird laugh, almost like he was choking. "One last time. Okay?"

Sheila giggled and hopped on. She wrapped her arms around his neck, and he hooked the backs of her knees with his wrists. She buried her nose against his neck. Daddy always smelled good — like cinnamon and oranges and maybe a little bit of vanilla. He smelled even better than the pumpkin pies Mom baked for holidays. She sniffed hard, filling her nostrils with the scent.

He moved through the hallway real slow, making the ride last, but they reached her bedroom sooner than she wanted to. He backed up to the bed, then gave a little buck. She plopped onto her mattress with a bounce and giggled again.

Daddy put his finger against his lips. "Shhh. Don't wake the boys."

Mom always said an earthquake wouldn't wake Wayne and Brandon once they'd conked out, but Sheila wouldn't argue with Daddy.

He tugged at her covers. "C'mon, climb under."

She burrowed beneath the comforter and nestled her head on her pillow. "Daddy, what were you and Mom doing?" It must've been important since he forgot to kiss her good night.

He tucked the edge of her comforter under her chin, brushing her jaw with his knuckles. "Nothing to worry about. Just getting our ducks in a row."

Sheila imagined a bunch of ducks all lining up like the kids did at school to go to recess. She grinned. "That's pretty funny."

He nodded. "It is." He leaned down and kissed her forehead, then stayed close, looking into her eyes. "Sweet dreams, punkin. I love you."

For a second, it looked like his eyes were wet, but her little plug-in night-light didn't put out much light. It was hard to tell in the dark. "I love you, too, Daddy." He stood straight, and she rolled to her side and closed her eyes. She waited for Daddy's foot to hit the squeaky board under her carpet when he left. But she didn't hear it.

She peeked over her shoulder. He stood beside her bed, staring down at her. Now she knew his eyes were wet. Was Daddy getting ready to cry? But daddies didn't cry. Or did they? A funny feeling wriggled through her middle. "Daddy?"

"Shhh." He smoothed her hair and smiled. His regular smile.

The weird feeling slipped away, and she smiled back at him.

"Sleep, now."

"Okay." She snuggled in and closed her eyes. "Good night." The creak let her know he left.

Present Day
Meghan

Meghan swallowed. Whatever else Anson Menke had been, he'd been a good dad. Did Sheila know how lucky she was to hold memories of a daddy giving her piggyback rides and tucking her into bed?

Greg said, "It sounds like maybe he was worried about something and wanted to make sure your mom was taken care of."

Meghan gave her head a little shake, forcing herself to focus on the present. She looked into the front seat at Sheila, and the tender expression the girl had adopted while she reminisced disappeared beneath a hardened veneer.

"Or he was planning to run and wanted to make sure she had all the doctors' contacts and everything since he was usually the one who handled stuff like that." She rolled up the window and set her gaze straight ahead. "I'm done here."

Greg put his hand on the gearshift, but he

didn't take the vehicle out of park. He turned his head and aimed a thoughtful frown at Sheila's profile. "Thanks for sharing that with us. I'm sure it wasn't easy, making yourself go back there."

Sheila didn't answer, but she gave a stiff nod.

"Here's the thing about dads, Sheila. They think they're the strong ones. That they have to carry the load for everybody and not worry anybody. So they keep stuff to themselves. They think they're protecting their family by staying quiet. Sometimes that makes wives and kids draw incorrect conclusions about what's going on."

Slowly, Sheila shifted her head and looked at Greg. "Are you saying Dad left to protect us? From what?"

He held up his hand. "I'm not saying anything yet. It's too soon to know. But you're plenty mad at your dad for going away."

She nodded hard. "I sure am. He totally messed up our lives."

"Since it's too soon to know why he left, it's too soon to be mad. Wouldn't you rather hold on to the good memories? The hugs? The good-night kisses? The piggyback rides?"

Meghan's heart ached with such ferocity

233

that she planted both palms over her chest in a feeble attempt to ease the pressure. Even if her father decided to step into her life tomorrow, she'd never have sweet childhood moments. The sense of loss nearly overwhelmed her.

"Here's the thing, Sheila." Greg spoke softly, his tone gruff yet kind. "Yeah, your dad went away. But for your first ten years, he was there. And during those ten years, he was, you said yourself, a good dad. Hold on to that. Don't let bitterness erase the memories. They're too important to lose."

Meghan glanced back and forth between Greg's fervent expression and Sheila's uncertain one. She'd been given a glimpse of Greg's fatherly heart, and her admiration for the detective grew. Even if Sheila didn't accept his advice, Meghan had listened intently. *"Don't let bitterness erase the memories,"* he'd said. She didn't have any memories with a father. But maybe, in the future, she'd have face-to-face time with him. Would she let bitterness about the lost years keep her from enjoying those moments?

NINETEEN

Carson Springs, Arkansas
Sean

"It shouldn't surprise us that someone else lives at the address from 1998." Sean leaned into the corner of the sofa and propped his feet up on the attached chaise. He'd called to catch up with Meghan, and hearing her voice, even though she sounded tired, was so welcome. The house was too quiet and empty without her. "But we're tracking them down. Or, I should say, Farber is. He's like a fox digging its way into a henhouse. He gives off this unconcerned, almost lazy vibe, but underneath, he's tenacious. Been good for me to see this side of him."

"I've been enlightened some, too, working with Greg." Street noise buzzed through the phone. She wasn't reclining in her hotel room for their conversation. She'd told him she had to go outside and around the corner from the lobby for privacy. Hardly comfort-

235

able. She sighed. "I miss you like crazy, but I'm kind of glad I'm getting the chance to know him better. He's really a pretty good guy."

Sean wasn't ready to describe Farber as a pretty good guy, but at least he wasn't seeing him as all bad. "Have you talked any more to your mom? How'd her meeting with Kevin Harrison go?"

"You're not going to believe this. She and Grandma agreed to redecorate the loft apartment in the building he bought in Vegas." Meghan's stunned tone matched Sean's gut reaction.

"What? Why?"

"She said it just kind of happened, but I don't know how a person *just happens* to sign up for a job like that. At least Grandma's involved, too. She'll make sure Mom stays safe."

Sean frowned. "Has she said something that makes you worry she might not be safe?" He presumed Meghan was speaking of staying safe emotionally, but what did they really know about this man? Other than he'd fathered Meghan, abandoned Diane, and gone on to build a successful business for himself.

"It's not so much what she's said. I mean, we've only talked through text messages —

I didn't want Sheila or Greg hearing my side of what's bound to be a personal discussion, so I texted while Sheila was napping this afternoon. But agreeing to work for him is bound to put them in regular contact. I'm not sure how I feel about that. Still . . ."

Something changed in her voice. Hesitance? Introspection? He wasn't sure, but his detective instincts revved into high gear. "What are you thinking?"

He waited, but she didn't answer. If it weren't for the traffic noises still coming through the connection, he'd wonder if she hung up. "Meg?"

"It's too complicated to sort through right now. And I'd rather have that talk when we're together, okay?"

Even though his worry increased, he shouldn't keep her much longer. She'd already stood outside for half an hour. "Okay. I'll put it on the calendar for your first night home." His attempt at humor worked. She laughed.

"Sounds good. Sheila agreed to stay in the hotel room tomorrow when Greg and I return to the bank. Hopefully the reps will be more forthcoming with information. He and I want to review some notes before we turn in, so I better let you go." A pause, then a trembling "I love you" made his heart roll over.

"I love you, too, babe. I'll talk to you again tomorrow night, okay?"

"Okay. Bye."

He disconnected the call, and immediately his phone rang. Farber's number flashed on the screen. Sean hit Accept Call. "Hey. What's up?"

"My blood pressure."

After listening to Meghan's sweet voice, Farber's growl was an attack. Sean cringed. "Why? What's going on?"

"I've found obituaries for Clark and Hilda, so we won't get any help from either of them."

Sean searched his memory. Ah, Clark and Hilda Dunsbrook — Stony's parents. "We've encountered roadblocks like that in other cases. Now we know to look for Stony himself."

"That's the thing." Farber's aggravation carried clearly through the connection. "Other than his name listed as a survivor in his father's obit back in 1983, there are no other online hits for the man. No place of employment. No record of traffic tickets. No address. It's as if he doesn't exist."

When Sean had called the detective tenacious, he hadn't realized how accurate his statement was. He assumed what he hoped was a calming tone. "We've got access to more information on the department computers. If he changed his name or ended up in a witness-protection program, we'll be able to find out. Why not set it aside for now and get some rest?" He forced a chuckle. "Your blood pressure will thank you."

Farber grunted. "No offense, Beagle, but I wanna get this thing wrapped up so I can cut you loose."

Why did every statement that started out "No offense, but" end up being an insult? Sean started to snap that working with Farber was no picnic, either, but the prayers he'd uttered for patience paid off. He scooted to the edge of the sofa and stood. "Obviously you don't have any choice except to let it go for now. So let's start fresh again in the morning. I'll pray for clear minds and —"

"Beagle, if you talk religion to me again when we're on the job, I'll file a suit."

Sean gave a jolt. Had he mentioned religion? He replayed his comments and inwardly groaned. The habit of prayer was so natural that he hadn't thought twice about praying. But he shouldn't have said it out loud. He knew Farber's feelings. Still, Sean didn't believe he'd done anything wrong. After all, they weren't on the job, and he hadn't preached Jesus's name to the detective. But to keep peace, he should apologize. "I —"

His phone screen went blank. Sean dropped back on the sofa, covered his eyes with the back of his forearm, and sighed. *Lord, let him cool off by morning. Help me guard my tongue. And let us find Stony Dunsbrook as fast as possible so I can shed Farber.*

His conscience pricked. He dropped his arm and looked at the starry sky outside his living room window. *That's what I want. But let Your will be done, Father. Your will, whatever that is.*

Las Vegas, Nevada
Diane

Diane pinched the credit card the way she'd pinch the scruff of a dead rat's neck and stared at Kevin across Mother's coffee table. She'd invited him to the house for a midmorning meeting to discuss details about the apartment, but she hadn't expected him to give her so much responsibility. "Did . . . did you say forty-thousand-dollar limit?"

He glanced at the card and then returned his blue-eyed gaze to her face. "Yes. I'm sure it won't be enough, especially if you make major changes to the kitchen or bathroom, but I'll track the balance online and keep it paid up so it won't slow down your progress. Consider your budget double that amount."

Diane nearly spluttered. She sent an aghast look in Mother's direction, and Mother returned it with a disbelieving shrug. She turned to Kevin again. "I furnished and decorated my entire apartment in Little Rock for a tenth of this card's limit." Of course, she'd shopped second-hand stores and yard sales. Even so . . . She stared at the rectangle of plastic. What if she lost it? She thrust the card at him. "It's too much, Kevin. I don't want to be responsible for it."

He shook his head. "Keep it."

She slapped it onto the table. The trio of dachshunds drowsing on the opposite half of the sofa lifted their pointed noses and snuffled. She absently patted the closest one's head. "I can't. I won't." The dogs settled, and she waved her hand at the card as if stirring embers to life. "That's equal to two years of my teaching salary. If I lost it, I'd —"

"Two years of . . ." Now he gaped at her. "Are you telling me you only make twenty thousand a year as a teacher? That's ludicrous for someone with a master's degree."

"I teach at a small private high school. They don't have federal funding."

"Why would you waste your life that way?"

Defensiveness struck with force. She folded her arms over her chest. "I don't consider investing in the lives of our country's future leaders a waste."

"But —"

Mother cleared her throat. "Kevin, rather than giving Margaret Diane carte blanche with your credit card, perhaps she could make selections in stores or online, share them with you, and allow you to make the actual purchases."

He didn't seem to hear her. His gaze remained locked on Diane. "Did you make more than 20K before you moved to Nevada?"

Diane frowned. "I don't think my salary is your business, Kevin."

He wilted against the backrest of his chair. "How did you raise a child on such a minimal amount? Were you ever able to take her to Disneyland? Buy her braces? Enroll her in dance classes?"

Diane turned her focus to the dachshunds, unwilling to meet his dumbfounded gaze. She hadn't given Meghan extras. Certainly none of the experiences she herself had enjoyed as a child. Mother hadn't been extravagant, but neither had she been stingy. More than once, Mother had offered to fund activities for Meghan, but Diane had always stubbornly refused, not wanting to accept "charity," especially from Mother. Meghan didn't seem to hold a grudge, and Diane had tried to set aside regret for denying her daughter the extras many of her friends received, but Kevin's queries sent a boulder of guilt rolling through her.

"Diane, I'm sorry."

The sincere admission startled her into looking at him. True remorse glimmered in his eyes.

"I should've helped you. I should've . . . supported her. I was stupid and wrong." He drew in a deep breath and released it in a whoosh, shaking his head. "I'm really sorry."

Why was it easier to face off with the overly confident Kevin? She lifted her chin and shrugged. "It's in the past. Obviously Meghan grew up okay. We might not have had luxuries, but we never went hungry, and we were always adequately clothed and sheltered. There's no sense in worrying about it now."

"That's exactly right." Mother's stalwart tone drew their attention. " 'My God will meet all your needs according to the riches of his glory in Christ Jesus.' That's Philippians 4:19, and I've always found it to be true. As have Margaret Diane and Meghan." She smiled, her eyes crinkling in the corners. "Sometimes it's a blessing not to have an overabundance of wealth."

Kevin huffed. "How so?"

"Oh, those who have much always seem to want something more or better. Those who have little tend to appreciate what they have. Even Socrates said, 'Contentment is natural wealth, luxury is artificial poverty.' It comes down to a matter of contentment." She tilted her head and pinned Kevin with a pensive look. "Are you content with what you have, Kevin?"

"Of course I am." He spoke with force, as if trying to convince himself. "And acquiring this building in Las Vegas makes me even more content. Or it will when it's filled with vendors and the apartment is ready for lease." He jerked his focus to Diane. "Which brings me back to decorating it. I want you to take this card" — he slid it across the table's smooth surface — "and use it at your discretion to make the apartment aesthetically appealing, up to date, and warmly inviting. If I'm to get top dollar in rent, the place needs an overhaul, and I trust you to do it right."

She sighed. "Kevin, I don't know."

He offered his engaging, convincing, heart-melting smile. "I do know. You and your mom were throwing around great ideas. Make them happen."

Diane looked at Mother.

Mother held out her hands in a gesture of defeat. "It's up to you, dear. It might be fun to play with someone else's money. And it will be a way to occupy yourself this summer."

Diane gingerly picked up the credit card and held it in front of her like a shield. "Have you contacted your credit card company? I don't want to be accused of fraud the first time I try to use this thing."

His face lit. "Does that mean you'll do it?"

She might live to regret it, but she did need a distraction. And who knew how the experience might be of use someday? Mother always said God didn't waste anything in their lives. "Yes. We'll do it."

He whooped and punched the air. The dachshunds came to life, yipping and jumping on the cushions. He cringed. "Sorry. Didn't mean to get them all stirred up."

"Here, now! Miney, Duchess, Molly . . . settle down. We aren't under attack." Mother's firm voice ended the melee. They whined but flopped into a furry bundle again and stared at Kevin with round brown eyes. Mother turned her attention to Kevin. "When do you want us to start?"

He stroked his stubbled chin. Diane had no idea how he maintained that slight shadow of whiskers, but it gave him a rugged appearance she found hard to ignore. "I have a meeting this afternoon to get a building permit. As soon as I have that in hand, the plumber and electrician are ready to go in and do what needs doing. The plumber agreed to start at the top and work his way down, so he should be out of the apartment by the end of this week if all goes well." He sat up and crossed his leg in the relaxed way men did — ankle on knee. "Obviously you can start planning right away, but you might want to hold off on doing any actual work until after the first of June. Then you won't have to worry about tripping over the plumber. But there is one small condition."

Diane fingered the credit card. "I won't do anything too girlie." As soon as the words were out, she regretted them. Why take a deliberate foray into the past? She waited for him to cringe, but instead a knowing smile softened his expression.

"I trust you on that. No, it's this." He

slipped his fingers into the patch pocket of his shirt and withdrew a folded piece of paper. A check? Her pulse skittered into double beats. He placed it on the coffee table and held it in place with his fingertip. "Your fee. And before you argue, keep in mind I would've paid a professional designer four times the amount on this thing. It's really more a token than anything."

Diane stared at the check, then aimed an uncertain grimace at him. "Kevin . . ."

"I'll kick you off the job if you refuse."

She rolled her eyes. "Mother, what do you think?"

An impish grin formed on Mother's face. "A workman is worthy of his — or should I say *her*? — hire."

Diane squelched a chortle and faced Kevin. "All right." If it was too much, she wouldn't cash it.

"Good." He rose and paced back and forth, the watchful gazes of the dachshund trio following his progress. "I've got the names and numbers of a couple of general contractors who're interested in helping if you decide to tear up flooring or change the shape of the doorways, like you mentioned. I'll text those to you later today, and — oh, yeah . . ." He reached into his pocket and pulled out a ring of keys. He handed them to Diane. "The key to the front door is marked with a one, the apartment itself has a two, and the one marked three unlocks the elevator. Please keep the elevator locked when it's not in use. A simple safeguard."

Diane bounced the keys in her palm. She released an amused huff. "Seems like they should weigh more, considering what they go to."

"Welcome to the world of corporate investment." He pointed to the keys. "There is a lot of responsibility resting in your hand, but there's a lot of pleasure in seeing an empty building come to life again." His eyes gleamed, and his chest puffed. "This acquisition exceeds anything my old man ever did. And I did it without bending a single law or paying one cent in bribes." He gave a jolt, and he turned a startled look from Mother to Diane. Then a nervous smile replaced the strange expression. "As I said, I have a meeting at the city building, so I'll scoot. Thanks for breakfast, thanks for agreeing to decorate the apartment, and thanks for . . . Well, thanks for letting me back into your life. It's been beneficial to me. I hope it proves so for you, given time. I'll be in touch." He departed, waving as he closed the door behind him.

Diane placed the keys and credit card on

the end table between the sofa and Mother's chair. Mother gazed at the items. Her brow puckered. Diane tipped her head and peeked at her mother. "Are you okay?"

"Yes. But something he just said . . ." She nestled into her chair and linked her hands in her lap. "That man thinks he has it all, but he doesn't. Not even close to all. Are you praying for him, the way you said you would?"

"Yes, for his salvation." She wasn't sure what else to ask for, since she wasn't sure if she really wanted him becoming a fixture in Meghan's life. Because that would mean, by default, he'd become a fixture in hers.

"And God's will."

Mother spoke so softly that Diane wasn't sure she'd meant to say it out loud. Diane didn't answer, but she rolled the comment around in her mind. God's will sometimes took her places she wouldn't choose to go. She'd stick to praying for Kevin's salvation. She wasn't ready to commit to the other.

TWENTY

Fort Smith, Arkansas
Meghan

Meghan and Greg had hoped the bank representatives would be forthcoming with answers if Sheila wasn't in the room, and so far they'd come through. But Meghan wasn't satisfied with their answers. Why did it seem as though they were reciting from a memorized script?

Certain phrases — "always worried about money," "complained about lots of doctor bills," "extra quiet and standoffish those last days" — popped up repeatedly even if the question didn't require that particular response. The longer she and Greg remained with them, the more uncomfortable she grew, despite the fact that the men seemed sincere and willing to cooperate.

After an hour and a half, Greg snapped the lid of his laptop closed. "Thank you, gentlemen. I know we'll have more questions as we go over the files from the Arkansas Bureau of Investigation, but for now we'll let you get back to work."

The pair rose and left the room. At the click of the door latch, Meghan turned to Greg. "Do you get the feeling they practiced answers before meeting with us?"

Greg laughed. He opened his laptop again. "I kinda felt like we were in a room with a couple of shyster politicians. They talked a lot, but they didn't say anything." He stared at his computer screen, his forehead crunching into a series of furrows. "But they're sure laying the blame on Anson Menke, aren't they? It's pretty obvious they want us to draw the same conclusion the judge drew, that Menke took the money and ran. But I'm not buying it."

Meghan scooted her chair closer to Greg's. She had the same gut feeling, but Greg was more seasoned. "How come?"

"First of all, the man's reputation." Greg turned sideways in his chair and fixed his serious gaze on Meghan as if delivering a formal lecture. "The ABI delved very carefully into Menke's financial and personal dealings. They went all the way back to his college years and couldn't uncover one single questionable act committed. If they couldn't find it, it's not there."

He tapped two fingers on the tabletop. "Second, Sheila's personal memories of her father. Sure, that last night he wasn't himself, but that only says he was worrying about something. Maybe something he knew could get him into hot water. I think he was wrestling with a truth he needed to share but was hesitant to let out."

Meghan nodded. "I agree. He was probably trying to protect his family."

"And most likely someone else who was important to him."

Meghan tipped her head. "You mean like a friend or coworker?"

"Exactly." Greg's expression turned grim. "I'm leaning toward looking at Menke's closest pals here at the bank. From everything we know about him, Menke was a loyal, honest man. If he found out someone who mattered to him wasn't so honest, he'd struggle with turning him in." He pointed at Meghan as if taking aim with a pistol. "Let's say he's a straight shooter, same as Eagle and you. What would you do in a situation like this?"

Their minister had taught the appropriate response when a Christian found himself in conflict with someone else. She couldn't recall the scripture, but she remembered the application. "Go to the person who's doing wrong and try to make it right. If he refuses, then get someone else and go again. The goal being to get the one who's in the wrong to repent and change."

Greg smacked his palm on the table. "Exactly. I don't care what the judge determined. I suspect Menke's wife hit upon the truth. I think Menke found out someone he worked with was stealing the money. I think he approached that person and encouraged him to come clean. And I think that person did away with Menke to keep his evil deeds hidden."

Could one of the men they'd spent the last ninety minutes with be a murderer? A chill crept up Meghan's spine. "It's a pretty ugly accusation, Greg. We'll need to back it up with fact before we actually say it to anyone who matters."

"I know. But I'd bet my kids' beloved standard poodle that Menke is innocent of embezzlement." He picked up his laptop and slid it into his briefcase, then sat and stared across the room, his forehead furrowed. "In the fifteen years since he disappeared, he's never been sighted. Neither has his vehicle. The ABI found no overseas accounts in his name or in any of his kids' names — a common ploy for embezzlers. He made no suspicious purchases. If he'd taken the money, he'd have made sure his wife knew where to find it. Then his family wouldn't have lost their home and experienced all the other problems that struck. Seems to me he cared too much about them to put them through the losses."

Meghan couldn't argue with anything Greg had said. "If Menke really was murdered by a bank worker and we ask who Menke's friends were, they're liable to close rank and not tell us. So who should we talk to next?"

Greg grinned. "Is that a rhetorical question?"

Meghan bumped her forehead with the heel of her hand. "Oh, duh. Blame it on the weak coffee at the hotel."

He laughed, closed his briefcase, and stood. "Shall we use my room or yours as the meeting spot?"

Meghan rose, grabbed her belongings, and headed for the door. "Mine, of course, since that's where we'll find our informant."

When they reached the hotel, Meghan asked Greg to wait in the hallway until she was sure Sheila was ready for company. Then she entered the room, calling Sheila's name. The younger woman was sitting against a pile of pillows on her unmade bed, playing on her phone.

She set it aside and gave Meghan a hopeful look. "Are you all done with the investigation?"

Meghan swallowed a chuckle. Sheila had a lot to learn about detective work. "Not yet. But you might be able to help. Is it okay if Greg comes in and we all talk?"

Uncertainty briefly pinched Sheila's face, but she stood and smoothed the covers up over the pillows. "Sure. Bring him in."

Meghan invited Greg in, and he crossed to the desk in the corner and sat in its squeaky chair. He pulled out his computer and placed it in his lap, fingers poised over the keys. Meghan sat on the end of her bed and patted the spot beside her.

Sheila sat, her frame stiff and her hands woven together. "Okay, what do you need?"

"Names," Greg said. "Think back. Who were your dad's closest friends at the bank?"

A scowl creased Sheila's face. "Dad didn't have a lot of friends. I mean, with Mom being so sick, they couldn't socialize much with other people. He had a high school friend he stayed in touch with, but that guy didn't work at the bank. The only one I'd say was a friend at the bank was Uncle Wally."

Greg tapped on the keys. "Wally who?"

Sheila shrugged. "I don't know. Dad just

told Wayne and me to call him Uncle Wally."

An alert dinged in the back of Meghan's brain. She tipped her head. "Did Brandon call him something different?"

Sheila laughed. "No. Brandon wasn't born yet when Uncle Wally was coming around. Before Mom got so sick, she and Dad invited Uncle Wally and his wife over almost every Saturday night. They played pinochle. Uncle Wally always brought us kids a little something — candy or books or a toy. Mom said that since he and his wife didn't have kids of their own, they needed somebody to spoil. They picked us, I guess." She turned to Meghan. "They were really nice to us. But then Brandon was born, Mom got sick, and we didn't really see them anymore."

Meghan gave Sheila's knee a light squeeze. "What did you call his wife?"

Sheila crunched her forehead. "Um . . . it was Aunt something, but I don't really remember. I was only, like, seven when I saw them last."

Greg closed his computer and stood. "Thanks, Sheila. If you happen to remember the wife's name, will you let us know?"

"Sure." Her shoulders slumped. "I didn't help much, did I?"

Meghan patted her shoulder. "You did great. No worries." She walked Greg to the door, then stepped out into the hallway with him. "What do you think? Does our theory about Menke struggling about turning in a close coworker still apply?"

"I'm not ready to dump any theory yet. But there's gotta be something we're not seeing." Steely determination flashed in his pale-brown eyes, darkening the irises. "We'll find it, though."

Little Rock, Arkansas
Sean

Sean glanced across the top of his computer screen to Farber, who sat scowling at his own computer. The other detectives were away on assignment, leaving the two of them alone in the office. It should have been a relaxing day — no Roach asking what Farber deemed stupid questions, no other conversations or phone calls creating distractions. Cap had even carried in lunch for them. But Farber had arrived wearing the scowl, and not even towering roast beef sandwiches, warm chocolate chip cookies, and soft drinks diminished the detective's foul mood. Farber couldn't find Stony Dunsbrook, and it seemed Farber was a sore loser. Sean's patience was nearly spent, and it wasn't even two o'clock yet.

"When someone goes off the grid, they're

reclusive, fanatical, or they've got something to hide. Wonder which applies here." Sean hadn't intended to speak out loud. Maybe the deathly silence of the room bothered him more than he realized. He wished he'd kept quiet when Farber shot a derisive sneer at him.

"You left one out. Dead, but nobody knows it."

Sean had already considered the possibility. "If he was dead, wouldn't he have been declared missing by somebody? Even if it happened after his parents' deaths, there should be a family member, friend, or coworker who'd question why he suddenly dropped out of sight."

"Unless nobody really cared."

What a dismal thought. Sean pushed the idea aside and dug for another reason why Stony Dunsbrook wasn't showing up in any of their standard internet searches. "I wonder . . ." Would Farber sneer again? Probably. Ridicule was his modus operandi. But they wouldn't turn over new rocks unless they explored new ideas. He gathered his courage and finished the thought. ". . . if something happened when he was still a youth. You know, when records can be sealed or expunged. And he changed his name before he reached the age of eighteen to further cover up his past. Anything done by a minor wouldn't —"

Farber banged his fist on his desk. "— be public knowledge. You might have actually hit on something, Beagle." The man didn't smile, but the stern downturn of his lips eased a little. "You dig in Arkansas, and I'll take California. Let's see if we can find anything sealed or expunged."

Although the cold-case unit had access to files the general public and even some other policing agencies were denied, expunged records were deeply buried. Sean and Farber spent the rest of the day digging, but by quitting time, neither had discovered anything usable.

Farber slammed desk drawers, flung his chair under the desk, and yanked up his computer case, all the while muttering under his breath. Sean was pretty sure some of the words were off color, and he sent up a prayer for the man to calm down before he got home. His family didn't need the kind of treatment Sean had put up with during the day.

Farber stomped toward the doors, and Cap trotted out of his office and stopped in the detective's path. Farber snapped, "What?"

The captain's face reddened, and his gaze

narrowed. "First of all, watch your tone with me."

Farber's jaw muscles twitched, but he gave a brusque nod Sean interpreted as an apology.

"Second" — Cap pointed to Farber's computer case — "leave that here."

Farber took a backward step, slipping the leather case halfway behind his back. "Why?"

"Because you need a break." The captain folded his arms and set his feet wide, a stubborn stance if Sean had ever seen one. "You've been going after this case like a bulldog after a bone. If you don't take some time away from it, you'll end up making yourself nuts." He angled his head. "Is there something personal at stake, or is it —"

Farber snorted a laugh. He waved one hand in Sean's direction. "I'm going at it hard because the detective you put on it to start with can't seem to find his way out of a paper bag. How many weeks has he been on this already and . . . nada. Somebody's got to get it done, and I intend to see that it happens."

Lord, gimme patience, and give it to me quick. Sean swallowed a chortle. At least he'd found some humor in the situation.

"Farber, I could argue with you, but I'm

not going to waste my breath. I am, however, going to deliver an outright command. Lay off the investigation until tomorrow morning."

Farber glared at the captain for several tense seconds, then huffed out a snort. "Fine. Here." He shoved the briefcase at Cap. "Put it on my desk."

To Sean's shock, Captain Ratzlaff took the case. "Good choice. Now go home." He put his hand on Farber's shoulder. "And get there safe, all right?"

Sean waited for an explosion. The captain's directions stepped across professional lines, and Farber never put up with people intruding into his life. Surprisingly, Farber hung his head.

"Not in the mood for that anyway." He stormed out without a backward glance.

Captain Ratzlaff remained in place, his gaze seemingly following Farber's progress, until the elevator doors closed behind him. "Dealing with him is worse than parenting a rebellious teenager."

Sean suspected the captain hadn't intended to speak out loud, but the comment hit him like a fist in the gut. Would he ever know the challenge of seeing a son or daughter through the rocky teenage years? He'd take it all — the good, the bad, the heartbreaking — if given the chance.

Cap trudged to the desks and laid the leather case next to Farber's computer. He looked at Sean, his lips forming a weary half smile. "Been a rough one."

Sean stifled a grunt. "Yes, sir."

"It's not likely to get easier. Working with him, I mean. Just giving you a word of warning."

Sean leaned back in his chair and examined his boss's face. The man knew something. The question was whether he would share. "I appreciate the warning, although I have to tell you, Farber's never been easy. Not on me. But the antagonism he threw around today can't all be because I accidentally mentioned prayer to him on the phone last night."

Cap's eyebrows rose. "You said you'd pray for him?"

"Not in those exact words." Sean repeated the exchange he'd had with Farber. Then he shrugged. "I didn't proselytize. I know better. But he took it as such and hung up on me after threatening to file a suit. I'm not worried about it. He doesn't have a case, and I think for the most part, he's more bark than bite."

The captain chuckled. "You're right on that. But it doesn't make listening to the bark any more fun." He glanced toward the doors, as if concerned someone might be listening in, then pulled out Farber's chair and sat. "Listen, Sean . . ."

Sean went on alert. If they were sliding into a first-name basis, Cap could be stepping outside professional boundaries again.

"I'm asking you as a favor — this isn't an official order, okay? — to go easy on Farber."

Sean crinkled his face in confusion. Didn't the captain have it backward?

"There's stuff going on. Stuff he can't control. And you know how he likes to be in control."

Yes, Sean knew.

"He isn't handling it well."

And taking it out on Sean, so it seemed.

Captain Ratzlaff pinned Sean with a penetrating frown. "What is it you Christians say about treating other people?"

Sean rocked in his chair and held his hands wide. "There's a lot. Love your neighbor as yourself, treat others the way you want to be treated, turn the other cheek . . ."

Cap braced his elbows on Farber's desk and linked his hands. "Yeah. All of that. That's what Farber's gonna need over the next few weeks, and I'm counting on you to stick to your convictions. There's not another detective in the office, including Dane, who could do what needs doing for Farber right now.

"I know I'm putting a lot on you, and maybe I shouldn't, since what I'm asking goes beyond the normal work partnership. But I think in the long run, knowing what I do about you, you'll be glad you had a role to play in this."

Sean sat up and angled his head, his flesh prickling. "Exactly what game are we playing?"

The captain shook his head. "I can't say. Confidentiality. But you're a smart man. I think you'll figure it out. Until you do, be civil. Even when he's at his surliest — and, Sean, we've likely not seen the worst of it yet. It'll all come to an end. Eventually."

Captain Ratzlaff seemed in need of assurance. Sean pasted on a wobbly smile. "You got it, Cap. I'll do my best."

The man released a slow breath. Relief sagged his features. "Thanks, Eagle. I appreciate it." He rose and headed for his office. "You go on home now, too. You need a break as much as Farber does." He paused and glanced back, smirking. "Maybe more."

Sean laughed. "Yes, sir." He gathered his belongings and strode toward the elevators.

For the first time since he'd tossed Meghan's suitcase into the back of his vehicle, he was glad she'd left town. At least she was spared attacks by whatever demons Tom Farber battled.

Battling demons . . . Today was Wednesday. Bible study night. Even though Meghan wasn't there to go with him, he should attend. He'd grab a burger somewhere, then head to church. If things would get harder than they'd been today with Tom Farber, Sean would need prayer support. And folks would give it.

He felt more confident already.

TWENTY-ONE

Fort Smith, Arkansas
Meghan

The evening was so mild that Meghan and Greg decided to walk to a little family-style restaurant near their hotel for supper. Sheila stayed behind, claiming she wasn't hungry and needed to call home and talk to her brothers.

Meghan didn't doubt Sheila's claim about wanting to check on her brothers, but she also feared that the young woman had very little money and couldn't afford to keep buying meals. At least the hotel offered a continental breakfast. Simple fare — store-bought rolls, boxed cereal, and apples and bananas — but at no extra cost, so Sheila could carry an apple or roll to the room for a later-in-the-day snack.

A sign inside the restaurant's foyer invited guests to seat themselves. Greg led Meghan to a corner booth. Menus stood on end between a sugar shaker and a bottle of ketchup. They opened them and made their selections even before a waitress brought silverware and glasses of water.

Greg gestured for Meghan to order first, and she asked for her favorite, a reuben sandwich and fries. Greg ordered the chicken-fried steak with mashed potatoes and a side salad.

"Dressing?" the waitress asked.

"Yes," Greg said.

The waitress, an older woman with rust-colored curls and too much mascara, gave him a mock scowl.

He laughed. "Ranch, please. Smother it. The way you smother a chicken-fried steak with gravy."

She rolled her eyes but laughed, too. "I'll see what I can do." She smacked the menus back into their resting spot and strode off.

Greg took a drink of his water, swiped his lips with the back of his hand, and huffed out a breath. "I'd sure hoped Sheila would remember some of her dad's friends' names, but I guess we can't blame her for drawing a blank. She was only a little girl, and a lot of time has passed."

Meghan pulled the wrapper off her straw and slid the length of plastic into her glass. "She did remember Uncle Wally, though, who wasn't really an uncle. Is there someone named Wally working at the bank?"

"No one I recall from the list of employees during Menke's time." Greg frowned, tapping his chin. "Maybe it was a nickname, though. What are names that could be shortened to Wally? Besides the obvious Wallace."

"Hmm, Walter. Waldo." Meghan used her finger and made a series of circles in the condensation on her glass. "Walker. Walton." She jolted.

Greg gave a start, too, and they chorused, "Wallingford." One of the men who'd been sent to answer their questions about Anson Menke.

Meghan check-marked the last circle, then set the glass aside. "That could be it. Do you remember what title he holds at the bank?"

Greg tapped his chin again, the taps fast. "I think he's the commercial-lending director, but when Menke worked there, they were both loan officers. I don't remember what kind — commercial or consumer."

"But they'd have worked closely enough together to know what the other was doing."

"In all likelihood."

The waitress put Greg's salad in front of

him. At least, Meghan assumed there was lettuce somewhere under the sea of white dressing. He gave the woman a double thumbs-up, and she walked off laughing.

Greg picked up his fork and plunged it through the glop of white. The tines came away with a chunk of drippy lettuce. He popped the bite into his mouth, chewed, swallowed, and grinned. "Perfect."

Meghan looked aside as he ate his salad. Watching made her stomach swirl.

Her sandwich and his meal arrived before he finished the salad. Meghan bowed her head and asked a brief blessing over the food, and then they ate without chatting. The sandwich, with its layers of tender corned beef and tangy sauerkraut, pleased Meghan's taste buds. She could have eaten the whole thing, it tasted so good, but she saved half of it and most of her fries, then asked for a to-go box. Sheila needed supper, too. Greg winked at her as she boxed up the leftovers, and she offered a sheepish grin in reply.

They paid their tabs, each tucking the receipt into their wallets, then headed for the hotel. Greg set a sedate pace going back, probably slowed by his full stomach. The chicken-fried steak had been the size of a hubcap. Not to mention the sea of gravy drowning it.

He linked his hands behind his back and angled a pensive look at Meghan. "If Mr. Wallingford is the man Sheila called Uncle Wally, I wonder why she didn't recognize him during the first meeting."

Meghan shrugged. "People can change a lot in fifteen years. Maybe he wore a mustache or beard back then. Maybe he didn't have glasses or his hair wasn't gray. Plus, like you said earlier, she was a little girl. She might have a picture in her head, but then again, given the stress and trauma of her life, she might not. She might've blocked a lot out."

"True enough." Greg opened the door, and Meghan preceded him into the lobby. They paused outside her hotel room door. "Pull up the bank's website on your computer and see if they have a pictorial directory of the major players at the bank. If they do, have her look at Wallingford long and hard and try to remember if he's the man she called Uncle Wally. Even if she doesn't remember, I want us to have some one-on-one time with him tomorrow to learn about his relationship to Menke."

He started for his room, then turned back, a sly smile creasing his face. "But if she does think he's Uncle Wally, then we need to take her with us to the bank tomorrow. Bring Wallingford in and ask the same set of questions we went through earlier, but this time with Anson Menke's little girl staring him down. His reaction should tell us a lot."

Las Vegas, Nevada
Kevin

The alarm clock blared, jolting Kevin from a sound sleep. He rolled over and slapped the offending box into silence. Then he groaned and buried his face in the pillow. Thursday already. His sixth day in Vegas.

"Time flies when you're having fun," Dad used to say with a grimace, which always put a sarcastic edge to it. But Kevin had discovered the truth of the old saying during his time in Glitter Gulch. He'd had fun finalizing the purchase of the building he planned to call Harrison Heights. He'd had fun setting the groundwork for renovating the building. He wasn't ready to return to Arkansas. And not only because of the building.

But he needed to get that side of his thoughts lassoed, hog tied, and tossed in a well, like the good guys did with the villain in last night's old-time spaghetti Western. He'd already messed up one kid's life by playing daddy. Why do the same to another one? Especially one who had it all together. Getting himself entangled with Diane would lead to becoming a fixture in their daughter's life. She was pretty hard to resist, though.

Strong. Independent. Confident. A lot like she'd been in college but with a maturity that made her even more appealing. After losing her in college, he'd gone after insecure girls. Ones who relied on him, needed him, were afraid of losing him. But his interest in them always waned. Eventually he'd figured out he wanted a partner who matched him strength for strength, wit for wit, spunk for spunk. The problem was finding her. Or maybe he had. Diane did all that.

She'd loved him once. Could she love him again?

He wasn't going there. She was better off without him. They both were. The recognition made him consider ordering a bottle of something strong enough to steal his ability to form rational thought.

He sat up on the edge of the bed, waited for a moment to let the usual first-thing-in-the-morning dizziness pass, then pushed to his feet and plodded to the bathroom. A shower and tooth brushing brought him fully to life. He considered shaving, but he liked the casual look a couple day's growth of whiskers gave him. His calendar didn't hold any formal meetings today, so the stubble could stay. He dressed in a pair of khakis and a striped button-down shirt. While rolling the sleeves to his elbows, he slid his bare feet into tasseled loafers, then returned to the bathroom.

He rubbed his hair nearly dry with a towel. Using a scant amount of gel spread on his palms, he finger combed the thick strands into a series of ridges that swept away from his forehead. Finished, he grinned smugly at his reflection. Fifty-two years old and not even a hint of a receding hairline. Thank goodness he'd inherited Mom's hair genes and not Dad's. Dad's hair had been mostly gone up top by the time he was forty. Mom said he worried too much and that's why his hair fell out, but Kevin wasn't sure he believed it.

One steel-gray strand drooped toward his left eyebrow, Elvis Presley style. Appropriate for the city, perhaps, but too unkempt looking for Kevin Harrison. He gritted his teeth, squirted out a little more gel, and smoothed the strand into place. He checked his reflection again and nodded. Even Tawny would approve.

With a grunt, he turned from the mirror and crossed to the dresser for his wallet and watch. He gave the drawer a pull, and three books slid forward. The writing on the spine of the largest one — *Holy Bible* — caught his eye.

Without warning, Hazel DeFord's comment about being content tiptoed through the back of his mind. She'd quoted something from the Bible to back herself up — in Philips? Philpins? Something like that. He chuckled. She was something else, Diane's mother. So angelic looking with her snow-white hair and serene smile, but those eyes of hers sparked with humor, and she wasn't afraid to say what she thought. Kind of like Diane.

And here he was thinking about her again. He jammed his wallet into his back pocket, stretched the band of his watch around his wrist, then bumped the drawer closed with his hip. A man would have to be pretty hard up for entertainment to take out any of those books and open them. He didn't intend to ever be that bored.

The plumber he'd hired was scheduled to work in the loft apartment today, and Kevin wanted to catch him before he got started. The man wouldn't arrive before eight, though, so he had time for a leisurely breakfast and at least three cups of coffee in the hotel's restaurant. Then he'd walk to

Harrison Heights.

He smiled as he set off up the hallway. Harrison Heights . . . It had a great ring to it.

Diane

Diane used the key Kevin had given her and let herself into the loft apartment. Inside, she dropped her bag on the floor, leaned against the wall, and waited for the ache to leave her leg muscles. Worried she might not be able to lock the elevator correctly, she'd used the stairs. Obviously she needed more exercise if climbing three flights of stairs winded her this much. She made a mental note to check out gyms in her area. Thanks to the check Kevin had given her, she'd be able to afford it. And buy new tires. Mother called the money a God-kiss. Using that terminology had erased Diane's reluctance to keep it. But she was determined to do the very best job possible in decorating. She'd make sure she earned every penny of it.

She scooped up her bag and carried it to the kitchen. She spilled the contents across the counter. Measuring tape, multihead screwdriver, spiral notebook, pencils, a dozen paint swatches she and Mother had selected from a home improvement store, and — she burst out laughing — two vegan granola bars. Obviously tucked in by Mother, who hadn't been happy about her skipping breakfast.

Diane shook her finger at the bars and imitated her mother's voice. "Breakfast is the most important meal of the day." Fifty-one years old and Mother still viewed her as her child. She couldn't blame her. Diane felt the same away about Meghan, who likely received Diane's motherly advice as graciously as Diane sometimes received Mother's.

Chuckling, she unwrapped the chocolate-coconut bar and took a bite. While she ate, she examined the main room in the apartment. She'd been curious about how much morning sunlight came in, given the row of windows facing east. So many tall buildings clustered together certainly blocked some of the light, but she was pleased to see fingers of sunlight reaching through gaps in the curtains. Once she'd taken down the ghastly balloon shades — seriously, bubblegum-pink chintz in a living room? — the place would seem instantly cheerier.

She popped the last bit of the granola bar into her mouth, grabbed the screwdriver, and stalked to the windows. Removing the curtains proved easier than she'd expected.

Someone had hung them on tension rods. A quick tug and down they came. And what a difference! She stood in the middle of the tumble of sheeny pink and stared in amazement. Her imagination revved to full throttle. She envisioned an entertainment armoire — maybe one with leather panels inset in its rich stained wood doors — on the north wall. An abstract painting above the fireplace. Matching leather armchairs flanking the fireplace. A long, low, overly-laden-with-pillows sofa facing the chairs.

In her mind's eye, she made the chairs smaller in scale, with rolled arms and tufted backs, in a bold yet tasteful burnt orange. The modern-style sofa would be covered in forest-green velvet. Pillows in both florals and geometric designs, incorporating earth tones with splashes of gold, would bring out the —

"Diane?"

She yelped and spun toward the open doorway, her hand on her pounding heart. "What are you doing here?"

Kevin took a few steps into the room, his gaze dropping to the pile of curtains and then returning to her face. "I could ask you the same thing."

How long had he stood there watching her daydream before he made his presence known? Embarrassment struck hard. She planted her fist on her hip and glared at him. "You paid me to redecorate this place, remember? I can't do that without taking measurements and getting an idea of what it looks like at different times of the day. Paint colors can appear different depending on the amount of light, you know."

A funny grin twitched the corners of his mouth. "Yes, I know." He stepped around the pile of curtains and gazed out the window. "Wow. It sure makes a difference, having the open view." He peeked at her over his shoulder, the grin still hovering on his lips. "And the sunlight coming in makes everything seem more . . . beautiful."

A provocative statement like that might have made her swoon when she was a teenager, but not anymore. So why did her stomach get all trembly? She grunted and scooped up the wad of pink chintz. "I had the same thought after I tore down these atrocities. Just so you know, whatever goes back up will not hide the view or block the sun. And it won't be pink." She tossed the pile into the hallway and then crossed to the kitchen counter.

She flopped open the spiral notebook and wrote *backsplash* on the top line. She tucked a pencil behind her ear, snatched up the measuring tape, and aimed a tart look at Kevin. "Why are you here, anyway?" She measured from the counter to the underside of the cabinets and wrote down the number of inches.

He slid his hands into his trouser pockets and ambled to the opposite side of the island. "The plumber is due to start replacing lines in here today. I wanted to talk to him about fixtures that are more conservation friendly."

"I wouldn't take you for someone who wanted to protect the environment." She stretched the measuring tape across the south wall, noted the length, and wrote it down.

"It's smart business to protect the environment." He leaned on the counter, observing her with his forehead pinched. "Why waste water? Up the usage, up the bill."

She tucked the end of the tape into the corner and moved along the west wall. "Ah. So it has to do with the bottom line, not the environment." The tape slipped, and she returned to the corner.

"Here." He rounded the island and leaned in behind her. "Let me hold that for you."

His nearness made her scalp tingle. She scuttled a few feet away. "Thanks."

He held the end of the tape flush against

the wall, his gaze so intense she wanted to squirm.

"What time will the plumber get here?" She blurted the question.

"Anywhere between eight and eight thirty. Why?" He must have lost his hold on the end, because the tape skittered across the cabinet and snapped into the case. "Are you nervous being here alone with me?"

She was, but she'd never admit it. "You're distracting me. I have a lot to get done."

"Well, since I'm distracting you anyway, let me totally steal your focus."

If he meant what she thought he meant, he'd better think again. She glowered at him, silently warning him to keep his distance.

"Why didn't you ever get married?"

Twenty-Two

Kevin

Whatever she'd expected, he'd taken her by surprise. Her frame jerked, her mouth dropped open, and she ceased to blink.

"W-what?"

Kevin leaned on the counter. "You heard me. Why did you stay single all these years? I mean . . ." He coughed out a self-deprecating laugh. "I took my time getting married the first time — waited a good ten years out of college — but between marriages? Never more than two years."

The stunned expression turned puzzled. "First time . . . How many times have you been married?"

He held up four fingers.

She slumped against the counter, her mouth falling open.

He nodded. "Yep. But you . . . not even once. Why not?" If she said he'd scared her off from men, he might regret the question,

281

but he wanted to know. How much easier her life would have been if she'd had someone to add to the income, someone to share responsibilities with her. "Why not, Diane?"

She folded her arms across her chest and pressed into the corner, her brown eyes sparking. "I don't think it's your business."

"I think it is. After all, you were raising my kid, raising her pretty close to poverty. If you could've done something to make it easier, then —"

She burst out laughing. A shrill, sarcastic laugh. "Are you kidding me? It's ironic, don't you think, for you to criticize how I raised her when you chose not to take any part at all? What happened to the apology you gave me for not helping? Was that just lip service?"

He cringed. "I phrased that badly. I wasn't trying to accuse you, and I'm not criticizing. I want to understand. Weren't you lonely? You were an attractive woman." She still was. "You were real social when I knew you." And now she lived with her mother — out of financial necessity or a need for companionship? "But you became a hermit. Why?"

"I didn't become a hermit, Kevin. I became a parent." She swung her arms wide. "Do you have any idea how many children

282

are abused, even killed, every day by someone their mother brings into the household? I couldn't risk that. Besides, every man I loved bailed on me. First my dad, by dying, then you, by —" She turned away and clamped her lips together.

Kevin waited a full minute, but she didn't speak. Didn't move except for her chest heaving in rapid breaths. He slowly closed the distance between them, anticipating her bolting. But he came within arm's reach, and she still hadn't moved. He could've touched her. Could've taken hold of her shoulders or rubbed her arm or even cupped her cheek. But he kept his hands in his pockets.

"When I said I was sorry, I meant it. I was young. Stupid. And mostly terrified about what my dad would say. Believe me, in my household anything but perfection was unacceptable." Which, in retrospect, was pretty ludicrous, considering what Dad had done. "I made a huge mistake, and there's no way I can go back and change it now. If I could, I would." He wished he had the courage to touch her. He really wanted to touch her. "I mean that."

She shifted her eyes and met his gaze, but her mouth remained fixed in a firm line.

"What about now?"

Her eyes sparked.

"Meghan's a grown woman, successfully making her own way. You're still young, still attractive." He removed one hand from his pocket and braced it on the counter. She followed its progress with wary eyes, then kept her gaze fixed on it. "You could have years of marriage if you wanted it. Don't you want it?"

Her gaze drifted from his hand to his face. She seemed expressionless, as if every bit of life had drained from her. He had a hard time not flinching, but he pressed hard against the thick slab of butcher block and refused to move.

"Again, I think you're prying into subjects that aren't your business, but I'll answer. Because if I don't, you'll probably ask again, and I'd rather get this unpleasantness out of the way for good." She angled her chin high and sealed him in place with an icy glare. "I'm content with my life as it is."

Content . . . that word again.

"I'm independent. I don't need anyone to take care of me."

Yet she depended on her mother. Or so it seemed.

"Even so, I'm not opposed to marriage. *If* I fell in love again" — her cheeks flushed pinker than the chintz — "and *if* the man was a Christian, *then* I might consider getting married. But I'm not in the market for a husband." She pointed at him. "So don't even think about trying to make me wife number five."

Ouch. He backed up a few inches. "Okay. And for the record, I don't intend to go there." Liar. If he could have Diane without Meghan, he'd be tempted to pursue her. Very tempted. All the reasons he'd liked her way back when were still in place but enhanced by a maturity even more attractive than Tawny's youth. But she'd chosen someone else over him then. No sense in setting himself up for a repeat performance.

"Good. Now . . ." She held up the measuring tape. "Since you're not doing anything, would you hold the end over there? And hold it tight this time."

He saluted. "Yes, ma'am."

They measured the entire kitchen backsplash area without speaking. As she recorded the last set of measurements, someone tapped on the doorjamb and hollered, "Anybody here?"

Kevin hurried around the corner. A man wearing tan dungarees, a blue shirt, a blue ball cap, and a well-stocked tool belt waited just inside the door. He had to be the plumber.

Kevin stuck out his hand. "Jim Connolly?"

The man shook his hand, and the tools in his belt clanked in accompaniment. "Yes, sir. You must be Kevin Harrison. Nice to meet you."

"Thanks for coming."

The fellow grinned. "Thanks for the job offer. I —" His attention shot to Kevin's right. To Diane, who'd left the kitchen and was moving toward the first of the windows lining the wall. The man whipped off his cap. "Excuse me, ma'am. I didn't know his wife was here."

Diane offered a wry grin. "I'm not his wife. I'm the interior decorator."

"Oh. Sorry, ma'am."

Kevin gestured between the two. "Diane DeFord, meet Jim Connolly. I imagine you might encounter each other in the building a time or two before this project is done, so you might as well know each other's names."

Connolly bustled across the floor, his tools clanking, and held out his hand. "It's nice to meet you, Mrs. DeFord."

"Miss," Diane and Kevin said at the same time.

Connolly sent a startled look between them. "Miss DeFord."

Diane shook the plumber's hand. "Please, call me Diane."

"And call me Jim." The brazen fellow smiled directly at Diane. "It's very nice to meet you."

Kevin cleared his throat. "Do you want to examine the lines in the kitchen or the bathroom first?"

Connolly turned, a discordant tune playing from his tool belt. "Seems to me we'll be in Diane's way if we stay in here, so let's start with the bathroom." He jerked his smile at Diane. "Unless you wanted to work in there now."

She lifted her measuring tape to the window casing. "Go ahead. I'll probably be out here for another half hour or so."

"All right, then." Connolly faced Kevin, thumbs hooked on the thick leather belt. "Lead the way, Mr. Harrison."

Kevin headed for the hallway, and clinks and clanks followed him. Then Connolly called, "Holler if you need help with anything, Diane. I'd be glad to lend a hand."

"Thank you, Jim."

The smile in her voice set Kevin's teeth on edge. He wasn't too sure about this guy. He might need to hire a different plumber.

"Didn't we answer these questions yesterday?"

Meghan smiled across the table at Darryl Wallingford and Michael Thames, focusing on Thames, who'd asked the question. "Yes, you did, but . . . well . . ."

Greg gave her a feigned look of disgust. "She accidentally deleted the file when trying to transfer it to her computer. New program . . . learning curve . . ."

She held out her hands in a gesture of helplessness, inwardly praying God would forgive them for fibbing. A lost file was the only excuse she and Greg could conjure that the bankers might accept as factual.

Wallingford harrumphed. "One would think a person in your occupation would have better computer skills."

Meghan shrugged and offered another smile. "We appreciate your patience. Your input was so beneficial that we wanted to be sure we had every piece of information you so graciously gave us."

Wallingford flicked a quick look at Sheila, who sat at the end of the long table, linked hands resting on the table's edge, gaze never wavering from the face of the man she might have called Uncle Wally when she was a little girl. He slipped his finger under his collar and pulled. "Mike and I have other duties requiring our attention." He started to rise. "If we're finished here, I'd —"

"One more question."

The man set his lips in a stern line and sank back into his chair. "Yes, Detective Dane?"

"Our investigation has led us to believe Anson Menke didn't really take the money."

Red climbed from Thames's collar up his neck. "Of course he took the money. The judge said he took the money."

Greg raised his eyebrows and aimed a sly smile at the pair of bankers. "Yes, a judge found him guilty based on testimonial, anecdotal, and analogical evidence, but remember the Arkansas Bureau of Investigation couldn't find any direct evidence linking him to the theft. So the case was largely circumstantial."

Thames scowled at Greg. "Then what do you think happened?"

"We're actually leaning toward the probability that someone framed Anson and then murdered him to keep him from being able to tell the truth."

Wallingford stared at Greg, almost expressionless, but Thames drew back and his jaw dropped. "Who would do something like that?"

"The person who stole the money, in all probability." Greg shook his head. "Pretty sad situation, targeting a man with a sick wife and three young children. Whoever did it is as low as a person can go, in my opinion."

Thames bolted out of his chair. "There is not a single person in the history of our bank's employment roster who would deliberately set up a colleague, especially one with Anson's difficult home situation, for prosecution. And murder? Out of the question. So you need to take your investigation in another direction."

"I agree with Michael." Wallingford rose. "And as I said, we have other duties. I trust you will be able to find your way out." The men left the room, and Thames slammed the door behind him.

Greg turned to Sheila. "What do you think? Was the gray-haired man your father's friend, the one you called Uncle Wally?"

Sheila sighed and sank against her chair's back. "Maybe. His voice seemed familiar. But he looks so . . . old. I always thought Daddy and Uncle Wally were the same age. I can't imagine my dad looking so worn out and ancient."

Meghan squeezed Sheila's hand. "If Mr. Wallingford is our true thief, he might be a lot younger than he appears. Carrying a load of guilt has a way of aging a person."

Sheila hung her head. "If one of those men really did set Daddy up, maybe even had him killed, I want to find out. I want to hold him accountable." She lifted her face, and tears trembled on her lower lashes. "But if they're innocent, I don't want to falsely accuse them. Because just thinking that's what happened to my dad really hurts. I wouldn't want to hurt somebody else like that."

Meghan's affection toward the younger woman increased. "You have a good heart, Sheila, wanting to find the truth instead of seeking vengeance."

Sheila offered a weak smile. "My folks wanted us kids to be kind. I'm just trying to think what Mom and Daddy would say if they were here." She looked at Greg, her expression hopeful. "Did it help to have me here? Did you find out anything that will lead you to the truth?"

Greg grinned. "Absolutely. Don't you agree, Meghan?"

She considered not only what the men had said but also how they'd behaved during the question-answer session. "Yep. Sheila's presence made a difference."

"And that means we deserve a reward." He waggled his eyebrows. "How about banana splits?"

Sheila bit her pinkie nail. "Um . . ."

Greg added, "On me."

A shy smile curved Sheila's lips. She was so pretty when she smiled. "That sounds really good, Detective Dane."

"Greg." He winked, rising and reaching for his computer. "C'mon, you two. Banana splits, and then Meghan and I need to dig into some fellows' financial records."

TWENTY-THREE

Little Rock, Arkansas
Sean

"It'd be easier to find a needle in a hay-stack."

Sean nodded in response to Farber's growling comment. Four hours yesterday and almost eight hours today hunched over the desk, digging through juvenile records from 1979, the year the twins died, through 1986, when their older cousin would have aged out of the juvie system, had put a serious crick in his neck. He rubbed a particularly tender spot with one hand and tapped the Down key with the other. A dozen new names lined up on the screen.

"The problem is," Farber groused, bouncing his fist on the edge of his desk, "we don't know all the places where the family lived in the seventies and eighties. We know where Clark and Hilda Dunsbrook went from here, but who knows what other places they called home from the time they left Arkansas until they died. We could be searching the wrong states, totally wasting our time." He banged his fist extra hard, then pressed it against his chin. His hand trembled. He thumped the desk some more.

Sean sat up straight and examined Farber. The man's skin looked pasty. The odd color combined with his persistent tremor raised Sean's concerns. "Farber, are you okay?"

"Yeah, why?" *Thump, thump, thump.*

Sean pointed to his pounding fist.

Farber jammed his fist against his chin again and twisted it, as if trying to pull out an imaginary beard. "I'm fine. Just peeved. We need to find this guy." He lowered his hand and angled his scowl at the clock. "Almost five and nothin' to show for a whole day's work." He hooked his hands behind his head and rocked his chair, glaring across the desks to Sean. "What're you doing in the evenings with the little woman out of town?"

Sean shrugged. "Mostly trying to stay busy so I don't think about it."

"She call every night?"

She'd only been gone two nights. "So far."

"Talk about the case over there?"

"Yeah."

"Is it going good?"

"It's still in the beginning stages, but yeah, I think it's going okay for them."

Farber grunted. "Good. Let 'em finish, get back here. Then we can swap out partners, put DeFord on this Dunsbrook case with you again, and set Dane and me on a new course."

Sean would be perfectly fine with that setup. Farber was wound as tight as the bolts on a semi's wheels, which put Sean on edge. He shrugged and searched for a noncommittal reply. "I guess we'll see how it goes."

Farber brought his chair to an abrupt halt and whammed his palms on the desk. "I'm hungry. Are you hungry? This is Thursday, right? Half-price chicken wings at Barney's on Thursdays."

Cap strolled toward their desks. "What's that about chicken wings?"

Sean repeated what Farber had said. "I can't say I've ever been to Barney's. Have you, Cap?"

"I have. It's definitely a hole-in-the-wall, but they do have good wings." A frown pinched his forehead. "Lots of beer on tap, too."

"Now, Cap, you gotta admit, ice-cold beer's the best drink for tackling a basket of habanero wings." Farber flung his arm in

Sean's direction. "Not even Beagle could argue with that."

Sean chuckled. "I can't argue, but neither can I concur."

"Never had habanero wings?"

"Never had beer."

Farber's jaw dropped. "You've got to be kidding. How old are you?"

"Thirty-six."

"And you've never had a beer?"

Sean shook his head.

Farber burst out laughing. "I knew you were goody-goody, but are you for real? I've never met another man your age who hasn't downed a beer or two. What a —"

Captain Ratzlaff held up his hand. "All right, Farber, enough. Sean's drinking habits are his own choice."

"He doesn't have a drinking habit." Farber started rocking again, grinning at Sean with a wicked gleam in his eye. "What do you drink instead? Coke? Lemonade? Shirley Temples?"

"Farber . . ."

"Okay, okay." Farber raised his hands in surrender. Their tremble was evident.

What had the man imbibed, swallowed, or snorted? But when could he have taken anything? They'd been together pretty much the whole day, including during the lunch hour when they walked to the sandwich shop and placed take-out orders.

Farber slapped his hands on his knees and pushed himself upright. "I really would like an order of wings. Who's in?"

The captain backed up. "Not me. My wife's got a roast in the Crock-Pot. I'll take that over habanero wings."

Farber looked at Sean. "I know for a fact your wife doesn't have a roast ready for you. So how about it, Beagle? Wanna get some wings?" He held up his fingers the way a Boy Scout pledged his honor. "No beer. Cokes instead."

Sean glanced at Cap. Their boss had advised Sean to go easy on Farber, but did that mean going to a bar with him? Even though Farber was being friendlier than he'd ever been, Sean wanted to go home, eat a sandwich, and wait for Meghan's call. "What about your wife, Farber? Isn't she expecting you?"

Like a switch being flipped, Farber's snarling attitude returned. "I don't need you telling me what to do. You don't want wings? Fine. Say so." He grabbed his car keys from the corner of his desk and shot off, muttering.

Cap hurried to Sean and grabbed his elbow. "Go after him."

Sean gave his boss a puzzled look.

"If I could, I would, but Marla's expecting me. I have to go home."

Farber was poking the elevator button. Even from the distance of twenty feet, Sean heard his muffled oaths. The last thing he wanted to do was spend an evening eating hot wings with Tom Farber, but it seemed he didn't have a choice. "All right, Cap. I'll go."

The relief flooding their captain's face convinced Sean he'd made the right decision. He took off at a trot. The elevator doors slid open, and Farber entered the car.

Sean hollered, "Hold the door, Farber!"

Farber blocked the door with his hand.

Sean stepped in next to his scowling temporary partner and forced a smile. "Thanks. If it's okay, wings sound pretty good after all. I'm coming with you."

Farber stared at him for a few seconds, his eyes narrowed to slits, then shrugged. "Suit yourself."

If the sauce on the wings didn't kill him, breathing the cigarette smoke might. Farber had chosen to sit at the bar, and of course Sean sat with him. The men on either side of them chain smoked, and Sean nearly lost Farber in the thick cloud surrounding them.

At least Farber kept his word about not drinking beer. Even though everyone else at the bar had an alcoholic beverage in front of them, he ordered soft drinks. And made a face every time he took a swig.

Sean made faces, too, but over the wings.

Farber jabbed Sean with his elbow and lifted another wing to his mouth. "Good, huh? Best wings in town."

Sean took a sip of his soda. The burn in his mouth remained. "I think you'd get less heat from chewing on a white-hot coal."

Farber laughed. "Aw, come on. Eat up. They'll put hair on your chest."

According to Meghan, Sean had enough hair on his chest. He pushed the rest of his basket aside and used a napkin to clean his fingers. "I'm done. Go ahead and finish mine if you want to."

Farber ate another wing, glugged the remainder of his soda, and hollered for a refill. "Sparky'll get you a box. Take 'em home with you. They're good the next day, too." He picked a chunk of meat from a wing and popped it into his mouth, then spoke around it. "Been thinking about Stony Dunsbrook, about the possibility that he did something to his cousins, and I think I have an idea of what could've happened."

"Oh, yeah?" Sean rested his elbow on the

bar and waved smoke away with his free hand.

"Yeah. You ever been to Riverside Park?"

Sean shook his head.

"I have." The bartender swapped Farber's empty glass for a full one. Farber dropped the half-eaten wing in the basket and picked up the glass. "Let's go to the park tomorrow, snoop around the spot where the twins were found. I'll tell you my theory then." He took a long draw of the soda, set down the glass, and reached for the wing. "The dirt in their lungs tells me they didn't die from somebody holding their heads under water. The coroner took one look at their damp hair and clean faces and chose the lazy way out."

"You could be right about that."

"What a job . . . doing an autopsy on babies. Enough to drive a man to drink." Farber put his focus on his glass of Coke, and Sean caught sight of the detective's hand on the soda glass. During their time in Barney's, Farber's tremors had finally stopped. Maybe he'd only been hungry and his blood sugar had gotten too low. Could Farber be diabetic and not treating it? That might explain Cap's concern. A physical ailment could explain the man's extreme testiness, too.

"You feeling better now?" Sean hadn't meant to ask, but the question found its way out of his mouth anyway.

Farber aimed a confused look at him. "I feel fine. Why?"

Sean forced a chuckle. "Earlier, before we ate, you were pretty shaky. I was worried about you." He swallowed, hoping he wasn't stepping onto thin ice. "I think Cap was, too."

Farber stood so quickly his stool scooted across the planked floor. He leaned in and pointed at Sean's nose. "If you don't want my fist here, keep that thing out of my business." He stormed out.

Sean stared after him, then looked at their wing baskets and glasses. He'd been stuck with the bill. "Thanks a lot, Farber."

The bartender wandered over and started cleaning up their mess. He lobbed a grin at Sean. "Never seen you here before. You a friend of Tom's?"

Not exactly a friend, but Sean didn't want to explain. "Yeah." He dug in his pocket for his wallet.

"Glad he's got somebody to hang out with. He's been bummed since his old lady moved out."

Sean paused and frowned at the man. "His wife left him?"

301

"Took the kids and headed for parts unknown." He swished a rag over the bar's surface, sending crumbs dancing. "Said she wouldn't live with a lush anymore." He laughed. "As if every man who likes his beer is a lush. Oh, well. Probably better off without her. Sounded like a real shrew." He tossed the rag over his shoulder and held out his palm. "Seven bucks each for the baskets, buck fifty for your drink, and three bucks for each of his, tax rolled in, so twenty-one fifty."

Sean counted out the bills and added a tip. "How come his soda costs more than mine?"

" 'Cause yours didn't have bourbon in it." He rolled the bills and tucked them in his shirt pocket. "Thanks. Come again."

Sean doubted he'd come again. He might never wear these clothes again. Would the smoke smell come out of the fabric? But at least now he understood Farber's surliness and trembling. The man was trying to detox from alcohol. And he'd sat right next to him and watched him fall off the wagon. Some help he'd turned out to be.

TWENTY-FOUR

Fort Smith, Arkansas
Meghan

"I know we'd planned to go home for the weekend, but . . ."

Meghan set her paper cup of coffee down and gave Greg her full attention. Sheila paused midchew and looked at him, too.

"I think we need to stay. Make ourselves known around town." He stirred his instant oatmeal with his plastic spoon. "If we keep interviewing people, requesting records, and generally snooping, our thief will get plenty nervous. If we're lucky, he might break and lead us to the money as well as" — his gaze flicked to Sheila, then settled on Meghan — "any other evidence."

Meghan had been looking forward to going home and having the weekend with Sean, but she agreed with Greg's reasoning. She could stay if need be, but she wasn't without concern for Sheila. "Can you do that, Sheila? Take more time off work?"

The younger woman chewed, swallowed, and then gave Meghan a sheepish look. "Probably. I've never taken a vacation from the time I started at the retirement home. Not like I could go anywhere, with Mom and the boys needing me, and I kinda needed the structure of my job, with so much unpredictability at home."

Meghan couldn't resist giving the younger woman's wrist a squeeze. Sheila was definitely unselfish.

"So I've got a whole month stored up. I'd have to ask my supervisor, but yeah, I could probably stay."

Greg nodded. "Call your supervisor. If she's good with it, then we'll plan on using your presence to make the thief squirm. If it means losing your job, though, Meghan and I will pitch in for a bus ticket and send you back to Little Rock."

Tears swam in Sheila's blue eyes. "You've both been really nice to me. Thank you. I know I can be hard to live with. My brothers tell me that all the time. I guess when you're always worried, it makes you . . . ugly."

Meghan leaned over and gave Sheila an awkward sideways hug. "You could never be ugly, Sheila. You've been through a lot, losing your dad when you were young, then watching your mother fade away and not being able to do anything to fix it. That's bound to make anybody stressed. Stress exhibits itself in lots of ways. Anger is one. But we understand, and we want the end result of this investigation to take some of the stress off you. Knowing the truth will help, right?"

"Yeah. And being able to get Daddy's life insurance money will help, too. If he's really dead." She dropped the half-eaten pastry onto her Styrofoam plate and sighed. "I don't know what I want there. Part of me really wants him to be alive somewhere instead of maybe murdered by somebody he trusted, and part of me needs this done and buried and with enough money to pay for Brandon's college."

Meghan understood mixed emotions. She wanted to get to know her father but at the same time was scared of what she'd discover. She peeled back the aluminum cover on a cup of blueberry yogurt. "What career field is Brandon pursuing?"

Pride glowed on Sheila's face. "He wants to be a rheumatologist. So he can help people who have diseases like Mom had."

Greg whistled through his teeth. "That's a big ambition. Good for him."

Sheila nodded. "He's the smartest of all three of us. He should do something really big. Me and Wayne, we're content with our jobs. Wayne is an equipment operator for a private excavation company. It's owned by a guy from our church, and he treats Wayne real good. As for me, I like working with elderly people, trying to make them feel better or happier. My job's not glamorous, and sometimes it really hurts, like when a favorite patient dies, but I can't imagine doing anything else."

Meghan again marveled at Sheila's compassionate heart. She'd been raised right, even if her childhood had been difficult. Or maybe it was the difficulties that built her heart of compassion.

"Well, if we're all in agreement about sticking around, I'll give Captain Ratzlaff a call and let him know our intentions to stay over. I better also extend our reservation with the hotel." Greg pushed away from the table and grabbed his empty coffee cup. "You two make your calls while I set us up for another week. Then I need another cup of coffee. Stuff's so weak it takes four cups to get enough caffeine in my system to do any good."

Sheila laughed as Greg strode off. "I didn't like him at all at first. I thought he was grumpy. But he's growing on me." Her smile faded, and her lips quivered. "His kids are lucky, I think. Being around him has kind of reminded me what it's like to have a dad, you know?"

Meghan didn't know, but she nodded anyway.

"Daddy wasn't ever grumpy that I remember, unless one of us did something really wrong. Then I wouldn't say he got grumpy, just stern." Sheila tipped her head and peered at Meghan. "What about your dad? Was he kinda crusty, like Greg, or gentle, like my dad?"

Meghan scooped a spoonful of yogurt and ate it. She spoke to the yogurt cup. "I don't have one." She took another bite.

Sheila leaned close, bringing her sympathetic face into Meghan's line of vision. "I'm sorry. Did he die?"

Meghan set the yogurt aside. "No, he's alive. He actually lives here in Fort Smith. But I've never met him. He left my mom before I was born." She could have added that he and her mother had recently spent time together, but she still wasn't sure how she felt about it, and she wasn't ready to discuss it with anyone except Sean.

"Wow, that's sad."

Meghan took a sip of her tepid coffee and

shrugged. "I've gotten along okay with just a mom. It's really fine."

Sheila's sorrowful face brightened. "Maybe you could look for him while we're here. We're already searching for my dad. Would it be that hard to look for yours, too?"

She should have known by now that Sheila was persistent. "There's no need. I know where he is, but I've gone more than thirty years without him in my life. I'm not sure I want to switch that up. Especially since I don't know if he's like your dad, or like Greg, or even like Frankenstein's monster." She laughed, and to her relief, Sheila did, too. She patted Sheila's hand. "It's kind of you to be concerned, but you know what? I've always had a dad, and so have you."

Sheila's forehead puckered. "We have?"

"Mm-hmm. Our heavenly Father. My grandmother says the name *Abba* actually translates to 'Daddy,' like I've heard you call your dad." Jealousy tried to sneak in, but she pushed it aside. Envy had no place in this conversation. "That's pretty intimate, isn't it? You don't call a father 'Daddy' when you don't have a close, loving relationship. But that's what we can call God because we're His children and He loves us so unconditionally."

Amazement bloomed on Sheila's face. "I'd never thought of that, but you're right. After Daddy disappeared, Mom started taking us kids to church. My Sunday school teacher taught us to pray, 'Our Father, who art in heaven . . .' That's talking about God."

"More than that, it's talking *to* God. And being the loving Father He is, He always listens." Grandma's voice whispered in Meghan's memory, and she rephrased her words for Sheila. "He never leaves us. He never lets us down." Meghan's nose stung, tears looking for escape. But who was she crying for — herself or Sheila?

Sheila beamed the brightest smile Meghan had seen on the young woman's face. "Thanks, Meghan. That really helps."

"What helps?" Greg stood at the edge of their table, a steaming cup in his broad hand.

Sheila jumped to her feet. "Oops. I haven't called work yet. I'll go do that now." She darted off.

Meghan pulled out her cell phone. "I haven't called Sean, either."

Greg rolled his eyes. "Leave women unattended and all they do is yak." He waved his hand at her. "Go. Call. Then let's get this show on the road."

Meghan grinned at him, then headed

outside to the spot behind a cluster of potted plants where she'd found some semblance of privacy for previous calls. The morning air was crisp and cool, and the wind carried the smell of exhaust from the busy traffic, but her nose detected the fresh scent of burgeoning plants. New life. She allowed the aroma to clear her tumbled emotions.

Sean's phone went straight to voice mail, which she'd expected, given the hour of the day — he never answered his phone when he was driving. She explained their intention to stay through the weekend, then said, "Sean, as much as I miss you, I'm so glad I'm here. I've learned some things, and Greg and Sheila are the teachers. I'll talk to you more about it later. Have a good day, honey. I love you."

She disconnected the call and stepped from her hiding place. Greg and Sheila were waiting on the sidewalk. Greg raised one brow. "Good to go?"

Meghan nodded. "Lead the way."

Little Rock, Arkansas
Sean
Sean listened to Meghan's voice mail while he walked from the parking garage to the unit's building. Disappointment fell like a

310

wall of bricks. He'd looked forward to having her home, to sharing his worry about Farber — who would've thought he'd be so concerned about a man who gloried in antagonizing him? — and bouncing case theories with her. He wanted to be glad she was gaining new insights, but jealousy that he wasn't part of the process left him more unsettled than grateful.

Roach and Johnson were already at their desks when Sean entered the unit, but Farber's desk was vacant. A prickle of unease worked its way up Sean's spine. He pointed to the empty chair. "Did Farber call in sick?"

Roach glanced at Johnson, and Johnson shrugged. "Cap didn't say anything."

Sean changed course and went to the captain's office. He tapped on the doorframe, and his boss gestured him in. "Hey, Cap, sorry to bother you, but Farber's not here. Pretty unusual for him. Wondered if he'd called in sick."

"Close the door, huh?"

Sean did so, then sank onto the edge of the sofa, where he'd sat for so many other meetings in Cap's office. Why did this one feel ominous?

"Farber's at Riverside Park, waiting for you."

Sean searched his memory. Had they

made plans to meet and he'd forgotten?

"He went straight to the park this morning because after he talks to you there, he's taking a leave of absence."

Sean fell against the cushions. Farber? The one who wanted to sit in the captain's chair? "Why?"

Cap angled his head and pasted on a "Really?" look. "C'mon, Eagle. Use your deductive skills. What's going on with him?"

Sean scratched his temple. "He drinks too much. I've always known that. But last night I found out it destroyed his relationship with his wife."

The captain's jaw dropped. "He told you that?"

"No, the bartender at Barney's did."

"That's it in a nutshell. So now you know he's lonely, he's detoxing, and on top of that, I'm pretty sure he's battling depression." Cap leaned heavily on his desk and sighed. "I've been trying for the past six months to get him into AA. He finally joined. Has even gone to a couple of meetings with me as his sponsor."

Sean jolted. The captain was a recovering alcoholic?

Cap nodded, as if reading Sean's thoughts. "I've been sober a little over twenty years. I know how hard it is to fight your way out of

312

the hole and then keep from falling back in. I hoped he'd listen to me, trust me, given how long we've worked together. But mostly he's thrown rage in my direction. That's not doing our work relationship any good, so I'll have to set him up with a different sponsor."

Sean cringed. "Yeah — and quick. Because he kept his word about not drinking beer with his wings, but he did have a couple of Cokes with bourbon."

The captain leaned back, raised his face to the ceiling, and shook his head. "That explains him taking time off. When you trip and fall, the guilt gets you." He looked at Sean again. "I gave him sick leave for today, but he put in for a two-week leave. I'll do my best to see that it's approved. Of course, this means you're on your own with the Dunsbrook case."

Sean stood. "Actually, I'm okay with that. Farber says he has a theory to explore. I'll meet with him, hear him out, then chase that rabbit."

"I guess you know Dane and Meghan are staying over in Fort Smith."

Sean gritted his teeth and nodded.

"All right, then. Thanks for trying to help with Farber. Might want to" — he glanced at the door, as if ascertaining they were alone — "keep him in your prayers. It's a mighty monster he's fighting."

In his years on the cold-case unit, the captain had never mentioned anything remotely related to religion. For him to do so now told Sean how deeply the captain cared about his detectives. He gave the man a thumbs-up. "Will do. You can count on it."

Cap nodded and turned to his computer.

Sean opened the door but then shot a grin over his shoulder. "By the way, you were smart to go home and eat roast last night. I've still got heartburn from the wings, and my Bronco smells like cigarette smoke, thanks to me leaving the windows rolled up for my drive home."

Cap released a short chuckle. "Yeah, the smoke and the wings'll kill ya."

Like Stony Dunsbrook might've killed his cousins? Sean touched his forehead in a casual salute and headed for the elevator. The drive to Riverside Park took twenty minutes, and he left the windows down the entire time. Maybe the humid air would wash the cigarette-smoke smell from his upholstery. He could hope.

He pulled in through the park's main entrance and spotted Farber sitting on a bench near a half circle–shaped gravel parking area. Leaning forward, elbows on knees, hands loosely linked and dangling, he looked dejected. Despite everything, sympathy struck. Sean angled his vehicle next to Farber's little sports car and left the engine idling, uncertainty holding him in his seat.

How should he greet the man? Should he pretend he didn't know anything about Farber's crumbling marriage and alcohol addiction? Or was it better to acknowledge it, let Farber know he was concerned? Because he was.

Farber pushed off from the bench and ambled to the passenger side of Sean's SUV. He propped his arms on the window's sill and scowled in at Sean. "Took you long enough to get here."

His drawling, sarcastic tone chased away Sean's sympathy. He was about to tell Farber he'd have been here sooner if he'd been given advance notice, but the prayers he'd sent up for patience paid off. "Sorry. Wanna hop in? We can drive closer to where the Dunsbrooks camped the weekend the twins died."

Without a word, Farber yanked open the door and climbed in. He pointed to a narrow dirt road off to the right. "Take that. It's not really for public use, but we've got our badges if anyone asks. It's a shortcut to the riverbank." He shot a wry grin at Sean. "My brother and me used to walk it when we came here."

Sean put the vehicle in gear and aimed it for the unmarked road Farber had indicated. His tires stirred dust, and it poured through the window openings. Sean coughed and reached to roll up the windows.

"Leave 'em. Stinks like an ashtray in here."

Sean swallowed a laugh. The man was full of contradictions. Farber gave terse directions, punctuating his words with finger jabs, and eventually they reached the end of the road. A grassy patch, shaded by towering trees, stretched ahead of them. A long grassy rise that looked like a giant mole path curved toward the east.

Farber reached for the door handle. "Park here, get out, then follow me." He exited before Sean had a chance to turn off the engine.

Sean left his keys in the ignition and trotted to catch up. Farber had climbed to the top of the rise and stood, hands in pockets, staring into the distance. Sean stopped next to him, then let out a low whistle. The river for which the park had been named flowed below them, its soft gurgle joining with the wind's whisper. Small twigs and leaves floated on the brownish water.

"The place where the twins were found is about a hundred yards north of where we're standing."

Sean shot the man a startled look. "You've been out here before?"

He snorted. " 'Course I have. When I investigate, I investigate." He pointed to a spot ahead where the grass was flattened, then headed for it. Sean automatically followed. "The Dunsbrooks' campsite was roughly a half mile from the river, in a designated camping area. This stretch here is supposed to be off limits, but . . ." He angled a wry grin at Sean. "Boys will be boys."

Farber paused on the patch of flattened grass, at the very edge of the rise. "I don't know if you spent time at Riverside Park when you were a kid, but I did. For at least a half mile along this riverbank, there are steep inclines like this one. The soil is sandy. Easy to dig in." Without warning, he dropped to his bottom and slid down to the bank below. He squinted up at Sean. "Come on."

Sean grimaced. He'd dressed in work trousers, not faded jeans like Farber was wearing. Meghan would have a fit if he stained them. But what else could he do?

He huffed out a breath of resignation and imitated Farber's actions. He landed, his shoes digging into the soft sand. He stood and brushed off the seat of his pants. He'd need to empty his shoes before he got back in the Bronco.

Farber gestured to the cliff-like wall they'd descended. "My brother and me made maybe a dozen little caves out here when we were kids. Mom had a fit every time we came home filthy from digging. She'd tell us that one of these days a cave would collapse and bury us both. It never happened to us. But . . ." He bent over and picked up a twig, then used it as a pointer. "Imagine the Dunsbrook cousins digging a cave . . . and what Mom said would happen to Tim and me happened to them. But it only fell on the little ones because the big one was smart enough to stay at the outer edge."

Recalling the dust filling his nose during their drive, Sean could imagine the panic of being smothered by sand and dirt. His chest went tight just thinking about it. "It's a logical theory and would explain why dirt was in their nostrils and mouths, but that would mean they died in an accident. So why not tell the authorities what happened?"

"Maybe it wasn't an accident. Maybe the older cousin was jealous of them. Twins get a lot of attention, you know. He might've gotten tired of playing second fiddle to them and deliberately caved it in." Farber chewed the end of the stick, his expression thoughtful. "Or maybe he only wanted to scare them and didn't expect them to actually die. Maybe he thought if he stuck their heads in the water it would revive them. Kids that age, they don't reason like grown-ups do." He turned his gaze to the opposite bank and fell silent, the end of the stick between his teeth.

Sean scooped a handful of the mixture of sand and clay from the bank and squeezed it, then watched it drop in chunks to the bank. Farber's speculations held merit. But they wouldn't know if either were actualities without speaking directly to Stony Dunsbrook. Somehow, they — well, he, since Farber was taking leave — had to find the man.

TWENTY-FIVE

Las Vegas, Nevada
Kevin

"So that's the scoop, Gentry." Kevin lounged on his bed, feet crossed, while a glass of orange juice — all that was left of the breakfast he'd ordered from room service — created a circle of condensation on the bedside stand. "I rebooked for next Friday instead. Can you handle things for another week?"

Kevin's return flight to Arkansas was scheduled to leave at six that evening for a projected landing in Fort Smith at midnight. When he booked it, he'd figured a full week in Vegas would be plenty to accomplish everything he needed to do to get the building purchased and the reno underway. But he hadn't anticipated getting involved with Diane DeFord.

"Of course, sir. Should I keep forwarding your email?"

He wished his newest receptionist sounded more confident, but things couldn't fall apart too badly in only two short weeks. Even if he had fires to put out when he got back, it'd be worth it to have a little more time with his old college flame. He nearly snorted at his own private pun. "Yes, do that, and if something important comes up and you can't reach me, my attorney has the power to act on my behalf, so give him a call."

A shuffling sound came through the connection. "Is your attorney David Bradley?"

Didn't the contact's name in the database have the title *attorney-at-law* behind it? Kevin closed his eyes, shook his head, and held back the sarcastic reply. "Yes."

"All right. I have his number right here next to my telephone now."

"Good girl." Kevin knew the comment was condescending, but he doubted naive Gentry realized it. She was a good kid, but after being around Diane, he'd lost his taste for kids. He wondered more and more what he'd ever seen in Tawny. Besides her physical attractiveness, which she had in spades, she was shallow, unmotivated, and pouty. And thanks to his stupidity, he'd be paying her alimony for the next four years. If he hadn't employed a prenup, it'd be worse, but still . . .

"Enjoy the rest of your time in Las Vegas, Mr. Harrison." Gentry's perky voice carried to his ear. "I hope it's all successful."

"Thanks. Bye, now." Kevin dropped his cell phone on the mattress and grabbed the glass of juice. He downed it in one swig, then slung himself out of the bed. If he intended to join Diane and her mother at Lights Plus, their agreed-upon location to purchase new chandeliers and sconces for the loft apartment, he needed to get ready.

Kendrickson, Nevada
Diane

Diane entered the living room and stopped in front of Mother's ottoman. She held her arms wide and turned a slow circle. "Well? How do I look?"

"Very nice. I've always liked that outfit."

Diane slid her hands over the hips of the trim-fitting Caribbean-blue capri pants, then adjusted the collar of her short-sleeved white blouse dotted all over with tiny sailboats in the same brilliant blue stitching. "It's one of my favorites, but . . ." She gave her mother an uncertain frown. "Is it too dressy? I mean, we are just light-fixture shopping, so I don't want to go overboard."

Mother laughed. "Interesting choice of

words, considering the embroidery on your top."

Diane didn't join in.

Mother sat up in her chair and patted the ottoman. Diane perched sideways. Mother took her hand. "You've been on edge since you came back from the apartment yesterday morning. If being around him makes you this uncomfortable, then why put yourself through it? Clearly he has the financial means to hire a professional interior designer. He doesn't need our help."

"But then I'd have to give back the money he gave me, and I could really use it."

Mother made a *pfffft* sound with her lips. "We aren't destitute. We'd find another way to fund your car tires. If you want to back out, do so."

Diane considered her mother's suggestion. Why was she so torn concerning Kevin Harrison? After their decades of separation and her total disinterest in connecting with him, why did she now make herself available to him? She wished she knew. "I hate to quit when I've made a commitment. Plus, I think it'll be really fun to redo that place. It's such a unique apartment, and there's so much potential."

"Then do it."

"But doing it means being in contact with

Kevin until the renovation is done, and that could take weeks. Maybe even months."

Mother laughed again. "Margaret Diane, you're talking in circles. Aren't you getting dizzy?"

Diane hung her head and chuckled. "I guess I am being pretty ridiculous. I mean, all he wants from me is a redecorated apartment." Her throat tightened, and she swallowed. "So I shouldn't care if my outfit is too much or not enough for an outing to Lights Plus."

Mother squeezed Diane's hand between her warm palms. "Honey, instead of thinking about what Kevin wants from you, maybe you should ask yourself what you want from him."

Diane gave her mother a puzzled look. "What do you mean?"

"Only that I wonder if your continued willingness to spend time with him holds an ulterior motive. Your relationship ended so abruptly thirty-some years ago. Much was left unsaid that has probably rolled around inside you for decades. Do you want to let loose those unsaid words but haven't had the courage to do so yet?"

"I . . ." Diane blinked. She licked her lips. "I honestly don't know."

"Have you forgiven him?"

"I think I have."

Mother gave Diane the pointed look she used to hate when she was a teenager — the one that asked if she was telling the truth, the whole truth, and nothing but the truth. Mother would have made an incredible prosecuting attorney.

Diane threw her hands in the air. "I said I think I have."

"Well, until you *know* you have, you better keep examining yourself. Because holding on to unforgiveness benefits no one, and least of all the carrier."

"I know all this, Mother." Diane rose and paced the length of the room. Duchess, Miney, and Molly hopped down from their spots on the couch and accompanied her, tails wagging and tongues lolling. "What did the author Marianne Williamson say? Refusing to forgive is like drinking a poison and expecting the other person to die? Something like that. I've been able to be in his presence without strangling him. Doesn't that mean I've forgiven him?"

Mother settled back in her chair, chortling. "It's certainly a start."

Diane flopped onto the ottoman again. Miney leaped into Mother's lap, Duchess hopped up with Diane, and Molly collapsed at Diane's feet. Diane tugged Duchie close and played with her silky ears. "He told me he's been married four times. He didn't say so, but I presume every relationship ended in divorce."

Sympathy pursed Mother's wrinkled face. "Oh, my goodness. So much failure."

Diane nodded. "He asked me why I'd never married, and I told him why. Afterward I got really mad at myself because my answer showed something I didn't necessarily want him to know."

"What's that?"

"That I loved him. I really, truly loved him. When he told me to abort our baby" — tears stung and she sniffed — "shouldn't that have killed every bit of affection I felt for him?"

"Love isn't so easily squelched." Mother braced her elbow on the arm of the chair and rested her chin on her fist, as if tiredness had suddenly claimed her. "Over and over my father disappointed my mother with his broken promises and drunken rages. Yet she never walked away. And she had the chance. She could have come with me and made a clean start when I left for college. But she stayed with him until the end, even though it shredded her heart to do so."

Mother sighed and sat up. "When we love

someone, the roots grow deep into our hearts, and sometimes getting over the person is as ineffective as pulling up a dandelion. We can yank out the flower, but under the soil the roots continue to thrive. Mama never loved any man except Daddy. Your daddy was my first and only love. It could be that despite everything Kevin Harrison put you through, deep inside your heart, there's still a root of love for him."

Diane gawked at her mother. "You mean I still love him now? After what he did, I should hate him."

Mother's dark eyes snapped. "Can you hate him and still love his child? She's a part of him, you know."

She might have been smacked, as hard as Mother's statement struck her conscience. Diane lowered her gaze. Molly's round brown eyes peered up with adoration. Apparently the dog had already forgotten about having her paw trod upon that morning when Diane stepped from the closet in the dark room. Complete forgiveness. Complete trust that the hurt hadn't been intentional.

"Believe me, in my household anything but perfection was unacceptable."

Kevin's wry comment, delivered in the midst of proclamations of regret, whispered through Diane's memory. He'd also admitted to being young and stupid. They'd both erred, engaging in a relationship outside marriage that produced another human being. His rejection hadn't been premeditated. It came in a moment of great emotional upset. Could the same be said about the feelings she carried today?

Was some of her resentment toward Kevin a means of absolving herself of blame? After all, she'd chosen to bring the pregnancy to term and raise Meghan, despite the hardships and loneliness. When people looked down at her, she'd smugly assured herself that she'd at least been the bigger person by protecting the baby rather than snuffing out her life, the way her father had demanded.

Diane covered her face with her hands. "Mother, if you're right, if part of the reason I'm still alone is because I never let go of my first love, then what do I do?"

Soft hands cupped Diane's head. Mother's breath brushed her face as Mother began to pray. She thanked God for the precious gift named Meghan, thanked Him for His ability to make beauty out of ashes, and asked Him for wisdom concerning Diane's involvement in Kevin's project. She spoke with the ease of one who knew her Listener and trusted Him completely. Then her voice turned husky.

"Our gracious Father, I praise You for wanting the best for Your children. You know we cannot be happy unless we practice Your teachings and strive to reflect Your glory. Please guide my dear child in her words, actions, and emotions. We give You control. Work Your will in her life, Lord, and in the lives of Meghan and her father. In Your Son's name I ask these things. Amen."

Diane opened her eyes, and tears spilled. Mother's cheeks were moist, too, but her eyes glowed. Smiling, she slid her hands to Diane's jaw. "Healing will come, Margaret Diane. For you, for Meghan, and for Kevin. I believe it. Just wait. You'll see."

"You'll see." Wasn't that what Diane had told Kevin about prayer making a difference?

Diane placed her hands over Mother's and nodded. Healing would come. She believed it. She released a shaky laugh. "Thanks. I hope I don't have to wait too long, though. It's already been over thirty years, you know."

Mother gave a brusque nod. "And that's enough time to wait." She kissed Diane's forehead, the way she had when Diane was a little girl in need of comfort, then let go. She set Miney aside and pushed herself upright. "I need to find my shoes. Even if we're only going to Lights Plus, I ought to wear something other than my bedroom scuffs."

Las Vegas, Nevada
Kevin

Kevin found Diane and her mother waiting inside the doors of the incredibly monstrous warehouse. He slipped his sunglasses to the top of his head and winced. Between the sunlight pouring through the floor-to-ceiling windows on two sides of the building and the glowing bulbs in the hundreds of fixtures hanging from the industrial-type metal beams overhead, the light was almost blinding.

He slid his sunglasses back into place and grinned. "Boy, Diane, you weren't kidding when you said they had a good selection. There are enough chandeliers in here to decorate every house in Little Rock with a few left over for sheds."

Her lips formed a weak smile, and she glanced up and down the aisles, as if she was expecting someone else. Had she invited the plumber to join them? The thought rankled.

Hazel handed him a trifold brochure. "This might come in handy. It's a map of the store."

Kevin unfolded it. A map to guide shoppers through a light-fixture warehouse. Now he'd seen everything. "This is smart. As big as the place is, a person could get lost in here."

Hazel chuckled. She tapped the page. "Along the edge is a key. Scan down the list and find the type of fixture you want. They have it all, from antique reproduction to ultramodern. It'll be less overwhelming if you choose a style and we go to that department instead of endlessly wandering in search of 'the one.' "

If he didn't know better, he'd suspect the older woman of delivering a dig about his numerous relationships. He'd spent the past thirty years trying to find "the one" who would complete his life. If he'd had a map back in the day, would it have led him to Diane? He cringed. Life itself had led him to her, and he'd foolishly let her go.

Kevin glanced at Diane. She hadn't said a word, which was out of character for the girl he'd once known and didn't seem to match the woman he'd recently met. He waved the paper, and she turned her attention to him. Finally. He smiled. "Miss Decorator, why am I the one holding the map? You're calling the shots on this, remember?"

She took the map and pointed to one section. "If it's up to me, I'd say explore the Classic department first."

"Okay."

"If nothing there appeals to us, we can go to Vintage."

Why did the casual use of the pronoun *us,* delivered in an impersonal tone, make such an impact on his pulse? "Sounds good. Lead the way." This time he'd be smart enough to follow.

Fort Smith, Arkansas
Meghan

Sheila climbed out of Greg's back seat and grinned at Meghan. "I wish my brothers were here. They'd have gotten such a kick out of going around town today and asking people what kind of lifestyles the bankers at UNB&T have. Their favorite game when they were little was Clue. Mom even bought them detective costumes for Christmas one year, with magnifying glasses, hats, trench coats, and everything. They wore them every time we played Clue, until the cheap fabric fell apart."

Meghan hadn't had the pleasure of playing games with siblings, but she smiled at the picture Sheila's remembrance painted in her head. Sean would probably like the idea of having a weekly family game night if they had kids someday. Her smile wobbled. "Sounds like fun."

"The game was fun, but doing it for real is even more fun. I can't wait to call Wayne and Brandon and tell them I got to help in a real investigation." Sheila's bright expression faded, and she blinked hard. "Do you think Mr. Wallingford's the one?"

Meghan folded her arms and angled her head. "What makes you think it's him?"

"Well . . . how many people said something about him taking a lot of vacations? More than anybody else they knew. That's kind of a clue, isn't it?"

Meghan nodded. "Yep. That is definitely a clue."

Greg rounded the vehicle and joined them. "What's a clue?"

Meghan repeated Sheila's observation.

Greg grinned at the younger woman. "Good call. Of course, we can't prove anything yet, but he worked the closest with your father back then, and he seems uneasy about us spending time at the bank. He also can't seem to look you in the eyes. My gut says we need to check into him more closely." At that moment, his stomach growled.

Sheila burst out laughing. "I heard that."

He grimaced and gestured to the hotel. They headed across the parking area.

Sheila rubbed her stomach. "I'm hungry, too. What I wouldn't give for a supersized pepperoni pizza from the pizzeria in Little Rock. Have you ever been to Ir—"

Meghan and Greg chorused, "Iriana's." Meghan's mouth immediately began to water.

Greg groaned. "Now you've done it. I can't get pizza off my mind."

Meghan looked up and down the street. "There's gotta be a pizza place around here."

Greg made a face. "I'm all for pizza, but it's Friday night. Any pizza places will probably be overrun with teenagers."

Sheila shrugged. "What about delivery?"

"Delivery would be all right." He crooked his finger, inviting the women to follow him, and entered the hotel. He crossed to the check-in desk. "Excuse me."

The young man serving as clerk hurried over. "Yes, sir?"

"We're in the mood for pizza, but we're not in the mood to go out. Is there a delivery service close by?"

The clerk nodded. "Less than two blocks away. Murray's. We keep their menus on hand because a lot of our guests order from them." He dug through a pile of papers and pulled out a rumpled photocopied sheet. "Here you go."

"Thanks." Greg showed the menu to Meghan and Sheila. "Tell me what you'd like, and I'll order it. We can get bottled sodas from the machine in the laundry room, then use the desk in one of our rooms for a table. That sound okay?"

Meghan nodded. "Sounds great. And I'm good with whatever you two want."

"Pepperoni," Sheila said, then hunched her shoulders. "I mean, pepperoni, please. With mushrooms."

Greg laughed. He tapped the phone number into his cell and handed the menu back to the clerk. "One large pepperoni pizza with mushrooms, comin' up."

TWENTY-SIX

Meghan

Meghan sat in the lobby and watched for the pizza deliverer. Greg had given her money to pay for the pie, then excused himself to call his wife since he'd neglected to let her know he wasn't coming home for the weekend. Sheila stayed with Meghan until one of her brothers called and she went to the room to talk to him. So now Meghan waited alone.

She didn't mind. She'd been around people all day without a moment to herself, and hiding out in a chair tucked in the corner was the perfect way to unwind. Mom had teased her more than once about being an introvert. *"You'd rather sit and watch the world go by than be in the middle of the action."* Mom was probably right, but all that sitting and watching had prepared her well for what she did now. So much of her job involved simple observation and drawing

336

conclusions from people's behavior.

Take Darryl Wallingford, for example. During their first meeting, he'd hardly said a word, deferring to his coworker to answer questions. Then the second day, when they'd left Sheila at the hotel, he'd answered boldly, almost overly confident, as if he'd spent the night rehearsing and was eager to share his lines. But on the third day when, once again, Sheila sat in the room, the man acted uncomfortable, but was it because he was hiding something or only because he didn't like revisiting the loss of someone who'd once been a good friend?

Sheila's comment about Uncle Wally being the same age as her dad lingered in Meghan's mind, too. If the men were close in age, then Wallingford would be somewhere between fifty and fifty-five. Yet his physical appearance more closely resembled someone in his late sixties. Guilt, and the worry of being caught, could sure bring on early wrinkles and gray hair.

Of course, certain illnesses or poor lifestyle choices also aged people prematurely. As far as they knew, he was healthy. She didn't take the man for a smoker — his teeth weren't stained, usually a telltale sign, and he didn't carry the scent of smoke on his clothes. A drinker? That was a little harder to detect.

The lobby doors opened, and the spicy smell of pepperoni filled the room. A young man scuffed in. The torn hems of his baggy jeans dragged on the floor, his shirt was half-untucked, and ragged strands of brownish-blond hair fell across his forehead, partially shielding his eyes. A plastic bag swung from his wrist, and a pizza box balanced on his palm. If it hadn't been for the spicy aroma wafting from the waxed cardboard box and *Murray's* emblazoned across the top in bright red letters, Meghan would have presumed the man was homeless.

He headed for the desk, and Meghan hopped up and intercepted him. "Hi, is that order for Greg Dane?"

The man — or maybe she should call him a boy, given the two pimples decorating one cheek and the abundance of peach fuzz covering his chin — squinted at the piece of paper taped to the top of the box. "Yeah." He turned his gaze on her and smirked. "Don't tell me you're Greg Dane."

Meghan didn't like the way he ogled her. If Sean were with her, the young man wouldn't be so brazen. She stood as tall as possible and stared him down, the way she'd been taught to confront uncooperative suspects. "No, I'm not, but I am his partner.

I'm paying for the pizza."

"Hmm." The guy gave her a head-to-toes-to-head-again examination and settled his weight on one bony hip. "Lucky guy." He slid the box onto the counter and flopped the bag on top of it. "Paper plates and napkins in there. Total is sixteen ninety. That includes the delivery fee but not my tip."

The way he was behaving, the only tip he deserved was advice on appropriate behavior, but from the looks of him, he needed every penny he could get. Meghan gritted her teeth and handed him a twenty. "Keep the change."

He pocketed the bill, grinning. "Thanks, sweetheart. You have a good day, now."

Meghan bristled. The obnoxious upstart! She started to demand change from the twenty — he needed manners even more than he needed a haircut — but the desk clerk spoke first.

"Hey, Kip, back at Murray's again, huh? I haven't seen you for a while."

An uneasy feeling attacked Meghan's midsection. She took a hesitant step backward as the pizza deliveryman leaned on the counter and grinned at the man behind the desk.

"Yeah, you know how it is. Sometimes I feel like workin', sometimes I don't. But you can only watch YouTube videos and play Xbox so long before the boredom gets you. So I signed on again."

The clerk laughed. "Lucky sap. If I had a rich daddy like you, I sure wouldn't deliver pizzas for Murray's. Not even if I was bored out of my gourd."

A sullen look fell over the young man's face. "You wanna be bored out of your gourd, spend an hour listening to one of my old man's lectures about responsibility. You oughta hear him." His lips twisted into a sneer. He lowered his voice in timbre and struck a pompous pose. " 'Son, I'm fed up with your lazy attitude.' " A sarcastic laugh left his throat. "Takes two or three months before he's fed up enough to say anything. Then you know what he does when he leaves? Hands me three or four hundred-dollar bills — supposedly to get myself cleaned up. But hey, he never sticks around to make sure I actually do it, so I spend the money how I want to."

The clerk laughed. "Sucker!"

Kip slapped the counter and roared with laughter. "I know, right?"

For a moment Meghan felt as though she observed the prodigal son who'd squandered his inheritance. So obviously rebellious and self-absorbed. Based on his appearance, he might've even recently rolled in a pigsty. She cringed. Had he put their pizza in the box? If so, it might not be wise to eat it.

The boy pushed off from the counter and saluted the clerk. "Good to see ya, Mason. Enjoy your job."

"Ha, ha — real funny, Kip. Take it easy, man."

Kip sauntered out, and the clerk turned a smile on Meghan. "No need to look so worried. Kip's harmless. He's just kind of a . . . well, a loser."

What had Mom called Kip? A brat. Similar to a loser. She picked up the box, but then she remained in place, staring out the glass doors where the boy named Kip had disappeared. Maybe it was coincidence that the pizza deliveryman had the same name as the boy her father had adopted. Still, how common was Kip?

She turned to the clerk. "What's his full name?"

The clerk eyed her. "Why? Are you gonna file a complaint against him? He flirted with you, but he didn't really do anything wrong."

She forced a smile. "No, I'm not going to file a complaint. He reminds me of someone. I wondered if he might be from the same family." Not a complete truth, but not a lie, either. He reminded her of Mom's description.

"Oh, okay. In that case, his name's Kip Harrison. Do you know the Harrisons?"

Meghan's stomach churned. "I know of them. Is Kip's father Kevin Harrison?"

"That's right. Kip's old man owns lots of businesses, makes a lot of money." He smirked. "Likes the ladies, too. So does Kip. But I guess you figured that out." He shrugged, and his expression turned thoughtful. "Kip and I ran around some in high school. My mom always said she thought he got into trouble because he had really poor self-esteem. But I don't know about that. Me and my pals always just kind of saw him as . . ." He shrugged again. "A loser."

"Then why'd you hang out with him?"

"Are you kidding? Hanging around Kip had its privileges. He always had money for movies or burgers or whatever we wanted to do."

How sad was that? Meghan thanked the clerk and carried the pizza up the hallway toward her room. By now it was probably cold, but they could reheat slices in the little microwave in their room. She doubted she'd be able to eat, the way her stomach felt. If

Kip was the outcome of Kevin Harrison's parenting abilities, she should be grateful she'd been spared living with him.

But gratitude refused to rise. Her hope that she might have inherited some good parenting genes from her paternal side had just crashed and burned.

The bank was open until noon on Saturday, and during breakfast in the hotel's little eating area, Greg suggested spending the morning in the conference room. "Make sure they all know we're still around."

Meghan shook her head. "I got to thinking last night . . ." She'd been awake until almost two o'clock, too uneasy to sleep, but it gave her plenty of time to think about the case. Now if she could gather her thoughts enough to make sense, given her drowsiness. "A man who absconded with hundreds of thousands of dollars has to have something to show for it. The people we talked to yesterday mentioned Wallingford's frequent trips out of town. We need to find out if he's made use of his passport. People with money usually take some pretty extravagant vacations. I'd like to know where he goes."

Sheila's bright-eyed gaze fixed on Meghan. "How come?"

"If there's another country he visits regularly, he might actually own property there."

Greg had chopped a cherry turnover to pieces while she spoke. He jabbed a chunk with his plastic fork and pointed at her with it. "Smart thinking. We should also go to the courthouse, see how many deeds are in his name, what kinds of vehicles he drives." He jammed the bite into his mouth. "I didn't uncover anything in the bank's financial records that stuck out, like one employee with unexplained deposits. Not that it'd be smart to put it in his own bank. But first-timers aren't always the brightest crooks."

Sheila poured milk from a half-pint carton over her cereal. "Is the courthouse open on the weekend?"

Greg speared another chunk of turnover. "Not usually. And since Monday is Memorial Day, it'll be closed then, too. I guess we'll have to wait until Tuesday to do any checking there."

Meghan groaned. Why hadn't she remembered Monday was a national holiday? They could've gone home for the weekend after all. If they'd left yesterday afternoon, she wouldn't have come face to face with Kevin Harrison's son. Oh, how she wished they'd left then.

Greg wrinkled his nose and put down his

fork. "This thing's bone dry." He folded his arms on the table and looked first at Meghan and then Sheila. "All right, then, it's decision time. Do we stick around, spend the morning at the bank snooping through financial records, make sure everybody knows we haven't gone anywhere? Or do we head for Little Rock and let them think we've given up?"

Meghan cringed. "If we leave, we might give the thief time to hide assets."

Greg nodded. "Or skip town if he's really worried we're onto him."

Meghan wanted to skip town. She needed to see Sean, to sort out the emotions her encounter with Kip Harrison had stirred. "Maybe —"

"Excuse me." A police officer stopped next to their table and sent his gaze across each of their faces. "I'm Officer Lang from the Fort Smith Police Department. I'm looking for some cold-case detectives from Little Rock — Greg Dane and Meghan De-Ford?"

Greg stood and offered his hand. "I'm Detective Dane, Officer, and this is Detective DeFord." He gestured to Meghan. She shook the officer's hand, too, but remained seated. "What can we do for you?"

"I'm here to escort you to the jail."

Greg scowled. "For what reason?"

The officer slid his thumbs into his pants pockets and splayed his elbows. "It's probably best to discuss all this at the station."

Greg pulled his cell phone from his pocket. "Before I go anywhere, I need to check with my captain."

Officer Lang shook his head. "No need for that. Little Rock's been notified. You can ride in my squad car or follow me in your own vehicle. But we need you to come in as quick as possible to get this mess straightened out."

Meghan slowly stood on shaky legs. "What mess are we talking about, Officer Lang?"

"The one you're stirring up about Anson Menke."

TWENTY-SEVEN

Diane tiptoed through the hallway to her mother's bedroom. Mother had always been an early riser — up by six, six thirty at the latest. So worry traveled with Diane to the closed door.

She pressed her ear to the door and listened for sounds of activity. Nothing. Her pulse pounding, she tapped on the door. "Mother?" She waited a few seconds, then tapped again a little harder. "Mother, are you all right?"

"What? Who's . . ." A few soft thuds and bumps and mutters.

"It's me — Margaret Diane." She gripped the doorknob. "May I come in?"

"Yes. Yes, come in."

Diane entered the dark room and crossed to Mother's bed.

Mother sat on its edge, her snowy hair on

end and bare feet dangling. She squinted at Diane. "What time is it?"

"A little after seven." She reached to pull up the shade and allow in sunlight, but Mother put out her hand.

"Please don't. I have a pounding headache."

Diane sat next to her and put her arm around her. "Are you sick? Should I call the doctor?" Mother had the strongest constitution of any octogenarian Diane knew, but almost four years ago she'd undergone an endarterectomy and fallen into a brief coma after the surgery. At Mother's age, illnesses could strike fast and overwhelm quickly. Diane wouldn't overlook symptoms the way she had last time.

"I don't need a doctor. I need an aspirin."

"You're sure it's just a headache?"

"Margaret Diane, the seasons are changing. I always get allergy headaches this time of year. An aspirin or, better yet, an allergy pill will take care of it."

Diane drew in a deep breath, deliberately tamping down her worry. "All right, I'll get you one. Orange juice or coffee?"

"For heaven's sake, no caffeine. I want to go back to sleep."

Diane stifled a chuckle at Mother's uncharacteristic crankiness. "Juice it is. I'll be right back." She hurried to the kitchen, poured a small glass of juice and another of water, grabbed the box of loratadine from the little cabinet above the refrigerator, and then returned to her mother's room. Miney extricated herself from her dachshund pals lounging in the sunshine in front of the kitchen patio doors and trotted after her.

"Here you go." Diane placed the items on the nightstand. Mother had already crawled back under the covers and lay propped up on pillows. "Miney came to check on you. Can she jump up?"

"Of course. She's my best medicine."

Diane hid a smile. Given the choice between the two humans in the house, Miney would hang with Mother over Diane every time. Strange how animals chose their special "one" and remained loyal. Her mind automatically zipped to Mother's observation about Diane's subconscious loyalty toward Kevin, and she patted the mattress a little more exuberantly than necessary to dispel the errant thought. "Here you go, pretty girl. Grandma says you're welcome to join her."

Miney leaped up, turned a circle, and settled next to Mother's hip. Mother stroked the dog and scowled at Diane. "As much as

I like her, I'm not this beast's grandma, you know."

"I know." Diane pushed a tiny white pill through the layer of protective foil into her palm and offered it to her mother with the juice.

Mother swallowed the medication, then held the juice glass against her bodice and sighed. "If I'm not up and ready by the time you're to meet Kevin at the kitchen-and-bath store, go without me."

Diane groaned. In her worry about her mother, she'd forgotten about their plans to pick out new sinks, faucets, and a tub for the loft apartment. "How about I call him and cancel? You might need —"

"I don't need a thing except sleep, so you can go without a moment's concern. But I'll be fine as frog's hair once this pill kicks in. What time are we supposed to meet?"

"Ten."

"I'll make it." She wriggled downward and tucked her arm around Miney. "Shut the door on your way out, please." She closed her eyes.

Diane tiptoed out but left the door cracked wide enough for the dachshund to leave if she had a mind to. Miney was like a cat when it came to closed doors — she'd paw at it and wake Mother. Diane returned to the kitchen and poured a fresh cup of coffee. She glanced at the clock. It would be almost nine thirty in Arkansas. And since it was Saturday, Meghan shouldn't be working. They'd texted back and forth only a few times since Meghan's arrival in Fort Smith. Curiosity about how the case was progressing, not to mention an odd yearning to hear her daughter's voice, struck hard.

Diane retrieved her cell phone from its charging station and pulled up Meghan's number. She hit Call, then tapped the speaker button. *"Hello. You've reached Meghan's voice mail. I'm sorry I missed your call, but —"* Sighing, Diane hit End. She'd try again later. After her meeting with Kevin. She'd need to hear her daughter's voice even more then.

Fort Smith, Arkansas
Meghan
Meghan glanced at the clock. Another fifteen minutes had passed since the last time she'd peeked. She, Greg, and Sheila had already been waiting an hour for officers to tell them why they'd been escorted to the station. If it was important enough to pull them away from breakfast, shouldn't someone have talked to them by now?

Sheila sat next to Meghan, gnawing at her

thumbnail. She'd already bitten her middle finger's nail to the quick. The younger woman's forehead wore a series of lines that seemed out of place on someone her age. Greg, on her other side, sat with his arms folded and his face fixed in a thunderous expression.

He caught her looking at him and grunted. "We're going to end up wasting our entire morning sitting here. This is nuts."

Meghan had no answer, so she only shrugged and offered a sympathetic grimace. She wanted to check her cell phone. The vibration a few minutes ago had made all three of them jump. If it would be a while yet, she might have time to call whoever had tried to call her. She hoped it was Sean. She missed him so much her chest ached.

Another glance at the clock, then a glance into her purse propped on the floor between her chair and Sheila's. She reached for the purse.

The door swung open and a tall, slender man dressed in a suit and carrying a briefcase entered. Two police officers trailed him. The man in the suit slapped his briefcase onto the table, then seated himself across from the detectives and Sheila. The younger of the two officers rounded the table and held his hand toward Sheila.

"Ma'am, would you come with me, please?"

"Why?" Sheila shot a frantic look at Meghan.

Meghan frowned at the officer. "Where are you taking her?"

"To the front lobby."

Sheila drew back from the policeman. "I'd rather stay here."

The suit-wearing man huffed. "This meeting is between my client and the detectives. Confidentiality will be breached by your presence. Kindly depart so our meeting can begin."

Meghan squeezed Sheila's wrist and whispered, "It's okay. Go on."

Uncertainty creased the younger woman's features, but she followed the officer out of the room. The second officer closed the door and positioned himself in front of it, his stance similar to a soldier at parade rest. Meghan's stomach tangled into knots. Were she and Greg about to be arrested for some unknown local infraction?

The suit-wearing man aimed a tight smile at Greg. "My apologies for leaving you waiting. I'm afraid the delay was unavoidable." He stuck his hand across the table. "I'm Attorney Philip Johnske of Bailer, Johnske, and Long Law Offices."

Greg gave the man a single pump of his hand. "I'm Detective Greg Dane. Of the Arkansas Cold Case Investigations Department."

"Yes, I know." Johnske didn't offer to shake Meghan's hand. He opened his briefcase and took out a stack of typed pages stapled together in the upper-left corner. He flattened the pages on the table, leaned forward slightly, and rested his linked hands on top of them. "I represent Union National Bank and Trust. I understand you've spent a significant amount of time there recently, interrogating employees and examining private records."

Meghan's jaw dropped. The bank president had been cooperative from the moment they'd arrived in Fort Smith. Why would he now sic a lawyer on them?

Greg cleared his throat and gestured to Meghan. "Mr. Johnske, this is Detective Meghan DeFord, who is lead investigator for this case. Why don't you direct your comments to her?" He sat back and folded his arms over his chest, his expression bland.

Johnske set his lips in a grim line, glaring for several seconds at Greg, and then shifted his dark eyes on Meghan. "What exactly is your purpose in Fort Smith, Detective De-Ford?"

Meghan met the man's icy glower. "We're investigating the mysterious disappearance of Anson Menke, who was an employee at UNB&T at the time."

"According to legal records, the 'mysterious disappearance' of Anson Menke in" — he glanced at the pages — "March of 2002 was declared intentional abandonment by a judge in the Sebastian County court system. Furthermore, Menke was found guilty of embezzlement by that same judge." His lips curved into a smug smile. "Detectives from a bureau outside Sebastian County have no authority to overturn that conviction."

Meghan smiled in return. "Maybe we can't overturn the conviction, but since the cold-case unit is a state rather than county agency, we do have the authority to investigate the disappearance of a man from Sebastian County, Arkansas. If our investigation uncovers what we suspect, we will petition the court to amend the indictment and absolve Mr. Menke of wrongdoing."

Johnske didn't even blink. "And what exactly do you suspect, Detective DeFord?"

She disliked the way he said her name, as if he questioned her credentials as a detective. She sent up a quick prayer to maintain professionalism. "I'm sorry, but since this is an ongoing investigation, we aren't at liberty to discuss details with anyone outside the agency."

He sat in silence for several seconds, as if waiting for her to change her mind and answer his question. Then he gave a little jerk and lifted the stapled pages. "Your presence at the bank has been disruptive, intrusive, and — to be blunt — nosy. The bank's board of directors has filed a stay-away order against the two of you specifically and the Arkansas Cold Case Investigations Department generally."

Meghan's jaw dropped. "Are you serious?"

Greg leaned forward and took the pages. He scanned them, his expression unreadable.

Johnske gave a firm nod. "I assure you, I am serious. More important, they are serious. The board is satisfied with the judge's ruling, and the bank employees have neither the time nor the interest in assisting you in an unnecessary investigation. Therefore, your presence is no longer welcome." He pointed to the papers. "You'll notice it is duly notarized and signifies a date of issuance."

Greg glanced at Meghan. "It's dated yesterday."

Johnske's smug smile returned. He closed

his briefcase and rose. "Since we have this matter settled, I'll leave you to pack for a return to Little Rock. Good day, detectives." He strode out, and the police officer followed him.

Meghan slumped into her chair. "A stay-away ruling. I sure didn't see that coming."

"Me neither." Greg plopped the pages on the table and shifted to face her, a secretive smile playing on the corners of his lips. "You know what this means, don't you?"

"Oh, yeah." Meghan released a soft snort of mirthless laughter. "Someone's running scared."

Greg grinned. "Yep. But guess what? We don't need to go to the bank to dig into personal property records. And this stay-away order doesn't include any building in town except the bank. So the courthouse is fair game."

"Except we can't get in there until next Tuesday."

Greg shrugged. "So let's let Johnske think he's won and go home for the weekend."

TWENTY-EIGHT

Las Vegas, Nevada
Kevin

Kevin trailed Diane and her mother through aisles showcasing an array of bathroom faucets. Diane paused only in front of the gold-plated ones marked "water efficient." Gold would best keep with the art deco theme, she'd said, and even though he preferred brushed nickel, he opted not to argue with her. What did he know about interior design?

The interactions between Diane and Hazel intrigued him. Things had changed in the mother-daughter relationship since Diane was in college. Back when he knew her, Diane overflowed with resentment toward the woman she derisively called a neurotic perfectionist. He'd related to her, having been raised by the male version. But apparently Diane had put aside her resentment or Hazel had shed the perfectionist title, because any fool could see that the two of them got along fine now, bouncing ideas back and forth, sometimes bickering but always laughing. At ease.

Oddly enough, he envied them. He'd never been at ease around his father, even though he did his best to please the man. Chuck Harrison was a genius in business. Except for the one decision that became his downfall. Then Dad's death ruined Kevin's relationship with his mom. They loved each other, but their interactions were stilted, hindered by the ugly secret they shared.

Diane looked over her shoulder at him and tapped the arched spout of a faucet set. "What do you think of this one?"

He peered past her at the faucet. It seemed pretty much like half a dozen others they'd already seen. "It's okay. Do you like it?"

She nodded, her expression serious. "I do. It has really nice lines, the spigot is high enough to get your hands under without having to bend yourself in half but not so high it resembles a kitchen faucet, and the handles have a shape that's easy to grasp. Plus, it has a spot-proof coating guaranteed to last for the life of the faucet. It'll be easy to keep clean, and that should appeal to anybody who's spent time scrubbing water spots from their fixtures before."

Why did her formal recital of the faucet's positive aspects tickle him? He forced himself not to laugh, and he struck a formal pose, like a butler in a classic movie welcoming dignified guests. "My, that is appealing."

She narrowed her gaze and eyed him. "Are you making fun of me?"

"Of course not." His lips quirked. He couldn't help it.

Her jaw dropped. "You *are* making fun of me." She propped her fist on her hip and gave him a saucy look. "Listen, mister, finding the right faucet is a big deal. It's only the central point of the entire bathroom vanity."

He knew he'd regret it later, but he burst out laughing.

She rolled her eyes. "Honestly. We should have left you out of this excursion." She pulled a little card from a plastic holder in front of the faucet and linked arms with her mother. "C'mon, let's go to sinks."

Hazel shot an impish grin at him. He winked in reply and fell in step behind them. They rounded the corner at the end of the aisle, and his cell phone rang. He recognized the name on his screen and grimaced. He pushed Accept Call and turned his back on Diane and her mother.

"Julie . . . hello. What's wrong?"

Her huff carried through the connection. "Why do you immediately think something's wrong?"

"Because there usually is when you call." He glanced and discovered both of the De-Ford women watching him. He lowered his voice. "Listen, I'm kind of in the middle of something right now. It's not a good time. Can I call you later?"

"It's never a good time with you, Kevin, is it?" She blasted his ear. His phone wasn't set to speaker, but he was pretty sure Diane heard every word.

He took a few steps away from the women. "I'm in the middle of a business deal. Let me call you this evening."

"It'll be too late by then. No business deal can be more important than your son, can it?"

He really didn't want to answer that.

"I need you to transfer three thousand dollars to my personal checking account."

He closed his eyes and hung his head. "What did he do now?"

"*He* didn't do anything, but a friend who was a passenger in his car had marijuana on him. Kip found out when he got pulled over for running a red light and the officer frisked them."

"For Pete's sake, Julie, that's a class A misdemeanor. He could get a year in jail." In his aggravation, he forgot to temper his voice. Two customers a few feet farther up the aisle sent curious looks his way. He shifted to avoid them and came face to face with Diane and Hazel. He glanced left and right, searching for a cubby to jump into and finish the conversation. Not one hidey-hole in sight. He set off for the front doors.

Meanwhile, Julie harangued him. "You think I don't know the laws, Kevin? I looked everything up before I called you. That's how I know what I'll need to bail him out. Even though it's his first time being caught with an illegal substance, it's the friend's third time, so —"

"When is he going to grow up and stop making such stupid decisions?" Kevin burst out of the store onto the sidewalk. More people were outside than had been inside. Was there no place in this town where a person could find privacy? He leaned against the building and hunched around the phone, hoping everyone else was too occupied with their own business to worry about his. "Have you considered leaving him there until he has his appearance before the judge? It might do him some good to —"

"Leave him in jail with drug dealers and who knows what other kinds of criminals? How can you even suggest something like that?"

Of course Kevin couldn't leave Kip there. Twice before in moments of angst, Kip had threatened to do away with himself. If he followed through while in a jail cell Kevin could have rescued him from, how would he live with himself? He carried enough guilt already. "All right, listen. You've got the number for my attorney. Give him a call and tell him he's authorized to take what he needs from my business account to cover Kip's bail. Have him see a bail bondsman and get Kip out. You stay out of it."

"Why can't I do it?"

"Because I want David to handle it, that's why. And since I'm paying for it, I get to make the decision."

"I still think —"

"Call David, Julie."

"But —"

"Call David."

"Fine!"

The connection went dead. Kevin gripped his cell phone and rested his forehead against the cool glass pane. Would it ever end? How many times would he and Julie be forced to pay Kip's way out of trouble before the kid grew up and developed some maturity?

"Kevin?"

He spun around. Hazel was over by the doors, but Diane stood only a few inches from him. He glared at her. "How long have you been there?"

"Long enough to know something is seriously wrong. What is it?" She'd lost her earlier feistiness and seemed genuinely concerned.

He dropped his phone into his pocket and moved toward the doors. "Nothing. Let's finish up in there and —"

She stepped into his pathway. "No, really. If something's happened with your son, you can go back to Fort Smith. Mother and I are capable of handling the apartment changes on our own."

She was capable. Completely capable. So was her daughter. While his son was nothing but a mess. He placed his palm on her lower back and urged her toward the doors. "My going back to Fort Smith won't make an ounce of difference. So let's finish our shopping and pretend the phone call didn't happen."

She moved in the direction he'd prompted, but she shook her head. "I'm not that good at pretending. And neither are you." She paused outside the doors and put her hand against his chest. "You're not going to be able to think about anything else, so why not unburden yourself? Mother and I are both good listeners, and Mother's had enough life experience to intelligently advise the president."

Hazel offered a solemn nod. "That's probably true."

Kevin swallowed a chortle.

"Why be stubborn and hold it all in when you've got help at your disposal?"

Her warm hand over his heart did funny things to his middle. He gently grasped her wrist and lowered her arm. "Thank you, but Kip's a . . ." He sought a word that wouldn't be considered vulgar by the older woman's generation. "Nitwit. He's always going to be a nitwit. No one can change that."

"You're wrong, Kevin." Hazel shook her finger at him. "Someone can change him. The same Someone who can change you."

Kevin drew back. "Not to be disrespectful, ma'am, but I'm not the one who needs changing."

"Wrong again." Hazel folded her arms and fixed a stern look on him that made him squirm.

The doors opened, and a man strode out carrying a large box. A woman and little boy followed him. The child swung the woman's hand and giggled. The sight twisted Kevin's stomach in a knot. He'd never seen Kip so carefree. Kevin couldn't ever recall being so carefree.

He turned his attention back to Hazel. Her bright eyes remained locked on him. The knowing curve of her lips made him believe she'd read his mind.

She slipped her hand through the bend of her daughter's arm. "I don't think any of us are in the mood to shop for bathroom fixtures right now. So let's postpone the duty and go to Brenda's."

Kevin frowned. "Who's Brenda?"

Diane chuckled. "Not a who, a where. Brenda's is a little sandwich shop on the Strip."

"But in the morning, they sell muffins the size of a head of cabbage." Hazel smiled at Kevin. "I'm particularly fond of the zucchini-walnut muffins. If you buy me one, I'll share it with you."

A laugh exploded from him before he realized it was coming. It startled him, but it felt good. He shook his head. How could Diane have called this woman neurotic? He wished he could adopt her as his grandma. Or maybe Kip's grandma. "All right, I'm in. Since you're the advisor, who should drive?"

"Margaret Diane. She knows where we're going. We'll come back here after our break. If we're in the mood, we'll shop. If not, we'll leave you at your vehicle. Deal?"

Kevin nodded. "Deal."

Diane

"I keep thinking he's got to grow up, you know?" Kevin held a cup of coffee between his palms and seemed to stare at the black liquid. "But instead, he's getting into more serious trouble. I mean, caught with an illegal substance? What's he thinking? His life . . . it's falling apart, and he's going to destroy his mother and me in the process."

They'd chosen a corner booth. The old-fashioned high backs created a cozy nook, and the intimacy of the setting must have wooed Kevin to a place of security. He'd shared Kip's behavioral and attitude issues dating all the way back to preschool. Diane didn't want to feel sorry for Kevin, but she did. Although he expressed his worries through a veil of anger, his genuine confusion told her he wanted something better for Kip. He just didn't know where to find it.

Mother had listened in silence, breaking

off tiny pieces of her muffin and eating while Kevin talked. Diane had chosen to stay quiet, too, mostly because she had no idea how to advise him. Only by the grace of God — and Mother's prayers — had Meghan grown into the amazing young woman she was. Despite Mother's overprotectiveness, the result of a deep-seated fear of loss, she had done well raising Diane. She'd taken her to church, modeled respectfulness and responsibility, and disciplined her appropriately. Even if Diane hadn't appreciated it at the time, she appreciated it now. She waited for her mother to address the things Kevin divulged.

Mother finally pushed the last of her muffin aside. "Kevin, when you buy a building, what's the first thing you inspect?"

Both Diane and Kevin gawked at her. Had Mother been listening or daydreaming? She'd gone completely off topic.

Kevin blinked twice, picked up his cup, put it down without taking a sip, then coughed a short laugh. "The first thing? The foundation, of course."

"Why?"

He gave Diane a quick "are you kidding me?" look. "Because if the foundation is bad, there's no sense in buying it. No sense in renovating it. A bad foundation means

the whole place is bad. Eventually it'll collapse."

"Foundations are important, then?"

"Yes, that's what I just said."

For several seconds Mother sat gazing
across the table at Kevin, her lips sucked in
and her forehead puckered. Then she nodded. "Your Kip is falling apart because he
doesn't have a sound foundation. And you"
— she pointed at Kevin, her eyebrows
shooting high — "don't either."

He sat straight up. He connected with the
booth's wooden backrest with a soft thump.
He remained pressed there, as if trying to
put as much distance as possible between
Mother and himself. "Me? I'm not the nitwit."

"I didn't say you were." Mother spoke
tartly. Then her expression softened. "Tell
me what you did for fun with Kip when he
was little."

Kevin crunched his forehead. "What do
you mean?"

Mother held out her hand. "I mean fun.
Recreation. Entertainment."

Kevin stared like he'd gone into a trance.

Mother sniffed. "Honestly, for an intelligent man, you can certainly be obtuse."

Diane hid a smile. Mother was winding
up for a strike.

"Did you take him to the zoo? Play catch with him? Go for bike rides? Work puzzles together?"

Kevin gave a slow shake of his head. "No. No, I didn't."

"Why not?"

"I was working." He sounded defensive. "A person has to make a living, you know."

"Yes, I know." Mother's expression warned him to watch his tone. "So when you talked to him, what did you talk about?"

Kevin snorted. "The stupid things he'd done. Believe me, we had plenty of chances to talk."

"So you only told him what he did wrong? Never what he did right?"

He scowled. "I don't think I like where this is going."

"I'm sure you don't. But I'm going there anyway. Kevin, if you never spent time engaging with Kip other than to correct him, you likely didn't take the time to first develop a father-son relationship with him. No one likes to be told what to do by someone with whom they have no real relationship."

"So it's my fault he messes up?"

Mother sighed. "Not entirely. He's an adult now. Each of us comes to a fork in life's road when we realize there's a choice to make — continue as we've been going or follow a new path. Past experiences and influences can certainly play a role, but ultimately we make our own decisions."

Diane cringed, realizing how her decision to do the opposite of what she'd deemed her mother's paranoid protectiveness had resulted in near neglect of her daughter. Her long-held hostility had robbed her and Meghan of a meaningful relationship with Mother for years. She couldn't go back, and she believed God had forgiven her, but sometimes she still regretted her foolishness.

"Then it's Kip's problem, not mine." He sounded smug.

Mother shook her head. "You're missing the point. Deliberately, I think." She folded her arms. "Let's go back to the foundation, shall we? Granted, once a building's foundation has crumbled, there's little point in investing in it. But lives are very different than buildings. Lives are always worth investing in. As long as Kip still draws breath, there's hope for change."

Kevin winced. An odd reaction Diane wanted to explore, but Mother went on.

"You said no one could change Kip, but I think what you really meant was *you* can't change Kip. You're absolutely right about that. You can't change him. His mother can't change him. The only one who can change Kip is Kip, but even he can't do it on his own. He needs a solid foundation on which to build his life. With the foundation in place, there's hope."

Kevin's gaze narrowed. He lifted his head slightly and peered down his nose at Mother. "Are you going to preach at me?"

"Yes, I am. And you're going to listen because you need the foundation as much as Kip does." Mother opened her purse and withdrew a tiny New Testament. She'd carried it for as long as Diane could remember, and the poor little thing was battered and dog eared. She laid it on the table facing Kevin and opened it to 1 Corinthians, chapter 3. She tapped a section of text. "See here? Read it to me."

Kevin looked like he'd rather take a beating than read the verse, but he leaned forward and scowled at the tiny book. " 'For no one can lay any foundation other than the one already laid, which is Jesus Christ.' "

"Yes, Jesus Christ." Mother smiled. "At the time of this writing, people in church were trying to follow other things, other people. And Paul set them straight. If they were trying to build their lives on anything other than the truth of Jesus, their lives would crumble."

She pulled the Bible close again. "Are you familiar with the cornerstone of a building?"

Kevin rolled his eyes. "Of course I am."

Her lips twitched. "Define it for me, please."

"A cornerstone is the first stone set when constructing a masonry foundation." He spoke flatly, the way Diane's students did when they were bored with a subject. "It's the most important stone since all others will be set in reference to this stone. In other words, it determines the position of the entire structure."

"You said it's the most important stone, yes?"

He sighed, reminding Diane again of her freshman students. "Yes."

Mother flipped a few pages and turned the Bible to face him again. "Look here at Ephesians 2:20. See what it says? Christ Jesus Himself is the chief cornerstone." Tears winked in Mother's eyes. "Our structures, our lives, are doomed to collapse unless we build on the cornerstone, Jesus Christ. With Him as our foundation, our lives become stronger, more purposeful, more fulfilled. In fact, in John 10:10 we have Jesus's words sharing a very important truth."

She riffled to a page so marked up the original text was nearly obliterated. Her voice quavered as she read, " 'I have come that they may have life, and have it to the full.' " She looked at Kevin, and the joy shining in her eyes brought the sting of tears to Diane's. "Life 'to the full' is what He wants for us, and He knows we cannot have it unless we have Him. You won't find fulfillment in owning lots of properties or even in having lots of wives. Ask King Solomon for confirmation. Kip won't find it in revelry and rebellion and spending money. Your relationship as father and son will never grow and develop until you put a strong foundation of mutual love and affection beneath it."

Kevin shook his head. "Hazel, this all sounds well and good, but Kip is twenty-three years old. There's too much time gone. I can't take him on bike rides or toss a ball around with him. We can't change any of that now."

"I'm not telling you to go backward. I'm telling you to go forward. Jesus Christ wants to be your cornerstone. He wants to be your life completer. If you'll let Him in, you'll discover the change He can make. But it's your choice. Continue living on the same crumbling and collapsing foundation, or build your life on the One who was, who is, and who will always be." Mother closed the Bible, returned it to her purse, then turned a serene smile on Kevin. "You're familiar with a building's construction. Which makes more sense?"

TWENTY-NINE

Kevin

She'd gotten to him. As much as Kevin hated to admit it, Hazel's talk about a cornerstone made sense. If a building — an inanimate object — needed a solid foundation, then it seemed to follow that people needed one, too. Had Dad's life gone the direction it did because he'd lacked a cornerstone?

His heart twisted in his chest. He'd done his best to emulate Dad in business dealings and business relationships. He'd emulated Dad when parenting Kip, too — set high standards, made the boy plenty uncomfortable when he didn't meet them so he'd want to avoid disapproval. But it hadn't worked so well with Kip. Was it because Kevin had known Dad loved him but Kip didn't have that assurance with Kevin?

Kevin hung his head. "I'll admit things were rocky between Kip and me from the very first days of my marriage to Julie. I knew he'd be there — for Pete's sake, he even went on some of our dates — but I didn't realize how much a three-year-old is *there,* you know? Unless they're asleep, they're right in the middle of everything you're doing. I think I kind of resented that."

Hazel nodded. "And more likely than not, he resented you being there, too. After all, up until then, he'd had no competition for his mother's attention."

Kevin hadn't considered Kip's feelings. He'd seen Kip as a child, not a person whose thoughts and feelings really mattered. He cringed. "I think what I said most to him that first year was 'Can't you go play and leave us alone?' " Small wonder Kip hadn't liked him.

"So suddenly he had a man in the house. A dad." Hazel's tone turned musing, as if she were looking at his first marriage through a peephole into the past. "A dad who was taking time with Mom away from him and told him, in essence, to go away. So he went away, but he still wanted attention, so he . . ." She fixed her gaze on Kevin and whirled her hand in the air. "Fill in the blank for me, Kevin."

He snorted. "He broke things."

"And what did you do?"

"Let him know without any doubt he'd messed up."

"You paid attention to him."

A light went on in the back of Kevin's brain. He gaped at the older woman.

She raised her eyebrows, and her expression said, *Mm-hmm.* She folded her wrinkled hands on the edge of the table. "I have a theory I call the potato chip theory. It's very simple. Every child likes potato chips, yes?"

He couldn't argue with her statement, so he nodded.

"They prefer crisp potato chips. Who wouldn't? But if all they're offered are soggy ones, they'll take them." She leaned in slightly, and he did the same without conscious thought. "Now, replace the crisp potato chips with positive attention and the soggy ones with negative attention. Children would rather have positive attention, but if the only attention they ever receive is negative, they will do what it takes to earn it." She sat back and offered a soft smile.

He rested his head against the high seat back and sighed. "And now Kip has formed the habit of doing negative things to gain his mother's and my attention."

"So it seems," Diane said. "But if habits can be learned, they can be unlearned."

He gave a start. Diane hadn't said a word the entire time he and her mother talked, but suddenly she inserted a comment that sounded as if it came from personal experience. He settled his gaze on her serious face.

"I developed the habit of pushing God aside, of ignoring the things I knew were right. I was rebellious and foolish. But Mother never stopped praying for me to return to the foundation of faith I'd accepted when I was a child. I was older than Kip is now when I realized my error and chose to reverse my steps. It's never too late, Kevin. It's never too late to begin a relationship with God the Father through His Son, and it's never too late to fix a human relationship that's gone wrong."

He didn't reply. He didn't trust himself to reply. Because he was afraid if he opened his mouth, the unspoken question making his pulse pound and his hands tremble might find its way out. How would she respond if he asked if it was too late for them?

Fort Smith, Arkansas
Meghan

Meghan put the last of her clothing in the suitcase and zipped it closed. She could hardly wait to see Sean. Even though she'd learned some valuable things from partnering with Greg, she'd also discovered she did not want to work apart from her husband anymore. They were a team in every way that mattered.

She lifted her suitcase from the bed and turned to Sheila. "Are you ready?"

Sheila's duffle was closed, and she sat beside it, her fingers resting over the handle. Tears swam in her blue eyes.

Sympathy struck hard. If the past days had been hard for Meghan, they had to have been doubly hard for Sheila. Meghan put her suitcase on the floor, crossed to the younger woman, and sat beside her. "Are you okay?"

Sheila shrugged, her chin wobbling. "I don't know. I can't decide. There's so much all mixed up inside me, you know?"

Meghan thought she understood, so she nodded. She took Sheila's hand, surprised by how easy she found it to comfort her new friend. "Lots of secrets have held your family in limbo for a long time. But those secrets will be revealed, Sheila. Secrets in the light of day lose their power. It'll take time, but you'll overcome."

"How do you know?"

"Because you've already overcome so much. You're amazingly strong and resilient." Meghan meant every word. Sheila had carried an incredible weight of responsibility for a long time. She was wise beyond her years. "And I'll be praying for you."

Sheila leaned close and rested her head on Meghan's shoulder. "Thank you. You know, it's kind of embarrassing to say this, and it's not like I think you're super old or something, but being with you . . . having you look out for me and advise me . . . has kind of been like having a mom again."

The sweet comment winged its way to the center of Meghan's heart and lingered. She swallowed and managed to rasp, "Thank you, Sheila. That means a lot."

Sheila sat up and smiled through tears. "Thanks for being so nice to me even when I'm a pain."

Meghan laughed and pulled Sheila into a hug. "That's what moms are for. But you know . . ." She released her and grinned. "So are big sisters. Since I'm not really old enough to be your mom, is it okay if I be your big sister instead?"

Sheila's tears disappeared behind her bright smile. "I'd really like that."

"Good." Meghan stood and pulled Sheila up with her. "Let's get home then, Sis."

Sean stood with the refrigerator door open, frowning at the contents. A bag of browning chopped lettuce, a shriveled slice of days-old pizza, and a half container of sweet-and-sour chicken were the most appealing options available.

"Blech."

Cool air flowed over him, raising goose-flesh on his bare legs and torso. He closed the door and ran his hand through his damp hair. After housecleaning and yard work, he'd needed a shower. He'd intended to spend the evening vegging out in front of the television in his boxer shorts, but maybe he should get dressed and go to the grocery store. Good thing Meghan wasn't there. He'd have nothing to feed her.

He sighed. He was too pooped to shop. He'd pop a bag or two of microwave popcorn for his supper, watch a little television, and head to bed early. Tomorrow after church he'd do some shopping. The decision made, he crossed on bare feet to the cabinet above the built-in microwave and pulled out the popcorn. As he removed a plastic-wrapped bag, the front door opened.

His heart fired into his throat. Hadn't he locked it before he got in the shower? He dropped the items on the floor and lurched for his work pistol, which lay on the cabinet next to the back door.

"Sean, I'm home!"

"Meghan?" He changed course so fast his feet slid on the tile floor and he nearly went down. He regained his balance and scrambled for the front door. Meghan met him in the wide doorway between the kitchen and living room and lunged into his arms, laughing. He rocked her, his face buried in her hair. "You scared me out of a year's growth. Why didn't you tell me you were coming?"

"And miss surprising you?" She pulled back and grinned at him. "Besides, at our ages, the only direction we grow is out, and I'm happy with the shape you've got now." She teasingly patted his belly, then melted against him again. "I missed you so much."

"I missed you, too." He slipped his arm around her waist and guided her to the sofa. He sat and tugged her down half on top of him. "But why are you here? Is the case done?"

While toying with the curling hairs on his chest, she explained the latest developments in their investigation. She nestled her head in the curve of his neck. "Since Monday's Memorial Day and we can't really do anything more until Tuesday, we decided to come back." She kissed the underside of his jaw. "I'm glad, too. I really needed to see you."

A hint of desperation colored her tone. He shifted so he could look into her face. "What's wrong?"

She shook her head, crinkling her nose. "We'll have plenty of time to talk later. For now, I'm hungry."

"Well, I can tell you, there's nothing in the fridge worth eating." He slipped free and stood. "If you want something more substantial than popcorn, I better get dressed." He turned toward the hallway.

She caught his hand. "Sean, I'm hungry, but not for food." Her grin turned impish. "And you're dressed just fine."

Laughing, he captured her in a hug. "Ah, Meghan, I love you."

She gently tugged a chest hair. "Show me."

He led her up the hallway.

After church on Sunday, Sean took Meghan to their favorite Italian restaurant for lunch, and then they visited the grocery store. He pushed the cart while she loaded it with lunch meats and cheeses, frozen vegetables, pasta, ground beef, boneless chicken breasts, cod filets, and a variety of boxed and canned goods. As she added a bag of rice to the cart, he shook his head.

"Babe, what are you doing? We've got enough food in here to last three months."

"No, we don't." She pulled the cart a few feet up the aisle to the selection of dried beans. She dropped a bag of mixed beans on top of the other items, then picked up a bag of black beans and tossed it back and forth between her hands. "Mom used to boil beans in the evening and leave them soaking on the back of the stove in the water all night to soften them. But there's gotta be an easier way to cook these things. Maybe a pressure cooker? Or a slow cooker?"

He rounded the cart and took the bag from her. "Meg, seriously, we aren't home for lunch, and a lot of the time we're home late for supper. Just cooking on the weekends, we won't use this stuff up before some of it goes bad. We're wasting money." He reached to return the beans to the shelf.

She plucked the bag out of his hand and added it to the cart. "If I'm going to cook more often, I've got to have things stocked and ready to go."

He caught her hand and looked in her eyes, searching for hints of what she was thinking. "Are you going to cook more often?"

"I think so." For a moment, uncertainty flickered in her brown irises. She slipped her hand free. "I want to. Is . . . is that okay?"

"It's perfectly okay. I like home-cooked meals."

"Good." She frowned into the cart. "I need onions. And potatoes. Not frozen, fresh ones." She offered him a quizzical look. "How about a bag of little white new ones — those are so good steamed — and some whole sweet potatoes for baking? Of course, we'll want brown sugar and cinnamon to put on top of the sweet potatoes." She wrinkled her nose. "They're pretty bland otherwise."

As much as he appreciated the domestic turn she seemed to be taking, curiosity got the best of him. He gripped the cart handle and held it in place. "Meghan, what's going on? Why're you suddenly morphing into Betty Crocker?"

She turned her head and gave him a view of her sweet profile for a few seconds, then faced him again. "It's time, don't you think? You've put up with fast food and boxed meals and frozen dinners for three years. Don't you want me to . . . well, morph?"

"Not if you're doing it out of some sense of guilt, like you're not living up to your obligations." He stepped around the cart and cupped her cheek with his hand. "I love you. Whether you cook every night or not doesn't change that."

"I know."

"So all this . . ." He gestured to the full cart. "Do you still want to take it home?"

"I do."

She commandeered the handle and pushed the cart around the corner and up another aisle. He followed her, still confused but unwilling to start a serious conversation in the Carson Springs grocery store. He glanced around. They weren't anywhere near the vegetables department.

"You're going the wrong way."

"No, I'm not. I forgot something." She turned one more corner. They'd returned to the meat counter. "I want a couple of steaks for you to grill for us tomorrow. Would you rather have a T-bone or New York strip?"

"A T-bone." He leaned on the edge of the counter while she examined the steaks sealed behind plastic wrap. They bought steaks only for special celebrations or the rare occasions they had guests for dinner. "Is someone coming over tomorrow?"

"No." She held up one steak. "This one's yours. I think I want a rib eye." She inched the cart forward, scanning the displays.

Sean trailed her, his confusion mounting by the minute. "Okay, no guests. So then what are we celebrating?"

Picking through the sparse selection of individually wrapped rib eyes, she barely glanced at him. "Memorial Day."

"We've never celebrated Memorial Day before. How come we're doing it this year?"

"Because I want to."

What in the world had happened to her while she was in Fort Smith? On one hand, she was still his loving, spunky, sweetly ornery wife, but on the other hand, a stranger seemed to have replaced her. He positioned himself into her line of vision. "Meg, what's going on?"

She bit her lower lip and blinked several times, her gaze aimed at the meat. Then she looked at him out of the corners of her eyes. "Not here, Sean, okay? We'll talk. I promise we'll talk. But not here. Maybe not even today. I gotta get my thoughts sorted out first." She begged him with her expression. "Okay?"

Even though he wanted answers now, he nodded. "Okay."

Why couldn't he sleep? Sure, noise from the Strip filtered through the walls and windows, the same as it'd done every night of his time in Vegas. Footsteps, voices, occasional laughter intruded from the other side of his door. But this restlessness under his skin wasn't caused by outside noise. No, a yearning — like an itch he couldn't scratch — kept him awake and uneasy.

"Life 'to the full' is what He wants for us, and He knows we cannot have it unless we have Him."

Hazel's comment repeated itself again and again in his mind, refusing to be stilled. The Las Vegas buzz of activity didn't drown it out. The television's drone didn't cover it. His own determination to focus on something else hadn't sent it to the recesses of his mind. What was it about the words that held him captive?

"Life 'to the full' . . ." People would say he already had it, given his wealth and status. Think of all he'd attained. Sure, his marriages had flopped, but that wasn't all his fault. Marriage was a fifty-fifty partnership, so his wives had to hold part of the blame. Yes, he'd made some mistakes along the way — who hadn't? But think of what he had.

Think of what he was adding to his list of accomplishments. He had it all.

So why did he feel so empty?

He clicked the television remote, removing one source of noise. He plodded to the bathroom and dug out a pair of earplugs from his shaving bag. Situating them in his ears shut out the sounds of the city. But the voice in his head continued.

"Life 'to the full' . . ."

That's what he'd always been after.

"He knows we cannot have it unless we have Him."

Kevin stared at his reflection in the mirror. At his haggard face, his lifeless eyes, his empty soul. "You want it, don't you?" The question rasped from his tight throat, and he nodded, observing the action in the mirror.

He sank onto the edge of the tub and buried his face in his hands. "I want completeness. I want a foundation. I want . . ." He'd never been one to talk to himself. Was he losing his mind? Or was he finally reaching for something he'd needed his whole life long? A groan emerged, and it took a moment before he realized he'd been the one to emit it.

He'd never get any rest until he satisfied this deep longing in his soul. Answers waited. And he knew where to find them. With a jerk, he bounded to his feet. He half stumbled, half ran to the dresser and yanked out the drawer containing the books he'd seen when he checked in. The Bible slid to the front. He lifted it out and flopped across the bed. But his fingers froze. Where should he begin? He huffed. Why not at the beginning?

He peeled back the cover, and the opening line on a piece of paper glued inside the front flap caught his attention. *Do you want to be saved?* An outline of step-by-step directions followed. And Kevin followed the directions.

THIRTY

Kendrickson, Nevada
Diane

Diane turned off the ignition and sighed. She turned to Mother, who sat quiet and somber in the passenger seat. "I wonder why he didn't come."

Mother sighed. "I don't know, but I'm as disappointed as you are."

Diane doubted Mother's disappointment matched hers. She never thought she would formulate a friendship, shaky as it was, with the man who'd abandoned her thirty-two years ago when she needed him most. But after the intense conversation they'd shared yesterday — the way he opened up and exposed a piece of his soul to them — she expected him to accept the invitation they'd given to join them for church and lunch afterward. But she and Mother had sat alone during the service, and they'd eaten alone at Mother's favorite buffet. No sign of Kevin.

He'd abandoned her again.

"Maybe . . . sometimes . . . it is too late."

"What?"

Diane hadn't realized she'd spoken aloud. She shook her head and pulled her keys free. "Never mind. We'd better get in and let the dogs out. They've been locked up for almost three hours. Duchess especially will need out."

They entered the house through the garage to a chorus of yips and yelps. Diane ushered the trio of dachshunds out the back door into the small enclosed backyard, then went to her room to change. She dropped her purse on the bed, and her cell phone bounced out. The little red light that signaled a missed call winked at her. Had Meghan finally called back?

She picked up the phone and pressed the Home button. The screen lit, and she pulled up the list of missed calls. At the top of the list wasn't Meghan's name and number but Kevin's. He'd called, but he hadn't left a voice mail. She chewed the inside of her cheek. Should she call him and ask what he'd needed? Or should she let it go and wait to see if he'd call again?

Mother wandered around the corner. "Margaret Diane, I just turned on my phone. I have a missed call from —"

Diane held up her phone.

"You, too?"

"Yes. Did he leave you a message?"

Mother checked her phone. "No, he didn't." She pressed the phone against her bodice, worry etched into her features. "Do you think something's wrong?"

If something was wrong, he wouldn't call them. He'd call his lawyer. "He was probably trying to let us know something came up and he wouldn't be at church, that's all." She turned on her phone's ringer and returned it to her purse. "If it's important enough, he'll call back."

"I suppose you're right." Mother ambled out of the room.

Diane scowled at her purse, envisioning her phone inside. "I hope I'm right."

Dallas, Texas
Kevin

Kevin checked his cell phone one last time. Still no call from either Diane or her mother. He grimaced and set the phone to Airplane Mode. He dropped it into his pocket, rested his head against the first-class seat's cushioned headrest, and released a long, slow breath. He shouldn't be surprised neither had called him. He hadn't left messages. For all they knew, he'd pocket dialed them by mistake.

"Sir, would you like a beverage? We have beer, wine, soft drinks, and a variety of mixed drinks." The pretty brunette in a stewardess dress held a notepad and pencil and smiled at him.

Strange how he had no desire to flirt with her. "No, thank you, I'm fine."

"All right. You let me know if you change your mind." She turned to the pair of men across the aisle.

Kevin closed his eyes and blocked the sight of passengers shuffling past with carry-ons. His phone seemed heavy in his shirt pocket. Should he call again? He quickly discounted the idea. No way he'd talk on the airplane. Not with so many other people around to overhear. He'd have to wait until he was back in Fort Smith.

He should've left a message the first time, but he'd lost his nerve. Especially with Diane. What voice-mail program had enough minutes available to make amends for what he'd done to her way back when? As for Hazel, it'd seemed too impersonal to put a heartfelt thank-you in a cell phone's voice mail. Since he wouldn't be able to see her face when he told her that after a night of wrestling with himself he'd decided to build his foundation from this day forward on Jesus Christ, he at least wanted to hear the joy in her voice.

He didn't make too many people joyful these days, and he wanted to carry the memory of having done so for her. Because he knew she'd be joyful. Maybe even over-joyful, if there was such a word. She was the kind of person who celebrated good things happening for others.

If he didn't get a chance to talk to either of them before Tuesday, they'd know he had left town when they went to the loft apartment and Jim Connolly — go figure, he had been able to reach the plumber — told them he'd flown back to Fort Smith. Last-minute flights weren't cheap, but the expense was minimal compared to the cost of bailing Kip out of trouble. As soon as he got home, he'd pay a visit to Julie and Kip.

He tried to imagine his son's reaction when he apologized for giving him soggy potato chips instead of crisp ones and asked for a chance to start over. Kip might laugh in his face, might tell him to get lost, might spew a whole lot of ugliness. But Kevin had made up his mind to listen patiently, not to give up, to build the foundation he should've built twenty years ago.

In the hotel room Bible, he'd come across

a verse spoken by Jesus to His followers. Something like, "Lo, I am with you always." The King James Version sounded a lot like Shakespeare. When he got home, he'd buy his own Bible. Probably King James. He intended to show Kip the verse and tell him that from now on, he could count on two people being there for him — Jesus and his dad. Always.

Kip wasn't the only one he needed to build a relationship with. It'd be hard — harder maybe than anything he'd ever done — but he wanted to contact Meghan. He wouldn't ask to be her father. He didn't deserve the title after what he'd done. But maybe she'd let him be her friend. That would be enough.

"Welcome aboard Flight 5957, with service from Dallas–Fort Worth to Fort Smith, Arkansas," the chipper voice crackled over the intercom.

Time to buckle up and fly.

Kendrickson, Nevada
Diane

At a quarter of ten Sunday evening as Diane changed into her pajamas, her phone rang. Visions of emergencies dancing in her brain, she snatched it up. Kevin's name and number showed on the screen. She hit Accept Call and jammed the phone to her ear. "Kevin? Where are you?"

"In Fort Smith. Put your phone on speaker and get your mom, will you?"

Diane pattered through the house to her mother's room, phone against her head. "We looked for you this morning, and we were worried when you didn't show. Why didn't you leave a message when you called? Mother's spent the whole day worrying." She tapped on the door. "Mother? May I come in?"

"I'm sorry. I'll explain as soon as you have her listening in."

Mother called "Come on in" at the same time Kevin spoke. Diane entered the bedroom, switching her phone to speaker as she headed for the bed. She held up the phone and showed her mother. "Kevin's on the line. He wants to talk to both of us."

Mother sat up and grabbed the phone. "Kevin, are you all right? You worried us."

Diane preferred he didn't know how he'd worried her, but it was too late now.

"I'm sorry about that. I did call — I tried both of you, but neither of you answered. And what I wanted to say didn't really work for a phone message. So I had to wait until I got home."

Diane glanced at the clock. "You're just

now getting home at almost midnight?"

"Yeah. Layover in Dallas. I guess I could've called from there, but what I have to say is too personal to be said in a busy airport."

Mother frowned and shook the phone. "Young man, it's late. Let's get on with it."

Kevin's laughter rang. "Yes, ma'am. You asked if I was all right. Well, I am. I'm more all right than I've ever been. I met Jesus last night in my hotel room. He's my cornerstone now, and I'll be building better things for the rest of my life."

Diane clapped her hand over her mouth to hold back her cry of elation. Mother didn't stifle hers. Diane's ears rang from the shrill "Ohhhhh! Praise the Lord!"

Kevin laughed again. "I have been. I've also been asking Him what I can do to make things right with my son. I plan to go see him tomorrow, to apologize and ask to start over. I don't know how he'll respond, and I confess . . . I have some trouble controlling my temper when someone gets obnoxious. Would you pray I handle myself well?"

"Of course we will." Mother nudged Diane. "Won't we?"

"Yes. Yes, we will."

"Thanks." Kevin's voice quavered. "Thanks for everything. Now, Hazel, I'll let you get to sleep. Diane, could we talk a minute longer?"

"Good night, Kevin." Mother beamed at the phone, her eyes glittering. "Thank you for calling and letting us know. All the angels in heaven are rejoicing with us." A smirk creased her cheek as she handed the phone over. "Here's Margaret Diane."

Diane turned off the speaker feature and put the phone to her ear. "Okay, it's just me now." She closed Mother's door behind her and hurried to the living room. She sat in Mother's chair and pulled her feet up. "What's going on? Why'd you go back to Fort Smith without saying anything?"

"I'm really sorry about leaving without telling you. As I said, I did try to call, but your phones must have been off. I can't really explain why I felt the urge to book a flight and go home so quick. I just kept feeling like there was more I needed to do here than there was to do there."

If the Holy Spirit had prompted him to go home, she shouldn't argue. But hurt lingered. "I'll be honest, Kevin. When you didn't show today, it took me back to college, to when you weren't there for me then, either."

"I'm sorry, Diane. I really am." The brokenness in his voice proved his sincerity.

Tears stung Diane's eyes. "It's okay. I understand you needed to go home."

"No, you don't understand. I'm sorry for more than leaving this morning. I'm sorry for every day you spent raising Meghan alone. I'm sorry for the financial support you didn't receive from me. I'm sorry for the shame you were forced to endure because of my stupidity. There's nothing I can do or say that will change the past, but if there's anything I can do to make it right, anything you need, anything Meghan or your mom needs . . . ever . . . call me. Okay?"

Diane sighed. "Kevin, that's kind but really unnecessary. You've apologized. I've" — her throat tightened as emotions rolled through her — "forgiven you. I don't hold any grudges. Honest." It was amazing how good it felt to say it all out loud.

"Thank you." His voice turned husky, as if his throat had closed up, too. "There's one more thing, and then I'll let you go because I am beyond tuckered. I'll be seeing my lawyer this week. I'm changing my will. Meghan's my daughter. She deserves half of my assets, equal to Kip."

Diane's heart skipped a beat. "Won't that create more issues in your relationship with Kip?"

401

A wry chuckle rumbled. "Kip doesn't know he's my beneficiary, so no worries there. Besides, there's enough to be split two ways and he'll still land in tall clover."

Diane didn't know how to respond to his statement, so she remained silent. The grandfather clock ticktocked in steady, rhythmic beats. One of the dachshunds — probably Molly — whined. Then Kevin spoke again.

"Thanks again for letting me sneak back into your life. You could've slammed the door on my foot and I wouldn't have blamed you. But you let me in. And I'll never be the same. Good night, Diane." The connection ended.

Diane stared at the blank screen for a few seconds, replaying his tender farewell. *"I'll never be the same,"* he'd said. She wouldn't be, either. She couldn't determine an exact moment, but sometime in the past two weeks, she'd stopped being angry at herself for the mistake she'd made in college. She was so much more than an unwed mother, and it was time to let go of the regret and simply appreciate being molded into the person God had designed her to be.

Would she have come to this place of recognition if not for having to encounter her past face to face? Maybe. But maybe not.

A sigh, one of contentment, eased from her throat. She tipped her temple against the padded headrest and whispered, "Good night, Kev. And thanks."

THIRTY-ONE

Meghan flopped into her folding yard chair, held her stomach, and groaned. "Oh, I'm so full. I should have saved half my steak for tomorrow."

"Eat, drink, and be merry, for tomorrow we diet." Sean grinned.

Meghan laughed. What a wonderful morning they'd enjoyed. Sleeping late, giggling while eating bowls of the kids' cereal she'd accidentally picked up in place of their standard raisin bran, then working together in the kitchen preparing their lunch. Sean grilled the steaks to perfection, and he complimented Meghan's tossed salad, steamed new potatoes, and whole green beans so many times that her cheeks were probably permanently red from blushing. But his praise lifted her heart. She *could* cook. She *could* do some of the things his

404

mother had done for his family.

She reached across the short expanse between their chairs and took his hand. "Sean, I told you about the case in Fort Smith, but I didn't tell you everything that happened. Are you awake enough to listen?"

He rolled his head to the side on the seat's woven back and erased the humor from his expression. "Of course I am. I've been wondering when you'd tell me what's bothering you."

"Well, first of all, nothing's bothering me. Not like a problem, okay?" She licked her lips, trying to decide how to begin. She'd turned her thoughts over in her mind so many times, but somehow articulating them didn't come easily. "It's kind of about Sheila, kind of about me, and mostly about us."

"Then I need to know what it is." He squeezed her hand. "Go ahead. I'm listening."

Meghan drew in a breath, filling her nostrils with the mingled scents of charcoal, fresh-cut grass, and cooked beef — an aroma she wished she could bottle. "Sheila told me something Saturday before we left the hotel that totally blew me out of the water. She said I reminded her of her mother." She searched Sean's face for signs of disbelief or doubt, but his expression remained unchanged. "She said I acted like her mother in the way I advised her and looked out for her even though she could be something of a, well, 'a pain' is the word she used."

A grin lifted one corner of Sean's lips. "I could see that."

Meghan grinned, too. "She can also be a real sweetheart. I decided that from now on she's my adopted little sister."

Sean's smile grew. "Works for me."

His easy acceptance gave her the courage to go on. "The thing is, I didn't think there was anything inside me that could be a good mother. I love Mom to pieces, but she was nothing like your mom was to you when you were growing up. Then I looked at the legacy of mother-daughter relationships from Grandma and her mom, to Mom and Grandma, and finally Mom and me. They all had conflict at the center. I didn't want to carry that legacy on with my child. Then I met my father's son and saw how he turned out —"

Sean's jaw dropped. "You met your father's adopted son? Where? How?"

Meghan explained ordering a pizza and it being delivered by Kip Harrison. "A chance meeting, but wow, it really shook me up. I had hoped maybe at least my father had some paternal instincts, something I might have inherited, but then I met Kip. Added to that, the desk clerk, who'd gone to high school with him, told me some things about him, and . . . Whew." She shook her head, blowing out a breath. "That pretty much let me know I wasn't going to inherit any great parenting genes from my father, either."

She closed her eyes, remembering Sheila briefly laying her head against Meghan's shoulder in the hotel room. "But maybe I put too much importance on my gene pool. I mean, Sheila saw something maternal in me. And there were moments during the week when I felt maternal toward her. Protective. Sympathetic. Even a little annoyed sometimes, like I wanted to tell her to straighten up, you know?"

Sean grinned. "That sounds like a mom."

Meghan laughed, then quickly sobered. "The thing is, Sean, you inherited some really great traits from your parents that need to be passed to the next generation. I inherited some good things, too. Like faithfulness, a good work ethic, moral values, even stubbornness."

He raised his brows. "Stubbornness?"

"Yes. *Stubbornness* is just another word for determination, and determination is a positive trait."

He squeezed her hand. "It sure is."

She pulled in another breath, savoring the scents that spoke of a new season coming to life. "All this is meant to say that I was wrong to refuse to think about having children."

Sean's fingers convulsed, and his body tensed. Hope ignited in his eyes.

"I based my decision on fear. But God doesn't give us a spirit of fear. I can't let fear get in the way anymore." Her lips quivered, but she managed to form a smile. "If our kids turn out half as handsome and kind and wonderful as you, I'll feel like the most successful mother in the history of the world."

Sean leaped out of his chair, swooped her into his arms, and delivered a warm, lengthy, joyful kiss. She clung, savoring the salty taste of steak on his lips. Or maybe she was tasting her own tears. Releasing her fear had sprung a leak. But she didn't begrudge them. Happy tears were always welcome.

He set her on the ground but kept his arms looped around her waist. She left hers around his neck and smiled up at him. The sunshine glistened on his dark-brown hair and brought out the rich, deep brown in his irises that usually seemed almost black. His square jaw showed a shadow, enhancing his manliness. Incredibly handsome, respectful, honest, even-tempered, God-honoring — he was as close to perfect as a man could get. And he was her husband. He would be such a wonderful father to their children.

"Sean?"

"Yes, babe?"

"I could never have imagined being so blessed."

He touched his forehead to hers and closed his eyes. "Me neither, babe. Me neither."

"Sean?"

His eyes slid open, but he didn't release his hold or lift his head.

"Greg said something to Sheila about her dad that's stuck with me. He said, 'Don't let bitterness erase the memories.' I don't know if I'll get in touch with my dad, but would you pray for me to know what to do? And that even if I don't ever have a relationship with him, I won't let bitterness about him taking off on Mom create problems in my other relationships? I don't want any of the memories I'll be gathering in the future to be tarnished by bitterness."

Sean kissed the end of her nose and drew her to the chairs. "Let's pray about that right now." She bowed her head, and Sean began, "Dear heavenly Father . . ."

THIRTY-TWO

Fort Smith, Arkansas
Kevin

Kevin pulled up in front of the house he'd shared with Julie and Kip for eight years. He killed the engine, then draped his wrist over the steering wheel and stared out the window at the brick 1980s cookie-cutter ranch. One thing about Julie, she kept things neat. Her gardener was doing a good job with the yard, too. The bushes out front were nicely shaped, no leaves littered the grass, and he didn't spot a single dandelion, even though the neighbors' yards were dotted with yellow.

After their divorce, he'd stewed about her taking the house and sticking him with an apartment, but now he was glad he hadn't fought for the house. Kids needed the stability of a home. He hadn't given Kip much else, but at least he'd given him that.

He hadn't called before coming. With it

being Memorial Day, the post office where Julie had clerked for as long as he'd known her was closed. So she'd be home. Murray's Pizza, however, was open seven days a week. If Kip was actually working these days, he might be gone. If he was, Kevin would get his son's schedule from Julie and come back at a better time. Sure, he could've gotten the information by texting, but he'd hidden behind impersonal texts for too many years. He wanted his ex-wife and son to see his face, to see his body language, to see that he had changed.

He felt so different it had to show, right?

He left the car and strode up the driveway to the front door. Sunshine beamed down, and a soft breeze teased — a perfect almost-summer day. When he was done here, he intended to drive to his mother's place and spend an hour or two with her. Memorial Day, a day of remembering those who had served. Dad served two years in the U.S. Army, required by every graduating male back in his day. Maybe they'd visit the cemetery. Dad wouldn't want flowers on his grave, but he and Mom could make sure the custodians at Memorial Gardens were taking care of his plot, maybe reminisce a little bit. He cringed. Or maybe not.

The porch, small and square, was deeply

inset and fully shaded. A tiny camera, something new since the last time he'd been there, blinked from the upper-right corner. He glanced at it, then pressed his finger against the doorbell button. Even though he hadn't lived here for a dozen years, it still felt weird pushing the doorbell. Before it stopped chiming, the interior door swung open and Julie, wearing a royal-blue lounging suit that brought out the brilliant blue of her eyes, stood framed in the full-glass screen door.

He offered a half smile and little wave.

She cracked the screen door. "Who died?"

"What?"

"Somebody must have died." She glanced up and down his length. "Black slacks, button-down shirt and tie . . . You're even wearing dress shoes. You look like you've been to a funeral."

Kevin released a nervous laugh. He'd spiffed up to set a good example for his son. He rubbed his fresh-shaved cheek. "Nobody died." Except himself to sin, according to the *What Does It Mean to Be Saved?* booklet he'd downloaded to his tablet and read while on the plane. "I came to see Kip. Is he here?"

"Yes." With a graceful sweep of her wrist, she tossed a heavy strand of highlighted blond hair over her shoulder. "But he might not want to talk to you. This is a rough time for him."

A sarcastic comment formed on Kevin's tongue, but he held it inside. He nodded, sending up a brief request for self-control. He sure hoped Hazel and Diane were praying, like they'd said they would. "That's okay if he doesn't want to talk. I'd still like to see him."

She shrugged and stepped out of the way. "Come on in, then." Kevin crossed the threshold and waited on the patch of tile inside the door while Julie went to the basement opening. "Kip? Will you come up, please? There's" — her shoulders stiffened — "someone here to see you."

"Who is it? I'm in the middle of something."

Kip's reply made Kevin wince. How many times had he used that excuse to put off answering his son's request for attention?

"It's your dad."

Moments later, feet pounded on the stairs. Only six thumps, which told Kevin that Kip took them two at a time. He rounded the corner, came to a stop several feet away, and gaped at Kevin.

Kevin couldn't help but stare in return. When had Kip last seen a barber? His shaggy hair fell over his eyes like a sheep-dog's hair, and his clothes were wrinkled and baggy, the pant legs dragging. But it was his bare feet that captured Kevin's full attention. Long, with dark hair growing on his big toes. A man's feet.

Sadness struck. So many years lost . . . He swallowed and forced a smile. "Hi, Kip."

Kip sauntered closer, giving his head a little jerk that shifted his bangs. "I s'pose you're here to bawl me out over the mari-juana thing." He set his bare man-feet wide and folded his arms. "You can save the lecture. I already know I messed up. That's what I do best, right?"

Kevin gestured to the floral sofa. "Can we sit? There's something I'd like to say, but I promise it isn't a lecture. Okay?"

His son seemed to measure him through slit lids, then gave a brusque nod. "All right. But make it quick, huh? I'm kinda busy." He scuffed to the sofa and flopped onto the center cushion.

Julie took a step in the direction of the kitchen. "I think I'll —"

Kevin held his hand to her. "No, please join us. I have something to say to you, too."

Uncertainty marred her still-beautiful features, but she changed course and sat next to Kip. Kevin chose one of the barrel

415

chairs facing the couch and seated himself. He leaned forward, elbows on his knees, and looked Kip straight in the eyes. "Son, I'm sorry."

The bored expression flashed to confusion, then twisted into a derisive scowl. "Oh, yeah. Sorry you adopted me, right?"

Kevin had expected as much. Maintaining eye contact, he shook his head. "I'm sorry I adopted you but then didn't treat you like a son."

Kip and Julie exchanged a glance. Kip flapped the hem of his stretched-out, holey T-shirt. "Whadda you mean?"

"I mean I should've spent time with you. Been more patient and loving. I treated you more like an intrusion in my relationship with your mother than as my child, and I was wrong. I only gave you" — he swallowed a grin, hearing Hazel's voice in his head — "soggy potato chips when you really wanted crisp ones."

Julie and Kip frowned. She shook her head. "You aren't making a great deal of sense."

Kevin kept his focus on his son. "I should've noticed the good things you did instead of only hollering about the bad things. You did a lot of good things, Kip. I remember how you used to draw and color

416

and build things with blocks and Tinkertoys. I wish I'd told you then, but since I didn't, I'm telling you now. You have a talent for making things."

Kip's hair drifted over his eyes again. He pushed it aside. "Okay. So?"

The insolence stirred Kevin's frustration. He glanced down and noted greenish stains on Kip's feet. He pointed. "Are those grass stains?"

Kip lifted his foot and peeked at its sole. "Yeah. Guess so."

Julie tsk-tsked. "I told you to wash your feet after you mowed this morning. You'll leave marks on the carpet."

Kevin sat up and stared at Julie. "You don't have a gardener taking care of the yard?"

Julie pursed her lips. "How would I afford a gardener? No, Kip takes care of the grass and landscaping."

Kevin turned a genuinely astounded look on Kip. "The yard looks fantastic. I noticed when I pulled up, and I inwardly commended the gardener. You're the gardener? Good job."

Kip blew out a snide breath. "It's just grass and bushes, Dad. No need to have a stroke over it." But something — gratitude? confidence? — flickered in his eyes.

Kevin laughed. He held up both hands as if surrendering, then dropped them to the chair's armrests. "Okay. The point is, Kip, I wasn't a very good dad, and I really want to change that. If you'll let me, I'd like to spend more time with you. Maybe go to a ball game this summer or take a weekend trip somewhere."

"Like where?"

"I don't know." Kip was too old for the standard weekend go-tos like amusement parks or zoos. "What sounds fun?"

Kip's lips twitched. "Las Vegas? Take in some shows, hit a few slots?"

Kevin grinned. "I'll think about it." Then he sobered and leaned forward again, propping himself up with his elbows on his knees, and settled his gaze on Kip. "There's something we should have done as a family when you were growing up, something that probably would have made a lot of difference in how things went down between your mother and me and in how I raised you. We should've gone to church. I'm going to start attending. I'll be . . . I don't know what to call it . . . shopping around for a church over the next few weeks. I'd really like it if you'd come with me. We could make Sundays our day."

Kip shook his head. "No, thanks. I remember 'our' Sundays when I was a kid."

Kevin remembered them, too. Kip locked in his room watching cartoons on the little television Kevin had put in there to keep him occupied while Kevin did paperwork. Remorse struck hard. "Those weren't really together days, were they? These would be different. I don't know you, and I want to get to know you. You don't have to answer right now. Think about it. But if you're not working at Murray's on Sunday, I'd like to pick you up, have you church shop with me, then grab dinner and . . . talk."

Silence fell in the room. Kevin waited, observing his son's lazy pose and bored expression. Yet his eyes — his vivid blue eyes that used to beg for someone to notice him — seemed to glimmer with something Kevin hoped was interest.

Finally Kip sighed. "I dunno, Dad. This seems fishy to me, you coming in after I totally messed up and not even saying a word about it. I'll think about doing the Sunday thing, but I'm not making any promises. It's not like I'm twelve and you can buy me off with a skateboard."

Kevin held up his hand, Boy Scout style. "No more buying off." He pointed at Kip. "And no more paying off, either. As you said, you're not a little kid anymore, so from now on, if you get yourself into trouble, you're going to have to get yourself out." He shifted his gaze to include Julie. "Your mother and I will always be here for you, to encourage you and advise you, but we've got to step back and let you be responsible for yourself. It's time."

She didn't speak, but a tiny bob of her head let him know that she'd heard him.

He stood, crossed the short expanse of carpet, and sat on the sofa's armrest. He put his hand on Kip's shoulder. "You're too smart to spend your life hanging out in your mother's basement. You're too talented to waste your time playing video games. This isn't a lecture, Kip. It's a suggestion. Ditch Murray's, look for a job that'll let you make use of the abilities God planted in you, and take care of yourself. You'll be a lot happier if you start building good habits instead of wallowing in these old, harmful practices."

Still gripping his son's skinny shoulder, Kevin summoned as much courage as he could find. "And listen . . . I want you to make a promise. From now on, no matter what happens — good, bad, or indifferent — there'll be no talk of doing away with yourself."

Kip flinched. He squirmed, but Kevin didn't lift his hand.

"Suicide is a permanent solution to a temporary problem. I know that sounds like a platitude, but it's the truth. Life is always changing. There's always hope for improvement, but if you end your life, you won't ever experience the good." He closed his eyes for a moment, reliving past memories and pain that made it hard for him to breathe. He looked into Kip's youthful, belligerent face. "My dad killed himself a few years before I married your mom."

Julie's mouth fell open, and Kip sat up, dislodging Kevin's hand.

Kevin cupped his shaking hand over his knee. "Money was always important to Dad — he thought it gave him power. He did business with some people who weren't on the up-and-up, and he did it on purpose because there was money to be made. The truth was about to come to light, and he was facing some significant jail time. Worse, in his opinion, his reputation would be tarnished. He couldn't handle it, so he got himself soused with one-hundred-eighty-proof whiskey and took a deliberate tumble down our cellar stairs."

Kip looked skeptical. "Sounds like an accident to me. How do you know he fell on purpose?"

"He told my mom and me so in a letter."

Kevin paused, his heart hammering in his chest. He was breaking a promise to Mom by sharing the whole truth, but Kip needed to hear it. "I've never told anybody else about that letter until now. But I want you to know how wrong he was. How much pain he caused."

Both Kip and Julie stared at him, and he was certain he glimpsed sympathy in Julie's expression, but neither spoke.

Kevin sighed. "My mother has never forgiven herself for not being more aware and stopping him. She lives every day with regret and heartache. I know you love your mom, Kip. Don't do that to her. Don't even think about doing that to her. From now on, when it comes to the subject of suicide, you don't think it, you don't say it, and you for sure don't do it. If you start to think it, you call me and we'll talk it through. Agreed?"

Julie gripped Kip's elbow. "Promise him, Kip. Promise me."

Kip glanced from his mother to his dad and then lowered his gaze. He nodded, his hair flopping. "Okay. Okay, I promise."

Relief flooded Kevin. He rose. "I guess that's all I came to say. Julie, please keep me updated on Kip's court dates. I want to be there for those. And, Kip, let me know about Sunday. I'd sure like to have your company."

Kip didn't look up, but he nodded.

Julie walked Kevin to the door. He stopped and set his hand on the doorknob. "Thanks for letting me come in."

Her lips quivered with a half smile. "Thanks for coming." She touched his arm. "Really, Kevin, thanks."

THIRTY-THREE

Little Rock, Arkansas
Sean

Sean drove Meghan to Greg Dane's house early Tuesday morning. They needed to pick up Sheila on the way, so Greg requested a seven o'clock departure. Sean slid Meghan's suitcase into the back of Greg's SUV, then pulled her into his embrace.

"Call me this evening. Let me know what you find out."

"I will. I'll be praying you get a lead on Stony Dunsbrook's location."

"Thanks, babe."

She kissed him full on the mouth. "Make sure you miss me."

"You don't have to worry about that. I miss you already."

Greg slammed the hatch lid closed and groaned. "You two could make a person gag." But he grinned, ruining the insult.

Sean waved the pair down the road, then

climbed into his Bronco and drove to work. The parking garage was largely empty, given the early hour, but one car stood out. A car Sean hadn't expected to see. He trotted the distance between the garage and the cold-case building and let himself in with his key. The elevator carried him to the fourth floor. The unit's doors were standing open, letting the AC flow into the landing.

He strode in and went directly to Tom Farber's desk. Farber sat hunched over his computer, red-rimmed eyes seemingly glued to the screen. Sean gave him a quick inspection and grimaced. How long had it been since the man shaved? Or changed his clothes? Farber had been away from the office for only a few days, but he seemed like he'd aged ten years.

Sean perched on the edge of Farber's desk and crossed his arms. "How long have you been here?"

Farber flicked a frown at him and returned his attention to the screen. "Since four or so. I couldn't sleep, and there wasn't anything to do at my house, so I came in. I needed a distraction."

If Sean's nose was working correctly, he also needed a bath. "Cap said you'd be out for a couple of weeks. Sure surprised me to see your car in the garage. It's good to have you back, though. Glad you feel up to work-ing."

Farber snorted. "It's not a matter of feel-ing up to it. It's a matter of this is all I've got, so I came in."

Sean glanced at the big round clock on the wall. Only a quarter past seven. They weren't officially on duty until eight. That gave him some leeway. He braced his palm on Farber's desk and leaned toward him. "Tom?"

The detective's bushy eyebrows de-scended. His gaze traveled from Sean's hand to his face. "Since when are we on a first-name basis?"

Sean held eye contact even though every part of him wanted to flinch away from the resentment blazing in Farber's pale-green eyes. "We're off duty. There's nobody else here. It won't hurt a thing for us to be friendly. And I have to tell you, Tom, if you're trying to make this job your every-thing, you're going to find it sorely dis-satisfying."

Farber pushed back from his desk and folded his arms tightly over his chest. He tapped his foot on the floor. The rhythmic thuds echoed in the large room. "Well, aren't you the bringer of cheer? Nice thing to tell a man whose family walked out on him. I can't even drown my sorrows since I gave up the sauce. I had to or Cap says forget being promoted. Can't you let me at least hold on to my position as detective?"

"I'm not trying to take it away from you. There's nothing wrong with finding pleasure or purpose in work. Even the Bible says hard work brings a profit. But this job is only that — a job. It's not going to fill the empty place inside that you tried to fill with alcohol."

Farber's expression turned fierce. He balled his hands in to fists. "What've I told you about preaching at me? I'll file a suit. I'll —"

"You can try. But it'll get nowhere because we aren't on the job right now. Not until eight, so I have the freedom to say what I want to say for the next forty-five minutes."

"And I've got the freedom to tune you out."

Sean shrugged. "You sure do. But do you really want to tune me out? Think of it this way. If you were walking blindfolded straight toward a cliff, would you want someone to call your name and keep you from stepping over the edge?"

Farber blasted a laugh. "That's dumb. I'm not blindfolded and walking toward a cliff."

"Not physically, but you are spiritually."

Sean sent up a silent prayer for guidance. He didn't want to say too much and scare Farber off, but the man needed to hear the truth. He needed to find a purpose in living. Farber needed Jesus.

Sean sat up and laid his linked hands in his lap. "Believe me, Tom, your spiritual life is much more important than your physical one. Physical life is temporary. It ends when we release our last breath. But spiritual life? It goes into eternity. Do you want to spend eternity separated from God the Father?"

Farber shot out of the chair and rushed at Sean. He gritted his teeth, nearly snarling. "I told you I don't want you preaching at me. I've heard it all before. There's another verse somewhere that says there's nothing new under the sun. Well, it's true when it comes to spouting your religious nonsense. My old man pounded the Bible into me when I was growing up. Oh, how upright and holy he made himself to be. But then he had an affair and left us. So what good was his so-called Christianity? It was worthless."

The detective carried hurt and hatred like the stench of body odor. Years of bitterness had hardened his heart, and it started because his father, the one who'd quoted Scripture and taught his son about God, had chosen a sinful path. His father had left, and now his wife had left. Sean hung his head. God was a great healer, but he hadn't realized how much healing Farber needed.

He lifted his head and met Farber's angry glare. "I'm sure sorry. When someone we love lets us down, it affects us. I'm gonna say one more thing, and then I'll be quiet, okay? God's not people. He doesn't leave us. He doesn't let us down. Whatever He does is out of His deep love for us and His desire for us to live lives of joy. So don't blame God for your father's choices. God didn't want that for you, either."

Farber stared at Sean for several silent seconds, his jaw shifting back and forth and his fists clenching and unclenching. He lurched, and Sean expected to feel a fist in his face, but Farber grabbed his chair, jammed it closer to the desk, then leaned on it. He cocked his head. "You done?"

Sean nodded.

"Good. Now it's my turn to talk." He pointed to his computer screen. "I might've found Stony Dunsbrook."

Fort Smith, Arkansas
Meghan
"Hmm, here's something. In Florida." Meghan leaned back and made room for

Greg to look at her computer screen. The tiny resource room tucked in an upstairs corner of the city library made a perfect away-from-home office. Not a soul around besides her, Greg, and Sheila. Their two hours at the Sebastian County Courthouse turned up nothing more than what they'd already learned about Thames's and Wallingford's upscale but not over-the-top property holdings in Fort Smith, but Greg's suggestion to search in every state in the U.S. proved lucrative. She wished she'd thought of it.

At the library, they'd decided to divide and conquer. Greg researched Michael Thames, and Meghan took Darryl Wallingford. Greg hadn't found a single hit, but Meghan's finds were proving telling.

"What is it?" Sheila left her chair and leaned over Meghan's shoulder.

"A three-bedroom house in Stuart. Beachfront."

Greg whistled. "That'd cost a pretty penny. Does it say when he took ownership?"

Meghan scrolled down a bit. "It looks like . . . January 1999. The title's clear, and according to the last purchase records, he paid not quite a quarter million dollars." She blew out a little breath. "It'd probably cost twice that now."

"So he bought that one three years before Daddy disappeared." Sheila straightened. "When did you say he bought the one in Breckenridge, Colorado?"

Meghan peeked at her notes. "In 1996. Paid a little over one hundred sixty-five grand, and the title is clear, same as the one in Florida."

Sheila shook her head. "Clear back in '96. How could he take money for so many years and nobody notice?"

Greg grunted. "I guess a little at a time." He tapped on his computer keys with his usual hunt-and-peck method. "So two properties purchased outright. That used up about four hundred thousand dollars, but that leaves a lot not accounted for."

"Do you think he has houses in other states, too?" Sheila chewed her thumbnail, her gaze zipping back and forth between Meghan and Greg.

"It's possible." Meghan turned sideways in her chair. "But a person could spend quite a bit on travel, entertainment, and smaller luxuries that might not stick out."

Sheila brightened. "Like a yacht?"

Greg laughed. "A yacht would definitely stick out around here."

Sheila made a face at him. "Not here. In

Florida. Meghan said it was beachfront. Someone who lives next to the water might want a boat. And a yacht would be better than a rowboat."

"Lots better," Greg said. "Let's see what I can find."

While Meghan researched Georgia, the next state in alphabetical order, Greg pulled up the database for yacht owners in the U.S. Meghan didn't find anything in Georgia, but as she typed *Hawaii,* he let out a yelp.

"Hey, look here." Sheila hurried over and peered at his screen. Meghan leaned sideways and looked, too. He grinned and pointed. "Mr. Darryl Wallingford of Fort Smith, Arkansas, is the owner of a 2007 Four Winns Horizon 290 OB. Not a luxury yacht — those run in the millions — but still a pretty nice boat to cruise around in. Sheila, you'd make a good investigator." He held up his palm, and Sheila laughingly high-fived him.

Meghan smiled. Greg's attitude toward Sheila had sure changed. But then again, Sheila's attitude toward the two of them had changed, too. "Does it say what he paid for it?"

Greg turned back to his computer. "No, but given the parameters for inclusion, it wouldn't show up in this particular database unless it was at least 150K."

"So even if we go by the conservative amount of one hundred fifty thousand, added to the houses we found, there's more than half a million dollars spent. By someone who brings in a salary of eighty-three thousand a year." Meghan closed her computer. "I honestly think that's enough to convince a judge we need to subpoena Wallingford's bank records."

Sheila gave Meghan a puzzled look. "But I thought you already searched his financial records and didn't find anything."

"We were given clearance to explore at the bank. But we need to know if he has accounts elsewhere. Because there's still a big chunk of change not accounted for."

Sheila nodded knowingly. "Ah. Okay."

"You know . . ." Greg rubbed his jaw, his brows low. "It's possible he could have inherited money, which he used to buy the properties. We should find out for sure. And there's something no one's said but is sure to come up when we start pushing deeper."

Meghan tilted her head. "What's that?"

"There hasn't been any embezzlement at the bank since February of 2002. And" — he glanced at Sheila, sympathy pursing his face — "Anson Menke dropped out of sight in March."

Sheila sucked in a breath and opened her mouth as if to protest.

Greg put up his hand. "I'm not making an accusation toward your dad, but anyone who defends Wallingford will certainly point it out. We need to be prepared for it. That's all I'm saying."

Meghan tucked her laptop under her arm and stood. "Let's get out of here, go back to the hotel, and call Captain Ratzlaff. He'll need to request the subpoena."

Sheila hooked her purse strap over her shoulder. "So you're not gonna look at Mr. Thames anymore?"

"Not unless our investigation of Wallingford clears him."

Greg snapped his laptop closed and rose. "While we're waiting for the subpoena, we can research inheritance records — see if anything pops up as a big payout to Wallingford."

Sheila sighed. "All this hunting through money records is kind of exciting, but when are we going to do something that actually leads to my dad? We still don't know where he is, what happened to him, or if he's alive or dead." Tears winked in her eyes. "Is digging into bank accounts really going to help?"

Meghan put her arm around Sheila's

shoulders. "Every piece of evidence helps, Sheila. Evidence confirms or disproves a theory, and either way, it helps us choose a direction." She smiled. "Don't give up, huh?"

Sheila nodded and stepped away from Meghan. Her head low, she scuffed out the door ahead of them.

Greg fell in step with Meghan. He pointed with his chin in Sheila's direction. "Maybe we should leave her at the hotel from now on. Especially if there's a legitimate reason for Wallingford to own all those properties. If things start pointing at Menke . . ."

Meghan gritted her teeth. Menke couldn't be a thief. The description didn't fit what they knew about him. She wanted to prove without a doubt Sheila's dad had been honorable. At least one of their absent fathers should be deemed an honorable man.

Thirty-Four

Little Rock, Arkansas
Sean

Captain Ratzlaff headed for the detectives' cluster of desks, his fist gripped around a rolled piece of paper and his grin wide. He stopped beside Farber's desk and whacked his shoulder with the paper tube.

Farber rocked his chair and smirked. "You got it?"

"Judge Clairmont agrees there's probable cause to bring Stony Dunsbrook, a.k.a. Fred Jones, in for questioning."

Sean chuckled. He couldn't help it. Farber's idea to search the Social Security database for name changes on Dunsbrook's assigned Social Security number led them to Fred Jones, who now lived in Sacramento, California. Stony had been thinking like a child when he changed his name to match a character's from the *Scooby Doo* comic strips. "Great catch, Farber."

Farber pointed at his temple. "This thing does still work." He dropped his hand to his mouse and worked the roller ball up and down with his finger. "Most kids are into cartoon characters. I remembered that one of the twins was found with a *Scooby Doo* magazine in his jacket pocket. So I followed the hunch. Glad we hit pay dirt."

At the word *dirt,* both Sean and Ratzlaff cringed. Farber muttered, "Sorry. Bad metaphor."

"It's okay." Captain Ratzlaff unrolled the tube. It separated into two sheets of paper. He handed one to Sean and the other to Farber. "The police chief in Sacramento's been notified. He assures me they'll serve a warrant for Dunsbrook at his workplace. Remember, he's a person of interest at this point, not a suspect." He gestured to the pages he'd given them. "Your flights've been booked, and I took the liberty of doing online check-in for you. I hate sending you on a red-eye, but I want you in Sacramento first thing tomorrow to meet with Dunsbrook. We don't want to give him the chance to disappear again."

Sean folded the paper and stuck it in his pocket. "Sounds good, Cap. I'm ready. How about you, Farber?"

Farber rubbed his heavily stubbled chin.

"I need to clean up some."

"More than *some,*" Cap said with a laugh. "Both of you, head home and pack an overnight bag. As you can see on your travel papers, your return flight leaves Sacramento at eight tomorrow evening. Only one day to get all the questions asked and answered. If he says something incriminating, then call me. I'll start the ball rolling for extradition."

Farber groaned. "After traveling all night, we'll probably be too tired to think of questions."

"Then write 'em down while you're still cognizant." Captain Ratzlaff turned and ambled toward his office. He called over his shoulder, "Grab a nap before you go if you think it'll help, but don't miss that flight."

Sean and Farber took a taxi to the Sacramento Police Department. A drizzle was falling, and the windows steamed over. Farber rubbed a spot clear and scowled out the window. "I thought the song said it never rains in Southern California."

The taxi driver, a dark-skinned man with a heavy accent, laughed. "You're in Northern California, man."

"I guess that explains it." Farber aimed his bleary gaze at Sean. "You ever been in California before?"

"Nope. You?"

"Nope." He turned to the window again. "Sure looks different from home."

The taxi pulled up in front of the station, and the driver popped the transmission in park. "Forty-three fifty."

Sean paid the driver and requested a receipt, which the man provided along with a toothy grin. "Enjoy your day in not-so-sunny California."

"Yeah, right." Farber slid out onto the sidewalk. He hunched his shoulders and cradled his briefcase against his front. "C'mon, Beagle. I already had my shower."

They entered the station house and crossed to the front desk. They showed their credentials, and an officer escorted them down a long hallway and into a small room. He started to close the door, then paused and shot a querying look at Sean. "You need some coffee? We've always got a pot brewing around here."

Sean opened his laptop. "That sounds great." He hoped he didn't appear too eager.

"Comin' right up." The officer left the door ajar.

Farber clicked open his briefcase and burrowed under a short stack of folded pants, shirts, and underclothes. He yanked out a long yellow notepad and pencil and slapped them onto the table. He glanced at Sean's computer and made a face. "I know most people have gone to recording everything on devices, but I think better when I'm putting a pencil to paper."

Sean tapped in his password. "Whatever it takes to think clearly. We don't want to leave any stones unturned."

Farber groaned. "Are you trying to make puns, Beagle?"

Sean started to answer, but the officer came in with their coffee, and a second officer followed. The second one ushered in a short man with thinning mouse-brown hair and a potbelly. His green jumpsuit, the kind auto mechanics wore to protect their clothes, bore a tiny patch on the right chest. White block letters in the center of the patch spelled the name Fred.

The first officer darted out, and the second one pulled a chair from beneath the table. "Here you go, Mr. Jones." He sent a somber look at Sean and Farber. "I'm Officer Horn. If you need something, I'll be right outside."

Stony Dunsbrook held up his pointer finger. "I'd take a cup o' joe."

The officer left without answering.

Dunsbrook sighed and slouched in the chair. He looked longingly at the cups of coffee. Sean slid his across the table, and Dunsbrook yanked it up, almost spilling it. "Hey, thanks."

"No problem." Time to get things started. Sean pointed to Farber. "Mr. Jones, this is Detective Tom Farber. I'm Sean Eagle. We're with the Arkansas Cold Case Investigations Department."

The man slurped the coffee, his watery hazel eyes shifting back and forth between Sean and Farber. "Hi. The policeman said you wanted to talk to me. How come?"

"We'd like to talk to you about your cousins, Dominic and Xavier Dunsbrook."

He set the coffee down and zipped his hands to his lap. "I don't have any cousins."

Farber drew squiggles with his pencil at the top of his notebook page. "Let's skip this part, okay? We already know you're Stony Dunsbrook, that your father and the twins' father were brothers, so Dominic and Xavier were your first cousins. We also know you were at the park for a family camping trip the last weekend of June in 1979, when the twins died."

"But —"

"Annnd," Farber said, raising his voice, "we know you changed your name from Stony Dunsbrook to Fred Jones in 1986."

"My name's —"

Farber thrust up his hand like a traffic cop stopping a semi. "No. Don't lie. Don't waste my time or yours. Capisce?"

Dunsbrook let out a hearty guffaw. "*Capisce?* I like that." He took a noisy slurp of the coffee. "All right. I had some cousins. But I haven't been around my family in years. So I don't know what you want with me."

Farber banged his fist on the table, making his notepad bounce. "We want the truth."

Dunsbrook jumped and stared, wide eyed, at Farber.

Sean cleared his throat. Farber had apparently decided to play the bad-cop role for the traditional good cop–bad cop interrogation. But Cap had said to treat Dunsbrook like a person of interest, not a suspect.

Sean set his computer aside and folded his hands on the table. "Mr. Jones, as Detective Farber said, we're trying to uncover the truth about who murdered Dominic and Xavier. I'm sure you'd like to have the mystery solved, too, considering you must've been friends with the twins when y'all were little."

Dunsbrook's rheumy eyes twitched. "Yeah . . . yeah, we were . . . friends."

"Then will you tell me everything you

remember about the day they died? Did you spend time with them?"

He nodded.

"Where did y'all play? What did you do?"

He lifted the cup and took a slow drink. "We, uh, we played all over the park."

"By the river?"

Another slurp. Beads of sweat appeared on his forehead. "Some."

Sean turned his computer so Dunsbrook could see the screen. "Look at this report, Mr. Jones. This is from the twins' autopsies." He pointed to a paragraph. "Can you read what it says there?"

He squinted at the screen, licking his lips. "Um, I don't have my glasses."

Farber grabbed the computer. "I'll read it to you. It says, 'Particles of dirt and clay found in boys' nostrils, throat cavity, and lungs.' " He lifted his scowl to Dunsbrook. "Now tell me, where did you play?"

The man's eyes swam with unshed tears. His chin began to quiver. All at once Sean felt he wasn't looking at an almost fifty-year-old man but a little boy. A frightened little boy. Sean spoke to him the way he would calm a nervous child.

"Mr. Jones, what's the matter? Did you see something scary that day?"

He nodded hard. His entire frame shook.

443

"What did you see? Anything you can tell us about what happened to Dominic and Xavier will be helpful."

He scrunched his eyes and put his fists against the side of his head. "I saw . . . I saw . . ." He shook so badly his teeth clacked.

Farber turned a disbelieving look on Sean. He whispered, "Is this guy all there?"

Sean was beginning to wonder if the man was an exceptionally good actor or if he had a below-average IQ. "Mr. Jones? Look at me please, Mr. Jones."

Dunsbrook's eyes opened, but he didn't lower his hands.

"What did you see? Tell me what you saw."

"I'm not supposed to tell anyone. My dad said not to tell anyone."

A sick feeling flooded Sean's stomach. "That was a long time ago, Mr. Jones. I think if your dad was here today, he'd say it was all right to tell us."

The man slowly lowered his hands. "Do you think so?"

Sean nodded. "I do. I think he'd want us to know."

He rubbed his nose, wriggled in the chair, and squared his shoulders. "The dirt. I saw the dirt fall down. Dom and Xavy were in the cave." His expression turned stern, and he shook his finger. "I said, 'Don't go in there.' Mom said never go in the caves. So I didn't go, but they did, and I said I was going to tell. I climbed the bank and I . . ." His chin quivered. "I must've stepped in the wrong spot, because the dirt fell down. It all fell down." He threw back his head and wailed.

Sean got up and rounded the table. He sat next to the man and put his hand on his heaving shoulder. "What happened next, Fred?"

He crossed his wrists over his chest and rocked slightly. "I pulled them out. It took lots of time, but I dug and dug with my hands, and I pulled them out. But their faces were all dirty. They had dirt in their mouths. I wanted to clean the dirt out, so I used water from the river and washed them, but —"

He sent a furtive look across the table at Farber. "You aren't going to tell anyone else about this, right? My dad told me I shouldn't tell anybody."

Farber lowered his brows. "Did your dad help you with the twins?"

"Yeah. I couldn't get them up the bank by myself, so I got my dad, and he carried them up the bank. We put them under a tree, where they'd be safe and someone would find them. But he said don't tell anybody. He said if people knew I'd killed the twins, I'd end up in prison for the rest of my life." He began to rock again. "Ooooh, I killed them. I should be in prison. I tried and tried to go to prison, but they never put me in."

Sean met Farber's gaze. He read the same understanding dawning for Farber that was blooming in his mind.

He squeezed Dunsbrook's shoulder. "Do you mean you broke windows and took things that weren't yours so the police would put you in jail?"

"Murderers belong in jail. That's where I should've gone. But Mom said I needed to stop trying to go to jail. She said since Dom and Xavy were gone, I needed to live for them. I needed to do lots of good things, as many good things as three people could do. So I decided to be Fred Jones. He's a good guy. He helps people." Hope ignited on his round, flaccid face. "Did I help you today?"

Sean patted his back. "Yes, you did. You helped us a lot."

"Then can I go back to work? I keep the floors clean, and I wash the cars, and there's a dog that comes in the alley every day looking for food. If I'm not there, the other guys'll chase 'im off and he won't get any dinner. So I need to go back to work."

Farber flipped the notebook around and laid his pencil on it. "Before you go, can you write down what you told us? For our records?"

Dunsbrook took the pencil and aimed it at the page. He wrote slowly, laboriously, his tongue poking out the corner of his mouth. Sean watched the words form.

The twins went into the cav. The durt fell on them. I dug them out and washed there faces. Dad put them under a tree. He paused, and then he scrawled, *I gave Dom my comic book to say I am sory.*

He looked at Sean. "Is that okay?"

Sean swallowed a knot of sadness. "Yes. Just sign your name now."

"My Stony name or my Fred name?"

"Your Fred name."

He put a few loops at the bottom of the page, then handed the notebook and pencil to Sean. He stood. "I need to go to work now. Thank you for the cup o' joe." He picked up the almost-empty coffee cup and walked out.

Moments later, the officer who'd brought Dunsbrook stuck his head in the door. "Hey, Jones is out here and says he can go. Is that right?"

Farber waved his hand. "We're done with

him." The officer left, and Farber aimed a flabbergasted look at Sean. "Can you believe he lives by himself? I think before we take this all as fact" — he jabbed his finger on the penciled sentences — "we ought to double-check with his boss, see if we've been scammed."

"Let's catch the officer, then, and get a ride to Dunsbrook's workplace."

The manager of the body repair shop that employed Dunsbrook, a.k.a. Jones, as the janitor confirmed the man was considered intellectually impaired. "He's slow, no doubt about it, but he gets along all right. He was left some money by his parents, and they assigned a lawyer to distribute those funds a little at a time. He rents a room, takes most of his meals at a little diner up the street, and lets the woman who owns the boardinghouse help him pay his bills. The guys who work here keep track of him and make sure nothing bad happens to him. He's as harmless as they come. I couldn't believe it when the police showed up and wanted to take him in. Did he do something bad?"

Farber glanced at Sean, then answered. "No. He was a witness to something when he lived in Arkansas, and we needed to find out what he could remember about it."

The man shrugged. "That's good to know. He told us he had a juvenile record, but we didn't believe him — figured he was trying to make himself look tough. Glad it's not true. Not sure I'd keep him around if he'd been involved in something illegal, even if he has been a good worker for me. I run a clean shop."

Sean clapped the man on the back. "You don't need to worry. He's trustworthy."

Farber trailed Sean to the edge of the sidewalk. He looked up at the cloudy sky and blew out a noisy breath. "I don't know about you, but this all feels very anticlimactic. All that searching for a murderer, only to find a mentally disabled man hiding a secret." He glanced over his shoulder. "Do you think he'll sleep better now that he finally told somebody?"

If Sean wasn't mistaken, Farber actually cared. "I know I will."

Farber gave him a startled look. Then he nodded. "Yeah. Yeah, I reckon so." He checked his watch. "Cap scheduled another red-eye flight, but I wonder if we could catch something earlier. Actually get home at a decent hour."

"I'm all for that."

"Me, too. Let's go, Eagle."

Thirty-Five

Fort Smith, Arkansas
Meghan

Meghan and Greg accompanied the court official who'd been assigned to deliver the subpoena for Wallingford's financials. Meghan had asked Sheila to stay behind in the hotel, and to her relief, the younger woman hadn't argued. Catching Wallingford at home, early in the morning, would save him the humiliation of being served at his workplace. She doubted he'd appreciate their consideration, though, and she wanted to spare Sheila any unpleasant exchanges.

The winding brick driveway shaded by mature oaks and maples led to the Tudor-style house she, Greg, and Sheila had driven past earlier. She'd marveled then — it was four times the size of her and Sean's cozy bungalow — and couldn't resist releasing a low whistle today. Wallingford had established a comfortable life for himself. But was it funded by his salary, from an inheritance, or through thievery? They'd soon know for sure.

The officer stepped up on the half circle-shaped tiled stoop and rang the doorbell. Several seconds later the door opened, revealing a middle-aged woman. Her welcoming smile faded when her gaze fell on the officer. "Is something wrong?"

"Darryl Wallingford, please."

She gripped the edge of the door and looked over her shoulder. "Darryl?"

Heavy footsteps pounded, and then Wallingford, wearing suit pants and a button-up shirt and tie, appeared in the doorway. He touched the woman's elbow. "Go finish breakfast, honey. I'll see what they need." The woman scurried off, and he scowled past the officer to Meghan and Sean. "What's this all about?"

The officer held out the folded subpoena. "You're being served, Mr. Wallingford."

Wallingford opened the document, scanned it, then threw it at the officer's feet. The veins in his temples bulged, and his face splotched red from his neck to his forehead. He shook his fist at Meghan and Greg. "You have no right!"

The officer took a step that put him between Wallingford and the detectives. Tall, barrel-chested, with a shaved bald head, the officer made a great defensive block. He picked up the pages and pressed them into Wallingford's hand. "The judge's signature at the bottom of this document says they do. If you don't hand everything over by eight o'clock tomorrow morning, you'll be in contempt of court."

"Get off my property." Wallingford hissed the command through clenched teeth.

"You've been served." The officer ushered Greg and Meghan toward the driveway, and the slam of Wallingford's door reverberated in her ears. When they reached the curb, the man wished them well in the investigation and left.

Greg turned a grim look on Meghan. "I wouldn't be surprised if Wallingford ignores the subpoena and decides to skip town."

Meghan chewed the corner of her lip. If he had money squirreled away, he'd have the means to do so. "Maybe we should have asked the judge to make him forfeit his passport."

"Too late for that now." Greg escorted her to his SUV, and they climbed in. He angled a thoughtful frown at Meghan. "We can't actually go into the bank, thanks to the stay-away order, but we can follow Wallingford and see where he goes. If he heads for an airport or bus station, we'll give the police department a holler. For now, let's move the car farther up the block and wait."

In fewer than five minutes, the sleek jet-black Lincoln Continental registered to Darryl Wallingford backed out of the driveway and turned in the direction of the town.

Meghan broke out in gooseflesh. "There he goes."

"And here we go." Greg pulled away from the curb. They followed, keeping some distance between the vehicles. Meghan's mouth was dry, and her pulse skittered. If Wallingford spotted them, he might be desperate enough to do harm. She found herself praying for protection as Greg's SUV trailed behind the Lincoln.

Wallingford turned onto North Sixth Street. Greg released a little huff. "He must be headed to the bank."

Meghan nodded. But he didn't turn left on Garrison Avenue, which would have taken him there. He drove through the intersection and kept driving.

Greg slapped the steering wheel. "Uh-oh."
"What?"

"I think this street leads to Highway 255. He might be heading out of town."

Meghan pulled her cell phone from her pocket. "Should I make a 911 call?"

"Not yet." Greg set his lips in a stern line and narrowed his eyes. "Let's wait and see."

Wallingford's Lincoln turned onto South A Street, then pulled into the parking lot of a brown-brick building with a red tin roof. Greg followed him in, then barked a disbelieving laugh.

Sunlight glared off the hood of the car and temporarily blinded Meghan. She leaned forward and squinted past the windshield. "What is it?"

"He led us to the Sebastian County Sheriff's Office." Greg made a circle and pulled into a parking space at the far corner of the lot, then left his SUV idling. He pointed. "Look — he's going in."

Wallingford strode across the pavement, his head high and shoulders square. Meghan shook her head, torn between disgust and disbelief. "He seems pretty sure of himself, doesn't he?"

"Yeah. Yeah, he does."

A sapphire-blue Mercedes-Benz pulled into the parking area. Wallingford paused beside the glass double doors of the office, his hand on the right door's silver handle, and seemed to observe the vehicle's progress. Its driver parked next to Wallingford's Lincoln, and none other than attorney Philip Johnske emerged from the car.

Greg whistled through his teeth. "Hoo boy. They're up to something."

Meghan nodded. "Probably trying to figure out a way to override the subpoena and run the two of us out of town on a rail."

"Good guess." Greg put his car in drive. "If he's with his attorney, I think we can safely assume he isn't going to skip town. So how about we head back to the hotel, check on Sheila —"

Meghan squelched a smile. Greg had grown fond of the young woman. He was a softy underneath.

"— and maybe try to pick her brain a little more? I feel like there's something we're missing about Menke's last days that's critical, but I can't put my finger on it."

"I'm good with following your instincts. Let's go."

The moment Meghan opened the hotel room door, Sheila bounded up from the end of the bed, where she'd apparently been watching the postage stamp–sized television on the dresser. She met them in the narrow entryway. "How'd he take it?"

Meghan released a mirthless chuckle. "Pretty much the way we expected he would."

Sheila's face pinched into a grimace.

"Mad as a wet hen, huh?"

"Yep." Greg gestured to the room. "Can you turn that noise box off? We need to talk to you."

Sheila grabbed the remote control and silenced the television. Greg pulled out the rickety desk chair and angled it toward the beds. Meghan sat on the end of her bed and gently tugged Sheila's hand. She sank down, too, earning a discordant squawk from the mattress.

Sheila's gaze shifted from Greg to Meghan to Greg again. She held her hands outward. "Well? What is it?"

Greg crossed his leg and cupped both hands over his upraised knee. "I need you to tell us about the last day you saw your dad. As much as you can recall, please share that with us."

Sheila stuck what was left of a pinkie nail between her teeth and bit down, her forehead scrunching. "Okay. Lemme think . . ."

March 22, 2002
Sheila

"Sheila?"

Sheila dropped the block she'd intended to put on the tower she and Brandon were building and got up from the floor. She crossed to Mom's recliner. Mom's eyes were closed, and her lips looked thin and white. Sheila touched her mother's arm. What Daddy called a barely-touch to keep from hurting her. Sometimes even a tiny touch made Mom wince. "Whatcha want?"

"Go look . . . see if Daddy's car is coming."

She'd already watched for a really long time. She watched until the boys got cranky and Mom asked her to entertain them. That's why they were building towers with blocks. But she'd check again because she wanted Daddy to come home as much as Mom did. Mom was hurting bad. She needed the special medicine Daddy kept in a locked box on the highest shelf of the bathroom cabinet. The kids weren't supposed to touch that box — only Daddy.

Sheila hurried to the window and pushed the curtain aside. She wished she could push the rain aside. She and Wayne had barely made it home from school before it started, and it was coming down in buckets, Daddy would say. Little wonder it sounded like a hundred soldiers were marching on the roof. She couldn't even see the street for the rain. She chewed her thumbnail and stared at the gray curtain of water, willing Daddy's car to pull into the driveway. He should have come home more than half an hour ago.

She glanced over her shoulder. Mom held on to the recliner's armrests the way Sheila held on to the bar of the Ferris wheel when it went to the top. Her stomach knotted, partly from hunger — it was past their suppertime — but mostly from worry. Mom needed the medicine now. Stupid rain. Daddy probably couldn't see to drive and was stuck somewhere, waiting it out.

Wayne swept his arm and knocked over his block tower. It fell into the tower she and Brandon were building, and those blocks scattered, too. Brandon sent up an angry wail. Sheila started to holler at Wayne, but Mom made an awful face, like a person made when they were trying hard not to cry. Yelling would only make Mom upset.

Sheila hurried to Mom, stepping around blocks. She gave Brandon's hair a quick ruffle and Wayne a sour scowl on the way by. She knelt beside Mom's recliner. "It's raining really hard, Mom. Probably too hard for Daddy to drive. I bet he won't come home until the rain stops."

Mom moaned.

Sheila stood and chewed her thumbnail, staring first at Mom's face and then at the rain beyond the window.

Wayne began to sing, " 'Rain, rain, go

away, come again another day . . .' "

The song wouldn't make the rain stop. Daddy wouldn't come, and Mom would go on hurting. Somebody had to do something. She jerked away from Mom's chair, balling her hands into fists, and marched to the bathroom. She climbed up on the toilet seat and opened the cabinet door. There on the top shelf, beside extra boxes of Ivory soap and the bottle of shaving lotion the boys gave Daddy last Christmas, was the little locked box. Her heart pounded as hard as the rain on the roof, and her hands shook, but she grabbed the box and hopped down.

With the box cradled against her chest, she darted to Mom and Daddy's bedroom. At the door, she paused. This room was supposed to be off limits to the kids unless they had permission to go in. But how else would she open the box? She'd seen the key in Daddy's sock drawer when she helped Mom put laundry away. She had to go in.

Her knees wobbling, she crossed to the dresser. She opened the drawer and pawed around, feeling like a thief. Her fingers found the little key, and she let out a sigh of relief.

The key and the lock were really tiny, and her hands were shaking so bad she had trouble putting the key in the little slot. But she finally did it, and the lock clicked. She opened the box, grabbed the plastic bottle of pills, then raced for the kitchen. The childproof lid gave her some trouble, but she followed the directions and popped the cap loose. She filled a glass with water and carried it, along with one of the pills, to Mom.

Mom didn't raise a fuss when Sheila helped her sit up and swallow the pill. She didn't even ask how Sheila got it, which told Sheila how bad Mom hurt. But Daddy would really scold her when he got home. He might even do more than scold. She'd broken two rules by getting the box and going into her parents' room. But somebody had to take care of Mom. Daddy wasn't there, so Sheila would do it.

Present Day
Meghan
Sheila's eyes glistened with unshed tears. She sniffed and rubbed her finger under her nose. "I made peanut butter and jelly sandwiches for supper, and Mom had me put the boys to bed. I didn't know until the next morning that she'd called the police and reported Daddy missing." She hung her head. "Our lives sure changed after that."

Meghan put her arm around Sheila's

shoulders. "You should be proud of yourself for how you took such good care of your mom and your brothers. I bet your dad would be proud of you, too."

A smile quavered on Sheila's lips. "I hope so."

Meghan gave Sheila a quick squeeze, then turned to Greg. Nothing in his expression indicated that anything from Sheila's reflections held meaning. Meghan's shoulders slumped. She'd been hoping his instincts were correct.

He thumped his foot to the floor and gave the armrests a light smack with both palms. "Thanks for sharing that, Sheila. I guess now we'll —"

Meghan's cell phone rang. She pulled it from her pocket. She'd never seen the number before, but it had the Fort Smith area code. She accepted the call and put the phone to her ear. "Detective DeFord here."

"Yes. Ms. DeFord." The stilted male voice sounded slightly familiar. "This is Attorney Johnske."

An image of the pompous lawyer formed in her mind's eye. Meghan waved her hand and captured Greg's attention. She pointed to the phone and replied, "Yes, Mr. Johnske, what can I do for you?"

Greg jolted to his feet, his frame tense and angled slightly toward her, like a runner prepared for the starting pistol shot.

"You can come to the Sebastian County Sheriff's Office. I'm here with my client, and he's ready to discuss his financial dealings."

Meghan grinned, waggling her eyebrows at Greg. "Thank you. We'll be there as quickly as possible." The call disconnected, and Meghan jabbed the phone in the air in a victory punch. "He's ready to confess!"

Sheila's jaw dropped. "He is?"

"Yep. His attorney says he's ready to tell us about his financial dealings."

Greg settled back on his heels and made a little *tsk* sound. "Well . . . that might mean a confession, but it might mean an explanation." He put his hand on Sheila's shoulder. "And I doubt it means he'll tell us anything about your dad."

Sheila sighed and hung her head. Meghan inwardly berated herself for jumping to conclusions. She knew better. She forced a cheerful tone. "But remember what I told you earlier — every piece of evidence is a step in the right direction."

Sheila gave a halfhearted shrug.

Greg folded his arms over his chest and fixed Sheila with a thoughtful expression.

"Sheila, Wallingford probably doesn't expect you to be with us, and he might say you can't come into the room, but if you're up to it, I'd like you to go along."

Sheila's head shot up. "You would?"

Greg nodded. "Your presence makes him uncomfortable. We've already seen that. I'm pretty sure he and his lawyer have decided what portion of the truth he'll divulge, but if he's uncomfortable, he might slip up and tell us something incriminating."

Meghan feared it might be too much for the younger woman after her emotional foray into the past, and she started to recommend Sheila stay behind and rest. But Sheila bounced to her feet and headed for the door. She grabbed the doorknob and sent an impatient frown over her shoulder. "Well? Are you coming?"

Greg grinned at Meghan and gestured for her to follow. She swallowed an amused chuckle. Greg had gone from wanting to leave Sheila in Little Rock to letting her lead the way. Sean would sure get a kick out of that. She followed the pair to Greg's SUV, and with every pound of her soles on the concrete, she prayed.

Truth, God. Let us find the truth.

THIRTY-SIX

Meghan

Meghan sat next to Sheila at a small aluminum table in what she was sure had been a broom closet in a former life. As Greg had suspected, Wallingford refused to let Sheila enter the room where he and his lawyer waited. He wouldn't even let Meghan in — said he'd talk to Greg and Greg only. Greg informed him that Meghan was lead detective and he should talk to her, but the man remained stubborn and said if they wanted his statement, it would have to be to Greg.

Meghan didn't much care. Getting the information was what mattered. Besides, she wasn't left out. A camera in the first room sent live video coverage to a small flat-screen television mounted on the wall of their closet. A speaker piped in every word. And Wallingford gave them a lot to hear.

"I admit, I stole the money. Back in the early nineties, I started making bogus loans that I let default. The bank then got reimbursed by the insurance company. The first one was small — only twenty-five grand. Kind of my practice run. When it went undetected for a full two years, I doubled the amount. Writing off a hundred-thousand-dollar loan every year or so didn't raise red flags with anyone. Except . . ." On the screen, Wallingford's face splotched red. He gritted his teeth.

"Anson. He came to me and asked me, as a friend, to turn myself in because he didn't want to do it. But he said he would do it if I didn't. I tried to tell him I wasn't hurting the bank, and the wealthy insurance companies could afford to pay out. But he wouldn't buy it. He said it was stealing and that stealing was wrong. I asked what did it matter since he wasn't the one doing the stealing." Wallingford snorted. "He said to know wrong and look the other way was as bad as doing the wrong himself."

Sheila's gaze was locked on the screen, and a single tear rolled down her cheek. "He told us kids that, too. 'When you see wrong, make it right. Don't be a party to wrong.' "

Meghan swallowed against a lump in her throat. Everything she knew about Anson Menke painted him as an honorable man, faithful husband, and loving father. Such a

465

waste that he'd left his children's lives so soon.

"So you took the money and you got caught." The camera's angle didn't allow them to see Greg, but they heard his voice. "Then you did away with Menke."

Wallingford jolted as if someone had yanked the back of his collar. A fierce scowl formed, and he shifted his gaze to the right, where Meghan presumed his attorney sat. The idea was confirmed when Johnske's voice boomed through the speaker.

"He's only confessing to embezzlement. He maintains his innocence in Menke's disappearance."

Wallingford gave a brusque nod and faced forward again. "I told him I needed to think about turning myself in. I asked him to give me some time. He wasn't happy about it, but he said because of our long-standing friendship, he'd give me two weeks."

Two weeks . . . Meghan nodded, understanding dawning. Those two weeks of waiting must have weighed heavily on Sheila's father, which explained his odd behavior in the short time before he disappeared.

The banker shifted in his chair, and a familiar *clink-clink* came through the speaker.

"What was that?" Sheila asked.

"It's his handcuffs, or maybe the chain connecting them, hitting against the table."

Sheila's blue eyes widened. "He's handcuffed? Like a real prisoner?"

Meghan nodded.

Sheila's expression turned hard. "Good."

Meghan returned her attention to the screen.

Wallingford's jaw jutted, his gaze narrowing. "I decided I couldn't turn myself in. I couldn't put my wife through that. So I told Anson if someone was going to squeal to the authorities, he'd have to do it. I also told him I'd laid out a paper trail that would lead to him. Out of all the employees at the bank, he was the most likely to need the money, so it wouldn't be hard to convince people he was the real embezzler." A cunning smile curved his lips. "I was right about that. Every finger pointed in his direction."

"And he wasn't here to defend himself." Greg spoke again, and his sarcastic tone made Meghan cringe. "How'd those fingers get pointed, anyway? If Menke never made it to the authorities, and we know he didn't, who alerted them about the missing money?"

Wallingford raised his chin in an arrogant pose. "I did. I figured the first one to talk would be the one they'd believe. So I told the bank president I'd caught Anson making false loans, and everything blew open from there."

Sheila was crying. Not a sound emerged, but her frame quivered and tears streamed down her pale cheeks. Meghan slipped her arm around the younger woman's shoulders. After all the years of wondering if her beloved father was a thief, his vindication must be overwhelming. But they still didn't know where Anson Menke was. Alive or dead? She silently prayed for Greg to draw the full truth from Wallingford.

"I'll be honest, Mr. Wallingford." Greg's snide tone came clearly through the speaker box. "This all sounds like a story concocted to avoid murder charges. You expect us to believe that you aren't responsible for Anson Menke's disappearance? You're the only one who would benefit from him being unable to speak to the authorities."

Wallingford set his lips in a firm line and glared.

"Where is Anson Menke, Wallingford?" Sheila shrank back at Greg's harsh demands. "What did you do with his vehicle? Where did you bury his body?"

Johnske stepped into view and put his hands on Wallingford's shoulders. "Detective, we're done here. My client has said as much as he's going to say."

Meghan half stood, overwhelmed by her desire to reach through the screen and hold Wallingford in his chair.

"You claimed to be his friend." Greg spoke again, no longer stern or snide or even wheedling. The genuine hurt and confusion in his tone brought tears to Meghan's eyes. She sank back in her chair.

Wallingford blinked several times, and red patches formed on his cheeks and neck.

"His kids called you Uncle Wally. They trusted you."

Sheila rested her head on Meghan's shoulder, and Meghan instinctively wrapped her in a hug.

"And you stole their father from them. You sullied his name."

Greg spoke so softly Meghan had to strain to hear his voice. She watched Wallingford's face for signs of cracking. *Please, please . . . the truth. Let him tell the truth.*

"Admitting you stole the money is a start." Greg's hand slid into view and patted Wallingford's clenched fists. "Now Sheila, Wayne, and Brandon will know their daddy wasn't a thief. That'll ease their minds. But don't you think those kids deserve to know where he is? They've waited fifteen years for him to come home. If he

469

can't come home, they should at least be able to give him a proper burial. Let them put this all to rest, Mr. Wallingford. Tell me where to find Anson Menke."

The man stared straight ahead, sullen and smoldering.

Several silent seconds slipped by while Meghan waited, watched, and prayed Wallingford would finally tell Sheila what she needed to know.

Not a word. Not even a flicker of remorse.

"All right, Mr. Wallingford, then let's put it this way." Although he spoke conversationally, even friendly, something about Greg's comment made Meghan's nerves buzz. "By your own admission, you stole the money. By your own admission, Anson Menke knew you stole the money. And according to public record, Anson Menke dropped off the face of the planet the same day you set him up for the fall. The ABI didn't uncover a single shred of evidence that the man still exists. So, even without a body, a good prosecuting attorney has enough to make a strong circumstantial case against you." Lengthy pause. "For murder."

Johnske leaned down and whispered in Wallingford's ear. Meghan bit the corner of her lip, her heart pounding. The lawyer and client shared a brief hushed exchange, and then Johnske stepped out of camera range.

Wallingford closed his eyes for a few seconds, and when he opened them, a flinty determination gave him a cold appearance. "He left the bank a full hour before closing. I presumed he was going to the police station, so I followed him. I planned to go in, too, and make my own accusations. But he didn't go to the police station. He headed out of town. It was raining cats and dogs, but I managed to stay with him until we got on a dirt road."

"What dirt road? Where was he going?"

The banker huffed. "How should I know? Just a dirt road. The rain was coming down hard, almost too hard to see."

Meghan sucked in a hopeful breath. His description matched what Sheila had said about the day, so there were elements of truth in his story. Had Greg convinced him to confess the whole truth?

"I decided to turn around, go to the bank president's office and tell him Anson had been stealing for years. But before I left Anson, first I had some anger to dispel. I was driving an SUV back then — considerably bigger than his Honda. So I sped up and gave his car's rear end a good bump. Then I came back to town." He shrugged. "I was as surprised as everyone else when he turned up missing. But it worked in my favor, so I stayed quiet." Wallingford stood, giving Meghan a view of his midsection and shackled hands. "I'm done here."

The screen went blank. Meghan stared at the gray square for several seconds, processing all Wallingford had said. If the man told the truth, then they had a place to search for clues.

She gave Sheila a little squeeze and let go. "Sheila?"

Sheila snuffled and sat up.

"Was there someplace in the country your dad liked to go? Maybe a friend he visited?"

"Yeah." She sniffed hard and swiped her face with the backs of her wrists. "That old high school friend I told you about? He lived outside of town. I think his name was Ken . . . or maybe Ben . . . Edwards. Daddy took the boys and me to his place sometimes when Mom needed quiet. Mr. Edwards had a huge pond, big enough for paddleboats and Jet Skis, and he kept it stocked. We'd fish for bluegill and crappie."

Meghan's pulse pounded. Rain heavy enough to obstruct vision. A slick dirt road. And a pond. A big pond. How deep? Puzzle pieces began to fall into place. She took Sheila's hand. "Do you think you could find his place again?"

Sheila frowned. "It was so long ago. I don't know." Then she brightened. "But I remember the name of the road because it matched something in *Anne of Green Gables*. His house was on Idlewild Drive."

The door opened, and Greg stuck his head in. "Did you catch it all?"

"We did." Meghan cupped Sheila's elbow, and they both rose and headed for the door.

"What Wallingford said about a dirt road . . . I think we should —"

Meghan led Sheila past Greg. "Yeah, we should. And thanks to Sheila, we know where to start. Get your search engine open. We're looking for a man named Edwards who lives on Idlewild Drive."

Meghan held Sheila's hand and followed Greg and Ben Edwards along the soft bank circling the surprisingly large pond. If someone had told her even a few weeks ago that she'd be comfortable holding another woman's hand, she would have laughed them off. But Sheila needed connection, and Meghan needed to offer it. So they held tightly to each other.

"No, I didn't see Anson on March twenty-second. But he did come out fairly regularly on Fridays."

Greg bent over, picked up a rock, and

skimmed it across the water. "Why Fridays?"

"My dental office closes at noon on Fridays, so I'm always home in the afternoon. He'd leave work a little early, and we'd meet out here. He said it was peaceful. It soothed his soul."

The dark-haired man sent a warm smile over his shoulder at Sheila. "That's why he brought you and your brothers out. He hoped you kids would find some peace out here, too, given how hard it could be at home with your mom's illness."

Sheila nodded. "It worked. We did." Her fingers tightened on Meghan's hand. Meghan squeezed back — an assuring squeeze.

Edwards pointed to an obviously hand-made wooden platform up ahead. "When the weather permitted, Anson and I sat there. I'd pray for him. He wasn't a weak man, but even warriors get weary when the battle doesn't end. Sometimes he needed me to, well, hold up his arms. So I prayed. For Carleena's health, for him to endure, for his kids . . ." He stopped and slipped his hands into his pockets, hanging his head. "I wish he'd come to me that day. I would've done my best to help him deal with the situation at the bank."

Greg propped his foot on a large rock and

cupped his hands over his upraised knee. "Here's the thing about the situation at the bank. We know he didn't steal the money."

Edwards's entire frame sagged. "Oh, thank goodness." He straightened and blew out a breath. "I never believed it. I couldn't imagine the man I knew being involved in embezzlement. But when a judge found him guilty, I — Well, it's a real relief to know I was right about him." He turned a curious look on Greg. "So why do you think he took off?"

Meghan stepped forward, drawing Sheila with her. "We're not convinced he did take off of his own accord." She squinted. She wished she'd brought her sunglasses. The sun glinting off the water hurt her eyes. "He disappeared. That's true enough. We thought he might've been murdered by the man who stole the money, but he denies harming him directly. So we're exploring other possibilities. That's what brought us out here."

Edwards gestured to a cluster of shade trees and a rough-hewn bench. "Let's go sit. Get us out of the sun." He led them up the bank and leaned against a tree. "Sheila, Detective DeFord, why don't you take the bench?"

Sheila released Meghan's hand and

perched on the edge of the bench. Too restless to sit, Meghan stood beside her. Greg ambled over and rested one knee on the other half of the bench.

Edwards turned his curious gaze on Greg and Meghan. "I'm not sure how else I can help you since I didn't see him that last Friday before he disappeared."

Greg gazed across the pond. "Sheila told us there was quite a rainstorm that day. What's it like out here when it's raining?"

The man laughed. "Have you ever been tempted to build an ark?"

Meghan and Greg exchanged a grin. Meghan said, "That bad, huh?"

"Sometimes." Frowning, he ran his hand over his short-cropped hair. "You know, I remember all the rain that day, too. It hit late in the afternoon, like the sky opened up and dumped buckets. My wife got caught in town at the grocery store. She ended up spending the night with her sister's family in town instead of risking the drive home. The road is awfully slick when it's wet, and in a rain like that, it would be downright dangerous to travel it. A person could get swept into the water."

Greg kicked at some new grass sprouting up from the sandy soil. "How deep is the pond?"

Meghan stiffened. The seemingly casual question sent chills of apprehension up and down her spine.

"I'd say maybe —" Edwards straightened so abruptly his knees popped. "My dear Lord in heaven . . ." The prayer emerged on a hoarse whisper. He pressed his hands to his stomach and staggered to the bank. "It's deep. Deep enough to hide a vehicle." He made a slow turn and faced them. "Will you need to drain the pond?"

Meghan shook her head. "Not yet. But we would like to" — she glanced at Sheila's stricken face, and her heart rolled over — "bring out some divers."

THIRTY-SEVEN

Meghan

The divers brought in to look for Anson Menke's car intended to begin their search by ten thirty on Saturday morning, and Meghan insisted she and Greg arrive well in advance of dive time and supervise the entire process. She asked Sheila to stay behind at the hotel — who knew what all they would find under the brownish water? — but the headstrong young woman they'd initially met returned. "He's my dad. I want to be there," she'd said, and Greg took her side. So all three of them watched the divers suit up, strap on air tanks, and waddle into the water.

As the pair of divers slowly sank beneath the surface, Meghan led Sheila to the bench beneath the trees, and they sat. She slipped her arm around Sheila's waist. The temperature was a muggy midseventies, but the young woman shivered, her body quivering from head to toe.

Meghan feared she'd vibrate herself into the pond if left on her own. So even though she preferred to be active in the search, she kept her arm around Sheila while keeping her focus on Greg, who stood at the edge of the water and communicated via some kind of walkie-talkie system with the two divers.

A kind of hush surrounded them. Away from city noise, the country was amazingly peaceful. Today, though, without even a breeze, it seemed unnaturally quiet. No squirrels chattered from the trees, and even the birds were silent. Meghan got the feeling everything held its breath, caught up in anticipation. She wanted to pray, but she wasn't sure what to ask for, so one phrase repeated itself in her mind. *Work Your will for Sheila and her brothers, Lord, please.*

Suddenly Greg's entire frame jerked. He swung his gaze in Meghan's direction. From the distance of forty feet or so, she spotted his smile. He gave the thumbs-up sign, and as if the gesture released a button, Sheila burst into tears. Her spine seemed to collapse. She covered her face with her hands and folded over her lap, sobbing.

Meghan's heart constricted. She rubbed the younger woman's back. "Shhh, shhh, it's all right."

Greg trotted to them and squatted on Sheila's other side. "That was insensitive of me. I'm always glad when we find the answers we've been hunting. I should've remembered that this time it's a little different. I'm sorry, Sheila."

She took a shuddering breath and sat up, lowering her hands. She turned her tear-stained face first to Meghan and then to Greg. "I'm crying because I'm happy. Now I know he didn't leave us on purpose. Like Mom kept saying, he really didn't walk out on us. But I'm also crying because I'm sad. He won't ever come back. The boys and me really are orphans now." A sob broke from her throat, and then she gasped. "But . . ."

Greg leaned close, worry evident in his frown. "But what?"

"I still have a Father in heaven." She fell toward Meghan, and Meghan held her.

Greg stood. He gave a nod to Meghan, then strode toward the divers, who were climbing the bank in their wet suits. The three men talked for several minutes while Meghan continued to soothe Sheila. By the time the divers headed to their vehicle, Sheila had calmed.

Meghan pulled loose and helped her stand. They crossed the grassy rise to Greg, but then Sheila changed direction and moved to the edge of the pond. She gazed across the water, her arms crossed and spine stiff.

Meghan sidled close to Greg. "What'd they say?"

"They found an older-model Honda Accord down there, and human remains are belted in the driver's seat." Greg kept his voice barely above a whisper and flicked glances at Sheila while he talked. "They said the back left bumper is pretty badly smashed in."

"So it matches Wallingford's story."

Greg nodded.

Meghan puffed her cheeks and blew out a big breath. "I'll want an autopsy performed. To make sure he didn't die some other way than drowning. You know, to confirm that Wallingford didn't do more than ram his car. And, of course, we'll want to do a DNA test to make sure it really is Anson Menke in the car."

"I agree." Greg's forehead crinkled. He aimed a pensive frown at Meghan. "One of the divers said the driver's-side window was down. If that's the case, wouldn't Menke have been able to unbuckle and swim to the surface? If he was alive and conscious, that is."

"No, he couldn't." Sheila climbed the

bank. Her eyes shimmered with unshed tears, and her nose was bright red. She stopped near them, blinking hard. "When Daddy was in high school, he cut off his right thumb on a table saw in shop class. So he had to unhook the seat belt with his left hand. He was a big guy, and it was a hard reach. We used to t-tease him about it." She began to cry again. "At least Daddy and Mom are together. They loved each other so much. They should be together." She sank onto her bottom, facing the pond, and fell silent.

Greg took hold of Meghan's elbow and guided her beneath a maple tree several feet away from Sheila. "We'll have to hand this over to the local authorities now. They'll most likely send out a team with equipment and pull the car from the water."

"I wonder if Wallingford's indictment will be amended since it was likely that his bump sent Menke's car into the pond." Meghan turned her attention to Sheila. Such a forlorn figure, hugging her updrawn knees and staring at the place where her father had been hidden for so long. "I hope she'll be okay."

Greg released a half huff, half laugh. "She will be. People with faith . . . they seem to make it through better than those who don't believe in any kind of higher power." He bounced his fist on the tree's trunk and took a step toward the house. "Let's go let Edwards know what was found. He'll need to give permission for the equipment to come on his property."

Meghan walked alongside Greg. Their feet stirred old leaves, and sunlight filtering through tree limbs dotted the ground. Beautiful. Peaceful. Incongruous with the car and its passenger trapped under the murky water. "How long do you suppose it'll be before Sheila and her brothers see the money from their father's life insurance policy?"

Greg made a face. "A while. Think of everything that has to happen first. They've gotta confirm it's Anson Menke. And there might be an investigation to prove he didn't commit suicide. Some insurance companies won't honor a policy if the person takes his own life."

Meghan sighed. "So they might not have the money in time for this coming school year."

"Yes, we will."

Meghan gave a start. Sheila had followed so quietly that Meghan didn't realize she was behind them. She held out her hand, and Sheila grabbed it. Her face was moist from tears and her eyes were red and puffy, but when she spoke, she did so with assurance.

"God knows we need the money to send Brandon to school. God knows Brandon wants to help other people. So He'll make sure we have what we need to get him enrolled this fall." A smile grew, brightening her entire countenance. " 'God will make a way where there seems to be no way' — Mom used to sing that to us. And I believe it."

Meghan put her arm around the younger woman's shoulders and squeezed. "I believe it, too."

Greg didn't say anything, but his thoughtful expression said enough. He also believed it would happen.

Meghan tossed the last of her dirty clothes into her suitcase and zipped it shut. It was so hard to believe their work in Fort Smith was done. She and Greg had spent all day Monday with the local sheriff, sharing the information they'd gathered and outlining a plan to complete the investigation. She trusted the local officials to take the reins. Time to return to Little Rock. To Sean.

He'd called last Wednesday and let her know he and Tom were finished and he would give her all the details when he saw her. She couldn't wait to see him, to return to their normal partnerships, and to talk more about expanding their family of two to three. Or maybe four. Her heart went fluttery.

"You ready?"

Meghan released a startled gasp. Sheila waited beside the hotel room door, her duffle dangling from a strap over her shoulder. Meghan grinned sheepishly. "Sorry. I guess I got lost in thought."

Sheila smiled. "It's okay. You were thinking about your husband, weren't you?"

Meghan received a second jolt of surprise. "How'd you know?"

The younger woman shrugged, her face blushing into a sweet pink. "When you talk about him, you get this look in your eyes and your lips form a special smile. Like you're talking about something precious. You had that same look and smile a minute ago."

Meghan hadn't realized her expression changed when she thought about Sean, but it shouldn't have surprised her. Sean was special. He held such an important place in her life, so of course it should show.

"I hope I meet someone someday who makes me feel the way your husband makes you feel. I can tell . . . you love each other. The same way my mom and dad loved each other."

Meghan crossed the carpet to Sheila, dropped her suitcase, and delivered a hug. "I'll pray for your future husband — that he'll be a loving, God-honoring, hardworking, faithful man, just like Sean and your dad."

Still in Meghan's embrace, Sheila said, "And super-hunky handsome?"

Meghan burst out laughing. She gave Sheila one more squeeze and let go. "And super-hunky handsome. Now, we better go. Greg's probably out there pacing and grumbling about us yakking again."

Sheila laughed, and they headed for the lobby. They rounded the corner and, sure enough, Greg was waiting by the counter. He glanced at his wristwatch as they approached and then aimed a mild frown at them.

"Checkout's at eleven. You barely made it — it's ten fifty-eight."

"But we did make it." Sheila's nose wrinkled with her impish grin. "So no need for fussing."

"Women's logic." Greg rolled his eyes, and Meghan and Sheila shared another laugh.

They placed their key cards on the counter

and turned for the doors, Greg in the lead. A tall, distinguished-looking man wearing a spring-green polo and tan khakis rose from one of the chairs in the corner of the lobby. "Excuse me . . . Detective DeFord?"

Meghan paused, a smile ready. "I'm Detective DeFord. Can I help you?"

His blue eyes developed a sheen, and his lips quivered. "I wanted to meet you. I'm Kevin Harrison."

Meghan's weight seemed to leave her body. Her suitcase fell from her hand, and for a moment, she feared she might faint. "K-Kevin Harrison?"

Greg appeared on her right. He braced his palm in the middle of her back and glared at Kevin, as protective as a mama cat defending its kittens. "Meghan, are you all right?"

She blindly flapped her hand toward Greg, unable to take her eyes off her father's face. "It's okay, Greg. I . . . I know who he is."

Greg slowly lowered his arm. "Are you sure? I'll get rid of him if you want me to."

"No. It's all right." The light-headed feeling was dissipating. "He's an old friend of my mother's. He just took me by surprise is all."

Greg still seemed uncertain, but he nodded. "All right, then. I'll put your suitcase in the SUV, and Sheila and I will wait for you there." He grabbed her suitcase and turned to Sheila. "C'mon. We'll give Meghan a minute or two." He shot one more glower over his shoulder and then ushered Sheila out.

For several seconds, Meghan stood stupidly and stared into her father's face. Lines fanned from the outer corners of his eyes, and his hair was completely gray — what Grandma would call the color of a galvanized washtub. But despite these signs of aging, he was a very handsome man. She understood why Mom had been attracted to him.

"Did —" Her voice cracked. She cleared her throat. "Did Mom tell you where I was?"

He gestured to the chairs, and she forced her shaky legs to carry her to them. They sat, and he leaned in with his elbows on his widespread knees and his fingers laced together. "No, I heard it from local scuttlebutt. The whole town's buzzing about the missing banker and the cold-case detectives from Little Rock who found him. The hotel received a bit of notoriety for hosting you."

He glanced around the lobby and pursed his face. "The next time you're in Fort Smith, please let me make your reservations.

I think we can find nicer accommodations."

Meghan didn't know when — or if — she'd be back. She stared at him in silence.

He stared at her, too, with the oddest expression in his piercing blue eyes. It was a combination of agony, embarrassment, and — the part that put an ache in her chest — pride. His thumbs tapped together. "What are you thinking?"

"Why am I so short?"

He blinked twice. His thumbs stilled. "What?"

Of all the stupid things to say. A nervous laugh found its way from her throat. "I'm trying to understand. Mom's actually fairly tall for a woman, definitely above average. So was my grandma before age started shrinking her. And you're really tall. But me? I'm five three, at the upper end of the petite scale. I'm trying to figure out how that happened."

He grinned. "My mother's petite. Not even five two."

"Really?"

He nodded. "Really." The pride she'd glimpsed earlier returned. "Maybe you take after her in that way."

"Maybe . . ."

They fell into silence again. The front door swung open, and Greg strode in. He searched the lobby, and his gaze connected with Meghan's. He crossed to her in two long strides and frowned down at her. "Are you ready to go?"

No, she wasn't. There was so much she wanted to know. Questions that had lain dormant inside her for decades pined for release. But maybe this wasn't the time. She held out her hand to her father. He took hold with both of his, sandwiching her hand between his wide, warm palms. A coiling warmth, what she could define as the feeling of being protected, climbed her arm and slid into her chest.

She swallowed against unexpected tears. "It was nice to meet you. Can we exchange phone numbers, talk to each other more later?"

He kept a light grip on her hand. "Or maybe I could drive you back to Little Rock. I'd like to take you to lunch, show you my office, maybe introduce you to my mother." He glanced at Greg, who was glowering at him with the most distrustful look Meghan had ever seen. "That is, if your bodyguard approves."

Meghan slipped her hand free, discovering a sense of loss as she did so. "Greg, you don't need to worry. Kevin Harrison is my father." Tears filled her eyes, distorting her vision. It was so freeing to acknowledge his title that she couldn't resist repeating it. "This is my father."

Greg leaned in and squeezed her shoulder. "All right, then. I'll get your suitcase." He offered a brief nod in Kevin's direction, then hurried out of the lobby.

Kevin — her father — smiled at her. "Thank you. I really appreciate the chance to get to know you." He extended his hands, and this time she took hold and held tight. "I'm sorry it took so long. If I could go back in time and do things over, I'd be there for you from the beginning."

His face twisted with regret. "I've asked God to forgive me, and now I'd like to ask you the same thing. Can you forgive me for abandoning you and your mother?"

Looking into his remorseful, moist eyes, Meghan experienced a wave of compassion. So many thoughts swarmed her brain — memories of lying in bed wondering about him, of trailing after the D.A.R.E. officer in lieu of following a daddy's footsteps, of wishing she could go to the father-daughter dances. The hurt of those moments wrapped around her heart and constricted, but at the same time, a recognition bloomed.

She stared for several seconds at their joined hands, then shifted her gaze to meet

491

his eyes. Without effort, a smile lifted the corners of her lips. "You weren't there, but my heavenly Father always was. He used my longing for an earthly father to draw me to Him. He also used elements of my lonely childhood to mold me into the person He designed me to be."

Kevin angled his head, curiosity lighting his eyes. "What do you mean?"

"I might not have become a cold-case detective if, in my desire for a father figure, I hadn't developed a relationship with a police officer at my grade school. That means I wouldn't have met Sean, the most wonderful husband in the world. I would've missed getting to know Sheila and helping her find her father, as well as helping countless other people who were caught in places of pain and loss. I would've missed so many blessings. So . . . yes, I forgive you."

The relief flooding his features touched Meghan more deeply than she could have imagined. His grip tightened, and he blinked rapidly. "Thank you."

She nodded, but her throat was too tight to speak.

Greg returned, Meghan's suitcase in hand. He placed it on the floor next to her. "There you go. We'll see you back in Little Rock."

Meghan released her father's hands and stood. "Thanks, Greg. Drive safe."

He nodded. "You, too."

Kevin rose, picked up her suitcase, and gestured toward the doors. "Ready?"

All at once, nervousness swooped in. What had she agreed to? An entire day with Kevin Harrison. With her father. She hoped she wouldn't throw up. She linked her hands and pressed them to her jumping stomach. "Yes."

As they exited, he said, "What would you like to do first? Lunch? My office?"

"If you don't mind, could you take me to meet your mother? My grandma is one of the most important people in my life." She offered a shy grin, nervousness fading beneath a sprinkle of excitement. "I'd love to add another grandma to my Christmas card list."

He laughed, a merry sound that lifted her heart and chased away the rest of her nervousness. "You bet. Let's go."

THIRTY-EIGHT

Kendrickson, Nevada
Diane

Diane laid the phone on her nightstand and swung her feet over the edge of the bed. Her entire body quivered, adrenaline still racing from her conversation with Meghan. Ignoring the movie still playing on her notebook, which she'd been watching before the phone rang, she trotted out of her room and through the hallway to the living room. Mother relaxed in her chair with Miney in her lap, balancing an open book against the dog's back.

When Diane entered the room, Mother glanced up and immediately set the book aside. She fixed a worried frown on Diane. "What's the matter?"

Diane sank onto the ottoman next to her mother's feet and clamped her shaking hands over her knees. "Meghan spent the day with Kevin."

Mother half sat up, and Miney whined. She stroked the dog's ears, her gaze pinned on Diane's face. "How did that happen?"

Diane repeated Meghan's explanation about finding Kevin waiting for her in the hotel lobby, then choosing to let him drive her to Little Rock. "She not only met Kevin, but she met his mother, who cried buckets when she learned she had a granddaughter. Meghan said his mother — her name is Melinda — went to lunch with them." She grabbed Mother's foot. "And get this. Melinda ordered Meghan's favorite sandwich even before Meghan placed her order. She already has something in common with her. Well, besides height. Melinda is short, too."

Mother chuckled. "I always thought Meghan got her height from my mother, who was, as they so elegantly say today, vertically challenged. But maybe it came from her paternal grandmother, too."

Diane nodded. "She said at first she was uncomfortable — for Pete's sake, who wouldn't be? — but by the time they finished lunch and toured Kevin's office, she felt as if she'd known them forever." Tears filled Diane's eyes, and she whisked them away with her fingertips. "I'm so happy for her. I'm so glad she feels at ease with her father."

Mother reached out and grabbed Diane's hands. "And I'm so happy for you."

Diane tilted her head. "For me? Why me?"

Mother smiled. "Listen to yourself, Margaret Diane. Do you hear the joy in your voice? No resentment. No jealousy. Only delight that your beloved child has united with her father. Do you realize how much your heart has softened?" She gave Diane's hands a squeeze and let go, then settled against the chair's back again. "I'm so proud of you. So very proud."

Diane ducked her head for a moment, contemplating Mother's observation. After all the worrying and wondering, she now recognized how fully God had prepared her to accept Kevin's presence in Meghan's life. And in her own. Forgiving him — and herself — made such a difference.

She looked at Mother again. "Well, there's more. Meghan invited Kevin, his mother, and Kip to Carson Springs for a Fourth of July get-together. She wants us to come, too."

Mother puckered her face. "Arkansas in July? The humidity will kill me."

Diane drew back. "You don't want to go?"

Mother huffed. "Did I say that? Of course

I want to go. But did you forget that my sister will be flying here for the same holiday? It's become our tradition, you know."

Diane groaned. "In her excitement, I'm sure Meghan forgot. Well, I'll have to call her back and tell her —"

"No, no." Mother waved her hands. "I doubt Emily has her plane reservation yet." She released a soft laugh. "She always waits until the last minute, bless her heart, and then complains about the high price. I'll call her tomorrow and tell her to book a flight to Little Rock instead. She's mentioned wanting to visit Arkansas. Maybe we'll rent a car and take a drive to Cumpton after the get-together at Meghan's. We can make it a reminiscing vacation."

Diane heaved a sigh. "Sounds perfect."

Mother wound her fingers through the thick hair on Miney's ruff and smiled, contentment evident in her expression. "Perfect, indeed."

Carson Springs, Arkansas
Meghan

Meghan carried a plate of uncooked hot dogs to the grill and placed them on the little shelf attached to the grill's base. She grinned up at her father. "Thanks for taking over here. Sean got a little sidetracked."

Kevin bounced a glance at the tag football game taking place on the opposite side of the yard. Sean and Kip were skunking Sheila's brothers, Wayne and Brandon, but from the whoops and playful insults filling the air, they were having fun anyway. "It's fine. I just hope everyone likes their burgers well done, because that's the only way I know how to cook 'em."

Meghan laughed. "Well done is fine." She headed for the house, smiling at the trio of older women seated around the picnic table under the protective canopy Sean had constructed for the celebration. Their chatter and laughter added to the noisy chaos in the yard. Grandma, Great-Aunt Emily, and Memaw, as Melinda insisted Meghan call her, had formed a quick bond, and Meghan especially delighted in seeing her grandmothers enjoying each other's company.

In the kitchen, Mom was digging in the refrigerator, and Sheila was adding dollops of mayonnaise to the huge bowl of potato salad Meghan had tossed together the night before.

Meghan opened the cupboard where she stored her serving platters and peeked into the bowl. "What's the matter? Too dry?"

Sheila bobbed her chin in Mom's direction. "She said so. She also said it needs

498

pickles."

Mom emerged from the refrigerator, holding a jar of pickles aloft. "Tada!" She handed it to Sheila. "Chop three of those and add them, along with a little juice, to the salad. Then it'll be perfect."

Meghan pulled a wedding-gift platter from the cabinet and shook her head. "Mom, for the love of Pete, you don't even eat potato salad because of the eggs and mayonnaise in it. So why should you care if it doesn't have pickles?"

"Potato salad isn't potato salad without pickles, Meghan. Everyone knows that." She picked up the covered platter of lettuce leaves, sliced tomatoes, and raw onion rings and headed for the back door. "Honestly. No pickles in potato salad? Who raised this kid?" The screen door slammed on her final mutter.

Sheila laughed and opened the pickle jar. "Your mom is so different from mine, but I like her. Thanks again for inviting us."

Meghan gave Sheila a quick half hug and then handed her a cutting board and knife. "Thanks for coming. I couldn't celebrate the Fourth without my favorite little sis."

Sheila pinched out a pickle and giggled — a girlish sound that made Meghan smile. Of course, she'd been smiling a lot already.

Having her whole family — Sean, Mom, Grandma, Great-Aunt Emily, Memaw, Kevin, Kip, and Sheila and her gang — under her roof was a joy she'd never have imagined. One simple search had brought so much change. And if the vibes she'd picked up between Mom and Kevin proved accurate, another change might be coming in the not-too-distant future. It might be fun to be a bridesmaid.

"Those beans are sure smelling good." Sheila's comment pulled Meghan from her reflections. "When'll they be done?"

Meghan checked the oven timer. "Three more minutes." She hoped they'd taste okay. She'd found the recipe for molasses baked beans in the cookbook Grandma had given her, but this was her trial run for making them. She leaned against the counter and crossed her arms, watching Sheila chop a pickle into small chunks. "What's the latest on Brandon's college admission?"

"He's been accepted to the premed program at the University of Arkansas. The financial-aid director said he qualifies for academic scholarships based on his high school grades and ACT scores." Sheila shot a nose-crinkling grin at Meghan. "Toldja he was smart." She fished another pickle from the jar. "Because our income's not so great, he'll also get some grants, and then he's eligible for student loans, but we're gonna hold off on those until we get the final word about Dad's life insurance."

"I think that's smart." The oven dinged. Meghan donned oven mitts and reached in for the bubbling casserole.

"Yeah, Mr. Meade at the bank is working hard with the insurance company to get the funds in time." She shrugged and scooped the chopped-up pickle into the salad. "But even if he can't, we know Brandon's in, and that's what matters most."

Shouts and raucous laughter exploded from outside and carried through the screen door. Meghan set the casserole dish on top of the stove and glanced in the direction of the sound, then turned her smile on Sheila. "Sean's having a blast with Wayne and Brandon. I think he's gonna want to have regular football games with them."

Sheila set down the knife, yanked a paper towel from the holder, and wiped her hands. "Sounds fine to me, but it'll be kinda hard without Kip here. You can't make two even teams with three people."

Meghan removed the oven mitts and chose serving spoons from a crock on the counter. "If you wait a few years, there might be a fourth person to join the game."

Sheila froze in place, her mouth forming an O. Then she sputtered to life. "Meghan, are you" — her gaze dropped to Meghan's stomach and up to her eyes again — "expecting?"

"No. Not yet."

Sheila seemed to deflate.

"But we're hoping we will be by Christmastime." She placed one spoon in the beans and handed another one to Sheila. "By then Sean and I will have all the paperwork in place to open Eagle Investigations."

Sheila squealed. "You're really doing it?"

"Yep." Meghan took the spoon from Sheila and stirred the pickle mess into the potato salad. "Sean's staying at the bureau for the time being. He says it's smart, and I agree — predictable income, good insurance. If the private agency really gets off the ground, he'll resign and join me. But working from home will give me the flexibility to get one of the bedrooms set up as a nursery so we'll be ready when the time comes. It'll be the best of both worlds, you know?"

Sheila clapped twice, then held her palms together under her chin. "I'm so happy for you. And I'm gonna pray for you to get pregnant quick. I can't wait to be Auntie Sheila!"

Meghan couldn't resist wrapping Sheila in a hug. Her life was morphing in so many ways. From only child to big sister, from having a father "somewhere out there" to her dad being active in her life, from resisting motherhood to embracing the idea. The rapid adjustments should have left her dizzy and overwhelmed, but instead she welcomed every new person — present and future — with enthusiasm. Proof of God's work in her heart.

The back door smacked into its frame, and footsteps stomped into the kitchen. Kip, sweaty and red faced, plunked his fists on his hips. "Hey, what're you doing? The burgers are ready. Dad needs something to put them on."

Meghan grabbed the platter and handed it to Kip.

He tucked it under his arm like a football. "He says to get everything else out here. As soon as the dogs come off the grill, we'll eat." He turned and stomped back out.

Sheila smirked. "For a minute, I thought Greg was here."

Meghan laughed. "We'll have to invite him and his family next time. The more the merrier, you know." Had she really said that? She was definitely morphing.

Sheila picked up the bowl of potato salad.

"You heard the man. Get those beans and let's go."

Meghan slid her hands into oven mitts, lifted the casserole dish of aromatic baked beans, and followed Sheila. The screen door slammed shut behind her, and she paused on the concrete stoop, struck by a wave of emotion. Every single person in her back-yard owned a piece of her heart. In her wildest imaginings, she wouldn't have guessed she would be part of such an eclectic group. She let her gaze rove the yard, taking in every bit of activity.

Kevin rolled scorched hot dogs back and forth on the grill with a pair of tongs while Mom supervised, both of them relaxed and smiling. In the center of the thick, freshly mowed grass, Sean stood with his arm slung around Kip's shoulders and chatted animatedly with him, Brandon, and Wayne. Sheila arranged bowls and platters on the picnic table, talking with Grandma, Memaw, and Great-Aunt Emily as easily as if she'd known them forever.

Joy pulsated from every corner of the gathering, and Meghan wished she were an artist so she could paint the sunshiny, full-of-happy-faces scene exactly the way she viewed it. She would title it *Family in Sonlight*. She closed her eyes for a moment, searing the images into her memory.

"The hot dogs are charred just right, so c'mon, everybody!" Kevin's cheerful command rang over the other backyard noise.

Meghan stepped off the stoop and headed for the picnic table. The sweet yet spicy scent rising from the beans mingled with the aromas of grass, charred meat, and sweat. Chatter and bursts of laughter filled the air. The combination of sights, sounds, and smells tantalized her senses, almost dizzying in its effect. She placed the casserole dish on the table, flicked off her oven mitts, then scurried to join the misshapen circle formed by those who'd gathered to celebrate the day.

They linked hands, Meghan between Sean and Kevin. Sunlight flowed down, illuminating every perspiration-dotted, smiling face, and she examined each one by one. From Sean to Grandma, to Great-Aunt Emily, to Memaw, Sheila, Wayne, Brandon, Kip, Mom, and finally to Kevin, who was grinning down at her.

"Who's going to ask the blessing?"

Meghan started to volunteer Sean, but Sean spoke first. "How about you do it, Kevin? After all, you're the patriarch of this motley crew."

Laughter rolled around the circle, but a

knot of emotion blocked Meghan's throat and brought the sting of grateful tears. Look at how many people would welcome their children, would love them and influence them. Part of the proverb Sean had read during their morning devotions trickled through her mind.

" 'The LORD works out everything to its proper end.' "

They'd unveiled shadowy pieces of the past and revealed a brighter present than she'd ever anticipated. And she couldn't help but believe that God would continue to bring them together to the end He'd intended from the beginning of time.

She swung her father's hand, something she'd wanted to do from the time she was a little girl, and nodded. "Yes, you should say the prayer."

He winked, gave her hand a gentle squeeze, and bowed his head. "Dear Father, thank You . . ."

READERS GUIDE

1. Meghan grew up in a single-parent household, which meant she didn't witness the give-and-take of a typical husband-wife relationship. Because of this, she felt ill equipped to be a wife. How could she have gained insights about being a wife? Have you ever been thrust into a role for which you felt unprepared? How did you handle the challenge?

2. Although always curious about her father, when armed with information to locate him, Meghan didn't seek him out right away. Why do you think she put off finding him? Was the timing of her search her timetable or God's? What makes you think so?

3. Sean often thought about his childhood and the way he was raised. He longed for a similar lifestyle with Meghan. Were his

desires reasonable or unrealistic? Why? Most people tend to take what they know from childhood and use it to mold their adult expectations. When is this healthy? When is it unhealthy? How can we break the cycle of unhealthy lifestyle choices?

4. Sheila held a great deal of bitterness about her mother's illness and the way her life changed after her dad disappeared. Was her bitterness understandable? Bitterness is a common response to out-of-our-control circumstances, but is it a helpful one? How can we use difficult circumstances to make us better instead of bitter?

5. Kevin was successful in business but a failure in relationships. Hazel tells him that he won't find contentment in owning properties or finding a wife and that he needs a solid foundation on which to build his life. Kevin initially scoffs at the idea but eventually comes to realize he needs Jesus Christ, the cornerstone and completer of life. What brought about his heart change? How does Jesus fill us when things of this world do not?

6. Kevin's father, when faced with the

destruction of his reputation and a possible jail sentence, chose to end his own life. Kevin and his mother carried a burden of guilt over his father's decision. Was the guilt theirs to bear? Why or why not? How would you advise someone who feels suicide is the answer to his or her problems? How can we minister to those left in the wake of another's suicide?

7. Meghan reflected how elements of her lonely childhood had prepared her to be a cold-case detective and how her position opened up the door to blessings for her. What elements of your past has God used to prepare you for where you are today?

8. Sean wasn't eager to partner with Tom Farber, who tormented Sean for his Christian faith. Have you ever been treated unfairly by someone because of your faith? How did you respond? What scriptures help you react in a God-honoring way when you're being mistreated?

9. Diane worked hard to build a successful life after becoming an unwed mother. Even so, underneath she tended to define herself by that one title. How can we keep from letting our mistakes define us? Hazel

told her she needed to forgive Kevin Harrison but also herself. Is it easier to forgive someone else or ourselves? Why?

10. Kevin's adopted son, Kip, was a troublemaker in childhood and continued to make unwise decisions in adulthood. Who was at fault for Kip's problems? Was Kip hurting others or himself more by his behavior choices? At what point do we have to assume responsibility for our behavior instead of using past experiences as an excuse for poor decisions?

11. Hazel reminded Meghan that she had always had a father in God, and then Meghan relayed this to Sheila. Many people aren't blessed with a loving earthly father, yet God is willing and able to fill the role when we allow Him to. How would you advise someone who lacks an earthly father to look to God to fill that hole in his or her life?

ACKNOWLEDGMENTS

Mom and Daddy, thank you for setting such wonderful examples of Christlike behavior. You viewed God as your Father, and because of your faith, I easily grasped the concept of a loving Father-God. If every child was blessed with the kind of parents God gave me, what a different world it would be.

Mom, writing this book in the throes of grieving your unexpected departure for heaven was the hardest task I've ever undertaken. But remembering your many prayers for me, your advice to lean on Jesus's strength, and your steadfast example of "I can do all things through Him" gave me the courage to finish the story. You're gone, but your legacy of faith remains strong. I'll see you soonly.

Kathy, I couldn't help but recall so many delightful excursions in Las Vegas as I wrote. I'm so blessed by our enduring friendship.

The Posse and my Sunday school ladies, you truly held up my arms. Thank you.

Tamela, Shannon, Julee, Kathy, and the entire team at WaterBrook, thank you for your support, your understanding, and your help in whipping this story into shape. I am grateful for every suggestion and every word of encouragement. Bless y'all.

Finally, and most importantly, *God,* thank You for being my strength and comforter through the difficulties of life. Thank You for being the Father who never leaves or forsakes His children. I pray my life and my stories always point to Your Son. May any praise and glory be reflected directly back to You.

ABOUT THE AUTHOR

Kim Vogel Sawyer is a highly acclaimed, bestselling author with more than one million books in print in seven different languages. Her titles have earned numerous accolades, including the ACFW Carol Award, the Inspirational Readers Choice Award, and the Gayle Wilson Award of Excellence. Kim and her retired military husband, Don, live in in central Kansas, where she continues to write gentle stories of hope. She enjoys spending time with her three daughters and her grandchildren.